T0129217

The assault on America begins with an attack on Red Harmon's family . . .

Trained to endure extreme danger and survive impossible odds, elite military operator Red Harmon has battled our nation's enemies for years. While in the Rocky Mountains for R&R, his family is violently attacked by an international squad of assassins. No ordinary wet-team, this group is only the vanguard of a power play threatening national security.

Danger is everywhere . . .

Red and his young daughter escape a brutal firefight, but are separated from his wife. Evading though the woodlands, stripped of his unit's support, Red puts his survival skills to the test all the way from Pikes Peak National Forest to Israel's West Bank. He must defend his country, protect his family, and identify the unthinkable forces that are willing to slaughter anyone in their path.

Visit us at www.kensingtonbooks.com

Praise for the Red Ops thrillers by David McCaleb

RECALL

"David McCaleb has a real winner here. *Recall* is a smart and well-plotted thriller, a fantastic read that I could not put down. Red Harmon is a guy I'd want on my side."
—Marc Cameron, best-selling author of *Brute Force*

"If you're looking for suspense, nonstop action, and a hero you can root for, the Red Ops series will clean your X ring."
—David Poyer, best-selling author of *Tipping Point* and *Onslaught*

"One of those wild rides where you strap in tight and leave your disbelief behind. Just my type of action thriller. I read it in a blur."
—*Deadly Pleasures* magazine

RELOAD

"With effusive writing and strong characters, McCaleb delivers a decades-spanning tale brimming with excitement, intrigue, and deception. Red Harmon is a keeper!"
—Alan Jacobson, best-selling author of *The Lost Codex*

"David McCaleb delivers with *Reload*! Red Harmon is a gritty hero who comes through in the clutch and McCaleb's gripping plot is the stuff of today's headlines. A must-read for all fans of thriller fiction!"
—A. J. Tata, best-selling author of *Besieged*

Books by David McCaleb

Red Ops Thrillers
Recall
Reload
Recon

RECON

A Red Ops Thriller

David McCaleb

LYRICAL PRESS
Kensington Publishing Corp.
www.kensingtonbooks.com

First Electronic Edition: August 2018
eISBN-13: 978-1-60183-866-7
eISBN-10: 1-60183-866-2

First Print Edition: August 2018
ISBN-13: 978-1-60183-867-4
ISBN-10: 1-60183-867-0

Printed in the United States of America

To my father. For teaching me how to cast bullets, reload ammo, sight-in a rifle, and clean a deer. For educating me how to arrange decoys so geese land near our blind. How to lead a duck, dress for cold, and stave off hypothermia after capsizing in the creek. For warning me with a grin that a .44 Magnum kicks like a mule...after I'd already pulled the trigger. How to bait a hook, cast a line, and fish. Well, sort of. I still can't keep straight what months to go to all those spots in the creek and which species are going to be there. And frankly, I never gave a crap. I simply enjoyed the time with you.

Thank you for cultivating creativity in our home, supporting your kids in their latest whims, and being genuinely excited when I started writing. Though you never saw my books in print, they are now. And they're damn good because, like it or not, experiences with you are stitched into each. Thank you.

Chapter 1

Betrayal

Frederick Johnson squinted through a scope mounted atop a Remington 783. The crosshairs wavered over a red-bearded man throttling a black Ford Explorer toward him on a dirt driveway wild as a cat escaping a bath. Out here in farm country with no other cars in view, a man could drive that way, Frederick supposed. A quarter mile of lush soybeans stretched between him and Red Man. A mist hovered a few feet above the leafy green carpet, the fog uncommon in June. The low angle of the early morning sun blazed it with gilded brilliance.

He shrugged off a cold shiver that crept up his neck. Sweat beaded on the bald spot atop his head and trickled down unshaven cheeks, dripping onto his blue jeans. Ever since he'd turned forty, he'd sweat just reading the paper.

The vehicle sped toward the end of the long driveway. "Brake...brake," Frederick whispered as the Explorer jerked to either side of the path, dodging potholes. A dust trail rose behind it and melded with the fog. The way this guy drove, the only chance he'd have of a clear shot would be when the vehicle stopped at the end of the lane.

"Five hundred meters," his spotter murmured. "This guy drives like a maniac." Wendy was crouched beside him in the hunting hide, shrouding her eyes behind rangefinder binoculars. Shiny, jet-black hair hung in a ponytail. Her bare arms were skinny as hell. Not the anorexic, lingerie-model brand. More like the steel cable, personal trainer, trying to prove women-can-do-anything-a-man-can-do-but-better kind of thin. Yet she'd been a quick study, even for a girl. And could think on her feet. On a prior job they'd been trailing their mark on foot when he'd made an unexpected turn. She'd choked him out with bare hands. Maybe he'd have to change his attitude about hit men being an all-male club. *Hit person?* Nah. "Three hundred fifty," she murmured.

Frederick kept the crosshairs over Red Man, then reached long fingers and twisted the elevation knob two clicks, zeroing the scope at two hundred meters, the end of the drive. The Remington was chambered in .243, a hyperfast, flat-firing round. He'd chosen ammo with heavier 115-grain bullets since the projectile would pass through windshield glass. The weightier shot would decrease deflection.

A wisp of haze, a specter's arm, reached from the foggy floor and floated across the scope's field of view. Red Man twisted the wheel, and the vehicle veered almost completely off the drive. Frederick chased him with the crosshairs. The Explorer wasn't slowing. "Brake, damn it!" At the end of the drive the SUV slid and accelerated onto the main road with a chirp of rubber. The speeding engine sang over the field, and a flock of crows exploded into the air from beneath the fog blanket.

"Shit!" he huffed, raising his head from the rifle as the vehicle raced away.

"Why didn't you take the shot?"

He lifted the bolt handle and yanked it back. The ejected round flew toward Wendy's head, and she snatched it from the air like a striking cobra. "No clear chance. I'm good, but no sniper. Even the best would have a hard time hitting a moving target like that. Plus, his wife wasn't with him."

She dropped the rangefinder so that it hung from her neck, resting between undersized breasts. "Worth the risk, though."

How much should he tell her? This was only their third job together. Still, tell her too little and it could bite him in the ass if she made a stupid move. "Red Man, and even his wife, isn't a target you take a risk on. They've been contracted before. Didn't turn out so well for those guys."

Wendy crossed her arms and leaned back, sitting atop an overturned five-gallon bucket against the plywood wall.

OK. Should have told her. He gripped the rifle barrel and lowered the stock to the floor. "Yeah, we're getting a huge payout for this. But I got no idea from who. Never do. But the instructions were written in broken English. Meaning it could be from an international business, or some government that can't reach here. This could be our break into the big leagues. But that means big risk. Every kill needs to be a sure thing. Double so on this guy. We wound him, and all the sudden we're the ones with a target on our backs. I don't know the whole story, but we ain't the first team that's tried to take him. And we only get paid if both are dead." He pressed the magazine latch, and it dropped into his glove. "And watching him these last few days…the bulge under the shoulder of whatever he wears. The way he drives five different routes to work. The way he cuts his eyes. Hell, just the way he carries himself. This guy's a predator. He ain't prey." Which troubled him. Frederick had skills, but he was no heavy hitter. Not yet. Why'd *he* been contracted? Was his team the only one working this job? Should he be looking over his own shoulder?

Wendy crossed her legs. Her tan calves were knotted rope. "Typical alpha male. I've taken his type before."

Frederick blew a breath. "Maybe. But if you want to stay alive, never take potshots."

"What're our options, then?"

Heat radiated from the wall behind her. Six o'clock in the morning and the rising sun was already warming the cramped space. The humid fragrance of decomposing timber filled the hut. They needed to get out of the field before anyone spied them. Deer season was long past. But still, no one raised an eyebrow at a man with a bolt action in rural Virginia, no matter what time of year. Likely just a farmer with a kill permit protecting his crop. And when they'd spy Wendy next to him, all suspicions would vanish. Only a guy teaching his girlfriend how to shoot. How quaint. That's why he'd chosen her. Couples were invisible.

"We could plant a bomb at the end of his driveway. But I don't know how to make an IED. There's a guy who can, but I don't want him involved on this one. And we can't get to Red Man at home. Too risky." They'd driven by his long driveway several times. Vehicle sensors flanked it, which meant more security up the way. A $250 frequency identifier showed surveillance system emissions from the house at 433MHz all the way up to 5GHz, plus some lower-frequency stuff on military bands. "And we can't get him at work. It's Langley. Plus, he drives as if he knows someone's after him. She's almost as bad."

Wendy squeezed her elbows and rolled her neck. "Options?"

He stood and ducked his head to keep from smacking pine branches stretched across the close box as a ceiling. His tall frame towered over the tiny woman. He pulled a worn Baltimore Ravens ball cap over thin brown hair. Lifting an olive drab cloth that covered a narrow exit, he stepped down atop a wooden ladder rung and stopped. "We wait till he's out of his routine. Away from here."

"How long's that going to take?"

How much to tell her? *Two can keep a secret only if one of them is dead.* Nah. She knew enough at this point. He managed a smile. "I know a way to speed things up."

* * * *

"So, you shot your wife?" the therapist asked, as if still confused who had actually been killed.

Tony "Red" Harmon leaned back in a low, hard, black vinyl chair. He'd explained it to the woman three times already. It wasn't that difficult to understand. Didn't she have five college degrees? He scratched his tight, curly copper beard. "I didn't shoot my wife. I only thought it was her." Which was the truth. And he'd done it trying to save the woman's life. "So, that's not the problem. Let's get past your maybe-he's-an-ax-murderer theory and get on with the session." There. Easy to understand.

The psychiatrist, Dr. Christian Sato, settled atop a high-backed wooden stool behind a vintage green enameled steel desk. The shrink needed the tall chair just to see over it. Red was short by most men's standards, but this woman of Japanese descent made him feel like a basketball player. *Old government* was the motif of her office. Red would go nuts if he had to work at a desk. Gray metal file cabinets covered one wall. The kind that would tear off fingers if slammed in the door, or crush small animals if tipped over. The corners of manila envelopes stuck out from the front of several in an effort to escape. Ancient, nicotine-stained vertical blinds hung in a window like prison bars.

As a military operator assigned to the Det, a fusion cell of three-letter government agencies and the Department of Defense, Red was required to undergo periodic psychological evaluations. The Det was short for Detachment Five, of Joint Special Operations Command. At most of these sessions he'd handled it a bit like an interrogation. Quick replies, not offering any additional information. But Sato was one of the good shrinks, meaning she never asked how long he wet his bed or whether his mother breast-fed him. He'd been endeared by her sick, sarcastic humor and direct, no-frills approach.

As commander of the Det, he'd requested she limit her inquiries to the task of ensuring his group of professional killers didn't have too many loose screws. A good operator was never entirely sane, and Sato seemed to recognize that. But today's session was on Red's dime and at his request. He'd woken up last week with a distinct understanding that, despite his best efforts, something was broken in his head that he couldn't fix. Sato being the only shrink he knew, he'd made the call.

His wife, Lori, sat up in an identical seat next to him. "It took a while, but we've gotten past that issue. A big mix-up. He thought he'd seen me die, and he'd contributed. But it's behind us. Tony's a good man. A great father."

At least Lori acknowledged he was trying. A half foot taller than Red, she somehow made sitting in a child-sized chair appear natural. She reached behind her head and pulled her mane of long, dirty-blond hair to one side. He leaned closer, and the scent of Extatic captured his attention. Her eyes were bright, but rimmed in pink. Taking time away from work for this session, she was dressed in office attire, a black skirt that hiked up to midthigh when she sat. She crossed long, slender legs that just last night had been wrapped around him for over an hour. On her calf, a round dot the size of a nickel marked where a 5.7-millimeter bullet from an assassin's P90 had passed through. An awesome wife, mother, and an absolute rock.

She lifted a finger. "But he's never present, mentally. At least not with me. He's great with the kids. I'm jealous of them. Other than sex, there's zero connection anymore. I'm an island."

All truth, though not for lack of effort. He'd date her, take her to dinner, even spend all Saturday with her at antique stores staring at furniture in various states of disrepair. *Yes dear, that chair is a great-looking piece of crap. It's a lot like the ten other pieces of partially dismantled crap we've got in the garage from our last visit. Let's bring this one home so we can shatter its dreams as well.* But those musings were unfair. They'd actually refinished an antique folding side table. He'd taken it completely apart and sanded everything down. She'd stained it and brushed on a polyurethane topcoat.

"It's not the table," she'd told him. "It's taking something broken and making it better."

Why couldn't he do the same with this problem?

Like the numbness of his thumb past a three-inch scar courtesy of an Ethiopian hunting knife, he no longer sensed a deep connection with her. His closest friends anymore were other operators.

A vacuum hummed outside the office door. Window glass rattled as the janitor smacked the machine against the wall. Sato placed her pen atop the desk and leaned forward on her elbows. "How long have we known each other, Red?"

Maybe he shouldn't have called this woman. This was going nowhere. "About a year, I suppose."

"And in that time, you've progressed from being an operator to commander of your organization."

Red grunted at her labeling the Det an "organization." As a fusion cell, it was moderately controlled chaos at best. A football field where three-letter offices and the military huddled together and cooperated for each one's gain, sharing intelligence, expertise, and most importantly, assets.

"How many operations have you executed during that time?"

A *whack* from the hallway, followed by tinkling of broken glass. "Fifteen major ones probably. Then there's training."

Sato scribbled something on a yellow-sheeted pad. At a $150 an hour, she probably had to have something to show for it. "And how long does it take," she continued, "from planning to execution to debrief?"

Lori leaned forward. "Two weeks at best. When he's planning an op, I never see the man. Then he's off to a place where the locals are trying to kill him. He comes home and we get the scraps. By then, he's an empty hulk."

Sato waved. "Red needs to answer the questions." Her eyes studied him now. Mascara was caked into her crow's-feet like black veins. She hopped down from the stool and waddled around the edge of the desk. He didn't have to look up to her, despite the fact he was sitting. She stood with her nose almost touching his. Her family must have had a much smaller concept of personal space. Her voice was grave. Breath of garlic. "You don't need me to diagnose your problem. Don't be an idiot. You thought you witnessed the death of your wife, just to discover it wasn't her. On top of that, you make your living in the profession of arms. You're the walking wounded. All your men sing your praises. But you're not invincible. Your symptoms are classic post-traumatic stress disorder. PTSD."

He leaned away from the garlic stench. "But I don't drink too much."

Sato's cheeks rose, and she cackled a laugh. "Not everyone with PTSD is an alcoholic."

Fine. Whatever. "So how do I fix it?"

A black cat jumped upon the windowsill outside. The angle of the sun cast its shadow as large as a mountain lion upon the carpet. Sato stepped behind the desk again. She stood on the stool's footrest and leaned onto the desk, arms braced as if doing a push-up. "You're not a machine. There isn't a quick fix. No magic solution. It's different for everyone. But for you the first step is time off. A vacation. And I don't mean Disneyland. You need time to be bored. To watch the sun go down. Time for your head to process what's transpired, instead of being constantly distracted."

Red raised a hand. "Now's not a good time. We've got—"

"For me, either," Lori jumped in. "We've lost ground at work. Maybe in a few months we could do it."

The shadow of the cat's tail swished like a whip crack across Sato's desk; then it leaped from the frame, as if to an adjoining office's balcony. The psych's eyes were slits. "Major, here's the sitrep. You've started to exhibit signs of PTSD. The path to recovery can be long, but if you don't start on it now, it just gets longer. Most operators, unless they take action, are in divorce court in six months. Within a year I have to declare many unfit for duty."

Wow. Maybe he didn't like her direct approach after all.

She flexed a pencil between thumbs. It snapped. "Funny, don't you think, how soldiers can be so dogmatically decisive when bullets are flying, but can't bring themselves to make basic life changes like the one before you now?" She pointed the splintered instrument at him as if it were a pistol. "Get away together. Don't take your work phone. Don't check email. Don't even tell anyone where you're going." She patted her chest. "Doctor's orders."

Just then, country rap music blared from Lori's black Coach purse. *Ho ya baby! You drive me crazy!* "What the—" she snapped, then yanked the bag off the floor, pulled out a phone, and lifted it to her ear. She plugged the other with a finger. "We'll be right there. Thank you," she said, then tapped the red button on the screen. Her mouth hung open. "Penny just slapped Jenny at school."

That made no sense. Penny was as gentle and tolerant as a kitten. And Jenny was her best friend.

"Teacher said she'd pulled out a chunk of Jenny's hair by the time they were separated."

Sato scribbled a note with the short pencil. "Has Penny done this before?"

Lori frowned, then stood and slung the bag over a shoulder. She grabbed Red's wrist. "Let's go. We'll finish this later."

Sato knelt on her stool, as if trying to appear taller. "You need time off. Both of you. Then we can talk about what's next. Make a decision. *Now.*"

Red stood. Lori stepped past him toward the door, but he pulled her to a halt. "School's out in two weeks."

The edges of her eyes glowed red. "No time right now."

"No shit. Me, either. But, if this is step one, let's do it."

Lori gripped the doorknob. Her fingers trembled. "OK. In two weeks, once school is out, we'll get away. Now, come on!"

* * * *

Martina Banderas wheeled a gray plastic trash cart down a narrow hall of Westwood Psychiatry. The carpet had recently been replaced. The playdough scent of vinyl adhesive still hung heavy in the air. She'd vacuumed earlier and the pile still looked new as— *Oh, Saint Zita!* Dark coffee had stained the rug outside an office. She bent and rubbed at the spot with bare fingers. Still moist. Good. She could spray it with cold water and dab the blemish up.

She straightened, then did a double take when she spotted the name etched into the door's glass. DR. CHRISTIAN SATO. A chill shivered her neck, just like the ones she used to get whenever she heard the voice of her manipulative aunt Florencia. Each time the janitor saw Sato's name, she heard it as if spoken in the annoying high-pitched voice of her dead aunt. The doctor spoke praises like honeysuckle to clients but flashed scorn to the help.

A dim light shone from behind the pane. Better knock to let the doctor know Martina needed to run the carpet cleaner. A tirade came any time Sato was working late and Martina made too much noise. She always had to bite her cheek to keep from laughing out loud at the Japanese lady.

She rapped on the glass timidly. No answer. She tried again, this time harder, the pane rattling in the frame. Still nothing. She cracked the door. "Señorita Doctor Sato?" The light on the baby-puke-colored metal desk cast a warm glow over a broken pencil and pad of paper.

Her heart quickened. This would mean an extra hundred dollars!

"It's just a way to get a message to a good friend without his wife knowing," Sato had told her three years earlier, blinking both eyes, as if attempting to wink but unsure how it was done.

Martina stalked inside, fearing Sato might actually not yet be gone. Another peek around, then to the desk. On the pad was written a number 3. Nice! Two months had passed since Sato had last requested a delivery, but location number three was Martina's favorite. She was to get a French manicure from the Vietnamese nail place next to Kroger supermarket, then "pay" with only a sticky note Sato would leave in the trash can.

She snatched up the wastebasket, lifted out a crisply folded pink square, and slipped it into her cleaning apron's chest pocket. She stepped over the coffee stain and dumped the rest of the contents into the cart.

Martina had tried to figure out which of the nail stylists Sato was seeing. But all the men there seemed so young.... She'd always been careful not to pry, but—really? That old lady and one of those Asian hunks? Her fingers drummed against the empty can. She reached in her pocket, pulled out the note, and unfolded it.

Package headed out in two weeks. Pick up. Discard both.

Chapter 2

Greenwood Park

Detective Matt Carter sucked in a deep breath and cinched his fall-arrest harness chest strap. The new nylon webbing was stiff, but he gripped the belt's tail with both hands, flexed thick biceps, and yanked again, edging it one notch tighter. He'd managed to score a worn pair of canvas Carhartt jeans at a hospice thrift store last week. Glancing at his reflection in the passenger window of the GMC boom truck, he looked like a real electrical contractor sporting a yellow hard hat, elbow-length rubberized gloves, and thick work boots. Not his typical Brooks Brothers staples, this stuff.

He'd parked the vehicle and chocked the tires on a brown gravel lot at Greenwood Park, outside Woodbridge, Virginia. Leaves on the tall hardwoods fluttered in a warm breeze. A child's distant laugh mingled with the buzz of cicadas, but it was still early enough that the lawns and athletic fields were mostly empty.

The door of the vehicle displayed HART ELECTRIC with a cartoon Dalmatian holding a lightbulb. If anyone were to do an Internet search for the company, they'd find a crappy-looking website with broken links and a "Contact us" form that didn't work—just what one would expect from a small-town business. But, if they called the phone number, the CIA had forwarded it to the Det where a geek named Jamison was sipping chocolate Yoo-hoo, waiting for the phone to ring. Carter shook his head, picturing the nerd in a dim com room, his lime-green Chuck Taylors propped atop the metal desk. The guy was so socially inept he couldn't get to first base on prom night.

Senior Master Sergeant Nolan Grind cinched laces on a black boot, propped on the truck's diamond-plate bumper. Tiny sweat droplets beaded on his smooth scalp. He pointed to Carter's getup. "Looks like a parachute harness, minus the chute," he said. Plump eyes bulging like olives, dark skinned with close-cropped beard and round belly, Grind had been with Air Force Office of Special Investigations, OSI, for fifteen years. They'd recently demoted him to classroom teaching escape and evasion at Quantico when Carter had come looking for an experienced detective a few months back. Eager to secure his own escape from "white-collar scurvy," as he'd called it, the man had proven adept at fieldwork.

Carter slipped wraparound sunglasses over his eyes. "Wouldn't know. I was intel for the few years I was in the Navy. Never jumped from an airplane. No desire." He tilted his head back and studied a brushed aluminum lamppost looming over them. There were forty of the poles scattered across the grounds. "Think we need to plant at least two cameras on the lights around these picnic tables. This place is huge. If you were meeting a handler here, where would you go?"

Grind pressed a broad, flat palm to his forehead, shading eyes from morning sun. He turned toward the parking lot and pointed. A twenty-something female in black running pants and skintight racer-back top was bobbing down an earthen trail next to it. "Depends. Just runners here now. They're not meeting till this evening, so the park will be different. Next come the moms and kids after breakfast. Some dads will wander in before dinner to throw ball. But by evening, it'll be empty. Folks gone home to eat. Some bums might be out. I'd say they'll park in that lot, just sit at one of those picnic tables. Won't be anyone around to eavesdrop, so—might as well."

Carter nodded. Not knowing the exact location of the meeting within the park, they had to cover all the most obvious spots. Months of electronic eavesdropping and surveillance were coming together this evening. Yesterday he'd intercepted an unsecured phone call between Senator Moses and a known Mossad agent, arranging a meeting at this park at 7:00 P.M. Within an hour he'd pushed through approval from the National Reconnaissance Office to task a thermal imaging satellite to monitor the area. They could track the men's position wherever they wandered.

Carter glanced around. Tall oaks in the distance leaned in a firm breeze. In another direction empty swings rocked, as if occupied by ghost children, stirred by the same gusts. Across from the playground a soccer field thick with blooming dandelions rippled as invisible fingers stroked its fuzzy yellow coat.

Clear skies now, but the Weather Channel predicted heavy, low clouds in the evening. So now satellite imaging had been nixed. And at the beginning of July there was still over an hour of daylight left at seven, so they couldn't hide in the shadows and trail the pair with a microphone. The only thing left to do was mount as many cameras as possible and stick mics under every table and bench.

The senator was wily; he knew exactly what he was doing. A dirty prima donna around whom the world stage revolved, in his own head. Carter's investigation had linked him to money laundering and intelligence leaks, not the least of which had nearly killed Red last winter. And the connections Carter had uncovered showed the man's infidelity stretched back decades, possibly even when he was still under the employ of the CIA. And like any lie, the scope of these breaches had grown. Now something huge was in play. It included a list of the identity of key military operators and the ops in which they'd participated. Moses was a traitor and his treasonous actions were a threat to national security. But it seemed only a portion of a larger conspiracy, and thus far Carter had only uncovered the fringes. Plus, all his evidence was circumstantial. But he was a patient hunter. He'd bagged big game before, and would pull it together again…somehow.

He stepped onto the bumper, climbed into the truck bed, and gripped the rim of a white fiberglass man-bucket. In a single smooth motion, he swung into the cherry picker. He swatted his harness's snap hook onto a D ring, securing himself to the hard point. Then, he imagined himself perched high above, working on the light. His stomach knotted, and he braced himself on the lip.

Sergeant Rick Mather stretched out one thin arm to lift a door on the side of the utility bed, rummaging like a squirrel through screwdrivers and wrench sets. Mather had been assigned to the Det along with Grind, a yes-man. A gopher. But what the kid lacked in know-how he sure made up in eagerness.

Carter slipped a com bud into one ear and flipped the tiny switch next to his lobe. "Com check."

Grind, then Mather, gave a thumbs-up.

"*I read you.*" From Jamison, back at the Det.

"You didn't put your tan on this morning," came Grind from below. Carter hesitated, but leaned over the bucket and glanced down. Grind wasn't talking to him, but faced Mather. "You look like the bride of Frankenstein. A lineman's got burnt arms and neck." He pointed skyward. "That glowing orb up there? We call it the sun."

"Sorry. I forgot," the kid offered. "What should I do?"

"Look the part. Slip on a pair of those arm protection sleeves to cover your whiteness. There's some sunglasses and a pack of cigarettes on the dashboard. Light one up."

"But...I don't smoke."

"You do now. And look bored. Type on your phone and shit. I'll yell at you every once in a while. But now we gotta get these outriggers down so Carter don't kill himself."

Which was quite possible, Carter thought. Borrowing the boom truck from the CIA had been all too easy. They'd picked it up only yesterday from in front of what looked to be a legitimate mom-and-pop lighting contractor's store. No display of credentials, no checkout log, just a slight nod from a man standing behind the front window. Keys were already in the ignition. Thank goodness Mather knew how to work a clutch or they'd still be there grinding the transmission.

Carter considered the five levers next to his hip. No labels. He squinted at tiny blue-and-red pictures on the handles. He bumped one, and the boom rotated rapidly, slamming the bucket into the side of a toolbox. He did the same to the lever next to it. With a jerk the thick metal arm rose a few feet higher.

Grind and Mather leaned on other controls. Long steel beams grew out and downward from the sides of the yellow steel beast till their pads pressed upon the earth and lifted the truck from its wheels. Now stabilized, Carter worked his levers to raise his perch farther skyward. He let go and it jerked to a halt. A mild wave of nausea roiled in his belly. He studied the horizon to shove away the memory of falling off his Cape Cod's cedar-shingled roof. And tripping down the wooden stairs of a towering waterslide at his son's twelfth birthday party. And snapping a tree branch where he'd leaned on a ladder while tying his daughter's rope swing. Nothing good ever happened this high up.

Grind's gruff voice hummed through his earpiece. *"Boss, the levers ain't just off or on. Ease 'em and she'll move slow. Don't screw yourself up."*

That was about as close to a concerned tone as Carter had ever heard from the man. To avoid peering down, he stuck a thumbs-up over the side of the bucket. But even when Carter didn't work the controls, warm breezes rocked the perch. As he eased higher, bagpipes droned like great bees from across the yellow soccer field. A man in black sweats marched in front of a goal, working the pipes and bag, as if sucking on a huge hookah. As Carter inched toward the head of the light pole, the twang of country music came from the truck cabin. He willed a glance down—damn, he was high—and Mather climbed out of the driver's seat, coughing violently, blowing smoke from both nostrils.

The aluminum light was huge. They looked nowhere near this big from the ground. Carter fumbled at his tool belt and selected a number three Phillips screwdriver. Within a minute he had the top cover off. Affixed to it was a light sensor that, he'd been told, turned the device on at night. "Jamison, there isn't much to this," he said. "Just three wires running from the sensor. They're screwed into a terminal block."

"Like I said. Sweet as pie."

"Mather, this won't take long. Get ready to turn the main power back on so we can test my work." The man jogged toward the parking lot, flipping a cigarette away onto the gravel path. Carter touched a voltmeter to the terminal block. It stayed at zero: no voltage. He spun off the sensor and replaced it with the new one, which sat somewhat taller, bearing a close resemblance to the old. But beneath its tinted domed covering, the replacement housed a miniature high-definition camera. The new device worked double duty, also turning the light on at night. Carter tightened down its wire leads. "Mather, hit it."

A low buzz hummed from the light head. Voltmeter read an even 240 now. Carter gently rested the cover back atop. "Jamison, you have eyes?"

The high-pitched spin of a tiny electric motor buzzed from the device. Carter stuck his ear close to it, trying to listen above the audio salad of wind, honking bagpipes, and modern country.

"All I see is a... OK, that's your ear.... Yeah, I can see everything. Nice definition. One down. How many you putting up?"

Carter straightened and sucked a deep breath, stiffening his stomach against motion sickness. With all the rocking, bile kept creeping up his esophagus like on his last deep-sea fishing trip. They'd been caught in a summer storm for six hours.

He eased the bucket down, jumped out, and leaned on the tailgate.

Grind laughed. "You look green as Mather sucking on that Marlboro. Scared of heights?"

Carter glanced at him, then nodded. "Vertigo. They make me dizzy."

"They make you ugly. Look like a corpse." He tapped his temple. "It's all up here."

No shit, Grind. Carter spat onto dry earth. Normally he'd have had a real lineman install the high surveillance. But he'd been careful thus far to limit awareness of this investigation to a select few. That meant doing things himself even when he'd rather not. Anything with heights fell into that category.

"If we can get some direct evidence this evening, I'll plant so many bugs Moses won't take a crap without us knowing. Till then, we keep surveillance at arm's length." The senator was dirty, all right. But, he'd worked for the CIA before being elected to senator, so a mere chat with a Mossad agent wasn't concrete evidence anything illegal was transpiring. However, the circumstances had become all too compelling. Moses was covering up something, Carter was certain. The man had ordered the death of his own daughter—Lori—in his efforts. The old man might be a skilled subversive. But Carter was patient.

* * * *

Steam thick as vapor rose from black coffee in an orange Hard Rock Café travel mug. Carter blew across it, then took a cautious sip. It had only taken eight hours to plant twenty of the cameras across the park. After the sixth, his nausea had subsided. Then Mather had stuck a wireless mic beneath every picnic table and bench on the grounds.

Carter glanced around Jamison's com room, tucked in a dark corner of the Det's basement. The geek must've spent the whole day wiring every spare monitor into his cave, covering two walls halfway up with poster-sized displays. The glowing mosaic spouted so much light it made Carter wince. He squeezed temples between thumb and finger, massaging a dull ache behind his eyes. Grind sat flipping through an edition of *Plane & Pilot*.

Jamison propped a lime-green hoof atop a folding chair, pounding a keyboard in his lap.

Carter squinted. "Those ugly-ass shoes give me a migraine."

Jamison took a final swig from a Yoo-hoo. The empty bottle clanked into a metal trash can. He pointed to one glowing screen. "That may be him." He clicked a mouse, and the image zoomed to a black Tahoe pulling to a halt in Greenwood's parking lot. Moses' unmistakable bulk loomed behind the wheel. From the high angle, only the bottom half of his head was visible below the roof, but he held a cell phone to one ear, mouth moving.

Grind tossed his magazine on a desk and leaned back in a maroon office chair, stuffing gaping through a worn hole in its side. "If we just bent the rules a little, we'd know who he was calling."

Carter clenched his jaw. Grind was right, of course. But anything they gathered needed to be admissible in court. He wasn't trying to figure out *if* the man was guilty, but rather laying a snare to ensure conviction. Get some evidence more concrete, *then* push through warrants. Spying on a three-term senator wasn't like listening to the cell conversations of an illegal immigrant.

Jamison pointed to a map of Greenwood Park pinned to the wall with twenty red pushpins indicating the placement of cameras, then studied an adjoining monitor. "We've got camera number eight as well. That should give us another angle on the truck." The image spun like a Tilt-A-Whirl, then came to rest on the same Tahoe. Jamison dragged the cursor across the vehicle, and within a second the truck filled the screen.

Grind huffed. "Be nice if a drone could've given us a bird's eye."

Carter's neck tensed. Why wouldn't the bastard let it rest? "You saw the clouds. Ceiling's too low. We'd run the risk of being spotted. Why all the harping on wiretapping and drones? We're doing old-fashioned investigating. You going geek on me? Want to transfer into Jamison's playgroup?"

Jamison turned to gape at him, hurt creasing his face.

Grind jerked his head toward Carter. "Screw you."

"Excuse me?"

"Screw you. Sir."

Carter smiled. "That's what I thought you said." He pointed at a monitor. A thin man in jeans and black blazer was stepping out from a squat red-brick building near the back of the parking lot. The men's restroom. He wiped his hands dry on white paper, tossed it in a canister, and jogged toward the Tahoe. "Where'd he come from? That the Mossad agent?" He'd expected him to arrive by car. They hadn't monitored foot traffic. How long had the guy been in there? Had he seen Carter and his crew replacing the light sensors?

The man opened the passenger door of the Tahoe and sat across from Moses. Carter pounded a fist on the table. "We can't listen to them there!" Months of patient stalking, waiting for the big man to make a misstep. Now something was calling the dirty senator off his worn path, necessitating a face-to-face with Mossad, and Carter couldn't even eavesdrop. He jumped up and waved at the wall of monitors. "We've got all the electrons in the universe focused on this damn Tahoe and for all we know they're exchanging cookie recipes."

Maybe Grind had been right. Maybe sometimes you had to bend the rules for the greater good.

Grind leaned closer to one of the screens. "Zoom in on the big guy's mouth. Do the same on the other screen to his friend in black."

What the hell? Both men's faces were half-hidden from the cameras. "What are you doing?"

Grind waved him off. "Shut up."

Carter clenched a fist. What was the worst that could happen if he decked Grind right now? The detective supposed he could give up the whole investigation and return to "retirement," working a lazy man's job for New Kent County Sheriff's Department. The thought evoked fresh air and freedom. Except Carter had no choice. He had to finish and find out who was trying to kill Red and Lori. Because in return, Red was removing evidence of Carter's involvement in the deaths of several terror suspects during interrogation not long after nine eleven.

Carter shook his head. He'd only executed his assignment, obeyed orders, extracted perishable intel from extremists, and saved American lives. But the media didn't have a damn clue what it took to ensure society's protection from scum like that. No one wanted to know the truth, that fanatics sometimes had to die in agony so that American kids could sip their Starbucks lattes without the shopping mall's food court being ripped apart by a backpack bomb at Christmastime. It'd be best if his name was simply never mentioned in the capital hearings. So, there was no backing out of this investigation for Carter, and no return to retired life. Just stale air and Grind's attitude.

He breathed a sigh. "Tell me what you're—"

Grind lifted a flat-bladed hand to stop him. "Lipreading, Detective." He nudged Jamison's shoulder. "You're recording this, right?"

Jamison slapped both feet onto the carpet and banged on his keyboard. Red lights flashed in the corner of both displays.

Grind studied the monitors in turn, head swinging between them as each man spoke. His own mouth moved as if trying to speak the same words. He pointed to Moses. "*Money stopped...two months' deposits. You guys not happy?*" Some words he seemed to decipher right away. Others he skipped over, speaking in sporadic phrases.

He pointed to the Mossad agent. "*Story isn't dead...still investigating your operations...damaged goods...*"

As Moses patted his chest on-screen, Grind continued his translation. "*I'll do it.*"

The man in black shook his head. "*We will eliminate...*"

After another minute of Grind channeling nonsense like the Oracle of Delphi, both men in the Tahoe leaned back in their seats, lips now still. A silver Jaguar XF pulled behind the truck. Without any movement of lips, the Mossad agent slipped out and drove off in it. Moses sat for several more minutes, rubbing the back of his neck. When he finally started the Tahoe, his shoulders hunched forward. He slid down in his seat, losing a few inches of height. One monitor was still zoomed in on his face. His eyes looked swollen. He rubbed them with a thumb, then backed the SUV up and drove from the lot.

"What the hell just happened?" Carter asked.

Grind stood and put a hand on Jamison's shoulder. "You got all that on film, right?"

The geek shrugged. "Not *film*. But yeah, I got it."

He turned to Carter. "My sister's deaf. Like, from birth. We used to play this game growing up, listening to others' conversations by lipreading. Easier if you know what people are talking about, or if you can see their whole face. Here I couldn't see any expressions or body language. So, I didn't get much, but we can review the tapes, maybe get more. Plus, I know some guys who're real good at this." He scratched his bald scalp. "What do you think he meant by the story not being dead? Is Mossad blackmailing Moses?"

"Maybe," Carter said. "But I don't think that's what he was saying."

Grind huffed. "What, you reading lips now too?"

"No. But I'll bet he said *Lori*, not *story*. As in: *Lori isn't dead*. So now Mossad is going to take matters into their own hands." Carter snatched up a black handset and punched the ten digits of Red's mobile number. He needed to reach him now, before Mossad.

Chapter 3

Truck Stop

Red glanced at movement in the rearview mirror of his Ford Explorer. His eyes focused on a small set of raised hands in the seats behind him. He straightened his back and saw they belonged to Nick, their five-year-old, grinning and waving arms as they rounded another curve on Interstate 64 headed into Charleston, West Virginia. They flashed by a white-and-black sign announcing a fifty-five-mile-per-hour limit. Speedometer read seventy, so he lifted his foot from the accelerator.

"This is like a roller coaster!" the child cried. Penny, ten, and Jackson, six, stared down at a screen with white-corded headphones in their ears, oblivious.

Red had driven this stretch many times. The graceful curves and dips of the pavement through the lush mountain valley begged for speed, despite the uphill incline. Lori's head leaned on the passenger window, the curved side of her neck stretched tight. That couldn't be comfortable. Though it was now three in the afternoon, she'd been sleeping, or pretending to sleep, for two hours. He glanced at her chest slowly rising and falling. They'd booked suites along the route, a separate bedroom for the kids. He smiled. A well-rested wife always meant a better chance for sex.

Carter had still warned him that Lori hadn't been completely forthright regarding her work at the CIA. The detective distrusted everyone, it seemed. He'd suspected her of being a mole, leaking financial intelligence, fintel. But it turned out she'd been a part of a CIA team investigating certain fintel leaks and had only *looked* like a mole. Nonetheless, Carter hadn't been convinced despite CIA reassurances and reminded Red often of his doubts. The detective's instincts had been dead on before, but Red reassured himself the mother of their children wasn't dirty. Still...

He reached a hand across the console to hers. "Driving always helps clear my mind."

No response.

They'd considered flying to Colorado Springs, their final destination, instead. But they hadn't done a road trip in years. Each had taken two weeks off, so Red suggested they go by interstate.

Outside Red's window a rolling green ridge rushed past. The calloused brown bark of white pines dotted stands of gray-striped sugar maples and the peeling skin of red ones. Across a frontage road sprouted a clump of birch, trunks wrapped with shredded linen-paper covers. The dark, coarse texture of a lone black cherry stood out among them, its crooked limbs wrapping around encroaching branches. He glanced at his palm, half expecting to see the ghosts of calluses from endless weekends gathering and splitting logs on the farm as a child. Red's father to this day maintained wood heat in winter. "It warms you twice," he'd say, usually out in the forest, as Red struggled to heft a weighty log into the weathered old farm trailer. Once unloaded in a heap in front of the woodshed, the song of sledgehammers ringing against splitting wedges would mingle for hours with the hollow *thunk* of axes sinking into wood grain. The air fragrant with the astringent vinegar of white oak, the mellow sweetness of sugar maple.

This labor, arduous as it was, had not been without effect. Red had built a compact strength that, throughout high school, punished many a linebacker who underestimated him due to his size. Later, climbing through special operations assignments, he'd often used that deceptive stature to his advantage.

He cracked open a window and inhaled the jumbled resinous scent of leaves and needles. Life in these West Virginia mountains seemed to force new growth continually through the earth's coarse skin, its fertile soil and humid air never allowing a patch of ground to lie bare.

Lori yawned and stretched her legs. Fuel gauge read just under a quarter tank. He steered onto an exit lane where a blue sign announced GAS—THIS EXIT. A gray Subaru Forester with New Jersey plates drove past once again. They'd traded pole position a few times over the last hour, its driver apparently oblivious to the benefits of cruise control.

Red pulled next to a green pump and slapped his thigh. "Bathroom break!" he announced.

Lori's eyes opened, and she yawned. "You doing OK? Need me to drive?"

"Nah. I'll stretch a bit and be all right for another hour or so. You can make it up tonight."

Her mouth curled devilishly. He hadn't seen her expression that intense for months. "Better get yourself one of those energy drinks, then." She adjusted her bra, stepped out, and leaned over, touching fingertips to toes. Her blouse slipped up her back and—damn. They should've taken a vacation a long time ago.

As Red grabbed the hose to fill the tank, Lori gripped the hands of their youngest two and walked across the lot under bright noonday sun, headed toward the convenience store's door framing a faded lottery advertisement. Penny bounced ahead of them. A cool breeze lifted Lori's blond ponytail. A skinny man with long white beard turned his head to gaze after her, stumbling as he twisted his ankle in a pothole.

Tank full, Red replaced the nozzle and noticed a gray Subaru Forester had parked near the faded orange awning of the store. The same vehicle they'd been passing so often? A tall man with a gut like a basketball under his white polo pressed hands to hips and arched his back, grimacing. Considering the vehicle's dark-tinted windows, Red had expected a much younger driver.

Were they being followed? The Subaru from the interstate had New Jersey plates. A West Virginia license was bolted to this one's bumper. Even so, he studied the man. Fair skinned, endomorph body type, feet at least size fourteen. The passenger door opened and a woman in close-fitting jeans, her tank top revealing sharp, defined arm muscles stepped out. Tight figure like a yoga instructor, long, jet-black hair fell to her bare shoulders. How did she end up with *that* guy? Then she turned sideways and her belly stuck out as well. Obviously pregnant, probably eight months judging by the huge baby bump. Even so, she walked easily toward the store, without the usual pregnancy waddle.

Red popped the hood and pulled out the long, hot dipstick. It was habit, even though the vehicle burned no oil. He always took care of whatever machinery he possessed. He'd never mentioned it to anyone, but he could actually bond with certain machines, connecting on some emotional level that he theorized sprung from the passion of their maker. On a recent op, an Ohio-class submarine had actually whispered to him. Or maybe his mind had made the whole thing up in a stress-induced nightmare. For this reason, he was careful to never talk about it. His own doubts about his state of mind were enough already.

He shut the hood as Lori and the kids wandered back, blue, red, and orange ice slushies in hand. Through the clear plastic cup, Nick's drink was as colorful as one of his finger paintings. Which was why Red had ordered the Explorer with the leather package and black carpet. He helped strap the boy back into his child seat, a contraption that looked ridiculously like the pilot's chair of an F-22 Raptor.

As they sped down a gently curved acceleration lane onto the highway, Lori turned her shoulders toward him. "Do you want any more kids?"

"No!" yelled Penny from the backseat, looking up from a gadget's screen, scowling.

Red put a finger in an ear, the family's sign for a conversation meant to be just between the parents. "I thought we were done. I mean, now they're getting older, where I can relate. Um—why? You want more?"

She turned to face forward again, studying the haze-topped mountain toward which the road was aimed. It was the only one with cloud cover, taller than the rest. "I don't know. I just saw this pregnant lady in there and she didn't look near as miserable as I remember it being. And, well, I always pictured us with a big family."

"Three isn't big?" Memories of being woken every two hours by crying, of stumbling out of bed, to feed Nick for the first six months of his life rushed back as if fresh from this morning. The kid had been a real chowhound, sucking even in his sleep.

"It's a good number." She nodded. "But so is four. Or five."

That could be a good sign, Red thought, that their marriage wasn't mired as deeply as Dr. Sato had suggested. Or was this Lori's way of subconsciously trying to fill a void he wasn't satisfying. Even he had to admit over the last few years the effort to romance his wife had slipped. Well, in ways other than sex. Or, maybe she was a traitor, selling secrets to foreign governments, trying to reassure her duped husband while secretly planning to cut his throat as he slept, then escape to Alberta with millions stashed in a Swiss bank account. The thought swirled around his mind like a soap bubble, then popped. Nah... Carter's intuition on Lori had to be misguided.

So, what was the right answer here? "Can you give me a hint?" he finally said.

"About what?"

"What I'm supposed to say."

She pursed her lips, but said nothing, only scowling.

"No, I mean, if you want more kids, then sure. Let's have more. If not, I'm happy where we are." He stretched a hand to cup her knee. "Either way, I enjoy the practice."

Another scowl.

"But, you know—work. We're both so busy. We'd have to be OK with hiring a nanny or something."

"Work doesn't play into this," she murmured.

A Kenny Rogers tune blasted from Red's jeans. Shit. The ringtone from Carter. He slipped fingers into his pocket, fishing for the phone.

Lori eyed his hand. "If you want to get something out of those pants and *practice* tonight, better leave that thing in there." She lifted her chin. "*My* work phone's off. Sato's right. They can deal without me for a couple weeks. Same goes for Carter." She jabbed a finger onto the dash. "This is our time."

But Carter had so far been good to not overburden Red with too much detail on the investigation. When he called, it was always for good reason. Red glanced at the white tip of Lori's index finger pressing the dash pad. She was right. He needed to match her attitude, to be as proactive about the family as she. He lifted the device, glanced at Lori, sighed, then held down the power button.

The screen flashed GOODBYE THEN!

Chapter 4

Cog Railway

Red gripped Lori's hand, careful not to squeeze her fingers too tightly. Cool morning air chilled his cheekbones. Standing next to a narrow mountain road in Manitou Springs, Colorado, he waited for a black BMW sedan to pass, then started across. Lori was on his uphill side, looking even taller than usual. Blond hair gathered to fall like a horse's tail down the back of her black fleece vest. Penny followed, looking bored, no doubt desiring independence. Still, she never lagged far. Her blue school backpack was crammed with snacks, water, and extra clothing for the ascent.

"It doesn't feel so cold," she said.

Red smiled. "Not down here." He pointed up the mountain, past the tree line, to a bare, rocky crown. "But at the top of Pikes Peak, some places still have snow. Trust me. You'll want that hat and coat once we're there."

They stepped onto the sidewalk, and Lori stopped. "Look at that, over the city." She pointed.

Deep gray clouds rolled from the south, stretching over half the valley below, dividing it into brilliant light and menacing shadow. From their current elevation, partway up the side of the mountain, the storm moved at eye level, a microcosm of darkness in an otherwise clear sky. Black streaks as from an artist's brush angled to earth, then disappeared halfway. The sky offering rain, then gobbling it up by evaporation before it ever watered soil. A brilliant lightning bolt flashed, arcing a crooked pattern to the valley floor.

It was amazing how far you could see in clear, dry air. On the East Coast, targets started to fade in a shade of hazy blue after just a quarter klick. Out here, it must be twelve klicks across the Colorado Springs valley, yet the green of the pines on the far side looked almost as deep as the spruce right across the road.

Jackson and Nick were most likely still asleep in the basement of Red's sister's house, down somewhere in the bright portion of that valley. She'd taken a few days off from her work as the Office of Naval Intelligence liaison to NORAD. Driving into town only yesterday evening, Lori had managed to score tickets on the cog railway to the top of Pikes Peak, but at the expense of having to get up at 5:00 A.M. to be ready in time. The boys were probably too young to care anyway.

They stepped beneath the weathered wood portico of the station and walked down concrete stairs to the platform. Two long, red train cars with wide, open windows rested at the bottom. It was the same bright shade of an Italian woman's dress in an oil painting hanging on a wall of their living room. Lori had been the artist, but since hadn't picked up a brush for years. *Lots of things get pushed aside when children come into the picture*, Red mused. Near the edge of the platform a woman, still plump with pregnancy weight, black tights stretched to the breaking point, struggled to fold a double stroller outside one car while her husband cradled sleeping infants.

Red pointed to the lead car. "Let's get that one."

They sat in high-backed wooden benches facing each other, like a restaurant booth without a table. The angle of the rails up the mountain eased him back into his seat. Morning sun warmed his nose. Through the window blew scents of cotton candy and springwater. He listened, but heard no burble of a mountain stream. Only the low hum of idling diesels and the creaking of branches sawing against each other, rubbed by wind. He closed his eyes and breathed a sigh. Penny leaned against him, and he took her under his arm.

"Tired?" asked Lori.

He cracked an eye. "Not bad. I'll catch a few winks on the way up."

"You can't, Daddy," scolded Penny. "You might miss something."

A corner of his mouth turned up. "You have fun. I've done it before. Spent more time than I'd like to remember around these mountains."

"Daddy's been driving a lot," Lori said. "Let him sleep. We'll wake him at the top."

Penny shook his arm. "No. I won't let you."

He leaned his cheek against a window post, skin to cold steel. The muffled vibration of the diesels spun higher as the train eased ahead.

Now hauling up the mountain, the car pitched back even more, till he was reclined as in a bed. Penny's tugging stopped and the gentle rock of the tracks took over. He closed his eyes as the conductor mumbled and the crowd laughed and the mule pulled....

* * * *

She was a large mule, eighteen hands high with muscles taunt and sinews thick from hauling her burden up the tracks. The animal glanced back to see what was upon the sledge but received a whip of leather on one flank. "Get up there, girl!" called the driver. The cart was stacked high with railroad ties just like the ones lying near her hooves. She was harnessed to a couple of horses, and another team like hers pulled from the opposite side of the railroad bed, tugging the load between them. Four horses and two mules in total, all with thick winter coats, like herself. Sweat ran down her legs and froze in crystals on the tips of her bushy brown hair.

Cool water gurgled across rocks and grass next to the tracks, the sound quickening her deep thirst. With winter approaching, the river seemed to sleep. In spring it would thunder again. But now the sound of a waterfall, weak as it was, spurred the entire team to pull harder, leaning into leather.

Soon the driver sounded the command they desired. "Whoooa." He pressed wood to wheels, unharnessed each team member in turn, and led them to a pool where they could drink as much as they wanted before continuing up the mountain. The mule lowered her head, whiskers brushing the clear surface, then plunged dry lips into the cold, delicious liquid. A blessing to thirst, but a curse to her stomach, the frigid fluid causing it to cramp.

A flash of sand-colored fur sprinted across the tracks. She jerked her head high at the unmistakable musk of mountain cat. The stupid horses, still in their harnesses, neighed and bucked, spilling the load, pulling one hitched team atop the other.

She tossed her head again, yanking the reins from the driver, and turned to meet the predator. Puffs of dust rose where she pawed the ground with a hoof. The cat...

* * * *

"You OK?"

Red jerked awake. He yawned and rubbed his eyes with thumbs. The window was still down. Penny was on Lori's side now. His wife's hand rested on his knee. "You looked like a dog chasing a rabbit in its sleep." Penny laughed. "You were funny, Daddy. Your leg was twitching. But Mommy said not to wake you. You missed the waterfalls."

Red lifted his arms and stretched. "Somehow, I don't think I really missed 'em."

Lori patted the seat next to Penny. "The view's better from this side now. Conductor said in a minute the trees will be out of the way and it'll be a good time to take a picture."

Red slipped in next to them and gazed out the window. The glass pane was still down, and the temperature had cooled since the bottom. A Korean woman from the opposite side of the aisle in a white tennis visor stood gripping a video camera in one hand, steadying herself on the bench with the other. Toward the rear of the car sat a thick-necked man with close-cropped hair and flattop, an Army cut for certain. Probably Fort Carson.

As Red turned back to the clear sky out the open window, he noticed a tall potbellied man behind Flattop. The lanky fellow sported black sunglasses and ball cap with the purple Baltimore Ravens mascot on the bridge. The face was familiar. He'd seen this guy recently. Red closed his eyes and let his mind flash through the morning, through yesterday, tracing their trail back down the interstate, dinner at McDonald's, breakfast at Denny's, slamming to a halt the previous day in Charleston, West Virginia.

He put a hand on Lori's arm, leaning to her ear. "Don't be obvious, but look at that tall guy at the back of the car. Ever seen him before?"

Lori smiled and took a photo out the window. As she lowered the phone, she stole a glance. They rested elbows on knees, hunching below the cover of the opposite seat. "No," she whispered. "Why?"

"Take a look at the woman next to him. She's wearing a purple cap and puffy green vest, but picture her with a round belly in tight pregnancy jeans."

Lori straightened and pretended to take another picture. Another glance. Her eyebrows lifted as recognition spread across her face. "That pregnant woman at the gas station. But she's not pregnant now. I *knew* she was making it look too easy. But it may not be her. Maybe someone who just looks similar."

Red stood and handed his phone to the Korean woman filming just over his head. "Excuse me, do you mind taking a picture of my family?" She smiled, nodded, and accepted the device. They switched seats so the rear of the railcar would be in the background of the picture. "Try to get the whole car, so we can show folks at home how many people were in here." She nodded again and pressed the button.

"A few more, just in case?"

Another nod, more photos, and she handed the phone back.

Cradling the device between them, Red and Lori reviewed the pictures, zooming in on the man and woman in the back. In each shot, their heads were down looking at a magazine or turned to the side, obscured by other passengers.

Lori turned up a palm, speaking low. "I think we're being paranoid. You can't tell from these."

"Which is why I think we're being followed. They're evading. They don't want to be photographed."

"Or they're just reading tourist brochures and you're being paranoid."

"I don't forget faces."

Lori leaned back, nodding slightly. "True. What do you want to do?"

"This train is a slow mover. I could grab one, jump off behind those boulders, and interrogate."

Lori blinked and stared at him blankly. "You shouldn't be allowed to roam in free society. What if you're wrong? Maybe my boss told them to follow since someone tried to kill me a few months back—they could be on our side. Plus, you're not the only one carrying a weapon. This is Colorado, you know. There's lots of other pistols on this train. One of them makes you as the bad guy, and you're a casualty of friendly fire."

"I could be nice. Just sit down across from them and ask. Play it as it comes."

Lori closed her eyes. She covered Penny's ears and whispered. "If I were a tail, that would be a definite sign of aggression."

"So?"

Another sigh. "Dial up the fact that we've got families here, ours being one. Plus, they'd lie and we'd have no way of proving it. A good tail has flawless backstory."

"Then what the hell am I supposed to do?"

"You? Nothing. Me? I call work and see if my boss ordered a tail. If not, we catch a better shot of them later, email it to my work, or to the Det, and have them run facial recognition through the databases."

Red pressed an arm against his side, hugging his pistol. Maybe Carter was right. For having been shot by a wet team in a brazen but disastrously executed hit a few months ago, Lori seemed unconcerned about the possibility of having a tail now. Maybe she knew who was following them and was disguising her lack of action under the pretense of protecting family. That's not the way you protect loved ones. If a threat exists, identify it, face it, and eliminate it. A simple, uncomplicated method; an operator's modus operandi. Red lived by it. But Lori wasn't an operator, he considered. She'd lived a stint as a field agent for the CIA, but that was financial intelligence, fintel, spook work. And a spy's instincts were cautious. To be invisible. Maybe that was why she wouldn't face this threat head-on.

Lori pulled the phone away from her ear. "What the hell? No signal."

"We're almost up to tree line, near the back side of the peak. Probably won't have signal at the top, either. Sure you don't want me to just ask them?"

Lori's eyes bulged. "No!"

He lifted both hands in surrender. "OK. We'll just sit here and play with ourselves. Gotta love vacation."

* * * *

Red gazed out the front train car's window as it approached the top of Pikes Peak. Tracks sloped upward next to a concrete loading platform in front of a sprawling visitor center. Weathered brown paint peeled from the wood trim of the low-roofed structure, which was lined with expansive picture windows. Ice melt pooled across the packed-clay path next to the train. From inside, the end of the tracks appeared as a ramp launching into pale blue sky. Twenty feet short of ramming the safety buttress, the car jerked to a halt. The conductor mumbled, "Sorry folks. New brake pads." Everyone stood and turned to the door as if deplaning.

The car's wide observation windows had been shut after reaching the tree line to keep in warmth. The conductor opened the door, and a cold rope of air wrapped around Red's shoulders. The visitor center roof still held a few inches of snow, plugging gutters. Morning sun was melting the mass, dripping from frozen stalactites at the corners. Ravens Fan was already inside studying souvenir coffee mugs next to a window when Red stepped off. Red straightened his back, trying to look tall.

They shuffled from concrete onto wet clay and hurried with the rest of the passengers inside. The souvenir shop was packed with displays of worthless tourist crap. Key chains and hoodies and polyester blankets. Korean and Chinese visitors teetered down narrow aisles between an occasional booted Texan, the men in big white hats, the women with hair teased and sprayed to match. An elderly man with an aluminum cane spoke in guttural German near the entrance to the bathrooms, pulling a wallet from a front pocket. Two slender men with sculpted calves spoke what sounded like French as they clattered across terra-cotta tile on lightweight bicyclists' shoes. Seven thousand feet vertical from Manitou Springs, the bikers must've started up the long road last night. But in the dark? Difficult, Red thought, since it was a crescent moon.

He gripped Penny's hand and hurried out of the stifling crowd, toward scents of sweet cooking grease and orange juice. "Breakfast? Let's snag some of those doughnuts the conductor was talking about." He ordered a dozen from a sleepy-eyed girl in a Colorado College sweatshirt. Penny plopped into a booth, and he squeezed next to her on a vinyl-clad bench, table scented with chlorine spray.

Lori stood, stretching a leg. "No thanks. Feels like I've been sitting for days."

The booth, built into one corner of the visitor center, provided a clear vantage of the entire shop, crowded as it was. Penny was licking powdered sugar from pink lips, red hair clips holding flapping pigtails. Damn. Ten already. Boys were still gross, but how long would that last? Red put mouth to paper rim, breathing in coffee steam, then rubbed the bridge of his nose. "I'm going to need a few more of these to stay awake."

Lori's chest rose as she inhaled. "Think I need a doughnut. I didn't have breakfast and now I'm light-headed."

Red was feeling it too, but not from skipping a meal. He was in excellent shape, but they'd lived the last decade at sea level and now were over two and a half miles in the air. He lifted his head. Ravens Fan was standing in a bathroom line at the far end. Red muttered across the rim of his mug, covering his lips, "You keeping an eye on our friend?"

Lori slipped intocross from him. "I don't think they're alone. That Chinese guy in the blue parka next to the entrance. He's just hanging out there, looking at the same key chains. Problem is, they're all tags with English names on them. He greeted that old lady in fluent Mandarin. I mean, he could easily know English, but…"

One way to find out. Red gripped the table and started to slip out of the booth.

Lori grabbed his wrist. "Don't. He's glanced toward the Ravens guy a few times. If it was CIA tailing us, they wouldn't send two teams. So we're going to test, to make sure. I'll go out the side door, to the observation deck. The parking lot is that way too. A tail would keep an eye on me, especially near a parking lot. Either one of them follows, then we know."

"And we snatch them?"

"No! Then…we just know."

Which gets us nowhere, Red thought, wiping a drop of condensation from his nose. "What? So I just take a nap until you say it's OK to do something?" "No. You sit here with Penny. I'll be back soon." She cradled her phone in one palm, pressed the camera app, dialed it to video, and hit RECORD. Red stared at her heart-shaped ass in low-rise black jeans as she stood and held the device inconspicuously, walking toward the side door, across the room from Mandarin. The Chinaman glanced at her and then studied the key chains more intently. He tapped a phone and lifted it to his ear. Right. There was no reception up here. Though he could be using an intercom function, Red considered, if his audience was close.

When Mandarin's back was turned, Red tapped the table softly and leaned toward Penny. "You stay here, sweetheart. Don't move. Have another doughnut." Red wasn't leaving her alone. He was only going a few steps away. He slipped out and stood behind a display of wooden puzzles with panoramas of Pikes Peak silk-screened onto them, the exhibit closest to Mandarin. Red peered between shelves, but couldn't hear what the man was saying into the phone.

Mandarin slipped the device into a belt caddy like a gunslinger returning a pistol to its holster. He started toward the side door, hands in pockets, lips pursed, eyes squinted to slits.

Red had enough of waiting and inaction. No way was he going to let this guy tail Lori. He wouldn't hurt him, but the man was about to know he'd been made. Mandarin neared a buxom woman bouncing a baby on one hip. Red slipped one foot onto the wheel of her empty stroller and shoved it in front of him as he passed.

Chapter 5

Mandarin

Red flattened against the puzzle display as Mandarin crashed into the carriage, yanking hands from pockets to break his fall. With all the tourist chatter in the shop, it seemed no one noticed the collision. A tiny Glock 43 with a slender silencer screwed onto the muzzle clattered to the ground between them. Shit. The man scrambled for it, glancing at Red with narrowed eyes. Red lunged to beat him to the weapon, but just then a jigsaw puzzle box exploded above his scalp, raining wooden shards upon his neck. A cream mug boasting I Hiked Pikes Peak in blue letters shattered with a *crack* next to his head.

Someone else was shooting at him—with a silenced weapon.

Red kicked Mandarin's pistol away and rolled behind the coffee bar. He yanked up his tight crewman's sweater and drew his own sidearm, a modified Sig Sauer 9mm. He thumbed off the safety. The ceramic-lined barrel was almost as fat as a .45 caliber but strong enough to take the higher pressures of Det ammo. Ducking behind a row of black coffee carafes, he peered carefully around the corner of the counter.

The loud rumble of a barista steaming two carafes of milk filled the room. Everyone was still turning displays of stuffed animals or pushing hot dogs into their mouths, oblivious to the silenced shots being fired nearby.

A young lady with kelly-green eyelids set a tray with a funnel cake next to Red's shoulder. Filling her coffee mug, she glanced down and did a double take at Red's pistol.

"Federal marshal," he whispered. "Get down."

Green flashed as her eyebrows rose. She gasped, then screamed shrilly. He whipped a leg against her ankle, and she fell to the terra-cotta tiles. A carafe wobbled as a stream of hot brew spouted from a fresh bullet hole, the same one a second ago the lady had been filling up from. Damn it. Where was the other shooter?

A flash of blue as Mandarin sprinted out behind a long chest of turquoise jewelry, hunched low. Red squeezed the trigger just short of the break point and trailed the man with his sights. For a split second, the room went silent as his bead caught up with the runner, then led him a mere half inch. Det ammo would penetrate two or even three bodies, so he had to wait for a clear shot. In his mind, quick as the beat of a wasp's wing, he reviewed firing a double tap through the chest. His grip tightened. Then, instinct collided with reality when the front sight passed over a blond girl with pigtails, stuffing a powdered doughnut into her mouth.

Penny!

A blink later Mandarin was out the door. Another carafe cracked open, spewing hot coffee on his wrist. *Enough of this shit.* Red pointed the pistol at the roof and squeezed twice. The loud crack of Det ammo whipped through the building.

He opened his wallet and held up a silver star. "Federal marshal! Everyone down!" The usual two-second pause as a hundred pairs of lungs gasped. Then came the screaming, the ducking, and scrambling to the floor.

There they were. The whole room stooped except for Ravens Fan in the bathroom line and his high-cheekboned yoga wife, who stood behind a sunglasses display. The weapon was at her waist, partially concealed by one palm, no doubt catching ejected brass to keep it from tinkling on the tiles.

"Daddy!" called Penny.

Red caught Yoga's gaze. The bitch smiled and puckered her lips into a kiss, glancing toward his daughter. Shit. They'd made Penny. He couldn't just run away and draw their fire; they'd grab her.

Now Ravens Fan drew a pistol from the small of his back. Ducking low again, Red lifted a round table and ran toward the jewelry counter. The slap of rounds hitting the top side cracked in his ear. Yoga and Ravens Fan were firing subsonic loads for silence, which meant slow movers. But if either slapped in a mag of regular ammo, the table wasn't going to do him much good. He squeezed off a few shots in Yoga's direction, aiming high since she was ducking now behind a cotton-topped couple, each gripping a cane and bent at the waist.

Kneeling next to Penny, he whispered, "Piggyback." She crawled on and latched arms and legs around him like a spider securing prey. He slipped toward the side door, table shielding their front. Ravens Fan reloaded. Loud muzzle barks followed; then wood splinters blew like thick dust into Red's chin. Pivot, squeeze, and two crimson petals bloomed from the man's chest. He dropped upon a table's edge, launching a hail of polished stones across the room. Red backed through the door into cold air.

Outside, Mandarin was running toward the far end of a packed-earth parking lot, head erect, swiveling, searching between cars. Too far for a good shot, and Red couldn't risk drawing fire with Penny on his back. A flash of motion in his periphery, and he swung his weapon toward it. Lori, crouching behind a car in the front row. He started for her, but she waved him away, mouthed *Penny*, and pointed down the mountain.

She was right. He had to get their daughter to safety first.

"Mommy!" screamed Penny next to his ear.

At the shout, Mandarin slid to a halt and turned back toward the visitor center. Red yanked a white-and-red road bike with low, curved handles from an outside rack. Yoga slammed the side door behind him, but he drove her back in with a quick burst. He mounted the bike and started down the road.

"You can't leave Mommy!" Penny wailed.

Red's fingers tensed on the handle brakes, but he didn't squeeze. Running from a fight felt completely wrong, though. He glanced back to see Lori jumping off a rock away from the parking lot, disappearing somewhere down the side of the mountain. Mandarin ran after her. She had a good hundred-meter head start. He'd have to be fast to catch up.

His legs pumped quickly, and soon they were screaming down the narrow road. Zigzagging across a steep ridge, they flitted continuously through shadow and blazing light as high rocks broke the sun's view, a beacon flashing warning. Breeze rushing up the mountain broke over a boulder ridge and condensed into thin fog, wisps of vapor like contrails from an airplane.

The bike's handlebars were thin and narrow. He'd only ridden mountain bikes before. The front tire of this one looked sharp as a knife blade. He squeezed the brakes around a cutback, but the front wheel locked when he crossed a path of windblown dust upon the blacktop. The wheels slipped out, and they toppled. He slammed his hip onto the road and skidded to a spinning halt, but Penny's grip stayed tight. Hopping up, he lifted the bike from a sharp granite boulder, then started down again. The steering was canted, but the tires seemed intact. In seconds, they were speeding down another straightaway. Next cutback, he leaned into the curve and stuck out a boot like a motocross racer. Cold drops hit the back of his neck.

"You hurt?" he yelled over the rush of frigid wind.

"Is she going to d-die?" Her breath warm on his ear.

"Mom? Shoot, no. She'll be OK."

"But, why'd you leave her?"

"She told us to go the other way. To get you safe."

Another cutback, then a long straightaway. Glancing up, he saw a white sedan stopped in the road, hood up, vapor rising. A small black pickup had squeezed next to it, as if trying to pass, instead completely blocking the narrow trail. No one was in sight. Red tightened his grip on the brakes. The rear tire locked, but he kept balanced. Leaning to one side, he started down what looked to be a centuries-old wagon trail. The wheels clattered over sharp rocks. He steered momentarily off the trail onto a thin carpet of pale green tundra. The bike slowed, narrow wheel slicing through the mossy surface like a pizza cutter.

A puff of dust. A rock skipped off the trail a few feet ahead. A few seconds later there came another puff, this one next to him. He glanced back. Yoga stood high at the top of the cutbacks, drawing a bead with her pistol. Any hit from this distance would be pure luck. But if the broken-down sedan was a trap, those guys could soon be taking shots as well. Red pulled off the trail behind an oblong rock, the sharp outcrop jutting from the tundra's surface like a giant's thumb.

"Hop off a sec," he panted. He drew his pistol and leaned against the rock's vertical surface. Flat green lichen crumbled onto one cheek as he peered around the edge. Yoga was no longer atop her lookout and— damn—the black pickup was backing up. Red watched it steer down the same wagon trail they'd just turned. Fight or flight? The bastards knew exactly where he was. If there were two, they could simply flank him. All the odds were not in his favor.

He jumped down and hugged Penny to his belly. Her arms were trembling. "Don't worry. Keep hanging on to me just like this." With her in front, his back would shield any lucky shot. He mounted the bike again and pedaled down a steep slope, toward a rock ridge that looked a half mile away. If he could get past that, they might be able to disappear altogether. The truck following looked to be only two-wheel drive, so it certainly wouldn't be able to make it over the crest. A few more thousand feet down and they'd be beneath the tree line. Once inside such cover, chances would start to lean his way again.

Halfway to the ridge the bike dropped several feet into a shallow washout thick with loose shale. The front wheel bent sideways; the forks buried deep in the rubble and stuck there. Red glanced behind them. The truck trailed only five hundred meters. He vaulted over handlebars and broke into a sprint. Soon, each breath came hard. At this altitude the air lacked substance.

The distant ridge ahead lay semisubmerged in a light mist, milling in the cold breeze. The rocks seemed to float on its surface, like stones marking the graves of specters fleeting about. As he pumped his legs harder, the entire ridge began to move. He skidded to a halt, sliding on slick green moss. Some of the brown boulders rose from the ground. Or...was he hallucinating? He blinked hard, then again. "What the hell?" he whispered.

"They're moose," Penny offered. "Like the stuffed animal Grandma gave me."

At last he recognized a herd of a hundred elk, not moose, as they stood from a rest and ambled slowly away, over orange-and-gray mounds. Antlers rose from behind a near boulder as a bull stirred to knees, then stood erect. The massive brown beast had a white patch on his rump and thick, black hair drooping like a shawl from his neck. The rack looked eight feet across. Easily an eight-hundred-pound monster. The animal curved his neck toward the herd and opened his mouth. His belly lifted in short bursts, barking a warning like a dog. The herd started to trot, hundreds of hooves trampling flora and rock.

A loud *crack* came from behind, and Red stooped low. The truck had bounced over a boulder, smashing one door, breaking a window. It continued its downhill course, though now with a front wheel wobbling, threatening to come loose. But in less than a minute they'd be in shooting range of him, even by pistol. And if these pursuers had a high-powered rifle, they were already too close.

Red stepped toward the beast. They had to get over the ridge. The bull lowered its head and stomped the earth with one sharp hoof, grunting from deep within that massive chest. Red had heard an elk's high-pitched bugle before, though never this basso growl. But the threat was quite clear. Red pointed his weapon skyward and pulled the trigger twice. The animal merely raised his head, as if in disdain. Red laid the skull atop his front sight.

"Don't shoot, Daddy!"

"We've got no time. It's not letting us pass."

"Tell it to shoo," she huffed.

"I don't mix well with alpha males. A gun is the only thing that works sometimes, honey."

Penny waved a hand. "Shoo, moose! Go away," she shouted.

Another *crunch* from behind. Red glanced back. The truck was high centered on the drop-off into the shallow ravine. Doors burst open, and two figures leaped to the ground, one in white pants, another in woodland camo. He turned his weapon once more toward the animal.

"I said shoo!" shrieked Penny, one hand still waving. "Bad moose! Go home."

It was an elk, of course, but Red wasn't about to correct his daughter. The animal jerked its head, vapor streaming from its nostrils. The bull turned and began to trot after his herd.

When Red sprinted after it, the animal seemed to spook, quickening its pace and trotting ahead. Red ran between two rocks that suddenly stirred from the ground and rose after he'd passed. Two more elk, latently heeding their leader's warning. Behind him, several other stragglers made chase to catch the rest of the herd. One of the animals caught up and passed close enough that it smelled of wet wool, snapping at Red as it went.

The herd's hoofbeats sounded like a great avalanche, thundering in his chest. Now, several more pairs passed as the stragglers gained speed. *Great*, Red thought. He'd made it off the top of the mountain with Penny just to get them killed by a stampeding herd of wild animals.

Gunshots cracked from behind. A stray bullet stung the bull's white rump, and he bucked. Thick blood oozed slowly from the wound. Red hugged Penny with one arm, pumping hard with the other. He changed direction like a running back every couple paces, zigzagging so as to not give the shooter a predictable target. The pair was still far enough away that it would have to be a lucky shot, but anything to increase the odds.

"One of the men is stopping, Daddy."

Not wanting to slow to risk a glance, he gasped, "Tell me what you see."

"He's leaning on a rock."

Not good. Pausing to aim, no doubt. Red couldn't zigzag any more radically or he'd risk losing ground. The other couldn't be too far behind. His lungs ached and head pounded. Ahead, a puff of dust on the trail. A ricochet whined as the projectile tumbled into the distance. Only a few hundred meters more till the ridge. He ducked behind a tall granite column and ran twenty meters in its shadow, shielded temporarily from the shooter's line of sight. Before breaking cover again he zagged and—sure enough—another ricochet. Right where he would've stepped if he hadn't changed course.

His legs were slowing despite his determination, as if mired in wet sand. Approaching the ridge, he chanced another glance back. The closest pursuer was the one in white pants.

Over the crest, another open field came into view, stretching for what must've been a solid klick before short evergreens began to dot the landscape.

Many elk were already halfway down the expanse, loping rhythmically in slow motion, bodies hovering over the terrain. The bull held his head erect, herding them on, the bullet in its rump of seemingly no consequence. No way Red could outrun the shooters any longer. His breath was coming in deep gasps, but those couldn't satisfy the oxygen craving. The guys from the truck had only sprinted a short distance, whereas he'd first biked and then run a long way, carrying Penny. There was only one hand left to play.

"Get down here," he said, shoving his daughter behind a boulder. A skilled hunter pursuing wouldn't follow their exact same trail. There were two natural breaks in the ridge where a person could easily pass. Red knelt behind the rock with Penny, hunching low until only his weapon and the top of his head broke the plane. He drew a bead on one of the openings, but his eyes flashed between the two, trying to cover both. Would White Pants wait for his buddy to catch up? The sight of his pistol wavered. His gut spasmed, but he clamped down the nausea between clenched teeth. He spit pink froth onto green moss, then slipped back and steadied his wrist against the boulder. But now he couldn't see the other break in the ridge.

It was a calculated chance. The break he was covering was downhill of the one through which he'd come; inexperienced hunters would gravitate toward the easier path without even realizing it. Skilled ones might choose it because Red was armed and they wanted to avoid following the same blind opening through which their prey had escaped. But White Pants hadn't seemed experienced. He was eager. A fast runner, sure—but there was more to it than that. Just too damned eager.

Chapter 6

Strength of a Child

Penny hunched till her shoulders hit her knees. She backed under a pink mountain of rock that towered overhead, looking like it would topple upon her any second. But Daddy had pointed to its base and said to hide. She pulled her ankles in and scooched lower. The chill of the boulder sank through her thin North Face jacket. Its color, Algiers blue, was just a fancy name for aqua, Mom had said. It was almost the same shade as the crumbly stuff rubbing off and falling down the back of her neck.

She braced her palms on the ground. Something slimy greased her fingers. She rubbed them on the cold stone, leaving brown streaks. "Eeew!" she whispered. It smelled like poo. Must have been one of those yucky brown marmots. They'd seen plenty on the train ride up, like ugly beavers without a tail. "Those varmints are gross," she'd said, scrunching her nose, after spying one chewing a leaf.

"Marmot, not varmint," Dad had corrected. "And I love marmots." The corner of his lip tightened, and one eyebrow rose, that smile whenever he had something else to say.

"What is it?" she'd asked, pulling on his arm.

He'd pinched her nose. "You'd love marmots too. They taste just like chicken."

"Oh, yuck!" Penny had giggled till her belly ached. It was the same joke he always used for squirrels and cats. The fat lady who'd sat behind them had scowled, though.

She wiped her hands on her jeans till the filthy marmot poo was gone.

"Sweetheart, get up. I need you to watch something for me." Her father's fingers wrapped all the way around her arm as he reached down and drew her out of her burrow with one smooth jerk. His smile looked too thin and wide, like Aunty Catherine's when she came at Thanksgiving. It wasn't... real. Daddy had never liked Aunty Catherine. Now, his face was as white as the vampires on *Blood Lust*, and he was panting like Heinz, Grandpa's dog, after chasing a rabbit. But Daddy was never scared, even when Mom wrecked their silver car. So, they must really be in trouble now.

He pointed back up the ridge. She sighted down his finger, pointing back in the direction from where they'd come. "See the space between those rocks? Keep looking there. If you see any bad guys, don't yell, just come get me. OK? I'm going to be on the other side of this boulder."

He was holding a gun. His special one. A big pistol. He'd gone to work with Uncle Jim not long ago, but then Uncle Jim had died. He'd always seemed so sad. Mom said Dad had taken his place now, at work. She hoped Daddy didn't get sad too.

Now he carried a gun wherever he wanted. Her parents didn't think she knew, but she'd felt it under his arm whenever she gave him a hug. Because he was one of the guys who protected the president. They didn't think she knew that, either. But that had to be the only reason why he could have a gun anywhere he wanted, she thought. But why would bad guys be after him when he wasn't at work?

That thought brought cold fingers up her spine. She studied the gap between the two boulders. It looked like a path. Many of the moose herd had run through it. No. *Elk*, Daddy called them. She could still hear their hooves trotting down the mountain now, clattering over loose shale. She glanced behind her. The herd was almost out of sight, moving like a big brown fishnet pulled across the bare land into the forest of short trees below.

She studied the two boulders again. Their round tops were like the smooth blue stones on that pretty silver bracelet she'd wanted back at the gift shop. Dad had seemed so scared when he caught her back there. He'd said to stay at the table, but she'd forgotten. Why did he shoot the ceiling, though? It had made everyone in the shop scream. Sometimes he did things that just didn't make sense. Like wanting to shoot that poor old elk. Anyhow, Mom had always said to never to let a horse know you're scared. So Penny had pretended she wasn't, and told it to shoo. And then Dad hadn't even thanked her.

A cold breeze whipped down from the tall boulder she leaned against. The bad guys might be coming any second. If Daddy was able to stop them, they could go back and help Mom. She'd seen the face of the one bad guy running after her. He looked angry. *But he'll never catch Mom,* she reassured herself. Not even Dad was as fast as she was. Two loud bangs came from the way her father had gone. She glanced at the two boulders, realizing she'd forgotten to concentrate on them, like she was supposed to. Echoes came from all directions. She hopped down from her perch and ran around the back of the rock. "Daddy! You OK?" He grabbed her arm and scooped her up to his chest again, running down the mountain the same way the moose herd had stampeded. "I got one," he said. "That should slow the other a little. But we've got to get into the woods." His face was shiny and white, kind of like he was sick.

"Don't carry me. I'm big, I can run." She wriggled, trying to get down.

"Stay put, sweetheart," he gasped between breaths, arms squeezing her tighter. Another minute of bumpy sprinting and then he placed her down behind a boulder and fell to his knees, panting, looking up toward the ridge behind them. Penny studied it too. Nothing moved there except for wisps of low clouds. A faint patch of white, kind of like a mound of snow, lay in a crack in the ridge, the one Dad had been watching. One of the men chasing them had been wearing white pants. So…that must be him. She felt light-headed as she realized what had happened. Just then, the white patch disappeared behind the ridge, as if someone had pulled it back.

"There's one man left, and he's not far behind," Dad panted.

He spat some frothy pink snot onto a patch of tan clay, and she was too scared to say, "*Eeeew.*" There was no way he could carry her anymore. She sprang to her feet and, leaping from rock to rock, ran down the hill toward the forest. It didn't look that far, and most of it was downhill. Her legs carried her as fast as when they'd visited Maine to watch the pretty leaves that had turned colors. Then, she'd ran alongside a riverbed for what seemed like an hour, Dad on the opposite bank, racing each other. The boulders there had been huge and gray, with sparkles in them when the sun was right overhead. Mom hadn't looked too happy when they got back. But these rocks were safe. Not smooth and slippery like the ones in Maine. They were dry and flat, but with sharp edges.

She'd been running almost a minute before she heard her father call, "Penny!" He must've not seen her get up. She glanced back; he was sprinting again now. She turned back to watch the trees ahead. But even though she stretched her legs as far as she could, jumping and flying, pretending she was in a steeplechase with Piebald in *National Velvet*, those trees didn't seem to get any closer. Her lungs started to burn, and her legs too. She tried to breathe deeply, but there just wasn't enough air around here. Maybe that's why Dad had been so white.

She reached a long patch of green carpet with a few small white flowers in patches. Most had been trampled to a slimy salad by the elk herd, and she stumbled as her ankles slipped. The tundra was springy, like running on a mattress. She'd almost gotten to the end of the green stretch when Dad caught up.

"You're almost as fast as your mom," he said, face not seeming so pale now. His eyes glinted playfully, the same look as back in Maine, when they were playing. "Bet you can't keep up." He ran ahead, widening the gap between them.

Penny knew he could run even faster than that. He was just being nice. But that was OK, because she was going to throw up for sure if she didn't stop soon. Her legs ached with cold even though her face burned hot as fire. She leaned one shoulder against a boulder and rested.

Dad stopped. "We're almost halfway there. You can't stop now."

Halfway? They'd been running *forever*. Was that stupid forest a mirage? Penny lifted tired, heavy arms. "Daddy...can you carry me again?"

A shot rang out from back at the ridge, and she suddenly found herself flying again, the throwing-up feeling completely gone. In a few seconds she'd caught up with Dad. "Should I zigzag like you were doing?"

"No," he gasped. "We're already doing it a little, running between rocks. The ridge is way back there now. He's just trying to scare us."

"Well, it's working," she said. *Bang!* A sound like the snap of a guitar string zinged ahead of them. "You sure?"

"It'd be pure luck if he—"

Bang! Dad suddenly tripped next to her and sprawled on a stretch of pale grass. His knees tore into the earth, gouging two lines of deep green. He put a hand on his back pocket. "Son of a bitch!" His face was twisted in pain.

She knelt beside him. "You OK, Daddy?"

He lay on his belly, face down, screaming into the grass. His knees kicked like he was trying to swim. Another shot from the direction of the ridge, then another guitar-string sound snapped behind them. Cracks came from further down the mountain, echoing off the trees. Then the air grew silent. Straight contrails of two jets crossed high above, the far-off roar of the engines the only sound now in the vast, open stretch of this cold, barren moonscape.

"You OK? Did you trip?"

But her father just bared his teeth at the grass, like a dog growling. She reached into the pocket of his vest and pulled out a phone, punched the PIN, then dialed 911. She listened to the distant roar of the jets, and then looked back at the ridge. A green dot was moving across it. *That must be the bad guy who was shooting at us,* she thought.

The phone beeped in her ear, and she glanced at the screen. NO SERVICE.

"I'll be OK," Dad said at last, pulling one knee beneath him. Blood oozed through a hole in his back pocket.

"You're shot!" Panic squeezed her belly. She was suddenly too tired to move.

"I said I'll be OK," he snapped.

But, he'd also said the bad guys couldn't hit them from so far away.

"Are you...going to die?"

He bent to look at his leg. Slowly, he pulled away the hand over the gunshot wound. "It's not bleeding fast, so it missed anything important. A long shot too. Probably not deep." He glanced at the forest again. "We'll worry about it later. Mom's probably already down there, waiting for us. She'll be mad if we waste time here. You'll be able to outrun me now. Enjoy it while you can."

He winked, and her throat stopped burning. Penny squinted up at the sun, only then realizing it was burning her cheeks. How could it be so cold on the mountain, but the sun still be as hot as at the beach?

"Come on. I'll race you down." Dad gave her another Aunty Catherine smile, pulled his good leg beneath him, grimaced as he stood to his feet, and limped away.

* * * *

Red's glute burned as if stung by an eight-foot hornet. Drops of warm blood trickled down the back of his leg, sticking cold jeans to his skin. His other calf ached, absorbing the added stress of compensating for the injury. He glanced back toward the ridge from where the shot had come, at least a mile behind them now. He thought he glimpsed a black dot moving near the pickup, now wrecked on the washout. The shooter must have run out of ammo.

The faint whine of a siren called in the distance. Ambulances and law enforcement should be scaling Pikes Peak any time now. Hopefully no tourists had gotten hurt in the visitor center. Collateral damage to human life was the ugliest part of black ops. Just one more reason they remained black. No citizen wanted to face the reality that, no matter how much planning and careful execution, sometimes killing a terrorist also meant slaughtering his family. But, despite Yoga's clear threat to Penny, Red had refrained from shooting directly at her because she was cowering among an old tourist couple. Now, with her likely in pursuit somewhere behind them, he hoped he didn't regret that decision.

Another warm dribble ran down his leg, and he increased the pressure of his fingers atop the wound. What a lucky shot. *No one* could make another like it. Especially with a pistol. Red had been shot in the other leg once before, but it had been a through and through. Another time, a fragmentation grenade had taken off the tip of an ear and sliced his head, but this shot hadn't seemed to penetrate far. It must have lost velocity during its long flight, or maybe it was a ricochet and the projectile was just below his skin's surface. Either way, it stung like a bitch.

He stopped next to a thin tree no taller than himself. He gripped the stiff trunk and breathed deeply, wincing as short needles stabbed his skin. Letting go, he pulled sticky fingers apart and inhaled the scent of pine sap.

Penny stopped a few meters ahead. "You OK?"

He nodded. How could a ten-year-old be such a trouper? Her temperament was just like her mother's. The girl had been running for what had to be over a mile. Granted, downhill, but from fourteen thousand feet. Her throat was pink where she'd unzipped her jacket. One hundred twenty dollars, that stupid thing. Better keep her warm now. Lori couldn't care less if the boys went to church with one shoe and holes in shirt elbows, but heaven forbid Penny not have the latest threads from whatever designer label was popular that month.

He glanced through the sparse evergreen forest. Trees wouldn't start to be thick for another half mile or more. They had to get lower, into deep cover. Up here, vegetation struggled to grow at all. Thin stems sprouted through bare rubble, like a field of Charlie Brown Christmas trees.

"Just needed to catch my breath," he said. "You're really moving."

"Why didn't we take that hiking trail back there? It would've been easier."

"Too easy. And too visible. If there were bad guys waiting on the road pretending their truck had broken down, there may be more bad guys guarding trails."

Penny pointed to the east. Colorado Springs lay in a sun-filled valley. An occasional flash shone as light glinted off metal or glass. The earlier thunderstorm and lightning show had blown through. At this distance the town was a fuzzy blend of muted gray squares. "There's the city. Why don't we head that way?"

Red stepped toward her, trying not to limp. "If you were a bad guy, where would you think we'd go?"

Penny turned and jumped onto another rock. "I don't know.... To the city, I guess."

"Exactly. You've got to think like they do. Understand?"

She cocked her head and frowned. "I never want to think like them, Daddy. Where are we going?"

"South."

Penny's lip curled. "To Mexico? We've got to find Mom."

"No, not there." Red glanced behind, studying the heights from which they'd come. Turning again to his daughter, he lifted an arm. "See that mountain there?"

"The one without any trees?"

"No, the one after that. It's smaller and has trees all over it."

Penny lifted a hand to shade her eyes from the sun. "Yeah. It looks like it has a bunch of antennas on top."

"That's where we're headed. And if we get separated, that's where we'll meet: beneath the tallest antenna." He placed a hand on her shoulder. "And if I'm not there, you go to the other side of that hill. At the bottom is Cheyenne Mountain. It's an Air Force base. You'll be safe there."

"What about Mom?"

Red sighed. "I'll bet that's the way she'll head too. Except she's faster than us."

Penny smiled and swung arms as she hopped again. "Let's go. It's not very far."

Red couldn't help but smile. "It only looks that way. It's probably eighteen or twenty klicks."

Penny turned atop a boulder like a ballerina on a music box. "What's a click?"

"I meant, the antennas are probably twelve, maybe fifteen miles. And since we're going up and down mountains, that's twenty miles of walking. Like going all the way to school and back twice, with your dad shot in the ass."

"What kind of antennas are they?"

"Radio, TV, maybe phone. I guess."

She pulled hands from pockets, his cell phone in her palm. "We couldn't see those earlier when I tried 911. Can we call for help?"

Red snatched the device from her grip. Why hadn't he thought of that? Must not be getting enough air to think straight. If he could call the Det, help would be here within the hour. But, this was just his regular phone, not his work one. It wasn't encrypted. Their pursuers may be able to overhear, even confirm their location. His gut tightened as the hard realization sunk in that even now the phone may be syncing with a tower, unwittingly giving away their position. He held the power button, but nothing happened. It was already off. Arriving in Colorado Springs last night, he hadn't plugged it in. Any remaining battery must've been eaten up early that morning, taking photos. Roaming would've killed it for certain.

He shifted weight off his cramped calf to his sore leg and reviewed their situation. He had no way of contacting the Det. Lori's status was unknown, but as long as she stayed ahead of Mandarin and out of sight from anyone else, she should be OK. If she'd forgotten to plug in her phone last night too, she'd have no way of communicating, either. He was shot in the glute, but clotting had been fast. Infection wouldn't be a problem for a few days. Worry was pressed onto Penny's forehead, but physically she was strong. They had twenty clicks to travel. A healthy team could cover that in a few hours at a run. But there was no way to know who to trust, so along the way they had to avoid anyone. With him limping, the hike could take days. This was beginning to look less like a sprint across no-man's-land and more like evasion behind enemy lines.

Chapter 7

Dark Canyon

Lambert "Lam" McNeil cranked down the window of his 1978 Jeep pickup, letting in cool, clay-scented Rocky Mountain air. Lam glanced at his watch: 10:12 A.M. Though the sun had broken the horizon around six o'clock, this brief section of Forest Road was still shaded by the towering orange shoulder of Pikes Peak. He squinted up at Windy Point, just over the tree line two thousand feet above the hood. Even in July, the old mountain's bald head was crowned with gray streaks of gust-blasted snow clinging in the deeper southern ravines.

He loved working in Dark Canyon, though he was scheduled there only once a week. His employer, Colorado Springs Utilities, had a small hydro plant here and today's punch list was the long one.

Thin dust floated aft as he navigated down the orange-pebble road. A deep hum rose from the floorboards and up through the seat like the bass aftershock of one of those Puerto Rican kids' pimped-out rides. But Lam's truck was no caco. *His* song came from the steady drone of rolling forty-four-inch Mickey Thompson Super Swampers. A rhythmic exhaust crackle from the AMC 401 power plant added a snare drum to the medley. The premium treads turned on black steel American Racing rims. No pretty-boy billet aluminum or cast alloy. On the trail, if his wheels got bent, they could be hammered back in place. Those limp-wristed aluminum ones would split or break off.

Andrea Snyder dozed on the passenger side. Everyone called her Andi, a fitting choice for a female mechanic. Her plump bare arms jiggled as he steered across washboard missed by the road dressers last spring. A tattoo of a yellow tiger, red mouth agape, stalked down Andi's left shoulder. She lifted her head, one eye closed. Palms pressed to her kidneys, she rubbed and winced. "Where we at?"

"Ten minutes out." He glanced at the gas gauge. Already down to three-quarters of a tank after only twenty miles on the rough incline. He shook his head. "Damn thing's more thirsty than a seaman on shore leave." He patted the tan-carpet-covered dash. "Company's mileage rate don't come near feeding this girl."

She raised an eyebrow. "When you getting your company truck back?"

"Tomorrow. It's just in for service. I didn't screw anything up."

Andi snickered. "Ain't had no elk hit you lately?"

Lam smiled, covering his embarrassment by scratching an unshaven chin. He'd run into a ditch last summer in a company pickup, having too much fun on these curves. In a panic, he'd lied and said an elk had jumped out of the brush and slammed into the side. Believable, sure—since it had been rut season. But pangs of guilt for the untruth still plagued him. He hadn't mustered the fortitude to confess it to his super.

Andi pointed ahead. "Watch out for the hiker."

A man in blue parka and black jeans waved from ahead. White tennis shoes? What was this tourist thinking? *So many of these damn flatlanders drive up to Manitou Springs thinking to hike Pikes Peak. Fourteen thousand feet, moron! If you can't breathe near the base at seven thousand, you'll wish you were dead at the top. Many depend too much on GPS, can't even read a map, end up getting lost, dehydrated, and end up like this dumb city slicker thumbing a ride back to civilization.*

Lam snorted. "Should just let the idiot figure it out himself."

"Might not be his fault. One of his friends could be lost or hurt." Sympathy… Andi was such an enigma. A woman in a man's job. But she'd held up better than most apprentices of either gender. A little pear shaped, but nimble as a donkey and just as strong. Once, she'd hoisted one end of a five-hundred-pound gearbox off his leg. Lam had strung it up with a block and tackle and was lying beneath it, like an idiot, draining the thick sulfur-scented gear oil. If she hadn't seen the strap about to give way and kicked a four-by-four beneath the metal casing, he wouldn't be walking now.

Lam lifted his foot from the accelerator. "I'll see what the guy wants."

The man stepped down, back from the built-up road bed into dry buffalo grass. *Some sort of Chinaman, or maybe Japanese*, thought Lam. Hell, they all looked the same.

The hiker smiled, beaming perfect white teeth. Probably had his dentist brighten them before the vacation. "Thank you so much for stopping."

Funny. No Chink accent. Lam squinted, studying the man. No backpack. No water bottle. As the hiker drew deep breaths, steam rose from his shoulders, quickly swallowed by the moisture-hungry air. "What you want?" asked Lam.

"So sorry. Have you seen anyone else on your drive?"

What kind of question was that? "Err. Nope...nobody. But that's not unusual. You lost?"

"Maybe. I'm looking for my party. A woman, a man, and their daughter."

"They lost, or you?"

"Both, maybe. She's blond and tall. He's about my height with red hair and red beard. His daughter, maybe ten, blond pigtails, blue jacket like mine."

"Nobody includes them."

"I see. Can I ride with you? Maybe we'll spot them. Where are you going?"

"Sorry buddy, but we're headed to work." Lam lifted his foot from the brake and the truck rolled slowly forward. The hiker kept up, walking next to the window.

Andi leaned forward in her seat, still rubbing her back. "You OK? Need water? Can we call someone for you? Police, maybe?"

"No, no." the hiker said, white teeth gleaming. "I...I can pay you."

Lam frowned. "Not interested, buddy. We'll be headed back out at the end of the day. It's early. If your party don't show up, wait here and we'll be back by. Take you to town then."

"But I really need to find them now."

"And I really need to make a living. Sorry." Lam offered his most condescending smile. "Enjoy the day. It's too early to worry. There're worse places in the world to be." The road leveled, and the truck rolled faster.

The hiker jogged to keep up. "Here, take my money. I'll pay you a thousand dollars just to drive me around a few hours."

Lam blinked and stood on the brake. A thousand dollars would get him that new 5.38 gear set installed. He'd have the most tricked-out rock crawler in the club. At least the best still used as a daily driver. He could motor this guy around for the morning, then do a short punch list in the afternoon. The skipped equipment would keep just fine till next week. He could do the long list then. "Lam's Taxi, at your service."

Andi scowled. "Lam."

"We're being Good Samaritans. That's what my pastor said was the right thing to do."

"You don't get paid for being a Good Samaritan. It's the other way around."

He shrugged. "So, I'm a work in progress."

The hiker nodded emphatically. "Thank you." He ran to the tailgate, lifted a foot onto the bumper, and hoisted himself into the bed as nimbly as a gymnast. The guy stood, bracing an arm on the cab roof. Lam slid open the rear window and held a flat palm over his shoulder. "Payment up front." No city boy was going to con him out of a free ride.

"Oh…yes, of course," came a murmur from the bed. Lam watched in the rearview as the hiker lifted the back of his parka, apparently reaching for a wallet. Only he seemed to be reaching too high, closer to his belt. Lam rested his foot on the accelerator. When the hiker brought his hand around, it was gripping a Glock with slim black silencer mounted to the muzzle.

Lam dropped his foot fast. Instantly, the 401 blew an angry roar, and the tach bounced against the rev limiter. The front of the truck lifted, and the hiker stumbled backward, falling out over the tailgate. Flashes came from the upturned muzzle. His tires dug a trench as they spun, the truck whipping sideways, carving a doughnut in the middle of the road. "Damn it," Lam muttered, steering to correct, trying to get forward motion. But the truck continued its useless circle. The hiker slammed onto the road, rolled to his feet, and raised the weapon again. Two more muzzle flashes, followed by two metal tom-tom drum raps on the cab. Then the driver side of the whirling truck slammed against the shooter. Massive rubber tire lugs grabbed and dragged him beneath their spinning fury, shooting him rearward with the rest of the orange dirt rooster tail. His limp body twisted flaccidly, landing in a stand of young aspen.

Lam stomped the brake, and the truck jerked to a halt. The loping engine sounded like a panting dog. Thick auburn dust drifted all around, lit on the top by a thin cut of the rising sun now peeking over the mountain. For several seconds, he listened to the tinkling of gravel landing on the road and the dry slapping of leaves high in trees. Was the guy dead? Was he coming back after them? Lam glanced in the side-view. A red streak of blood was drawn like spilled motor oil across one section of the scooped trench. If the guy wasn't dead, he would be soon enough.

But, what about his friends? Were they Jap gangsters too? Lam scanned the woods around them. They could be hiding anywhere. In the rearview in the far distance a green shape ambled out onto the road, obscured by the floating dust-fog. It rose, seemed to stand upright, as if human.

He pointed toward Dark Canyon. "Andi, which way should we go?"

No answer. She was leaning out the open window, dust settling into a red streak running from her neck. Shit. He gassed the accelerator and steered toward the power plant. With his free hand he pulled her toward him. "Hold on, girl." He could turn around and take her out of the forest himself. But what if that green person back there was the hiker's friend, and armed? Anyhow, they were still at least forty minutes from any hospital, twenty minutes till his cell phone would even work. The old caretaker's house had a radio for emergencies, though he'd never used it. He could call and maybe get a helicopter Life Flight to pick her up. He pounded the dash with a fist. What dumb luck that he hadn't been able to drive the company truck today. It still had a CB radio.

Andi slid toward the floor.

"No, no," he said, reaching for one arm. But he couldn't lift her. He stood on the accelerator, screaming up hills, drifting around corners like the racers in the Pikes Peak Hill Climb. He ducked his neck, chancing glances up the sides of the valley, hoping not to see anyone moving there.

Damn it! Andi's chest wasn't moving. Could she be dead? But she wasn't bleeding much. The cottage had a first aid kit.

Just a few more miles. Nearing a sharp turn around a tall Engelmann spruce, he smashed the brake pedal and slid off the road, right into a thicket of young juniper. Blueberries small as buckshot rained in through the open window, covering his lap, falling down the back of his shirt. The resinous evergreen perfume mixed with hot oil and gasoline. "Damn," he whispered. The tank might have been shot. The gas gauge only read half full. Hopefully it would leak slowly enough for him to still make it to the cottage.

He turned the wheel toward the road and dropped the pedal again. Another five minutes and he was skidding to a halt, next to a small pond formed by the damming of Sheep Creek. He leaped from the cab and opened the passenger door, cradling Andi's head. He lifted her under her shoulders and dragged her out. Her favorite brown cowboy boots, the ones trimmed in turquoise stitching, flopped to the earth. A small pool of blood dribbled down the rocker panel.

He laid her on the dusty ground, pressed two fingers to her jugular, and bent an ear to her mouth. No pulse. He sighted down her chest—it didn't rise. "What the hell," he whispered. The thin smear of blood on her neck looked to be only from an abrasion. He put a hand at her nape and tilted her head back, pinched her nose, and cupped his mouth over hers, tasting mint. He blew two breaths, then went to work pressing palms rhythmically against her sternum. In CPR class he'd been taught to keep elbows straight to avoid fatigue. He remembered how one instructor had said he'd done the exercise for an hour before paramedics arrived, but it saved his patient's life.

Two more breaths, then back to compressions.

His lower back started to ache. He glanced down the road. Caloric waves rose from the hood of the truck, making pines in the distance waver as in a mirage. He certainly hadn't made a quiet escape. How long till the hiker's friends caught up with him? Or did killers like him have friends at all? Maybe he was a solo act. But no backpack, which meant he must have had a base camp, which meant there were others. And the way sound traveled in the mountains, anyone within five miles had heard Lam's ruckus.

Two more breaths. An ant riding a swell of crimson slowly washed from beneath Andi. He checked her pulse and breathing again. Still nothing. "Come on," he growled. He rolled her on her side, and the back of her green tank top was soaked through with blood. He ripped open her shirt, and more of the liquid oozed from two holes atop her bra strap. Shit. The compressions were just pumping her dry.

Another quick pulse check. It was then he felt the chill of death rising on her skin.

He struggled up and turned toward the lake. Held up both arms and tensed his chest, preparing to scream. Instead he sealed his lips, eyes searching the far side. His gaze came to rest once again where the dusty road bent out of sight around a stand of brown bristlecone, killed three years ago by pine beetles. If the hiker did have friends, they'd be coming from that direction.

He ran for the whitewashed cottage, then slid to a halt. No. He couldn't leave Andi on the ground like that, alone. He yanked at the chrome handle of his tailgate, and the door dropped. He lifted shaking hands in front of his face, willing them to still, but the effort only produced a chill between his shoulder blades. He gripped her beneath her arms again and hoisted her halfway onto the gate. Then hopped up, pulled her the rest of the way in, and propped her head upright. It leaned against a brick, straight brown hair flowing over it like muddy water. *She'd like that view*, he thought. To be able to stare at the pale blue sky. She had always studied it, remarking on how clear it was at altitude. Describing what shapes she saw in the clouds.

At least he'd been able to kill the bastard who got her. Even though he'd done so by accident, it still somewhat leveled the score. Andi would've been proud of that, as competitive as she was. He already missed her gruff presence. Though he'd always enjoyed the predatory solitude of a hunt, now he understood why elk ran in herds. But he didn't intend to become a prey animal now. He turned his gaze away from her still body. The clear, empty sky washed over the lake, its chill breath stirring ripples upon the surface, blowing cold upon his face, filling the valley with a sense of dread.

He crossed both arms over her belly, then slammed the gate shut. The metallic crack echoed like a gunshot from across the lake, and he hunched low. He hunted elk not far from here every fall. Slowly, cautiously, like game catching a scent, he glanced again toward the dead bristlecone pines.

Still nothing.

But that *was* the direction from which they would come. He had no idea who, or how many. Just that it would be soon.

Chapter 8

FIDO

Red leaned to the side and, with one hand, slowly lifted his stiff injured leg, dried blood still sticky between his fingers. A rock gave way under his foot, and his full weight jarred down upon it. An electric arc shot from ass to heel as the muscles locked in pain. He wiped cold beads from his forehead, squeezed from pores by agony and exertion. Reaching out, he touched the rising hill. His hand pierced through a warm crust of pine needles and pressed upon cool dirt. His skin prickled as if it had been asleep. He shook a dozen black ants carrying plump, white larvae from his arm.

Lifting his gaze to the crest of the short ridge ahead, he watched Penny scramble a few yards before him. Though the trek had been generally downhill, ridges like this one gave occasion to curse. Each step had become an exercise of willpower. So he reminded himself of previous hells passed through. Several ops where contingencies had not favored his team, pushing their physical endurance further than he could've imagined. But he'd never caught a bullet in the ass before. He hugged the pistol holstered beneath his arm to reassure himself. He could still protect his daughter should they run across the wet team again.

Her thin legs were beginning to wobble with fatigue. The thought of a violent ending to her life chilled his neck even as it hardened his resolve. They'd have to kill him first. However, Mandarin had seemed intent on chasing Lori, not Red. Maybe no one was hunting him at all. But he had to protect her.

He grabbed a forked branch from the ground, then swung it against a trunk, snapping the soft wood to the right length for a crutch.

"You OK, Daddy?" whispered Penny, a few meters ahead. The knees of her jeans were smeared with clay. One of her red pigtail clips had broken apart an hour ago. Dirt rimmed her fingernails as she crawled on all fours up the hill.

"Yeah," he grunted. Though every stride burned his glute like a welding torch. He took a step with the new crutch. It gouged the earthen blanket. Shit. The tip would leave a trail, so he tossed it aside. "FIDO," he muttered.

"What does that mean?"

"Forget it. Drive on." He wasn't going to tell her the crude version. Even here, several thousand feet lower than the summit, air was still thin and his leg had begun to refuse commands. Missteps like the one he'd just taken meant a painful cramp for several minutes. "Now's a good time to stop," he said. "Remember what I told you?"

She turned, brushed off a gray rock sticking from the needle carpet, and plopped her bottom upon it, as if declaring it her own. Then dusted her hands, smearing off the heaviest of the filth. A deep breath, and she closed her eyes. "Stop, look, and listen."

"Just like before you cross a street."

"I've been looking, but all I see are stupid trees. What am I supposed to listen for?"

The pain in Red's leg gradually eased till he could draw it up. Instead of a rock, he lowered himself onto soft dirt, lying on his side, so his wounded butt cheek didn't touch the ground. He relaxed his neck with a grunt, staring through crooked pine limbs to deep blue sky. He spat out a green wad of aspen leaves, the mild painkiller looking like cooked spinach. "You listen for everything. One night in mountain training, they made us memorize a map, then blindfolded us. We had to try to go two klicks to our objective without our eyes."

"Could you do it?"

"No. My team was half a klick off. But it taught me how much we ignore sounds. What do you hear?"

She kept her eyes closed, nose wrinkled. Finally, a smile. She pointed. "Birds. An airplane. Something crunching on leaves over there. Wind rocking the trees, like they're fighting."

He nodded. "Good. But even more important than that, listen for something that doesn't fit."

A pause. "Sirens." She opened her eyes and stood.

"Better. I can barely hear them over the breeze. Now, for the *look* part." Red stifled a groan as he grabbed the trunk of a pine sapling, lifting himself. "See that tree at the top of this ridge? Wait till I get up there, but I want you to climb it."

She frowned, the playful pouty one she learned from her mother. "Mommy says not to climb trees."

He smiled. For a former field agent based in London, Lori was an overly conservative parent. "I don't think Mama will mind if you climb just once," he said. "I'll watch you. I know you've got arms like Spider-Man. Once you're up there, don't yell down what you see. Understand? You'll be up in a tree, which makes you easier to spot, so move slowly. Only step on big branches. Don't make noise. Get up there, look around, take a picture of it in your mind, then come down and describe it to me."

He stretched his leg out straight, feeling as if a bee stinger the size of a KA-BAR was still seated in his glute. Another couple minutes of walking up the ridge on all fours, and he leaned against the thick-crusted trunk. Cereal-sized flakes of bark rubbed onto his shoulder. He cupped his hands, and Penny set one fuchsia Nike into it, ready to scale up.

He lifted her pants leg to reveal black socks. Her jacket was unzipped, green long-sleeve T-shirt beneath. "Take off your shoes. You could see those things from orbit. And strip off your jacket."

She did, then climbed to his shoulder, head, and finally up the tree. He gazed after her, marveling at how effortlessly she moved. Ballet had lost appeal. Gymnastics classes had held her interest—and Red's charge card—for the last several years. He never would've guessed she'd be putting those skills to work at age ten, climbing a tree to recon for her injured father in the middle of Rocky Mountain National Forest while evading—he shook his head. Who the hell were they evading, after all?

If he could just get a signal to the Det—any sort of distress call. A Special Forces Group was billeted at Fort Carson. Which one? Didn't matter—the Det could have boots on the ground within an hour, if he could just get a call out.

He'd followed the squatty little psychiatrist's orders, though. He didn't bring his work phone. And his tag, a passive tracking device the size of a postage stamp implanted deep within the buttock of every Det operator, was useless in a few areas in the world, the Front Range of the Rocky Mountains being one of them. Something about minerals in the soil that reflected the same narrow slice of the electromagnetic spectrum, making tracking impossible. Which, Red had to admit, was one of the reasons a vacation to the spot had been so attractive. He'd relished the thought of being completely off the grid, no one watching. But now? Not so much.

As Penny climbed higher, he thought through standard distress calls. Smoke or noise would attract their pursuers as much as it would help. A rush of relief flooded his chest as he recalled how he'd flashed his US Marshals creds before the shootout. The visitor center had CCTVs for certain, to watch for shoplifters. He must've been caught on video. They'd wire his image to US Marshals Headquarters in Richmond to ID him. If the footage was high enough quality, they could run it through facial recognition and find him. Only a cover file, of course, set up as condition of the US Marshals being a cooperative agency in the Det.

But his smile faded as he thought through a plausible timeline. His file was classified, so the proper authorities would need to be notified. Days could pass before the Det ever found out he was involved.

He rubbed his forehead with chapped knuckles. No matter which angle he took, the toolbox was empty. He had a bullet in his ass. And a wet team chasing him. And his only daughter to protect. Who was in a tree, forty feet overhead. Still, he had to play his advantages, few that they were. Rocky Mountain National Forest was a great place to disappear. The farther they got from the peak, the better. As long as he and Penny stayed out of sight, they'd be safe, for now.

But another priority would soon be setting in...water. In the dry air, a hiker could start to dehydrate in a matter of hours. And you only drank water from a stream or pond as a last resort for fear of Montezuma's revenge, which would dehydrate you into delirium. They'd be fine for a week or more without food, but would need water before nightfall. A loud *crack* shot from overhead.

* * * *

Penny placed each step carefully as she climbed a tall pine tree. Dad had said if she moved slowly, bad guys wouldn't see her. Rough bark had already pricked the arch of one foot through her socks. She tested each branch after that, making sure it had no sharp points. But one had snapped with a *bang*.

She glanced down at her father. How slow was she supposed to go? He seemed lost in thought, but shot a frown at the broken limb and put a finger to his lips. After a few minutes, she could see over the tops of most other trees. The trunk was narrow up here, thick only as the branches had been at the bottom. A cool breeze rocked her perch, then a gust shook it so hard wood crackled. Not quite high enough for a good view, so she stepped up two more limbs, whispering, "Go away, wind." Maybe from up here she could see Mommy.

She gazed across a dark green landscape, like a prickly pine tarp draped over a humongous room of furniture. Only here and there did the trees open, allowing a glimpse of earth or rock. Toward the radio tower mountain, the pines parted, revealing a deep ravine. Fallen logs lay across a rocky streambed where the mountain walls creased. A falcon soaring below her swiftly cut across and then, without even flapping its wings, began an upward spiral toward clear blue sky. Within a minute it was as high as her. If only she could fly like that! Studying the soaring bird, she felt as if she could step off the branch, into the rising breeze, and follow it to Cayenne Mountain.

How silly. Why name a mountain after a pepper plant, anyway?

Instead she propped her foot on a different branch and turned to peer up to Pikes Peak. Its sharp pink rocks from one ridge loomed over them, looking like they might tumble down any second, slicing paths through the forest. But she knew they wouldn't, because her science book said they'd been there a long time already. So had the valleys, trees, and everything else she turned her head to study. The pain in her punctured foot drifted away as the falcon banked again, soaring even higher.

Maybe this forest was a safe place. Nothing out here had tried to hurt them yet, and thick trees shielded them from the searching gaze of those evil men. Above the timberline, bad things had happened. Down here, she was invisible.

What would Jenny say now if she could see her high in this towering tree? That backstabber had pretended to be her friend, then texted a picture to the whole class about how huge Penny's feet were. She smiled as she remembered pulling out a tuft of Jenny's blond hair. Mom had really been mad, but Dad had only pretended to be. "Sometimes we do stupid things." He'd shrugged. "Jenny and you will be friends again soon."

Maybe. Maybe not.

For a split second, the tree trunk vibrated under her hand, like a big truck was rumbling by. She braced her feet and glanced around. It happened again. She gazed down and... Oh. Dad was waving at her. He must've been pounding on the bark to get her attention.

She stole one more look at the falcon, now high overhead. It tucked its wings and dropped like a missile, shooting past her face in eerie silence, disappearing into the dark ravine. Resisting the urge to step out into the air and follow it, Penny slowly lowered her foot to the branch below and crawled down.

Dad looked a little angry, but he kept his voice low. "You take a nap up there?"

"No, silly. Just looking around."

"What'd you see?"

"Trees."

A pause. "And?"

"No one. An ambulance was going up Pikes Peak, but I didn't see anybody or any cars anywhere else. I think I moved slow enough no one saw me, either."

He nodded. "That's the truth." He grimaced as he shifted his weight to the other leg.

"But I did see a dirt road. Not far down from here. It wasn't a big one. Maybe we could find someone with a car down there."

"Not likely. Even if we took a chance and found someone we trusted, no telling who we might run into on the drive out. And even though the city is just over those next mountains, no roads run that way. You've gotta go all the way behind Pikes Peak to get anywhere. Anyhow, bad guys will be watching the roads."

She pointed in the direction where she'd seen a chimney. "But someone lives that way. I saw their roof."

His forehead wrinkled. "A house? Couldn't be…well, maybe. How far?"

She shrugged and took a step in that direction. "Don't know. Looked like two hills between here and there." She held up fingers like tweezers. "The roof was this big."

Dad smirked. "OK. Be nice if we had a compass, but you pointed toward that rock with a black streak running down the middle. Since we can't see the house over those hills, we'll walk to that rock and sight another line from there. If we keep doing that, we should stay straight enough to see the house after a while."

She grinned. "And then we'll ask to borrow their car!"

"No. Remember. Think like one of the bad guys. Stay away from the roads. All we need is a phone or radio. We'll watch the house this afternoon and, if all looks OK, sneak in at night. It's a risk, but if we can call my office, we may be able to help Mommy too." He took one step with a heavy limp. "We're pretty far from the peak now, so we can walk slower. Keep pretending you're sneaking into your brothers' room to steal their Halloween candy. Don't step on any dry sticks or pinecones. Don't even breathe hard."

She nodded. Her legs ached from climbing. As she slipped her shoes back on, she realized Mommy was going to scream at her when she saw how dirty they'd gotten. She'd even torn a hole in her new jeans. She carefully padded after Dad, imagining slipping along the forest floor as silently as the falcon had swooped past her nose. She gazed up, feeling again the warm, welcome hug of the forest.

Chapter 9

Water

Red paused within a thick grove of aspen, leaning one hand upon white bark, stripping green leaves from a low branch with the other. Though chewing the mash might dehydrate him more quickly, the mild herbal painkiller seemed to be helping. It was supposed to thin blood as well, reducing altitude sickness. Now, headed in the direction where Penny had spied a rooftop, their path cut across the mountainside, instead of descending, much more difficult going with his wounded leg. He didn't know for certain how much farther the structure would be, but based on her description, he hoped they were at least halfway.

"I'm thirsty." Penny's arms dangled like wet rope. Her face was pale. "My head hurts."

Beginning signs of dehydration. He'd recently become aware of his own dryness. The sun shone directly overhead. In the field, you knew your body's needs, but learned to ignore them when not convenient. They'd been walking for hours. They could still survive for several more days without water, but confusion and brain fog might make them careless if they didn't find some soon. "We're almost to the rock with the black streak. I think we'll find water there."

"Up at a rock?" She pointed downhill. "Wouldn't it be down there in the valley?"

"Maybe. But only as a last resort. It might make you sick." He'd picked up a bug from a cold, fast-running stream once, water he'd figured stood the least chance of infection.

After ten more minutes of hiking, a gray boulder six meters high stuck out from the side of the mountain like a spent cartridge ejected onto grass. Red reached up and touched a moist, black stain streaked down its front, dripping in a leisurely flow. Penny knelt and cupped her hands beneath it. Red pushed them away. "Not yet! We've got to see where it's coming from."

He stepped next to the boulder, staying beneath the cover of junipers, to its crown where the spring ran over its rim. Tucked atop, small rocks rimmed the mouth of a narrow opening in the hillside, like a harvest cornucopia. Water pooled in a shallow scoop in the top of the boulder.

She tugged on Red's arm. "Can I get a drink from there?"

"No. See all the white stuff around the pool? That's a bath for every mockingbird and magpie in the forest. The water comes out of that little cave and gathers there, then runs down the front of the rock, making that black streak." He nudged her. "And *you* wanted to drink it."

She shrugged and shivered. "But I'm thirsty."

He bent to hands and knees and crawled up to the opening like a three-legged dog, his injured limb stiff and straight. He stuck his head into the darkness. The inside was tight, but large enough for two or even three adults. Searching the ceiling for bats, he saw none, nor any brown-rice guano.

He'd gotten that cold-river drink down in Venezuela. Within eight hours his gut burned so hot his only fear was that he wasn't dying fast enough.

Now, except for the bleached bulbous skull of a raccoon, this cave was sterile. Water dripped steadily from a pointed roof, almost a small stream. No algae or mildew clung to rocks, and only a single tree root hung from a nearby crack. Pebbles dug into his kneecap as he worked his way across the opening. The wet floor soaked his jeans. He waved for Penny to follow. "See how the water drips from the ceiling? It's OK to drink from there. This is where the spring comes out of the mountain."

She wiped her palms on her pants.

"Don't use your hands. Just let it drop in your mouth. You crawled through bird poop to get here."

She scrubbed them harder, then kneeling, opened her mouth like a baby bird, swaying as a wobbling top to follow the uneven dripping. She giggled quietly, and drops blew out her nose. She inhaled deeply and put her hand to her mouth.

"Don't cough!" he whispered.

She doubled over, but she held it back, as if stifling a sneeze. After a minute, she swallowed and gasped, "It went down the wrong pipe. You sure this water is OK? It stinks worse than Grandma's at the farm."

"That's just sulfur. Some people say it's good for you."

She wiped her lips on the sleeve of her jacket, then opened her mouth again. The two drank till they were full, then he made them drink more, till Penny said she'd puke if she had another drop. He thumbed outside and was moving that direction when she touched his hand. She'd frozen, eyes staring toward daylight.

Pointing out the opening, she cupped a hand over his ear. "I hear something."

Red snatched his pistol and pointed it at the glowing brilliance. A few seconds later a boot stomp, then small rocks on the hillside cast with a puff of dust. He aimed his weapon toward the cloud. The Yoga bitch, now in brown leather hiking boots, worn gray flop hat, and cargo shorts crossed their trail, headed away from the cave. A black stick, or butt of a pistol, bulged from under a brown canvas backpack. She stepped with purpose, as if knowing where she was headed, tan dust clinging to olive-skinned calves.

He'd killed Ravens Fan, her partner. Yet here she was. Persistent. No stranger to the forest, either. Part of a trained, professional team. But why such an extreme effort? There were more efficient ways to kill an operator than in broad daylight in a tourist area. Yet, Red had instigated the conflict by tripping Mandarin. Still, it meant whoever was trying to kill them was well funded but desperate, without time on their side. Who was it? He'd have to figure that out later.

With one arm, Red pulled Penny tight and laid a hand across her eyes. Drawing a bead, he brought the front sight up to Yoga's back. So easy. But she might not be alone. Anyone with her would have the upper hand since he was stuck in the cave. Not a defensible position.

But the wet team would've split up, maximizing their search area. This bitch had threatened Penny. She had to die. His finger tightened on the trigger.

Still, a shot could bring others to the location. Sure, Yoga would be dead, but he had a bullet in his ass, so they wouldn't be able to make it very far from the area in time. Staying hidden was the only hand he had to play. He couldn't risk alerting others to their position.

Yet he kept his aim, held a breath, anticipated the weapon's kick...

And what if the takedown went wrong? If she got off a few shots into the cave before Red finished her? Could she hit Penny? Following her for a few strides, he released a breath and loosed his grip on his daughter. Her safety was the higher priority. Yoga's fate would come another day. Still, he'd regret not killing her when he had the chance.

Once Yoga was down the hill and out of sight, Penny whispered, "She looked nice. Couldn't she help us?"

Red held a finger to his lips, mouthing *Shhhh.* After listening for several minutes, he turned to her. "You ever see her again, run. Understand? She is *not* a good guy." He touched her ears. "You did well, though. Those young things are sharp." Just like he'd taught her, she'd heard something out of place. "All we need to do is get to that house and make a call. That's it. We don't know how much farther it is, and we can't take risks. Understand? Mama's depending on us. We can't get caught."

She shrugged. "I was hoping it *was* Mommy." Cupping hands to ears, she resumed a distant stare. "I don't hear anything else. You think it's safe?"

"Yeah," he lied. Red holstered his pistol beneath his sweater and inched toward daylight.

Chapter 10

Naked Dream

Lam leaned against his truck and gazed upon Andi's body once more. Her mouth curled slightly into a smile, but the flesh of her cheeks drooped. Placing his fingers upon her eyes, he pulled the lids down, the soft orbs feeling like chilled grapes. A pause. She wouldn't want them closed. She'd loved staring at the clouds. For Andi, it didn't seem right. Though it chilled his skin, he pushed them open again.

Lifting his head, he studied the bright white two-story cottage. An open porch with low bannister spread across the front. Cold from the truck body seeping through his shirt dissipated as he remembered the warmth of the old oil furnace standing in the living room. These chilly mountain mornings, he always looked forward to lighting the thing up. Even in winter it heated the entire cottage, small as it was, with a kerosene scent that reminded him of the one in his dad's mountain hunt shack they visited as a kid. He'd jump out of the bathtub and hold his T-shirt over the hot air vent, filling it like a balloon, warming the garment before he put it on. Guilt panged his chest for the pleasant memory.

He started toward the house. Halfway across the packed-clay parking lot, he was sprinting. He slowed, trying to calm his nerves, but his legs still seemed to carry him faster than when he'd run the fifty-five-meter hurdles in high school. He slid to a halt. What if the hiker's friends had already been here? What if they were inside? He slipped behind a stand of tall mountain sagebrush. On all fours, he crept between stalks, inhaling their minty scent, till he spied the side door. The paint seemed gray now, and the newel post at the base of the front porch steps leaned sideways, snapped at its base. Lam snorted when he realized how stupid he'd been. Hell, if any hiker friends were in that house, they'd have heard his truck's racket and would've already tried to kill him. How foolish, displaying Andi's body and hefting it into the bed.

But that didn't mean they weren't close. He stood and ran to the white door, gripped the knob, and leaned into it, cracking a bubbly pane of antique glass. *Shit. Forgot to unlock.* Quivering fingers fumbled to release a jingling bundle of keys anchored to a belt loop. He grasped one hand with the other, steadying it, only then able to select the key with the green plastic tab. The door swung open in silence, Lam having freshly oiled the hinges two weeks earlier.

He placed one foot on the threshold and hollered, "Anyone here?" What self-respecting mugger would answer such a stupid question? He huffed at his repeated stupidity, then stepped slowly inside. Only a few places to hide. He peered behind the furnace, cold and lifeless, then walked into the galley. Stepping lightly up oak treaded stairs, he peeked inside both bedroom closets, tucked on either side of the chimney, the ceiling sloping down sharply. Alone, he ran downstairs and rummaged through a musty utility closet.

He lifted a burgundy metal radio the size of a twelve-pack cooler, surprised at its weight, and set it on the kitchen counter. The piece looked as if pulled from a fifties police station. The cord was wrapped in gray cloth, but in good repair. Inserting the plug into a yellowed socket, he frantically turned dials. The beast lay dead.

He slammed a palm onto the counter. How could Colorado Springs Utilities have such a piece of worthless trash for an emergency radio? Joey, the safety manager, was such a useless ass-kissing stuffed shirt. As a lineman, Lam had been required to be CPR certified as well as first aid trained, and he'd spent countless hours listening to EMTs drone on about how to treat burns, breaks, and high-voltage trauma. But now, he'd trade it all for a damn CB radio!

The stainless steel splash shield behind the kitchen sink reflected a yellow glow. He turned the antique radio slowly, and radiant heat warmed his wrist. Through cooling slits in the rear of the case, he glimpsed the warm orange burn of vacuum tubes. Static crackled through a woven black-and-white speaker cover. In his panic, he'd forgotten the old girl had to warm up.

Splintered plastic tape held a white envelope to the side of the device. Lam stuck in fingers and pulled out a frayed paper. Hurriedly he unfolded the note. It was handwritten in pencil on company letterhead. *Operating Instructions* was double underlined. The graphite gray characters were thick and faded, at least twenty years old. If he got this thing working, would anyone even be listening? At the bottom of the paper was a list of numbers beneath the heading *Frequency*, specifying dial settings for utility headquarters, Colorado Springs and Woodland Park police stations, plus a misspelled *Rangerrs*. *Emergency* had a box around it.

Lam scanned the instructions, then found the narrow black antenna lead hanging from the ceiling next to the chimney. He'd just connected the box to it and was setting the dials according to a crude drawing when something plinked against the side door. He stopped. Frozen vapor blew from his nose and hung in the chill air like a ghost. He slowly pulled out a shallow drawer beneath the counter. Why hadn't he thought about finding a knife earlier? Another *plink plink*, as if stones were smacking against the window. Could the glass he'd cracked earlier be falling out of the door? He wrapped a fist around the white plastic handle of a steak knife.

Plink plink plink...plink.

What the hell? He slid toward the edge of the refrigerator and peered around the corner. A blue shadow the size of a man's hand hovered near the bottom of the door's milky window. It rapped the glass with another hollow *plink*. He stared at the shape, then glanced to the other panes near the front. Only thistle brush swayed in a breeze. Suddenly, the shadow grew, flapped quickly, and flew away.

"Damn magpie!" he grumbled through gritted teeth. Turning again to the radio, its speaker still gushing static like falling rain, he worked to set the knobs as in the picture. A tiny black one for RF gain, another for squelch, a larger brown one for frequency, band spread, and something called XIT in the middle.

He held the mic stand next to his chin, pressed TRANSMIT, and the speaker went silent. "Hello?" he said, imagining his voice beaming from the slender antenna strapped to the chimney. Damn, would the hiker's friends be able to hear him doing this? He gripped the power cord and was about to give it a tug, then stopped. Reaching in his pocket, he pulled out a Leatherman and unscrewed the radio's back panel. Gazing inside, he shook his head. Only three of the five vacuum tubes were glowing. He tapped them with a fingernail, then wriggled them down, firmly seating their base into sockets. A minute passed and they still stood cold. He rummaged through the closet and more drawers, coughing on dust, looking for spares, but found only rusted batteries and matches.

He glanced at his watch. Eleven. How to get out of this alive? He closed his eyes and put a thumb to his forehead. *Think, damn it!* Maybe the hiker had lied about his friends. Maybe there weren't any more Jap gangsters out there. But no one came up the mountain alone. There must be others. And if they found the lifeless body of the hiker lying in the scrub near the edge of the road, they'd follow Lam's fresh tracks up to this cottage. He could start hiking toward Colorado Springs, though twelve hours was a long time to be in the open.

But he knew these woods. If he could get far enough, they'd never catch him. He could hole up in that little cave he'd run across two years ago near Lake Moraine. But then, no one would know where he was. What was his strategy? He pounded his forehead with his palm as he paced the kitchen, glancing out the front windows toward the drive, next to the stand of dead bristlecone pines. He'd stalked elk. Only last year, he and his buddy Troy had run seven miles, tracking a spooked lone bull, sneaking up downwind, then bagging the monster with bow and broadhead, just like the Apaches. But the game was different when he was the prey. Three years as a mechanic in the infantry hadn't taught him much, but he knew how to dig a foxhole and hide.

The generator building! It was mortared stone with a thick antique plate-steel entry. He could lock himself inside. No one would find him there. Once he didn't come home tonight, his wife would call work and they'd send someone up here.

He cracked the side door and put his eye to the slit. His Jeep stood silently at the edge of the packed-clay lot. Holding his breath, he closed his eyes and listened. The only sounds were a breeze through the tall grass and the high buzz of a mosquito close to his ear.

To hell with it. He swung it open, stepped down the stairs, and ran toward the truck. Halfway there, the feeling of exposure was as intense as childhood dreams where he'd find himself at the front of his third-grade class during show-and-tell, naked. His eyes fluttered to man-sized rocks upon the ridge, a magpie swooping low into the yellow-fringed leaves of a thick clump of golden currant, and again to the stand of dead bristlecones.

The creak of the Jeep's door echoed through the shallow valley. Leaning on the seat, he reached for another ring of keys, heavy as a maul hammer. He closed the door slowly and leaned upon it till the latch clicked and the interior light went out. Gasoline vapors swirled thick around him. Ducking low, he studied a pool of fuel under the tank. A single drop glistened in sunlight as it fell from where a bullet had passed through the truck's side.

Hell, even if he wanted to take a chance by racing back down the road, he'd have no gas. Holing up here or chancing an escape into the forest were his only choices. He glanced at the generator house's thick walls. It'd be better to hide.

A last glance into the bed. Andi's bangs fluttered in a breeze. Should he bury her? But what if the hiker's friends came by? He shouldn't leave her in the open, or did it matter? A faint crackle echoed. The sound of an engine maybe? It seemed to come from all directions. Could be a broken muffler running up the Peak. Still, he couldn't stay exposed.

Running toward the building, he stopped at a previous set of his own footprints. The parking lot had no traffic except once a week, and a recent rain had erased all other evidence of prior visits. He clutched the keys to keep them from jingling, then changed direction and sprinted toward Dark Canyon. If he were to follow that valley, he'd eventually end up in Manitou Springs. Anyone looking at his trail should assume that's where he'd headed. Once off the parking lot, he stepped across the rocks that had been pushed up during its construction, concealing his tracks. He ducked below trees, careful to not disturb the delicate bed of needles, and came out behind the squatty generator building. Grasping a bundle of dry grass, he broke it off and backed toward the door, sweeping away his footprints.

Slipping a key into a padlock big as a fist, he removed the heavy device and gripped a black handle. He braced himself against the jamb and gave a hard yank. A heavy *crack-ca-chunk* fired as the steel door edged open. The moist scent of dust and machine oil poured out, accompanied by the low electric hum of the Gilkes hydro generator. A last glance around the empty valley, and he sealed himself inside.

Chapter 11

Repeater

Carter pressed a fat thumb onto a carved brass doorbell switch outside 1533 Gabled Meadow Court in Arlington. Beneath the two-story portico of the massive red-bricked Georgian, he adjusted fake Prada frames on the bridge of his nose. Finally, video surveillance glasses that didn't look like BCGs. Though they didn't go with his blue-shirted alarm contractor uniform, a man had his standards.

A short lady with black skirt and white apron opened the door. The dark skin and wide cheekbones suggested Hispanic; the uniform shouted *maid*.

She smiled. "Can I help you?"

Carter had practiced all morning talking through his nose like Jamison. He drew a pencil from his chest pocket and pointed behind her. "Yeah. Uhhh. Here to fix the system."

"Pardon?"

"Yeah. Fire and burglar alarm. Just the burglar part."

She shook her head. "Did Mrs. Moses call you?"

"Yeah. Well, her system did. ABC." He tapped the green, red, and yellow logo of a bouncing ball embroidered above his shirt pocket. The goal was to plant some bugs and get out, leaving no trace. Everything else was just cover. "Your alarm company. Got a fault. It should be flashing on the keypad."

"Wait here, please." She closed the door.

He rocked from toes to heels, glancing back at a white Ford Transit Connect van, stenciled with the same bright, meaningless logo. A minute later, the home's massive door opened again. In the gap stood a small-waisted medium-height blonde in tight yoga pants, bare feet, and breasts enough for two.

"*Quit drooling*," growled Grind through the hidden earpiece. The other detective was back at the Det, watching through the micro camera bored into one arm of the Pradas. After their surveillance at Greenwood Park, Carter had gotten the warrant to bug Senator Moses' house. Maurine, his wife, had *trophy* stamped across her chest. The venom in her gaze indicated she was used to nurturing suspicion.

"Can I help you?"

Why was she staring at his glasses? Could she see the camera, or maybe recognize they were Prada knockoffs? "Yeah. Uhh. Need to check your system."

"The maid told me. We didn't call."

He pointed behind her with the pencil. "Yeah. Well. Nothin' we can fix remotely."

"Sorry, but there's no problem with our alarm."

He raised an eyebrow. "It's not on your keypad? Probably an intermittent fault. It'll show on the diagnostics screen. Either way, should be flashing a code at you. Can I take a look?"

She studied his shirt pocket, then lifted her chin to glance at the van. Opening the door wider, she pointed to a small white box on the far side of a white-marbled foyer flanked by wide oak staircases. An oil painting hanging above the controller, a canvas in muted tans and blues, portrayed Army infantrymen surrounding a small water hole on the old western plains.

"Are you also here to appraise the art?"

Carter blinked. "Yeah. No. Sorry. I've got a client never stops talking about his collection. He's got us set up Fort Knox in his basement. Always showing off new stuff he's got. Kinda rubbed off, I guess." The painting was a Frederic Remington. An original, as best as he could make out while fingering the keypad below it. If so, an expensive piece.

He'd studied a similar security system all yesterday, slipping a couple of Ben Franklins to a real ABC Alarm employee to get Carter familiar with it. "Nothing illegal. Just make me look like I know what I'm doing," he'd told his instructor.

Now, he pressed the SYSTEM screen and scrolled through the settings, dropping into menus and back out, no one selection showing on the display more than a second. He pushed the frames back up his nose. "Yeah. You've got a code twenty-three. Means one of your sensors has a problem. I usually see this when one on the window goes bad. One client had a twenty-three, but only during storms. Come to find out the wind would flex the window just enough to throw a fault." He threw her a broad smile.

She remained bitch faced. "Where's that accent from?"

Damn. She was shaking him down. "Yeah. Accent? Didn't know I had one. Grew up in Nevada, near the strip. Got outta there five years back on an intercompany transfer. Guess that's where."

A slight smile. "And now?"

"Live off King Street in Rose Hill." Carter's mind raced through his cover details: Joking Joes, his favorite pub. The closest Walmart off Route 180. Divorced eight years ago. Family still back in Vegas.

She glanced at the neck of his shirt. "I like the crucifix. What church?"

Shit. That was one he hadn't expected. Moses had trained her well. Or maybe living with a traitorous, cheating stuffed shirt had understandably made her paranoid. Hell, the man had betrayed his country by selling national secrets to North Korea and may have ordered the death of his own daughter. Now something even larger and more ominous was in the works that involved Mossad. And this woman could've even been in on it. Of course she'd ask questions.

"Church?" He thumbed through another couple menus, pretending to be distracted at one of their readings, scowling.

"*Blessed Sacrament Catholic, on Braddock Road*," whined Jamison's voice in his ear. Carter looked up at her again, then averted his gaze, as if vaguely ashamed. "Blessed Sacrament, on Braddock. Don't get to mass much, though. Gotta work most Sundays."

Red lips parted into a full-toothed smile. Looked like he was in. She pointed at the control box. "So, what else do you need?"

Carter nodded. "Yeah. Right. This one should be easy to diagnose. I'll just need to get to the windows. Got a new tester that doesn't require we—"

She held up a hand. "Look, sorry, but I put my exercise video on hold. Do your thing. I'll be in the gym. Have the maid get me before you leave." She padded down the hall and turned; muffled footfalls upon carpeted steps sounded her descent. She hadn't cut him any slack. That must be where Lori picked up her elusiveness. Came by it honestly. A pang of guilt pitted his stomach for thinking ill of her secretive nature. He'd be screwed up too if he'd been raised in a house where parents interrogated every visitor.

Carter glanced around the foyer. Two tiny white cameras hung in corners, one aimed at the front door, the other at him. He hadn't actually done any diagnostics, hacked into the system, or anything else that might raise a flag.

He returned to the van and clipped a canvas tool belt around his waist. Back inside, he pulled a black metal device the size of a cordless mouse from a leather holster. A small LED display glowed in its center. He knew his target, the senator's personal computer, was in a home office, probably somewhere near the back of the house, but a real contractor would start at a front window and work each one in turn. He would do the same. A long, narrow dining room was just off the foyer, with four deeply cased windows gracing its length. The sensors were mounted on each sill, the size of a cabinet's magnetic catch. He held the fake tester next to each, pressed a button, and a green light shown on its face.

He stepped through a side door into the kitchen. The maid was standing next to a center counter, apparently surveilling his moves.

"Wife's calling her alarm company," Jamison said excitedly. *"You didn't charm her."*

Kind of hard to do when your cover is an imitation of a pencil-necked hacker. Grind's gruff voice sounded as if speaking through a pillow in the background, but Carter made out the greeting. *"ABC Alarm."* Jamison had rigged her telephone system to reroute the call to his surveillance cell in the basement of the Det. Grind had to convince her the repair visit was legitimate.

Carter continued pretending to test the sensors in the kitchen. The maid watched him as he flashed the green light next to the little white box on each window, plus several French doors overlooking a herringbone-bricked patio lined with massive potted red hibiscus. After he worked through a living room, the next door on the hall was closed.

"This one have any windows?" he asked the maid, still following.

She nodded. "Just one."

Carter cracked open the door and stepped onto a red-and-black Persian rug. Half the walls were paneled, the other half built-in bookshelves. Two forty-inch flat screens, one atop the other, sat inside a casing above a cherry desk. A single window blazed brightly, spotlighting the workspace. Carter walked into its glow, as if emerging from a cave into brilliant noonday sun. An eight-by-ten photo of the family rested behind the keyboard, one, almost two decades old, judging from the wide style of Moses' collar. The man was in front of a marble column, shaking hands with Bill Clinton, his family neatly lined behind him. A champagne glass suggested a party; election night possibly. Even though facing the camera, the father's bulk towered over his family. Maurine, then smaller chested, Lori, and a younger sister. Lori stood a full head taller than her mother, and looked to be just parting the awkward teenage years. What was it like to grow up where ambition overshadowed family? It had to have an effect. Was Lori's unwillingness to share information trained into her by Maurine's skepticism? Did her driving ambition flow from her father's bent? Or had she chosen her own path?

The maid cleared her throat, shaking Carter from his pondering. Shading his eyes with one hand, he held the tester next to the sensor as he had the others. This time, he hit a different button and a red light shone upon its face.

He turned to the maid standing in the doorway, holding it above his head for her to see. "Looks like this is the one." The sensor was held to the window by two small screws. He pulled out a compact drill driver and pulled the trigger. With a dead battery he'd intentionally loaded, the device didn't turn. He glanced around the room. "Battery's dead. I got a spare, but mind if I plug this one in?" Without waiting for an answer, he removed a charger the size of a brick from his belt, pulled back a leather executive chair from a desk, and dropped to his knees. He ducked his head and slid under, next to a small Dell desktop. The power button glowed, but having nothing displayed on the screens meant the computer was probably in standby. Spying six spare USB ports in its back, he plugged a tiny dongle into one. A bug. It filled the port and concealed it nicely, looking as if part of the back of the case. Now, only a close inspection would reveal a port existed there at all. Carter allowed a slight smile of approval at Jamison's handiwork.

Next, he spied a spare outlet in a surge protector and plugged in what looked like a mobile phone charging cord, another one of Jamison's devices. It would recharge a phone, but that wasn't its main purpose. It doubled as a signal repeater. The tiny USB bug couldn't broadcast more than fifty feet, so this repeater, feeding off full household current, would take that signal and boost it over a mile. Lastly, he plugged in his drill driver's brick. Before backing out, Carter dropped his cheek to the Persian carpet. Bare feet now stood in the doorway.

With a fist, he smacked the underside of the desk, pretending to hit his head. "Damn it! Oh. Excuse me." He backed out from under the furniture and rubbed the back of his skull, as if he'd smacked it, hoping to distract Maurine from the fact he'd just been below the desk. He slipped in a spare battery into the drill driver. "Just needed to plug in my brick." He loosed the screws on the window and adjusted the position of the sensor ever so slightly, pretending to test it after each adjustment. Several times he selected the red light till, moving it right back to where it had been, he hit the green button, holding it high over his head once more, in triumph. "That should do it!" He started toward the door.

"Don't forget your battery charger," Maurine said, smiling.

"Yeah. Thanks for reminding me." He slipped beneath the desk, unplugged it, and stole a quick glance at the USB bug and the signal repeater, reassuring himself they were properly installed. Standing up, he wrapped his charger's cord, dropping the spare battery onto the senator's keyboard as he'd practiced. Reaching to pick it back up, he was careful to bump the mouse. One of the flat screens lit up, displaying a logon screen, and a low whir sounded from under the desk as a computer cooling fan spun up. "Yeah. Sorry. Hope I didn't hurt nothing," he said, walking back to the door.

Jamison had told him all he needed to do was get the machine out of standby and he could start hacking. He would make it simulate going back into hibernation, but in the background he'd be downloading the senator's hard drive. And, while there, he'd adjust the network's settings so Jamison could monitor the home's computer traffic, with or without the senator's desktop running, just in case. Jamison might have been a socially inept geek, but he was a belt-and-suspenders kind of hacker. An asset to the investigation.

To appear thorough, Carter checked the rest of the downstairs windows as well, but green-lighted them all. While in a marble-floored bathroom with plate glass shower, Jamison droned, *The bug and the repeater are active. It'll take a while to gain direct access, but that's all we need on-site. Clear to go.*

At the control box, Carter rapidly flipped through more menus, Maurine never less than twenty feet from him. He gave an occasional smile or *Hmm* of approval, then said, "Yeah. I think we fixed it. Thank you for your business. No charge, of course. It's all a part of your service fees. We'll let you know if another problem shows up." He stepped back outside, moving toward the van, pretending to thumb his phone, being careful to stumble on a crack in the sidewalk.

Chapter 12

Rabbit

Red's knee burned, sanded by the damp denim of his jeans. He'd been low-crawling for a hundred meters across yet a third ridge, injured leg stretched stiffly, rubbing off patches of skin. A few yards ahead a yellow-and-black butterfly soared on a pine sap–scented breeze, fluttering more in random staggers than coordinated flight. It swooped past a thick green bush with crimson thorns, then turned to light upon a lone pink flower. A perfectly synchronized landing. A slender siphon unwound and probed between the petals, wings flapping, flashing yellow and black. A few seconds later it mounted the breeze again, dropping out of sight behind the gray granite slab toward which Red crept.

He glanced over his shoulder. Penny smiled back, only her face visible next to a thick spruce trunk, its low dirty-blue branches blanketing her body. He'd left a scrawl in the earth after him like a sidewinder upon hot sand. Up to now, he'd been so careful not to disturb the forest floor, but low-crawling with a bum leg made it impossible.

They'd be most visible while crossing these ridges. He inched forward to the edge of the sun-warmed slab, ducking below an overhanging branch of a long-needled pine rooted in a fissure. He timed his forward thrusts with the breeze, moving when wind rocked the branches. Peering over the boulder, he pushed a sigh of relief through tight lips. Thank God. The red metal roof of a small two-story cottage came into view near the bottom of the shallow ravine. A narrow clay-packed road led to it. A lake lay to one side like a shining meadow. A small brown stone outbuilding sat near a narrow cut of water.

Sunlight glinted off the rear cab of a tan pickup pulled across what could otherwise be three parking spaces. Skid marks lay behind the huge tires. An older-model Jeep, jacked skyward in the style rednecks favored. Hard to tell for certain from this distance, but splintered reflections made the rear window appear shattered. He stared at the vehicle for several minutes, trying to make out some sort of cargo in the bed. Actually looked as if someone was lying in it, taking a nap. Or, someone could have killed the truck's owner, stolen the vehicle, and stashed the body in the back. No—it couldn't be a body. The wet team wouldn't leave a corpse in plain view. It would warn their prey.

He scanned the far wall of the narrow valley, then across the lake, and back down the road. The scene reminded him of a recent op in North Korea. It had been winter then. And the valley had been snow-blanketed meadow, not silver lake. He didn't like to recall it. Other than completing the mission, not much had gone well.

He shook his head and drew his thoughts back to the present problem. Down those blunt boulders, there were so many places a hunter could be waiting. Watching the house and valley. Assuming the hunter knew it was here.

He lowered his arm and beckoned to Penny.

* * * *

Blue-green needles pricked Penny's cheek. Their color matched her jacket, at least before it had been stained by grass and clay while she was crawling on her belly. A stinkbug landed on one sleeve, but she didn't dare swat it away. Dad had said being on top of a hill was dangerous. That someone could see them a mile away.

It had taken him forever to crawl to the boulder. His leg must be getting worse. He pretended it didn't hurt, but couldn't bend it much now.

They should've seen the house from the last ridge. Maybe she'd pointed them in the wrong direction. It had taken *so long* to get here, carefully placing her feet every step. Dad had glared if she even snapped a tiny twig. And she had to watch the woods around them. "Keep your eyes up," he'd whispered. But how was she supposed to keep her eyes *up* and not step on pinecones? There was no way Mommy knew all this stuff. She was probably rattling through the forest like a squirrel on coffee.

Penny moved her hands into a patch of warm light. The sun was about to sink behind a mountain. If they didn't find the house from here...

Something moved near the branch next to Dad. He was waving her forward. She crawled just the way he'd told her, belly on the ground like a snake. Mommy was going to yell when she saw the ruined new jacket. Dust tickled her nose, and she stifled a cough. A few minutes later, needles of the branch next to Dad brushed her neck.

He smiled and leaned close to her ear. "You did that better than a lot of the guys I know. I couldn't even hear you."

Eeew! His breath stunk. Since when did the guys that protect the president need to crawl through woods? Maybe that's not what he did now, after all. But where'd he learn all this hiding-in-the-woods stuff? Probably growing up on the farm with Grandpa.

She inched forward, toward the sun. The big rock on which she lay warmed her belly. She pressed her ear to it, resting her head for a second.

"Can't go to sleep now. We need your sharp young eyes. The house you saw is just down there."

Excitement leaped in her chest. Still, she didn't pick her head up off the rock for a minute. At last, she pushed forward and peered over its edge. "Yep, that's the one." A square, white-painted chimney stuck from its red roof like one of Jackson's Lego houses. "Can we go down and call for help?" she whispered.

"Not yet. Think like the bad guys. What would they do?"

She shrugged. "Wait inside the house?"

"Maybe. But being inside a house makes it harder to see and hear stuff. They'd probably wait outside and watch for us."

Penny glanced around the valley, studying the shady bases of trees. "So, why'd we come here, then?"

His beard twisted in a smile as his eyes still searched the distance. "You and I need to be better than them. Study everything. Take a picture in your mind of the trees. Then, if something changes, you'll notice. Right now, this rock's warm from being in the sun all day. There're lots more hot rocks along this ridge too. So, we're fairly safe if someone has thermal optics."

Penny wrinkled her nose. "Has what?"

"Special binoculars to see heat and cold. We're hot, and right now so are these rocks, so they won't be able to tell us from them. But when the sun goes down and the rocks cool, we'll need to move beneath thicker bushes. Then, we'll try to make it to the house."

She frowned, not liking this plan. "But, you said the bad guys would be watching the house."

"Maybe. Or, maybe they already left. What I'm really hoping is they didn't climb a tree like a gangly girl spider, so they don't even know about it." He turned his head to her slowly and smiled. "We're safe for now. But, to stay safe later, study the valley. Take pictures in your mind. Whisper to me if anything changes."

* * * *

Red slowly dropped to one knee. A fingernail paring of the moon hung high over Pikes Peak. Even so, the sky was clear enough he could've read a newspaper beneath the glow of the Milky Way. He glanced back toward a stand of tall grass, but could no longer see Penny's silhouette. She'd be safe up there. If someone caught him, she was tucked down far enough they'd never find her, even in daylight.

Tufts of grass and pine needles showered from his sleeves where he'd woven them into the sweater to break up his form. He crawled below a thicket of scrub oak on a hillside above the parking lot. The plump form of a chipmunk, or maybe a rat, scurried out of a burrow, toward the pickup truck. A brown-and-white flash descended. An owl's claws scraped the sand next to the creature. It dashed into the shadow of one of the massive tires.

Red stretched his neck over a branch and peered into the bed. Damn. Two empty, open eyes dully reflected starlight. The corpse was a woman, not one of the shooters at the visitor center, arms crossed neatly over her stomach. Not much blood on the floor, so she'd been dead when they'd placed her body. Whoever had put her back there had done so carefully, respectfully. Not the work of the enemy, whoever they were.

Should he chance checking the body for a cell phone? Maybe an old CB radio in the truck? Exposing himself in the open would be a risk, but making a call out would put an end to this mess.

Slowly, he crawled down the short slope, leaned over the bed, and felt the front pockets. The body was stiff; full rigor. Fingertips brushed metal lumps, and he pulled out a small key ring. Maybe for the truck? No, the shanks were shorter, like for a house.

Another glance around the valley and he vaulted into the back. He straddled her thighs and felt beneath for the back pockets. One held something flat and stiff. He yanked out a cell phone. Cradling it tightly to his chest to hide any escaping light, he pressed its face. Nothing. He held the power button, and for a split second swirling dots appeared, but quickly faded. Dead battery.

He shoved the device into his own pocket. Never know if a charger might be in the house and could bring it back to life. Easy for a cell phone. Not so much for a life. From her other hip he pulled out a man's wallet. He flipped it open, and a photo of the woman fell onto her cold belly. In it, she was kneeling in front of a jungle gym, flanked by a freckled boy in a Superman T-shirt and blond girl gripping a Barbie by the hair, all smiles.

He pinched the bridge of his nose. Who was doing all this? Such an intense effort meant government funding and support. But which one? And why? How could you murder an innocent mother just to… He shook his head. Couldn't go there. To an operative, the woman was collateral damage. Unfortunate, assuming the gunman had a conscience at all. But the mission came first. Such an enemy would continue until Red and his family were eliminated.

Briefly, a glimmer of light reflected from the side of her eyes, like she was staring at him. A chill ran up his arms. Rage heated his belly. *Focus on the present*, he told himself. Anger was like adrenaline. It provided only a momentary boost, but drained you in the end. When things go to shit, an alert mind makes the difference. He had to get Penny out alive.

A large metal toolbox lay at the front of the bed. He opened the top and grabbed a screwdriver. Might need it to break into the cottage.

A rust bubble pocked the metal bed. This Jeep was old, so it wouldn't be difficult to hot-wire. The enemy may be watching the roads, but they couldn't keep their eyes everywhere. It was worth a chance. As he swung his good leg over the side rail and stepped back down, gasoline vapor burned his nose. He slipped beneath the rear bumper and peered up at the tank. Too dark beneath to see, but the odor was strong. He lifted a hand and softly tapped the bottom. A hollow *twang*. Empty. Must've drained out and evaporated off. He smacked the back of his head upon the gravel, chest tense, wanting to scream. What was God trying to do? Why couldn't he catch a break?

He rolled out and shuffled back beneath the cover of sage-scented scrub oak. A last glance back to Penny's hideout, then to the house. If the wet team had already been inside, they'd have destroyed any phone or radio. But on the outside chance someone had left a phone charger, one that would fit his or the dead woman's, maybe he could get a signal to make a distress call. With his bum leg, that plan might provide his only chance of getting out with Penny. He had to try.

He ducked again and crawled around the small parking lot, approaching the far side of the cottage. Two dry, scraggly bushes grew against the foundation, branches flailing as a gust of wind whipped around the house.

Red scurried behind them, into the shadows, like the rat. Held his breath to listen, but nothing sounded over the gusts. He squeezed under the porch rail, rolled to the threshold, reached up, and tried the doorknob. It turned easily, and he crawled inside.

* * * *

Penny stared at the cottage's side window, lit a glowing green. It felt like Daddy had crawled from their grassy hideout a hundred years ago. But being afraid made time go slow. And now, she was even more scared than the time she'd snuck out of her room to eavesdrop on that movie with the serial killer that Mommy and Daddy were watching. So maybe it hadn't been as long as she thought.

That dim green glow still hovered in the window like the shiny eye of a huge monster. Daddy had said it was probably from a clock or microwave. Once inside, he would cover the light to let her know he was safe.

They'd ripped off handfuls of stalks with long, narrow leaves, sticking them all over his sweater and legs, even tucking them down his neck to cover his face. He'd smelled like the hay bales back at her riding stable, but with bad breath.

She peered through a slender gap in the leaves and…yep, still glowing.
Crunch!

Something moved near the front of the hideout. She pulled her knees beneath her, ready to spring like a rabbit and run. But no… Daddy had said to stay still, no matter what. That no one would see her here, that the grass covered her even from those special binoculars.
Crunch. Crunch.

Like boots on dry leaves. She gripped some stalks and stared out the narrow path, toward the house. The green light was still on. She'd been careful to stay back, away from the edge, just like Daddy said. How had they found her?

Last month, while walking Heinz with Grandpa, she'd spied a skinny bunny at the edge of a freshly mowed field. The rabbit held still as a statue. The half-blind dog had trotted right past it, nose to the ground, sniffing eagerly back and forth as if smelling but not seeing it. The lab never spotted his prey.

Penny's fists quivered in rhythm with her racing heart. Her tongue throbbed too.
Crunch. Cruuunch.

It was closer. She would stay still, like Daddy had said, like the bunny rabbit. But she was ready to spring if spotted.

Crunch.

A squirrel hopped into view a few feet away from the grass shelter. She blew out a sigh, only then realizing she'd been holding her breath. "Stupid squirrel," she whispered.

A second later, it scurried away, tiny claws scratching bark as it scaled a tree. She just loosened her grip on the grass when another *crunch* sounded from the opposite side, this time louder. Her heart leaped again.

Just another stupid squirrel, she told herself.

Chapter 13

Clay Pigeon

Carter yanked the steering wheel of his white Malibu, dodging a pothole. The passenger tire sank into the soft shoulder of Meadow Ridge Drive like a plow harrowing soft earth, threatening to pull the vehicle off the road. It'd been fifteen minutes since they'd turned at a sign that read BULL RUN ESTATES, one of Washington DC's thousands of bedroom communities. But they had sped past the suburban mini-mansioned development and now were cruising through old farmland. He hadn't expected the scenery to turn rustic so quickly. Black and brown cattle rested in the shade of a sprawling maple. Knowing they'd be in the sticks, he'd left his tie at home. A hideous orange polo hung untucked over Grind's trousers. So bright, he resembled a school crossing guard. The bottom half of the undercover uniform consisted of baggy jeans with faded knees. The man must shop from a thrift store trash bin.

Carter steered the vehicle back onto the road and tapped the GPS stuck beneath the rearview.

"I doubt that thing works out here," Grind mumbled, studying a mailbox as they passed.

Carter shrugged. "I need to update the maps. Daughter hasn't taught me how to use the one on my phone yet."

"It's been five minutes since Bitching Betty told us to turn down a driveway that didn't exist. Go 'round and try again."

An Appaloosa raised its head from behind a split rail fence. Pastel green moss blanketed the low plank.

Grind pointed to a mailbox with brass numbers on its side. "That's the one."

Carter turned down a white stone driveway. "Never seen so many trees. Makes me claustrophobic."

Grind scratched the nape of his neck, pink with a mild rash. "Worried about that shooting in Colorado?"

That, and more. Jamison had already found a library of audio files on Senator Moses' computer. The traitor had bugged Red and Lori's house. Apparently it had gone on for years. The hacker had said it'd take weeks to synthesize everything, but he'd discovered one audio file that sounded like Lori at her office in Fairfax. Carter had tried to call Lori and Red, but no luck. "News is calling it a 'domestic terrorist event.' It came out too fast. A cover story if I've ever heard one."

"We've got no indicators Red was involved. Let it go."

Carter rolled down his window and spat into tall grass. Ammonia swelled into the vehicle. Did horses always smell this bad?

Grind put a finger across his nostrils. "Hogs. That smell never goes away."

Carter breathed through his mouth. "If Red was in the area he would've given us a call by now to say he was OK."

"So, because we *didn't* hear from him, you think he was the shooter?"

Carter rode the brake as he steered across a cattle guard spanning the opening in a white-railed pasture fence. "It's just a feeling. I don't like that we can't reach him. We'll know for sure in a day once the feds get it organized. Earlier if we can get the cooperation of the locals. In the meantime, we keep moving."

Grind massaged a thumb, popping the joint. "So, how we going to play this one?"

Good question. It was a late Saturday morning, and they'd just turned down the driveway of Stacy Giles, Lori's supervisor. He needed to confirm Lori's cover. Suspicion had burned Carter's chest ever since he'd met Red's wife. Some variable was rattling in his subconscious, like a marble in a locked box, clanging against steel walls. He'd strained to pry the latch open ever since. And now its racket had become unbearable. Even Red had admitted suspicion that Lori was working more than fintel for the CIA. She'd have reasons for keeping secrets, he'd said. A good friend, but Lori was making him look like an idiot.

Still, Grind's question stood. *How do we play it? What would make Stacy open up?*

As he steered around a stand of white oak, a blue Cape Cod with cedar-shingled roof stood atop a green earthen mound. Carter pulled behind a silver Toyota SUV and stomped the parking brake. "I'm going to give her the benefit of the doubt. Assume she's a patriot and gives a crap about her analyst. I'll give her enough to appreciate the situation and see where it goes from there."

Grind swung his door halfway shut, then froze. "You going to tell the truth?"

"That's the plan."

Grind huffed. "Gimme lies any day. Want me to take the lead?"

He studied the thick curly stubble on his partner's face. The man claimed he had a skin condition that prevented him from shaving. In the sun, his blaze-orange polo made Carter squint. "You look like a color-blind dealer strung out on meth. Just take notes. And try not to scare the kids."

An annoyed grunt.

The bell rang, and a bright-eyed skinny man in tight khakis opened the door. Exposing only half his body in the gap—was he hiding something back there? A weapon? His smile quickly faded when his eyes landed upon Grind. "Avon?" he said, with a curt curl of his lips.

Carter smiled. "I'm sorry to bother you on a Saturday, but is—"

Two shots boomed. A tall pine full of blackbirds took to flight, wings buzzing. Grind flinched, but the skinny man stood still. "Yes?"

Carter cleared his throat. "Is Stacy available?"

"And you are?"

"We work with her." A broad smile to cover the lie. But not a complete untruth. The Det's CIA liaison had set them up with files as independent contractors. "Stacy won't know us, but she'll want to talk."

Skinny didn't flinch. "I'll ask." Then the door shut with a solid *ca-chunk*.

Maybe he should've left Grind in the car. A minute later, a short, middle-aged brunette with a fair complexion and crow's-feet, in blue jeans and neat white blouse, opened the door, gripping a twelve-gauge Remington pump action by the forestock, pointed to the ceiling.

She glanced at Carter, then eyes locked with Grind. "Who's the stiff?"

His partner smirked, white teeth beaming in contrast to dark skin. "Sorry. It's as loose as he gets."

She faced Carter. Words snappy, confident. "Is it something that can't wait till Monday?"

He resisted shifting his feet. "I'd like to talk about Lori Harmon."

Her face remained smooth. No change in expression or sign of nervousness. "She's dead. Car accident, six months ago."

He clasped fingers in front of his belt. *If that's how she wants to play it.* "Understand. Nevertheless, we have questions."

"What's your interest?" A glance at Grind. "You're not IG."

"Promise it won't take long. May we?" He stretched out a hand.

Stacy lifted her chin a beat, then stepped aside. "We'll talk out back. We're breaking in my birthday present, dusting a few pigeons." She led them straight through a warm hallway lined with wood-framed pictures of kids and babies, out a back door. Following, Skinny reached behind it and drew out a second shotgun, this one with pistol grip and ten-round magazine.

They stepped down flagstone pads onto a grassy, flat lawn trimmed as tight as a cemetery. Its edge disappeared down a hill like an infinity pool, spilling into a wide valley filled with low clouds. Over a mile away, rolling green mountains sprung back up from beneath the white blanket.

Carter's feet sank into the dense grass. "I'd prefer to speak privately."

She raised her shotgun toward the valley and leaned into it. "Pull!"

Skinny yanked a string on a red machine the size of a lawnmower. A whir wound up, and two orange pigeons flew from the bottom. Tracking them with the barrel, she fired twice, puffing them to pepper flakes that sank onto the green carpet. "Out here is private. And my husband's staying." She ejected a blue plastic shell. "What's your angle? You talk too polite. Gives me the idea you don't have a right to be here." With practiced coordination, she slid two fresh loads neatly beneath the receiver. "You came to me. Talk."

Carter glanced at Skinny, assault shotgun hanging from his fist. Glad he'd brought Grind after all. But though Stacy's voice was steady, her fingers trembled slightly as she reloaded. Anger, fear? She seemed the polar opposite of Lori, who always struggled to cover her feral nature with a smile and floured apron.

"You know why someone might have wanted to harm Lori?" A dramatic pause. Often, subjects felt the need to fill silence. She didn't bite. "She ever mention she was scared of her father?"

Her response was quick. Reflexive. "Moses? Don't know anything about him. Who you really with?"

Carter raised eyebrows, hoping to look genuine. "CIA."

She swung the barrel in a circle. "Yeah. All of us. What part? Who's running the investigation now? I was told it was closed months ago."

Carter sensed Grind's gaze upon his back. *Sometimes you have to give a little to move forward.* "We're with a fusion cell, and CIA is a cooperative member. Lots of other co-ops as well. DEA, FBI, military. Maybe you've heard rumors?"

Lips parted just so slightly. She glanced at her husband, who dipped his head. Was that a good sign? Or did it mean *let's dust these guys and feed them to the hogs?*

She squinted. "K..."

"Lori's not dead. She's still working for you."

Stacy's stare was blank, as if waiting for him to continue.

"We're investigating attempts on her life. Right now, I'm asking about her father." More silence. "I've made significant progress."

The corner of her mouth turned up. Even her eyes seemed to smile. Still, she said nothing.

So much for giving a little. But Stacy was Lori's supervisor. If anyone would have inside intel... He'd try once more. "Six months ago, during an op in North Korea, we killed a CIA asset. One of yours. We think that was a setup for Lori."

Stacy lifted the weapon to her hip and punched in three more shells. Must not have a plug installed. "Where you going with this?"

Carter shrugged. He'd stuck his neck out far enough.

She snapped on the safety and rested the weapon across her forearm. "You've got proof Moses was involved?" She raised a finger toward him. "It'll never stick. That man's got dirt on everyone. He could shoot the pope during Christmas mass. Saint Valentine would grant the pardon." She stepped closer and brushed a fallen green leaf from his shoulder. "Watch your step. A man who'd kill his own daughter...you're just a sneeze to him. Which is why, I suspect, you haven't brought him in. You don't have ironclad evidence." She brushed his jacket once more. "But if you have it, do this country a favor and make the dickless skirt-chaser disappear. Your organization can handle that, right?"

Maybe this woman wasn't Martha Stewart after all. "That's not the way we work."

She gripped the forend and raised the barrel. "Seemed to work for *my* asset." A pause. "You ever hunt?"

"Nothing besides ducks."

She thrust the weapon into his chest. "But a hunter, nonetheless. I'm a detective too. Lori and I, a team. We were on the scent of a mole leaking tradecraft—how the CIA tracks financial transactions—and were getting close." She tapped his chest. "Just like you say you are now. But two years of planning would have gone to hell because Lori got hurt. A bullet in her calf. *She* was supposed to make that appearance in North Korea. I couldn't send a wounded agent, so I sent Karen, one of my other girls. So few people knew about our little fintel op, her cover was rock solid. We could still pull it off. Sound familiar?"

Too familiar. He was keeping his own investigation tightly wrapped. He swallowed, trying to relieve the irritating prickle at the back of his throat.

Her lips barely moved now. "Know what people think of you guys? You're the CIA's hit squad. Whenever they need a bigger hammer."

Carter gripped the shotgun and stepped next to a blue mosaic of spent shells. "How does that affect our conversation?"

She straightened and cocked her head. "You murdered Karen. And now you want help figuring out who's trying to kill your squadron commander. You don't give a shit about Lori. But I do. I want the guilty party dead."

A quiver ran up Carter's neck. "We don't act singularly. All ops are cleared through channels. Karen's dead because you didn't clear your little project through your chain of command. Our team did their job that night." He considered saying more, but clenched his jaw.

She stepped close to Skinny, shotgun resting on his belt. "This is where the conversation always breaks down. You want info from me. I don't trust you. You get dick. Nobody's happy."

Carter lifted the barrel toward the empty valley. "Pull!" Two pigeons flew. Chasing their path, the front sight overtook the targets. Aiming a foot ahead, he squeezed the trigger and pumped the action. The gun's booming echoed from the edge of the woods, sending another tree of blackbirds to flight and spurring a munching rabbit to sprint beneath a holly shrub. A rude interruption to an otherwise peaceful countryside. The weapon bucked his shoulder three times to bring them down, peppering the air with the scent of spent powder. She'd loaded five shells, so two shots left.

He turned back to the pair. Her arms were crossed so tightly her blouse was about to tear. Time to shift his approach. "Or maybe we've both been duped and the real threat is enjoying seeing us piss on each other."

She shook her head. "Lori's a solid gal, married to a half-cocked nutcase. Other than her taste in men, she's earned my trust. Suppose I share, what's in it for me?"

"Lori's safety. And Red's. That's the goal."

"She'll never be safe as long as she's married to that guy."

Enough. He kept his volume just under a shout. "Last hit was after *Lori*. Not Red. Sending agents into North Korea? That's no job for fintel. Lori does more than stare at dollars on computer screens. Quit the posturing. Someone's after *her*. We're trying to do some good here."

She stared at Carter, then glanced at Skinny. He shrugged. Grind's hands twitched uneasily in his pockets, no doubt gripping his .357 Mag.

She stepped over the small pile of shells and pointed down the hill. He walked next to her for a minute. Leafy tops of hardwoods sprung from the green horizon as they neared the lawn's edge. Her lips stretched tight.

"Normally, at this point in negotiations, I'd threaten you with IRS audit triggers for three generations. But I don't have to do that, do I, madman?"

Fear iced his chest. She'd spoken the word warmly, but her threat was clear. Marble Hill Madmen was the name the national media had given the current Senate hearings on the deaths of six terror suspects. Carter had performed several of the interrogations, obtaining perishable intel that saved over fifty American lives. But prisoners had died, and now, three years later, the media was having a feeding frenzy.

She lowered her head slightly, staring beneath eyebrows. "That's right, *Detective*. What I'm going to share stays between us Girl Scouts. Got it?"

Carter swallowed.

"Follow the money."

He winced. "That it?"

"Want to flesh out a terror system's network, follow the money. Where it flows. It can paint a clearer org chart than you can get tearing off fingernails or acid baths. It shows the real chain of command. You think Moses is dirty?" A shrug. "Join the club. The man's campaign contributors read like Hoffa's payroll. Legit on the surface. Even stand up to a good shakedown. But he's been my personal hobby for years. He could teach drug cartels how to launder money. He's got it coming in from overseas. North Korea, China, Iran, and other nasties. They get run through Bahamian accounts, bitcoin, and eventually come back to the US in small packages that stay below campaign finance reform's radar. Not long ago we noticed he started getting greedy, risking larger transactions."

"Why haven't you brought charges?"

"Like you, no proof beyond doubt. I thought we'd have him with that deal in North Korea. We were planting gear behind their firewall. A little time on their servers and I'd have the smoking gun. But someone had to kill my agent and burn down the entire North Korean data center."

A thought jolted his mind. He shuddered. "You saying we were played?"

"Your op was legit. But someone took advantage of the situation, fed you massaged intel, and set your boys up to kill Lori. Instead, you killed her replacement. I faked Lori's death stateside to give her breathing room. Get the huntsman off her back." She tapped a temple. "I follow money. Your poison is the trail of intel. You follow who provided it for your op in North Korea. Somewhere along that path you'll find the real mole. Dig him out, and I'll bet he looks a lot like Moses. Cut off his head, then bury him again."

Carter punched the weapon's safety. He'd forgotten after his first shots. "You have any indication Moses is into more than money laundering or illegal campaign contributions?"

Her expression remained flat. Not even the dilation of pupils. "Such as?"

"Such as selling national secrets? Specifically, a list of active military operators and the ops in which they'd participated?"

"I was told your op in North Korea plugged that leak."

"But we never nailed the source. I suspect Moses' involvement wasn't just to cover up his money laundering."

She tapped her fingers on her thumb, as if counting. "My interests are in fintel. Anything else would be outside my purview. However, national secrets are highly lucrative. And money flows from that man's pockets like a fire hydrant."

Back up the hill, Carter held the weapon out to her. "Nice action."

She snatched it from his grasp.

He turned toward the house and stepped away. Glancing back, he said, "You have a way of contacting her?"

Skinny remained a statue. Stacy stepped next to the pile of shells. "No. Off the grid for two weeks."

Carter stopped. "You haven't heard?"

"Heard what?"

"Take a look at CNN. There's been a shooting on the top of some mountain in Colorado. I can't hail either one. They've gone dark." He kicked a mushroom, and it puffed gray spore atop his black Gucci leather lace-ups.

She raised the weapon toward the valley and leaned into it. "It's a big state. No reason to suspect they were involved."

Carter glanced at Grind, then jerked his head toward the house.

As they walked across the stone patio, Stacy shouted, "Pull!" Two shots boomed. Over his shoulder, Carter glimpsed a single black-and-orange disc sinking like a setting sun beyond the lawn's horizon.

Chapter 14

Recoil

Lam placed a metal chair in front of the black steel door and lowered himself into it. He'd threaded a crowbar through the handle, preventing it from opening, then secured that tightly with a C-clamp. If any more hoodlums showed up, hopefully they wouldn't notice the empty padlock hinge on the exterior and realize he was inside.

Now, his outstretched neck ached as he rested his forehead upon the metal slab, eye to an old key slot, gazing toward the cottage. He'd turned off all the lights of the stone room so his vision could adjust to the dark, allowing him to see, even if only faintly by starlight, when help arrived. The Gilkes generator hummed behind him, though it couldn't drown out a gust of wind as it whipped across the roof, blowing dust beneath the eaves. It had picked up in the last few hours, though the sky was still clear. The shadowed forms of trees near the cottage bent in unison, the roof howled, and a puff of dusty air shot through the keyhole, stinging his eye.

When would someone come for him? It had gotten dark three hours ago. Sure, he'd gotten home late before, especially when working up here, but his wife should've expected him already. Maybe she'd put his daughter, Jessica, to bed and they'd both fallen asleep. Damn. If so, she wouldn't know he was missing till morning. Hell, it might be noon tomorrow by the time someone arrived.

A dark form marched into view, planting himself in front of the porch. The colors of his clothes were muddled, like camouflage. Hair fell to his shoulders in a knotted mop. Probably dreadlocks. He towed a kid in one hand, about the same height as Jessica, a ponytail drooping. She followed at the distance of her outstretched arm, as if he was pulling her across the parking lot on skis. He wrapped an arm around her waist and knelt behind her, facing the cottage, back to Lam. Was this the man and little girl the Jap gangster had asked about? Was he a thug too?

The guy hollered, but the rustle of aspens and the scream of the wind drowned out his words. He must think Lam was still in the cottage. A minute later the dark figure yelled again, then lifted a—

Shit! He held a pistol to the kid's head. Lam edged forward and felt for the C-clamp. Quickly, he loosened its grip. This guy had to be looking for him, because he'd killed that Jap. The gunman must be threatening to kill this kid if he didn't—

Another shadow stepped from the dark porch, outline like a walking bush with leaves jutting from his sides and head. But...Lam had never seen anyone go into the house. The bushman held hands up in surrender, stepping slowly to the edge of the parking lot. The gunman hollered again, shaking the kid.

Wind was gusting now, stirring starlit powder. A glowing dust devil churned through the parking lot behind the gunman, tugging on his dreadlocks, like a demon pulling him down to hell. That's where Lam would plant the crowbar. If he could sneak up from behind, with a good swing the bar's sharp foot could penetrate a skull. He'd be dead before he could pull the trigger. Lam slid the steel tool free, feeling in the darkness to ensure its proper orientation and a solid grip upon its shank. He paused for another gust to rattle the roof, drowning any sounds of his movement, then yanked open the door. This asshole was about to be reunited with his Jap gangster friend.

* * * *

Red held his arms up and stepped down the porch steps toward the parking lot. His fingers choked his pistol's grip, weapon aimed toward the night sky. His chest was tight, as if filled with ice water. In the middle of the barren lot, a gunman knelt behind Penny, holding her tightly in front of him.

Her arms reached out, tear-streaked face pleading. "Daddy!" she screeched.

The wind muffled the gunman's voice, but he sounded as if he was from the Caribbean. Jamaican, maybe. "Weapon. On the ground!"

Red had no clear shot at the man. He stood thirty feet away, and even his head ducked behind hers. Loosening the grip on his pistol sickened his gut more than running from the firefight at the peak. At least then, he'd been protecting Penny. But now, tossing it onto packed gravel, he was giving up hope.

A total loser. A Jamaican gunman, probably strung out on amphetamines, held his daughter's life by the tendon of his index finger.

Red's pistol clattered as it fell. "Let her go. It's me you want."

A shrieked laugh, and the man stood, still holding Penny against his chest. How'd he fit behind his little girl? The Jamaican was huge. Penny's feet barely hung to his belt. His triangular torso widened to broad shoulders. His neck was thicker than her head, dark cords of hair blowing in the wind. "You? I don't want you. Who you think you are, little man? Where's the girl?"

Red scowled. "You're holding her."

An angry growl. The Jamaican grabbed Penny's foot and, folding her in two, pulled it close to her face. The muzzle pressed against her shoe. "Don't waste my time, little man, or I blow off your daughter's foot, right here where she can see!"

The Jamaican whispered in Penny's ear, and she shrieked. The wind blew hard, frothing the lake's surface. How was this happening? Nothing was within Red's control. He had no angle to play, completely in the grasp of a hired man. His calf started to jitter. "Please, let her go. I'll tell you whatever you want."

Another screeched laugh came from the Jamaican, as if from an owl. "Yes, you will. Tell me where the girl is, and I won't hurt your daughter. You die either way, but she might live. If you waste my time, I blow off pieces until you tell me what I ask." He straightened even more, stretching himself higher. "Now where is the girl? Your *wife*."

Lori? What the hell did they want with her? "I don't know where she is. She ran when—"

"Wrong answer!" The Jamaican cocked the pistol. In a panic, Red waved his arms and shouted, "Wait! I do know. We had a rendezvous set up." *Think fast. Make it up. Where the hell could it be?* He pointed toward Manitou Springs. "If we were separated, we're supposed to meet in front of the Creamery in Old Colorado City."

"You think I'm an idiot? We've got eyes all along that route. No one has come off the mountain we didn't see."

Shit. He had no idea where Lori was. And even if he tried to answer, this man was going to blow off his daughter's foot. He'd move to her knees, arms... He'd never seen it done, but had witnessed the remains of ISIS terrorists left behind by a team of Russian operators.

A spark of hope glimmered as a dark shape stepped from the shadowed doorframe of the stone building across the parking lot. Red kept his eyes on the Jamaican, not giving the gunman a hint that someone was marching up from behind. Was it a policeman? Park ranger? Whoever it was, if he tried to shoot the Jamaican, Penny could be killed in the process.

"Wait!" Red shouted. "If you've got eyes on the way down to Manitou, she wouldn't have tried to move that direction. She's still on the mountain. I can help you find her."

The dark figure stepped more quickly now, striding in confidence. A crooked bar swung from an arm like a hay baler's hook. JEEP stretched in light-colored block letters across his shirt's dark background. This guy must be the owner of that pickup.

The Jamaican spat onto the ground. "You don't know where she is, do you?" His lip drew into a sneer. "That means you're just dead weight. The both of you."

A few more steps and Jeep Man would be behind the Jamaican.

Red held up his hands. "I know her. Where she'll go. You'll find her faster with me. But, if you hurt—"

Jeep raised the weapon, as if winding up for a baseball swing. The Jamaican smiled and spun, shooting toward the man's chest. Red ducked and rolled toward the gunman, springing to his feet under his arm. A yank and twist on his wrist and the pistol dropped free, though the thick radius bone didn't snap as he'd hoped. The Jamaican screamed and threw Penny aside, next to Jeep Man's body.

Red pummeled the Jamaican's kidneys with quick blows, but his core was hard as plywood. The Jamaican took a step back to get a clear swing, but Red closed again, staying tight and working his stomach. He couldn't let the gunman back away or he'd be vulnerable. With a bullet in his ass, he'd have no kick to speak of. But one punt from this guy and Red would land in the trees.

Another step back. Red ducked and planted an uppercut into the man's groin. It smacked plastic. Damn it! He was wearing a cup. Before he could step back again, Red planted two more strong shots on the same target. The last sounded a *snap*, and his punch sank in. *Got you!*

A knee caught Red in the chest and lifted him from the ground, lobbing him like a tennis ball tossed for a serve, shaking twigs and leaves from his sweater. Before he landed, a fist the size of a brick caught him aside the head and sprawled him upon gravel. He rolled to one side, dodging a foot stomp, then hopped to his feet again.

Sure enough, the Jamaican threw a side kick directly at Red's bum leg. A seasoned fighter, he'd seen his weakness. Red ducked, and the blow glanced off his back. Another shot to the Jamaican's groin, and another knee slammed into Red's belly, emptying his lungs of air and sending him skyward. This time, the Jamaican chose an uppercut as Red fell back to earth. He shielded his face with his arms, and the blow crashed into his triceps. Landing, his head smacked the clay surface. He opened blurry eyes just as the gunman raised his boot. This strike would end him.

Bang! A flash came from the direction of where Jeep lay. The Jamaican gripped his stomach, dropped to knees, then fell back. Red rolled to his feet and patted the man down, pulling a slender black throwing knife from a sheath and a .357 Magnum revolver from a calf holster. No way this guy was getting a second chance. The big man's breathing was fast and shallow. Good riddance.

Red scooped up his own pistol, then limped to Jeep and dropped to a knee. He pressed an ear to his chest. The guy was still breathing. Penny sat on the ground nearby, sobbing. "You'll be OK, sweetheart. But we've got to help this guy now. Go in the house. Find a bed and bring me the sheets."

She didn't move.

"Now!" he yelled.

She rose to wobbly legs and ran, stumbling up the porch steps.

Jeep moaned, trying to peer down past his cheeks, studying the scarlet stain on his shirt. The injured man would've been hard pressed to make that shot considering his wound. Maybe it had come from the trees. If the Det had located them and had a sniper out there, he wouldn't give away his position in case another enemy operator was nearby. The Jamaican's Colt 1911 lay beside Jeep's head. No. This guy must've squeezed off a round, somehow.

He tore off the man's bloody shirt and rolled him to his side. A white twig of bone, like a broken pencil, lay splintered inside the exit wound. The shot had been high and passed clear through. Bleeding was steady, but not in gushes.

"What's your name, buddy?" Red muttered.

Jeep's voice was a hoarse whisper. Red lowered an ear to listen. "Lam."

Red gritted through his own pain, trying to keep his tone upbeat. "Lam, my daughter and I owe you our lives. The good news is, you're gonna live. The bad news is, once shock wears off, you're gonna wish you hadn't."

No sooner had Penny run inside than she was back out the door trailing white fabric. "It's just a tablecloth," she blubbered.

Red forced a smile. "You did good, sweetheart. Sit down now. You'll feel better in a bit."

Within a minute, he'd torn the covering into strips, packed the wound, twisted a length of the cloth into a doughnut, placed it over the hole in the man's flesh, and tied it securely. Another strip went around the man's neck as a sling. "Just lie on your side for now."

He turned and pulled Penny into his arms, smoothing her hair back. "Thank God you're OK. I am *so* sorry. I thought for certain no one would find you all the way up there in that thick grass."

For a minute, she was stiff, frozen. Then, she opened her mouth, reached in, and pulled out a tooth. She cupped it in a quivering palm. "Is it one of my permanent ones? I bit his finger when he shot that man with the stick. I thought...I thought..."

A dribble of blood trickled down her forehead. Red wiped it off with a corner of clean tablecloth.

"I thought...I was shot." She blinked.

Taking her hands in his, he stretched her arms wide, looking her over. "No. You're not shot. Just the big man." He blotted away her tears, then hugged her again. "You don't seem hurt. You thought he shot you?"

She broke down now, sobbing. "Is he...is he going to die?"

"Lam? No, he'll be OK."

More sobs. She pointed to the fading operator. "N-no, the big man."

Red glanced at the Jamaican, whose belly quivered as it rose and fell. "I sure hope so."

More sobs. "B-but he was going to kill you."

She was in shock and needed to lie down. Her face looked pale enough that she might pass out. He gave her another hug. "Listen, you did good. You got the tablecloth. Rest a minute. Lam saved our lives, shooting that big bad guy. You don't need to feel sorry for him."

She shook her head. "But I shot him!"

What the hell? Red stared at his daughter. A greenish light glinted dimly in the corner of her eye.

She held up quivering arms. "The gun was h-heavy, so I used b-both hands. Like with Jimmy's BB pistol." She touched the spot where Red had wiped away the blood. "It hit me here, in the head. I saw stars. I thought I shot myself." She stared at the fallen mass of flesh in the parking lot.

Damn. Penny was the shooter. The recoil smacked the slide into her forehead, carving a twin-forked gouge atop a growing purple goose egg.

He shook his head. He'd have to deal with all this after they were out of the open. Now, they needed to get back undercover. "You did the right thing. Now run inside, sweetheart. Look for any medicine you can find. Rubbing alcohol, anything."

After she trotted off again, Red turned to the Jamaican. Who was after them? And why? The shooting at the Peak was the third attempt on Lori's life. And now this prick had threatened his daughter. Enough! He held the man's own black blade to his throat, pressing till it began to pierce skin. "Who you working for, asshole?"

Heavy eyelids slid open. Bloodshot orbs searched the sky. "Traitorous shit."

Red bent one of the man's thick fingers back till bone snapped. "Wrong answer. Who do you work for?"

His face contorted, and he coughed. "Uncle Sam, dickhead."

"Wrong again." He twisted more and another splintered.

This time, the Jamaican didn't seem to notice. His eyes met Red's, but they didn't focus. "What's happening?"

"You're bleeding out."

His mouth opened in a downturned arc, as if in dread. Everyone feared death. No one went quietly. One thick fist grabbed at Red's collar. "Don't let me die." No. Red needed information first.

He pulled up the man's shirt. Blood welled from a small hole near the operator's belly button. Red plunged in his middle finger, through meaty abdominals, and twisted, probing, pushing over and around slimy intestines. A pulse against his skin. Frantically, he dove and looped his finger against the source of the flow, clamping it against the inside of his abdominal wall. Almost instantly, the man drew a deep breath. *Can't let you die yet.*

Keeping the artery pinched, Red stretched his arm and leaned close to the operator's ear. "Here lies a stupid shit, shot by a ten-year-old girl. That's what I'm gonna carve on your sorry-ass grave." He gripped the blade over the man's eye so he could see it. "No, hold on. You're not getting a headstone. I'm gonna quarter your ass with your own knife and bury the pieces so deep not even worms will find them. Your own mother will never know what happened." He took a breath. "Unless you tell me who you're really working for. Think hard, because I'm holding your life pinched with my middle finger."

Now, the darkened pupils seemed to narrow. "CIA. FBI. DEA. Pick one. Like you. Except I'm not the traitorous shit."

Red tightened his grip on the knife's tang, ready to plunge the blade through the operator's eye.

Gravel crunched nearby. Penny stood a few feet away, green toolbox with a red cross in one hand, eyes as wide as the dying man's, staring at her father. "Shit," Red muttered, and tossed the knife aside.

The clamp of the Jamaican's fist relaxed, his thick arm fell to the ground, and his stare drifted distant again.

No. Not now. Red pressed fingers to his neck and listened for breath, but none came. He slapped his face, trying to wake him. "I need more than that. Gimme a name!" Nothing.

"Damn it!" He pounded his fist onto the dead man's chest. He could try CPR, but he'd have to release the artery. All options were counterproductive.

He pulled his finger out of the corpse's stomach and glanced around the valley. Others could be out there. Since the shootout at the peak, he'd counted six operators, which meant sophistication. Which necessitated coordination of movement. All signs were pointing to some form of government involvement. The Jamaican probably made a call to a command center before he grabbed Penny. But when Red had patted him down, he didn't find any com gear or night optics. So, those items were laying in the dead man's nest somewhere halfway up the mountainside. The fact Red hadn't been sniped simply confirmed the Jamaican had been surveying the cottage solo.

He knelt next to Penny and drew her into a hug. She was shivering. The last thing she needed was to be told to suck it up, but they had to get moving. "Did you see where this bad man came from?"

A sniffle. "No."

"Did he drop anything when he carried you down here?"

She shook her head. "Don't think so."

He lifted Lam to his feet. The wounded man's legs gave way, and he dropped to one knee. "Leave me here," he whispered. "I won't last out in the woods. Someone from work'll come looking for me in the morning. Just get me inside the generator house." He winced as he held out his good arm. "Gimme that gun the girl used. It's lucky."

Fair enough. Red handed over the 1911, and Lam's fingers closed on the handle as if they knew it well. He straightened, and Red wrapped an arm around his shoulder, adding counterbalance as they hobbled toward a squatty outbuilding close to the water's edge.

"Who are you? You live here?" Red asked.

Lam winced with every step. "Mechanic. Me and Andi. We take care of the plant." He stopped and glanced back to his pickup. "Well, took care of it, anyways. Now just me." He turned back, and his eyes studied the dark, flat parking lot before him, like a child, an orphan, afraid to take another

step. A low growl rose from his belly; he winced and started toward the
stone building again. As they neared, a high-pitched hum sounded over
the blowing wind. The wide door stood ajar: a thick black steel slab, like a
smiling mouth leading into a grave. The three hobbled out of the whipping
gusts, down into pitch darkness.

Chapter 15

No Rest

Red's eyes searched the empty darkness inside the small stone building, but found nothing. A loud hum filled the space, like a huge electric motor. One arm still around Lam, he pushed the door closed behind them. The mechanic leaned away. "You OK?" Red asked.

"Just trying to find the switch," came a hoarse reply.

"Can we take your truck?"

Metal clanked to the floor. "Bullet in the gas tank. You wouldn't make it far."

A second later, fluorescents glowed a few feet above their heads. Shielding his eyes, Red recoiled from the brightness, but in a minute the gray and pink earth tones of rock walls came into focus the same colors they'd run across for what seemed like hours above the tree line. Floors were concrete, swept more cleanly than even his OCD father's garage. Against a far wall stretched two metal workbenches like stainless steel gurneys, above which hung a calendar of a pickup truck with massive black tires crawling out from a muddy ravine. A glossy blue electric generator, at least as tall as he, droned in the middle of the space. A thick cable ran from an open electrical box at the generator's base, the other end tack welded to the steel door. Another one through exposed rafters to the metal roof. A sweet scent, like gun solvent, hung in the air.

Lam glanced at the same black wires. "Fixed that up this afternoon. Outside, the ground's always wet, being so close to the lake. I close that switch, and the door gets charged with seven thousand volts. Fry the nuts right off any sonofabitch stupid enough to…" His voice trailed off. Pointing to the polished worktables. "Lay down there, on your stomach."

Red waved a hand. "You got a phone out here?"

"No," Lam said.

"Inside the house?"

"No. And the radio's busted."

Red pulled out his cell phone along with the larger one from the dead woman in the back of the truck. "Chargers? Anything that could get these things going?"

Lam's eyes stared at the bigger phone. "Don't have nothing that'll bring 'em back to life. I checked for that already inside." His fist pounded the table. "Now, lay down."

Red shoved them back into his pocket. "We need to get moving. I'm only here to get you set."

The man turned with a grimace. "You patched me up, now I'm gonna do you."

Red grabbed the first aid kit from Penny's quivering grasp and opened the top, snatching a fistful of alcohol wipes. "Thanks. But no time." He stepped toward the door.

Lam's voice hardened. "That wasn't a request." He jabbed a finger at stainless steel. "Lay your carcass on that table. If you're going to run around in those woods, you'll be a lot faster without a chunk of metal in your ass."

"We gotta go." Anyone could've heard the gunshots. The Jamaican no doubt had called his team before he moved to pick up Penny. It wouldn't be long till someone showed up, and no amount of wiring would keep a trained operator from breaching the door.

Lam pointed to Penny. "She'll have a better chance if your wound ain't on fire from an infection setting in."

The man had a point. Red held up fingers. "Three minutes." He unzipped his pants and pointed to Penny with a twirling motion. She turned around, and he pulled them down past the wound. Laying his belly upon the table, cold steel ice his testicles. He stretched his arms out front, gripping his pistol, and heaved a sigh. The day couldn't get any worse, could it?

* * * *

Penny turned back around when the man with the arm sling placed a hand upon her shoulder. His voice was soft. Kind. What had Dad called him? *Lam.* "I'm going to need your help, darlin'."

He pointed to a hole in Dad's butt, smeared with blood, surrounded by a huge purple bruise. Dark-stained paper towels were in a heap next to him. A bright red drop rolled down his cheek, but Lam quickly wiped it away. Alcohol scented the air now, like when Mommy would pull out splinters. Daddy's face was pale. Lam held up a slender pair of shiny pliers with a small chunk of metal in their teeth. "I got the bullet out, but we need to check for frags."

"We'll do that later," Dad said with a frog in his throat.

Lam rested his hand upon Daddy's back. "It'll only take a second."

Dad didn't protest. He looked so...exposed. Weak. But, he was the one that always made everything OK. Last winter, he'd killed those guys in the parking lot who had tried to rob them. And tonight he'd attacked that mean man twice his size. But now, he looked like he was about to pass out.

Lam look her hand, tore open a white packet, and rubbed it down with a cold wet-wipe. "I found the bullet about two inches in," he said, pointing to her second knuckle. "That's a little more than this deep."

"She can't do this," Dad said. "You check, then we gotta go."

Lam held up his pointer, as thick as a tree branch. "I'd tear you a new asshole. She's got skinny fingers. Plus, there ain't nobody else close out there or they'd have come after us already."

Penny wasn't going to stand frozen like a bunny rabbit any longer. She'd held still when that big man came looking for her, just like Dad had said. But he still found her. If she'd run that guy never would have caught her. That's what Mommy would have done. What would she say now? "I'll do it, Daddy." She stared at Lam. "What's a frag?"

"Stick your finger in that hole and twist around a little. If you touch anything like metal, let me know where."

She pointed at the bloody, scab-crusted wound. "You want me to put my finger in there?"

"You don't need to do it, sweetheart," Daddy said.

Lam lifted his voice. "Shut up. She'd already be done if you'd clamp it!"

Penny glanced at her father. His eyes were pink, but he nodded and looked straight ahead.

"There you go, darlin'." Lam pulled her toward the table.

She stuck her finger out like she was pointing. When she touched the edge of the hole, Daddy's cheek tensed, and he grunted.

"Go ahead," Lam said. "Your daddy's a tough man. This'll help him."

She slid her finger in to the first knuckle. The scab scratched at her skin and crumbled a little as she twisted. She looked away and spotted a picture on a wooden shelf of Lam with a woman and little girl a few years younger than Penny, all standing next to Mickey Mouse. She stared at Mickey, pretending she was seven again at her birthday party when she'd stuck her finger into a warm blueberry pie to find the ring Daddy said he'd hidden in there. There hadn't been any ring.

"Is that the bottom?" Lam asked.

She shook her head and pushed to her second knuckle, then a little farther. She twisted it halfway around, and something hard scratched against her finger pad. She yanked out.

Lam quickly wrapped her blood-smeared finger in a wet-wipe and cleaned it off. "You feel anything in there?"

She tried to swallow, but couldn't. She managed a nod.

"Where was it?"

She pointed to the spot.

"Could it have been bone? You were in there pretty far."

She patted her own butt. "I don't think there's a bone there, Mr. Lam. The bottom was still squishy. This was on the side."

Lam swung a desk lamp down close to the open wound. "You're right, darlin'! You moved things around enough I can see a little speck of metal." He plunged the skinny pliers into the wound and in a snap pulled out a shiny paper-thin square. It looked like a metal sticker. He held it to the light. "What the hell kinda bullet leaves this?"

Daddy glanced back, beads of sweat dripping onto the table. "Gimme that." He grabbed it from him. "Just pack the wound," he squawked.

Lam opened a brown bottle and poured it into the hole. Daddy yelled at God and most of the saints, several whose names Penny had never heard. Lam pressed cotton patches over the bubbling froth and taped it down with white strips, then helped Daddy sit upright.

"The only thing we got for the pain is ibuprofen."

Daddy opened the bottle, dumped several into his hand, then swallowed them dry. Lam tossed him a brown bag and a bottle of water.

"What's this?" her father asked.

"My lunch. If you're gonna be runnin' around them woods, you guys need it."

Chapter 16

Gone Dark

Carter leaned on the stainless steel handle of the entry to the Det's foyer, exiting the cramped millimeter wave scanning room. Light spilled in from the bright marble-floored entry. The slam of the door behind them echoed like a gunshot. Grind's blue Skechers scuffed against the heel of his Guccis. Why did the man insist on walking so close? No concept of personal space.

A thick-armed marine with M4 and full battle rattle nodded as the pair passed. Head down, Carter stepped toward a dark side hall, his temporary office at the end. But as long as this investigation had dragged, the stronger the area's stale scent of permanence. Glancing at the doorjamb, he noticed a yellow sticky note with *Carter* written in black Sharpie hanging from an otherwise empty name tag holder. He yanked it down and crumped it into a palm. Grind squeezed by him through the door and plopped into a bright blue executive chair with coffee-stained armrests. Against his orange shirt, he looked ready for a Denver Broncos football game.

From the morning's shotgun-accompanied introduction to Lori's supervisor, Stacy, he had grasped one overt takeaway: Find out who had given the order for the op in North Korea and he'd be on the trail of who'd put the contract on Lori. And be one step closer to Moses. Jamison had installed a stealthy keystroke recorder on the senator's computer and discovered the man frequently utilized TOR, a dark web browser, to converse through anonymous chat rooms. His communications were cryptic, but it appeared he was selling a list of military operators and foreign operatives. US spies.

And he had a buyer. The deal would close within a week. If correct, the leak could be the largest intelligence breach in US history. Jamison hadn't been able to uncover the list on the hard drive yet, and even on the dark web, the senator communicated in ambiguous terms. Lots of people used the dark web, even for legal purposes. Carter needed solid evidence to provide to the appropriate authorities.

Grind scratched on a flaky pastry smear on his pants. "Stacy not sayin' much carries meaning."

True. The importance of what was unsaid could eclipse the spoken word. Stacy had embodied confidence, but she couldn't hide a certain level of tension. Her jittering fingers as she'd loaded the shotgun. The missed targets as they were walking out. And her husband... Come to think of it, Stacy's file had said she was divorced. A live-in maybe?

Carter rubbed his neck.

"Detective!" came from around a corner, back near the foyer. The purring voice sounded like Grace, Red's admin. Carter frowned as he remembered it was Saturday afternoon. She didn't routinely work on weekends, but one tended to work around the needs of the Det. He pointed to Grind, picking at yellow stuffing sticking from a tear in the seat. "Who was that guy with Stacy this morning? She called him her husband, but her file said divorced. Find out if she was married recently. I'll be back in a few."

Walking to the vestibule, he turned a corner and a tall woman in a black suit with a white collar met him halfway across the hard floor. It *was* Grace. Jet-black hair, lightly salted, pulled up in a bun. He'd never noticed how long her neck was. A hurried smile. Anxious? Carter had never sensed it in her before. Tautly muscled calves carried her with long strides.

He lifted his chin. "What're you doing here?"

She waved at him with a *follow me*, then walked toward her desk at the far end of the entry. As she turned, her dark brown eyes caught his gaze. She possessed a self-confidence he'd rarely seen in anyone working an admin position. Behind her the cubicle village buzzed, a rumble of activity humming from pale blue squares. "Didn't you notice all the cars in the lot? Something's come up."

Must've missed it. Walking in, he'd still been musing over the morning's meeting with Stacy. "And?"

She lowered herself into a small black leather swivel chair behind an L-shaped reception desk, mahogany top matching the foyer's paneling. "We're active. A tasking came in."

Carter rested forearms on the raised counter. "Where to?"

She shrugged, but gave a coy smile. A glance at the Marine guard standing at the far end of the room. Her blouse opened so low he noticed a new freckle amid her cleavage. She leaned forward to whisper.

He held his determination; his eyes stayed locked to hers.

"Don't know. They've been in the command center for hours. You heard from Red?"

Why was she whispering? He shook his head. "No. Still no luck tracking his tag?"

Her smile withered. "No. Ran recordings, but his marker just melts into a big bright blob once they got west of I-95. They could be anywhere along the Front Range." Her warm breath smelled of peppermint. "You have any other way of contacting him?"

"Me? No."

"Nothing at all?"

What was she getting at? She was his admin. If anyone had an emergency means of contact, it'd be her.

She leaned back, crossing a leg. "He's gone dark. I don't like it."

"Dark" meaning off duty, or off the grid in this case. "So, you're telling me the Det has no way to contact its commander?"

She nodded.

Carter knit his fingers together. "Maybe it's time you stop hoping he wasn't involved in that shooting on Pikes Peak, and assume he was. Captain Richards share our concern?"

She snatched up a pencil and tapped the eraser on a notepad. "Not yet. Plus, we're maxed out right now. He's planning the op. He'll be tied up for a few days at least."

"And in the meantime?"

"Based on what I see on CNN, the FBI has control of the scene in Colorado. If he *knew* Red was involved, Richards would pull every string in the Hoover Building to get at what he needed. But if not, it'd be detrimental to the mission."

Right enough. Like most classified organizations, the Det's modus operandi was to stoop below anyone's wandering gaze. She bent forward in her chair again, feet flat to the floor, eyes darting across her desk as if deep in thought. What was she hiding? "Something you're not telling me?"

She leaned close again, left breast brushing against his knuckles as she approached his ear. The lily fragrance of Diorissimo was on her neck. "This is the first op the captain has planned as the lead. Red needs to be here for it."

Carter stood abruptly, out of the woman's reach. "I've seen the captain work. It's his time. Plus, you know Red. If he were here, he'd be in the middle of the whole thing, suiting himself up. He needs to back off. It's better this way."

She crossed her arms and plopped back. The cushion hissed. Maybe he could use this. "I'll get Jamison to do some digging. He should be able to get Red's sister's cell phone number, the one they're visiting out there in Colorado. But if I do that, you help me."

She sat upright. "Now you're talking my language."

"How can I find out who authorized last winter's op to North Korea?"

"Who? You were here when we got that one. Red did. Remember?"

"No. I mean from Higher."

A coy grin. "For that, you'll owe me big."

"I don't see it that way."

"I don't care how you see it. I hold the cards. I come out on top."

Fair enough. "Whatever. I'll owe you," he mumbled.

Her brown eyes widened as she licked a lip. "Admiral Javlek. He authorized it. He's the one all the ops used to funnel through. Was the chair of the JCS, but retired a few months back. He gave the green light to Red."

No shit. "Further back than that. I know Javlek doled out the taskings. How do I figure out who put the request in to him?"

"That's all we'll have." She pointed the eraser toward his chest. "You'll need to talk with him."

He glanced at her computer. "Why? Can't you just look in the file and see who it came from?"

She giggled, then cleared her throat. "Cute. Written? You've been here for months and you still haven't figured it out?"

"Figured what out?"

"No tasking comes in on paper. It's all verbal, and never recorded. We communicate with the cooperatives through written means, but taskings are never in print. It's the old-fashioned way. For an organization that's not supposed to exist, it maintains deniability when things go bad. It's who you know. And Javlek knows them all. Talk with him."

Nothing written? This wasn't good, on so many levels. "And he is?"

She cocked her head. "Running for Senate. Spends his spare time on a sailboat, I'm told. Now, get me that cell phone number. You owe me."

Chapter 17

Big Cat

Red ducked beneath waving branches with stunted pine needles, like blunt cattails in dim starlight. They scratched his neck like a wire brush. He dropped to a knee and patted the ground. "Down here, sweetheart."

Penny stood still in the tree's shadow, her silhouette barely distinguishable from the muted backdrop of trunks and bushes. Too tired to move, perhaps? But she'd kept up for the last hour since leaving Lam at the power station.

He stretched a hand toward her. "You OK?" Stupid question. Though he kept his whisper low, he hoped the rising inflection in his voice would inspire hope.

She took a step back.

He kept the arm out and wiggled his fingers in a *come here* gesture. "You need some rest. Just an hour or so. Then we'll get moving again. Maybe get another klick before sunrise."

Her shoulders drooped. She sniffled and wiped the underside of her nose on one forearm. Her hand reached out to his fingertips.

"We're safe for now. Daddy will stay awake."

Shoe soles scuffed twigs as her feet slid across the pine bed. She fell against him so hard Red had to steady an arm against a rough pine trunk. Her chest heaved as she sobbed into his armpit. He patted her head, stroking tangled hair, combing it lightly, fingers snagging dried leaves and unruly strands from pigtails. He closed his eyes, but jerked them open again and scanned the forest behind. *Never relax your guard.*

She'd been through so much in the last twenty-four hours. Witnessed him kill several operators, was manhandled by the Jamaican, then ended that man's life using his own pistol. Even dug what she thought was a frag out of his butt cheek, but was actually Red's tag. Whatever credits he had in Penny's account at the start of the day were certainly exhausted now.

He patted his chest pocket where he'd slipped the tag. The small square of metal was gouged across its shiny face. But maybe that was what it was supposed to look like. He didn't know for certain.

Penny's breathing slowed, and the grip around his neck eased. Sleep would be best for her now. He laid her upon the ground and, using his fingers, raked a pile of dry pine needles next to her body.

"What's that for?" she slurred.

"To keep you warm." He stroked her neck. "When you wake up from cold, pile these across your legs. They'll be like a blanket."

Another sniffle, but gradually her chest settled into a calm rhythm. He waited a minute, then stood, grasping a low branch above him. It crackled, but the rush of air through her nose didn't break cadence. He limped uphill forty, maybe sixty feet, then knelt on the edge of an overlook. Sliding to his belly, he rested his chin upon a rock the size of a softball. If he fell asleep, his neck would relax and arch back painfully, waking him again.

Above, wind stroked pine needles, stirring terpenic scents, waving their clusters like a child counting on fingers. Penny, only ten years old. He'd seen the hollow eyes of kids her age rummaging the filthy streets of Sierra Leone, their only family a gang of peers, lives spent hiding from adults. High on whatever drugs the militias pumped into them, consciences seared through witness of continuous violence. Killing another as natural as taking a piss. No. Not Penny. It had been a lot for her, and it wouldn't be without effect, but Red and Lori gave her a stable family.

He huffed. Stable? What other family had wet teams targeting their mother? And where was Lori now? Why was someone so intent on ending her life when she was only a fintel analyst? Or was she? Carter must have been right about Red being ignorant, putting so much faith in her word. No one would be so bold as to attempt the contract killing of a CIA analyst twice, on American soil. What the hell was going on? What was she hiding? She'd kept his own past hidden from him for six years; who knows what rotting corpses she'd buried.

Fatigue weighed upon his body, but his mind kept firing. Over the last hour as they'd hiked, he could only see Penny when she moved, camouflaged against the forest's dark background. With so many roving inconsistencies, Lori's lies were becoming evident. She needed to come clean. To be honest.

A shot of pain ran down his leg. This shit had to stop. If she was a spook, he could handle that. But she owed the family the truth. If men were going to continue to threaten Penny and the boys because of her, she needed to do the right thing and leave.

He studied the dark line of trees under which they'd trudged, jagged tops tearing the sky. A deep breath, and he closed his eyes to listen. A breeze rumbled low, like the aftershock of a distant explosion. Or like waves upon rocks, sound blunted by tall dunes. An owl's screech surged from the shallow valley below.

When he opened them again, the sky seemed a half shade brighter. He could almost make out limbs from trunks. Had his vision adjusted?

His chin rested on the ground, softball-sized rock against one cheek. He'd fallen asleep! Gaze darting down to the tree under which Penny slept, he drew back arms to push himself up, but froze.

He tightened his grip on his pistol, straining to focus on a near line of shrubs, subdued outlines of sullied green and brown. What was it he saw?

Nothing. He hadn't seen a thing. Only a sense. A feeling of a near menace.

He brushed it aside as paranoia from waking, but it pressed like a fist into the nape of his neck. An animal instinct he'd learned to trust. Like a dog catching a scent and sniffing to determine its direction. Like the heat he felt from the alpha mare near the stable where Penny took lessons. Now the same hotness burned his belly.

A breeze climbed the hillside, its cool air watering his eyes, stirring tall shadows cast upon grassy earth. Ten meters below, one section of a shadow remained frozen. A boulder? One hadn't been there earlier. A minute later, as trees stilled in calming wind, the blocky form dissolved into a slender body with four lanky legs, dragging a long tail. A dog maybe? Wolf? Its fluid trot was silent as it climbed toward him.

Did the animal see him? Was it readying an attack? No telltale stalking. Its head swung loosely at the end of a short neck, jerking with each step, more like a security guard running a routine beat. If the beast came too close, he couldn't shoot it or he'd risk alerting other operators to their position. His only knife was in his pocket. He couldn't get to it fast enough, and any movement would broadcast to the animal his position. Two paces ahead, it froze, one paw just touching the ground, like a pointer spotting a covey of quail.

Shit. A blunted nose and small ears, this was no dog. A cat, and black as its shadow. The animal's bulk must have been at least ninety pounds.

But the tail was long and curled at the end. No bobcat. Too small for a mountain lion, and too dark. What the hell was this thing? If he had to shoot it, he'd press the muzzle into its pelt to muffle the shot. He'd tangled with many a wild man, but never a cat, with switchblades mounted to all four paws and a mouth full of razors. It turned its head away from Red, into the waft, and lifted its nose. The downwind breeze was probably the only thing that kept Red hidden.

Rounded ears turned one fore, one aft. Red's stomach seared. This beast knew danger was near. Cats could see at night, but there must be just enough darkness to obscure his presence…as long as he didn't move.

Another low gust brought the beast's perfume of musky cat urine. If Red sprang now, he might catch the creature off guard. If he failed, he'd meet the fury of paws and teeth slashing faster than any human could react.

He stayed put.

The animal swung its head back around, glancing directly where he lay. Another few strides and it stopped at the base of a tree. Turning, it lifted its tail, and two puffs from scent glands blasted the trunk. Cat piss and buttered popcorn. A bit of the mist sprayed Red's cheek. Maybe he should shoot the thing anyway. He held his breath.

The feline turned, staring toward the trees from which Penny and Red had hiked. A statue except for the ears, swiveling constantly, scanning the distance. What was it hearing? The cat ducked its head with a jerk, as if dodging a blow, then leaped uphill in bounding strides.

Slowly, Red drew his knees beneath him, arms shaking as if he'd done a hundred push-ups. Hobble-sprinting, he slid beneath the dusk of the tree where he'd left Penny. She lay motionless, covered by pine needles. He shook her arm, but it flopped lazily. He rolled her to her back, panic swelling his chest, and shook again, lifting her head from the forest floor.

An arm brushed across her face. "Leave me alone, Jackson," she moaned. "I'm trying to sleep."

Red's shoulders dropped as he allowed a quiet sigh to escape clenched teeth.

Behind him, a muffled metallic jingle, like keys in a pocket.

Chapter 18

Splash

Carter squinted against dawning light. He slowed and steered his white Malibu beneath a faded baby-blue-and-white sign with a silhouette of a trawler atop the words SEASHORE MARINA. Tires bumped a muddy-green telephone pole lying flat on the ground as he broke to a stop. Laying end to end, several of the tall posts outlined the harbor's crushed oyster shell parking lot. Early Sunday morning, only a few pickups with empty aluminum trailers rested at one end. Sailboat masts and rigging fractured dawning rays, glowing yellow and white, like spiderwebs laden with early morning dew. As the slow wake from a sparkling gray motor yacht disturbed their sleep, each rocked gently back and forth, as if leaning to its neighbor to whisper a secret down the line.

He opened the car door, and shells crunched under brown Ferragamo loafers. Knowing he'd be on a boat, he'd picked the ones from his closet shelf with the softest soles for better grip, not quite able to condescend to cross trainers. Guys that wore those things in public sported buffet bellies and had just given up on life. He tugged the collar of his Ralph Lauren polo so that it snugged his neck.

A salty breeze lifted his gaze eastward, clear skies to the horizon. Muddy marsh scent, oddly vacant of the oil and diesel concoction he recalled from his few years in the Navy. But he'd worked intel then, never much enjoying anything to do with water. Couldn't even swim well, but had somehow kept from drowning through boot camp. He stared at a single contrail stretching beyond a Canadian flag flapping atop a stubby mast.

What was that saying his bunkmate always said? Something about *Clear skies in the morning, sailors take warning.* Yeah, whatever…

He crossed two piers, turned down the third, then started to the end, skipping over a tangle of green hose. Drooping white lines moored *Mistress Two* near the end, a blue-hulled Bermuda forty, her owner had called it. He supposed that meant the boat was forty feet long, and from the dock it appeared to be a reasonable assumption. Her bow scooped in a gentle arc, curving up at each end, the same way crime scene photos in a murder book curl with age. Two masts, main one mounted amidships, short one astern. Sails of white nylon were wound and lashed tightly, spiral wrapped like stripes on a candy cane. A gray-haired man in a red T-shirt with BEARDED BELLY BAR across the back held up a seat cushion in the open cockpit, hunching over the cooler below. With practiced precision, he yanked green bottles from six-packs of Beck's beer and shoved them beneath ice. Not a top label import but better than water.

Javlek was the man's name. Carter didn't know his first. It'd just been *Admiral* before his retirement. His dealings with this prior chair of the Joint Chiefs of Staff had been brief. But several months back the man had doled out a tasking to the Det for an op in North Korea that had almost resulted in the death of Red and his wife, Lori. No telling how far back Carter would have to trace the trail, but whoever had originally proposed that op to Javlek was probably the one gunning to kill Red and Lori. And Carter reminded himself Javlek could be a suspect as well.

Carter cleared his throat.

Javlek jerked upright. Tanned skin creased his cheeks like the tongue of a leather boot. A glance ahead. "Grab that bowline, will you?" A brisk smile.

Carter loosed the cord from a heavy black cleat. Javlek stood behind a spoked stainless wheel three feet in diameter. He swung a shiny lever. A low rumble, then a puff of black smoke from astern. Now came the familiar diesel scent. Javlek jerked a finger toward the bow, and Carter tossed the line onto it. He did the same at the stern, then stepped aboard as the boat crept forward. A cool headwind swept his cheeks, and they motored east toward a glimmering yellow horizon, watering his eyes, bringing the aroma of chlorine bleach and sea spray. Gripping a shroud line, Carter glanced around the deck. All the rigging was taut, vibrating like a long piano cord in the rising breeze.

A splash of spray, and the eye of panic cracked open. What the hell was he doing on such a small boat? He'd weathered six months aboard the aircraft carrier USS *Abraham Lincoln*, even enduring two typhoons in the South China Sea. During one in particular, he'd stared for an hour at more waterspouts than he could count, fish falling upon the steel flattop like rain from a starless, lightning-filled sky. But the sheer bulk of the ship had been enough of an anchor to calm him.

Now, edging beyond stone breakwaters, an electric motor whined and the main sail climbed the mast, uncoiling itself from the boom. The bow began to sink and rise, crashing through ocean swells. Carter took a breath, held it, then locked eyes to the lifeline. Hand over hand, he made his way to the foredeck. The bowline was tied to a cleat but trailed alongside the vessel in the surf. He pulled it in and arranged it in a flat spiral, matching every other loose line on the boat, hoping the distraction would calm his nerves.

Javlek was messing with other lines near the mast. The boat's wheel rocked gently back and forth. *Hope this thing knows how to steer itself.* Shouldn't there should be more than the two of them? Even if Javlek was a sailor and not just another retired Navy officer who thought commanding a destroyer qualified him to pilot a sailboat, that still meant only one crewman knew what he was doing.

He stood behind the wheel again and leaned back, staring at the top of the mast. An electric whir and both sails started to climb. They flopped flaccidly in the breeze, then halfway up seemed to catch and billowed out. Carter ducked beneath the curling fabric and stepped down into the cockpit. Javlek's eyes stayed skyward till the trailing edge of the sheet stretched taut. The boat heeled, and Carter planted both hands on a railing.

"Thought you were a Navy man," Javlek said with wrinkled grin, still staring upward as he spun the helm.

The man certainly wasn't a talker. "Not much of a swimmer, sir."

Javlek wrapped a line twice around a shiny pulley and tugged, his sixty-year-old arms still nimble and wiry. "But you went for a dip in Iran, I hear."

Nice segue. "Wasn't my choice, then. You know how Mayard could be. Plus, we had some scuba gear. Never had a problem with diving, just swimming."

"Mayard..." The retired officer's eyes came off the mast and stared at the bright horizon. He scratched his forehead, then pinched his shirt at the navel, or maybe it was a hurried cross. "I miss that cantankerous sonofabitch."

Carter loosed one hand in an effort to appear nonchalant. "I'll agree with the sonofabitch part." Should he soften him up a bit more before jumping into the interview? Maybe talk about that op in Iran? Or Mayard? The dead man was the only common ground the two held. Screw it. The guy was a retired admiral and would respect a direct approach. "Sir, I'm investigating threats against Red and his family, the Det's commander. You know who put in the request for last winter's op into North Korea?"

The sailor's lips peeled back from yellow teeth. Blue eyes glanced aside, but only for a second. The strengthening breeze rippled his shirt, but his flattop remained stiff. "I like you. That why you came out here at five thirty on a Sunday morning? Ever since you called yesterday, I've been wondering what your angle was." A pause. "You religious?"

What the hell did that have to do with it? "No. Not particularly."

Javlek glanced up and spun the wheel, and the ship heeled more, leaning till the tips of waves rolled near the opposite gunwale. "Why not?"

Carter shrugged. "Never much time to think about it." Where was this going?

The wheel slipped beneath Javlek's palms a few degrees. "I hear that a lot. But statistics don't lie. You're gonna die." A cold glance. "You'd better make your peace with Jesus *before* you meet him."

That made no sense. Diversion. A weak but common counterinterrogation tactic. Plus, how the bloody hell could you meet a dead man?

"Mayard knew Jesus," Javlek spouted with a lift of his nose.

"Didn't seem to help him any." Too crass, but too late.

Javlek sighed and pointed at the mast. "This boat? Wife told me after a month of retirement to get the hell out of the house." He lifted hands like a prisoner surrendering. "How'd you like that? Work your whole life to retire and spend some quality time together just to find out she loves you, but only when you're not nearby. So now I've got a boat as a mistress."

That's not all, Carter mused. "I hear you've thrown your hat into politics." Javlek was running for senator, a last-minute decision with elections in only five months. But the Virginia constituency, not happy with any of the choices put forward by the parties, had shown favor to him with 25 percent of the vote after only one month of his announcement. Sometimes the enemy you don't know can be more appealing than the one inside your fence.

Javlek shook his head. "Hell, that's the last thing I *want* to do. But politicians now don't know dick about military. I mention blue water, and they think I'm talking about cleaning toilet bowls. War on terror is going OK, so everyone's getting lulled into a false sense of security. Nobody's thinking long term." He balled a fist and slammed the helm. "What about China? They got more money than sense. Own half the whole damn nation! Still a bunch of little commies." A finger wagged the air. "*There's* the new cold war. We won the last one by outspending Russia. As much debt we got ourselves into now, we can't even afford to pay attention. *That's* why I'm running, secretly hoping I don't win. It's duty."

The man was skilled at stalling. "Who gave you the request, sir?"

A sly smile. "I like you. Like one of them English bulldogs. Once they get their teeth in, won't never let go... Yeah. But, I remember J2 lecturing me for a full day when I retired about what I could and couldn't disclose. What you're talking about is firmly in the latter category."

"I wasn't aware J2 knew about the Det."

Javlek nodded. "Sharp too. You're right. Only a couple in J2 know about you guys. But the distance from my mind to my mouth has been known to be a short jump, so I've learned to be guarded. The answer to your question is something I can't discuss. Buried deeper than nuclear waste."

Not getting off that easy. "I'm not asking for details. Just who requested it. Where'd it come from?"

A red channel marker slipped by to port. Javlek turned the wheel and pointed the bow directly at the low sun. "You know, that's the beauty of how we set that up. The Det. We got shit *done*. Word of mouth. One person to another. Relationship. People think intel is having enough satellites floating in space, drones hovering in the air, listening posts, wiretaps, video cameras out the ass.... But that don't get anything done." He pointed to Carter, then himself. "You see, we got no history. No relationship. Therefore, nothing gets done. Know how I got so far up the voters' polls so fast?"

The man wasn't going to share without coercion. In only a month he'd seamlessly jumped from military into politics and was seeming more a stuffed shirt the farther they sailed, worried about covering his ass before the election. Carter might just have to endure the lecture. "No."

The sailor's weathered cheek skin flapped in a gust. "You know Virginia's other senator? Not the one I'm running against?"

Of course. "Moses." Why hadn't he made the connection before? The op in North Korea had served two purposes. To destroy a massive counterfeiting operation plus a data center run by their Ministry of State Security. A list of CIA spooks and military operators had been leaked to North Korea's MSS, and the Det had been sent to clean up. Now a similar list had been found on Moses' computer.

Javlek landed another slap on the helm. "Moses and I, we've got history. A relationship. The two of us get together, shit gets *done*. That man's got more connections than the Internet. His endorsement got me where I am today." He passed one hand over another, and the boat heeled even more. The foamy peak of a swell ran across the gunwale. He shouted over the breeze. "You understand what I'm saying?"

Carter would have to be an idiot to miss the insinuation. Javlek couldn't rat out his colleague. Moses had put in the request for the op in North Korea. The same one that almost killed his daughter, Lori. But could a senator wield that much influence? He'd been under the employ of the CIA before stepping into politics, even making it up to one of the deputy directorates. Maybe Moses used old contacts to pull strings. It wasn't hard to justify an op for reasons of national security given the right connections and... maybe falsified evidence? He had a list of operators now, so could he have planted a similar list earlier? Could Moses have created the need for the op, hoping to kill his daughter? But why her? She was fintel.

Carter held nothing actionable. The man who knew the answer, the key to the next step in his investigation, was only feet from him. Twice violence had been attempted against Red and Lori. And at that point, relationship dies away. If Moses requested that op, Javlek should want to distance himself from the man, not cozy up. Then again, he needed the senator's endorsement for the election....

"I respect your loyalties. But this isn't dying. My employer doesn't take kindly to attempts at killing him or his family. This is coming to a head sooner rather than later, and you *will* be called to testify. It'd be better at that time, especially if you're in office, to have helped with the investigation instead of stalling. I need hard evidence. In the absence of that, I need testimony. So my question is, are you willing to provide that?"

Javlek grasped a four-foot aluminum pole resting against a handrail, a flagstaff maybe, and shook it like a police baton.

Guess not.

He pointed it toward a pulley mounted to the deck near Carter. "We're gonna tack soon. You're gonna trim the jib. That means when I yell, you turn and pull that line 'round that winch till that front sail quits flappin'. Got it?"

Easy enough. Carter nodded, though he didn't like the idea of turning his back to the man.

The bow rose and fell with each passing swell, more rapidly as the wind strengthened. Cool salt spray cut across his face. He licked briny drops from his lips. Javlek stared toward the bow, ducking his head to see below the sail, one leg braced on the side of the cockpit, aluminum pole still firmly in his grasp. He smiled at the bright sun, still low on the horizon. A snapshot, and the man looked adept. He shouted, "Ready about!"

Carter gripped the line. "I start pulling now?"

"Not yet. I'll tell you in a few seconds."

He laid the pole back down and started to spin the wheel. The boat straightened as it turned into the wind. The sails went limp.

"Pull now!"

Carter turned and yanked the line. It didn't move. Was this a joke? Maybe the thing was stuck, or he needed to flip a release lever.

A goading chuckle from Javlek. "Pull, damn it!"

He wrapped the line around his hand, gripped it with the other, and heaved backward. *Smack!* A flash of light and his head jerked forward. He fell across the gunwale and splashed into cool water, fingers refusing his command to clutch the grab rail. A base consciousness flickered, considering it strange that he'd fallen overboard. His eyes closed, and suddenly even that flame of awareness was quenched.

Chapter 19

Reunion

Red dropped Penny to the ground and spun wildly, steadying the aim of his pistol in the dark toward the brassy ringing. What was it, the jingle of a dog collar? Did the operators have hounds after them? Maybe that was the reason the cat had beat such a hasty escape.

Low branches of the pine sagged near the tips, almost brushing the ground. Blocking any searching eye, he hoped. Which was why he'd selected this spot for Penny to catch an hour of sleep. But it also meant he couldn't see much past the barrier. Protecting, but blinding.

Penny's deep, even breathing rose again. The jolt hadn't roused her. Three green eyes of his tritium sights glowed dimly back as he aimed the weapon. He held his breath, listening. Dried leaves rustled as a gentle wave of air washed over distant trees. Others, closer, leaned in rhythm as the chill breeze picked up. The branches of their own pine started to sway as the blast finally hit them, flashing the dim starlight beams upon the ground dotting the tree's shadow.

"Red?" The voice was hoarse and shallow.

He swung the weapon, center green eye leveled toward the sound. A figure stood near the edge of the branches, just inside their perimeter. The boughs rocked silently behind whoever, whatever, had dared too close. His finger tensed, ready to make his name the intruder's final words. A whiff of a flowery scent gave him pause. Familiar, but what was it? Shampoo. Lori's was—

"Red, that you?" The voice was scratchy, like they were intentionally masking it.

He centered sights on what he thought must be the chest. "Don't move." What if the intruder had a weapon? He thought of lifting Penny and throwing her behind the shelter of the thick trunk. No, that would draw attention to her.

"It's me." A woman's tone, but too hoarse.

"On your knees. Slow. Hands up."

The dark figure bent low. "It's me. Lori."

The voice was nothing like her. "Shut up. Face down on the ground. Hands out front."

"Don't be ridiculous! I've spent all day and half the night running from a damn Chinaman and prissy-ass bitch because you couldn't keep your pistol in your pants. Where's Penny? Is she OK?"

Yep. That's Lori, all right.

But…how'd she find them? A fast runner, sure, but she'd have had to escaped both operatives without a weapon. Were these real attempts on her life, or a cover to get rid of her husband? He kept his weapon raised. The dark form might indeed be Lori, but if so, who the hell was she really? A threat to Penny too? His wife's true identity lay as dark as the tree's shadow. No, he wouldn't lower his guard again. "The truth. Now."

"What's your problem!" she coughed. "It's *me*!"

"Exactly." He cocked the hammer for emphasis. "Who are you? No damn fintel analyst, for sure. I want the whole truth."

Penny wriggled next to his thigh, then sat upright. "Mommy?" Red gripped her shoulder, but she strained against his hand. "Mommy!" He let her slip from his grasp. She scrabbled on hands and knees to the edge of the branches. Lori's dark form absorbed Penny's, arms wrapping her in an embrace, then a hushed *thump* as the two fell onto soft earth, giggling. Penny's laugh was muffled, as if her face was pressed to Lori's chest.

Finally Penny asked, "Where were you?"

She was the mother of their kids. It had to count for something. He decocked the hammer with a *click* and holstered his weapon. At the sound, the two shadows parted. Red scooted closer. Near the limbs' edge, his eyes adjusted enough to make out Penny sitting cross-legged. Lori's hair was still pulled back in a ponytail, but the scrunchie had loosed and strands were dangling, tangled with leaves. Even so, she was gorgeous. He felt a pull to embrace her like Penny had, but the voice of reason had finally risen to a shout. Carter had been warning him for months: *She's not who she claims. She hasn't been forthright.* But he loved her. And you always trust your team. That had to go double for family. He started to lean toward his wife, to take her into an embrace, then froze.

He pointed at his daughter. "Answer Penny. Where've you been?"

"Water," Lori rasped. "You have any?"

He grabbed Lam's bottle, still full, beside the pile of pine needles and handed it to her. She downed half in a gulp. "You guys OK if I finish it?"

Penny stroked her hand. "It's mine, Mom. You can have it."

After she chugged it, her voice softened. "Around the back of the mountain," she said, pointing toward Pikes Peak. "I came that way."

"You went all the way around the back?" Depending upon her route, that could've been ten or fifteen klicks. "Why that way? How'd you find us here?"

She dropped onto her butt, stretched both legs out before her, and leaned back on her arms. "I knew you wouldn't head down the front of the mountain, since that's where they'd expect you'd go. NORAD still has a unit under Cheyenne Mountain, so it's the nearest military base. It made sense you'd head to it. That's where you're going, right?"

"Yeah, but—"

"You always talked about traveling across a ridge two-thirds of the way up the side. Better positioned to make an escape over the crest or down through the valley. Well, there's one big-ass gully running this direction. Guess we both picked the same side. I stopped when I thought I heard snoring."

Penny giggled. "Sorry."

Lori cocked her head. "But I figured you'd be to Cheyenne by now. Why so slow?"

He tried not to grunt as he lowered himself to the ground, lying flat on his good side.

She jumped up and loomed over him in a second. "What's wrong with your leg? You wrench your bad knee?"

He grimaced. "Something like that."

"Daddy got shot!" Penny blurted out, then covered her mouth with a hand, as if realizing she'd spoken too loudly.

"You let yourself get hit?" she hissed. "What the hell?"

Nice. Love you too, dear.

Penny leaned over to pull her mother's arm. "Don't be mad, Mom. He got two of the bad guys. I saw him."

Lori gasped. "You saw that?" She pulled Penny closer and glared at Red. "You shot someone in front of our daughter?"

Damned if you do, damned if you don't. "I figure better than the alternative."

Penny's voice, muffled by Lori's sweater, still sounded almost gleeful. "I dug out the frag."

Lori covered Penny's ears and curled her lip at him. "Our daughter should not know what a frag is."

He shrugged. "May come in handy with you as a mother."

Penny wriggled free of her mother's grasp. Red caught her gaze and lifted an eyebrow, as if to say *Don't you dare mention that you shot the Jamaican.*

"That is...absolute shit!" Lori yelled, slicing her hand in the air like a blade. "You are leaving the Det. Erasing any memory of this part of your life. I'm tired of the danger bleeding through and affecting our family. This is exactly why I never told you how you'd been discharged from the Det years ago."

Red gritted his teeth. He'd been an operator in the Det when he'd first met Lori. The two had married and not long thereafter, along came Penny. Then Red had been captured on an op inside Iran. It had taken a few days, but the Det managed to extract him. But torture and beatings had pulverized his face until it resembled a cantaloupe. He'd endured a broken shin, several broken fingers, burned nipples, and countless other injuries. Waking in a secluded wing of Sentara Norfolk Hospital, he held no recollection of the Det whatsoever.

Reasons for his loss of memory were hypothetical, but the Det in-processed all new operators and agents through a protocol. That protocol utilized a combination of sedatives and hypnosis to bookmark memories of the Det. When reassigned out of the Det, operators were out-processed and run through a similar protocol that pushed those bookmarked memories back into subconscious. Their minds filled in the rest. It didn't work perfectly, but it was another layer of security to minimize leaks and maintain the organization's low profile. And it had proven marginally successful.

But Red had never been out-processed.

The medical team theorized the torture and beatings had triggered his mind's suppression defense mechanism, somehow also silencing memories of the Det, an out-processing of sorts. They had given him a medical discharge, explaining his injuries as a result of an accident in a warehouse by a shelving system collapsing upon him. For six years Lori had never hinted that he'd been anything more than a supply officer in the Air Force.

Until memories started breaking through. He joined the Det again, and now was the commander of the whole top-secret fusion cell, a nonorganization.

What kind of wife keeps her husband's past buried for six years? Red thought. Whose team was she on? And she was accusing *him* of being the reason for the shooting on Pikes Peak? None of this crap was because of his doing.

Grimacing, he rose to a knee. "Well, they ain't after me, princess!" he yelled, not caring how loud. "You're the one who's bleeding through. That Chinese guy was after you." He jabbed a finger into her shoulder. "Yeah, sure, I'm an operator. A damn good one. And I saved your ass up there, for the third time! Don't go pinning this on me. The Det's tight. It holds its water. You're the Jonah here. 'Cept you're too tied up in lies to throw yourself overboard. You're taking the entire boat down with you, kids included."

She swung at him, but he caught her wrist before the slap landed. She pushed Penny away and lunged at his chest. Red fell back, still clutching her wrist. Pain seared his ass as the wounded cheek struck the ground. She straddled him on her knees as her other arm flew free and fast, slapping his face and punching his ribs, too quickly for him to snatch it.

"You hit like a sissy," he taunted between her strikes. Her free hand swung harder, and she drove a knee into his kidney, halfway knocking wind from him. She pounded his shoulder and chest, but her blows began to weaken. Good thing her off hand was the only one loose. A few more strikes, and she fell upon him, heaving quietly, stifling sobs. She pressed her head next to his and pulled him into an embrace, coughing back tears. After a few seconds, he loosed his grip and rubbed her back, fingernails snagging on the knots in her sweater.

Lori rubbed her nose across her sleeve. Suddenly, she jerked upright and turned to Penny, as if remembering her daughter's presence.

Penny's voice was low and timid. "Don't be mad, Mom. He didn't mean to get shot."

Lori snorted, then held arms out to her. "It's not that. Mom just needs sleep. Daddy and I were only...playing."

Usually rough play meant Lori's clothes were off and the bedroom door was locked, Red thought. Somehow this wasn't nearly as satisfying.

Dawn had to be less than an hour away, since in a dim golden glow he could make out the smile on Penny's face as she leaned on her mother again.

Red tried to roll. "My ass is on fire."

Lori hopped off. "Shit. I mean, sorry. You need me to dress it? I've got—"

"No! It's just fine," he snapped, surprised at the new, sincere tone in her voice. "I'm a slow mover, but still faster than Penny. If you can carry her a while, we'll make good time. Could be there by noon, latest. And silence those keys in your pocket. I heard them rubbing together."

She frowned. "We shouldn't move during the day."

Right. Standard escape and evasion. Move when least likely to be observed. "But there's time to consider—or the lack of it, in this case. Every hour we aren't captured near Pikes Peak, the enemy's field of search will widen. Once they figured we haven't headed for the city, their next logical assumption would be Cheyenne Mountain, just as you reasoned." If they didn't move fast enough, it would be easy for their pursuers to set an ambush along the way. That was what Red would do, at least, if he were working for the other side.

"Plus, we had a Jamaican operator spot us in the dark. He had to have night optics to do it. Any additional risk of moving during daylight is negated by getting out of the woods faster. The sooner we're inside the air base's fence, the better for all of us."

"Is he the one that shot you?" Lori asked.

Red exchanged a knowing glance with Penny. "No. I'll tell you about it later. After a couple glasses of cabernet." He rolled over and pulled his good leg beneath him, then stood like performing a one-legged burpee. The limb jiggled with fatigue. "Just wish I knew who we were up against," he added as he limped to the edge of the shadow cast by the branches, raising both forearms to shield his face from the needles' scratch.

A heavy breath from Lori behind him, almost a sigh. "I may have an idea."

Chapter 20

Truth

"You what?" Red spun to face Lori's dark outline. She gripped Penny's legs, holding her piggyback, blanketed by the huge tree's shadow.

She let go, and Penny slid down her back. "Mossad. I think they're the ones on our trail."

Red reached overhead and clutched a prickly pine branch. "On *our* trail?"

She drew a deep breath. "OK. On *my* trail."

Thoughts fired as he tried to comprehend the magnitude of this cloud. "As in, *all* of Mossad, or one rogue agent?"

"I don't know. Both are possibilities."

This was very bad news. One didn't clean up a problem with the Israeli Secret Service by knocking off a few of their operatives, as Red had recently. They tended to frown upon the practice. "Why would Mossad be after you? Your guys help them, cooperate on financial intelligence. Your accounting geeks give numbers to their money grubbers, and they provide the inside scoop on stuff like that national bank in China...and other crap." He waved his hand in a rolling motion. "Why would they be trying to scratch you out?"

Lori glanced at Penny, now sitting back on the ground, head hung as if falling back asleep and poking at the dirt with a twig. Lori stepped close to him. "We do that. But more."

A moment of silence passed and, once again, a breeze brought the lilac scent of Lori's shampoo. He resisted an urge to sweep dangling bangs from covering her eyes. Maybe she was hoping he'd fill the quiet by moving to a different subject.

He didn't bite.

Eventually, she gave an annoyed huff. "I'll explain later. For now, understand these guys may be Mossad operatives. But more likely, a skilled outsourced team. Assume we're up against the best. Well equipped. Throw in a sniper for good measure."

He'd felt better when she was silent. Sweat was burning the bullet hole in his glute. "Sometimes you're not much fun."

"Be serious."

"I am. Hard to imagine this could get worse, yet you're telling me it just did. How'd you earn the wrath of Mossad? Misplaced decimal point? Couldn't you've picked on Chechnya instead?"

"It's not important now. I just wanted to warn you before we head out, about what we may be up against."

"I've got a hole in my ass cheek screaming like a hot poker that says it *is* important. And what if it was Penny they'd hit? What if we'd had the boys with us? I've been too patient, too long. Tell me the whole story. Now."

She glanced back at their daughter, who was lying on her back on the ground now. Probably about to fall back asleep. Gripping Red's arm, Lori pushed the two a few steps farther away. Leaning her head to one side, she said, "I'm a mole. But not the kind you might think of."

He closed his eyes and rubbed swollen lids. "So, not the traitorous, deserves-a-firing-squad, on-the-run-from-CIA kind of mole?"

She shoved his chest, hard. "You asked, so hear me out. US policy on sharing financial intelligence with Israel is too strict, most everyone in the field agrees. On both sides. I provide fintel to them in an unofficial capacity. Info that's in US interests for them to have. It's not officially CIA sanctioned, but it's been going on for decades. We call it a back door, one that's good to keep open in case the front one gets blocked. And I'm the gatekeeper."

"And this back door, I'm assuming it's not an entrance?" He rotated his wrist as if turning a key. "The kind with a brass knob? One I can breach with explosives?"

"Secured communication system, like email."

"And how does all this lead to a two-hundred-fifty-pound Jamaican manhandling Penny and threatening to blow off her feet?" Even in the dim light, Red could see the whites of Lori's eyes grow wider. "Yeah, so how 'bout I tell you *that* story after you explain what you did to piss off Israel."

"I didn't piss them off!"

Hmm. Defensive. And louder than he'd like.

"Every agency has its problems," she added. "Mossad has theirs. I provide financial intel for counterterrorism: hard-to-track bank account info, numbers, transaction amounts, dates. They asked me to verify some accounts from a report passed to them. I confirmed, providing the next few layers of detail at the same time, though they hadn't asked for it. Why? Because the request had seemed urgent, and it came when Al-Qaeda and other terrorist groups were rattling sabers. I gave a year's transaction amounts, sources, and destinations. The account was from Belize. None of the names or addresses ever prove legit, so that's not important. But whoever the account belonged to, I stumbled into a hornets' nest. Several inquiries followed, then stopped. And the back door closed. Locked tight."

"Yeah. Well, I still don't see the threat."

A snort from Penny and both turned to her. Her chest lifted and fell. Must've been a snore.

Lori continued. "A month later, I get a ping from my contact at Mossad." She shifted her weight to one leg and back again, as if stalling to choose her words carefully. "We had a routine. Routine is trust. Trust is everything. He'd broken routine with silence for three weeks, then just popped back onto the grid all of a sudden."

"And? Get to the point."

"It was a warning, in brief. *Disappear.* The door closed again. From then on, all communications bounced back."

"So maybe you misunderstood. Maybe your contact was the one who disappeared."

A long wisp of hair blew across her lips as she shook her head. "Too coincidental. It happened right before everything went to hell, when the wet team hit our house, and I was dragged off to Iran."

Red's stomach cramped at the memory of waking in their home's hallway, head bloodied, Lori gone. "But, we've still got the guys responsible in custody. And that op last winter to North Korea, it was supposed to fix this."

"It tied up some loose ends, but didn't eliminate the problem."

Red pursed his lips and grunted. This was why he could never be a spook. Just give him a weapon, an objective, and get the hell out of the way. "Who do we need to take out to get these guys off our backs?"

"That's why I've never brought this up. I can't wave my hand in the air and yell for help from the CIA, or else when the backdoor information sharing comes to out, they'll all turn tail, deny any knowledge of it, and I'll be stuck looking like a real mole. If I stay quiet, Mossad's still chasing my ass. You see, there are some things an op can't remedy."

Bullshit. He spat upon the pad of dry pine needles. "There're few problems a well-placed copper-jacketed bullet can't fix."

Another sigh. "My section chief and I've studied this from every angle. But we're only seeing part of the picture. Our fintel is irrelevant without Mossad's perspective. And that door's been closed. We've tried official channels, but our inquires get blocked at every turn. So all we've got is a bunch of numbers."

She reached a hand slowly to stroke his beard, the same cheek where ten minutes earlier she'd aimed a fist. He leaned back, breathing shallowly. His throat stung as if he'd inhaled salt water, and ribs ached where her knee had struck him. Or maybe it had been the rabid Jamaican. She stretched her arm, cupped his head, and drew him into a kiss. This time he didn't resist. Her lips were warm, but her chapped skin scratched against his own. *Always trust your team* shouted a stern voice in his head, the echo of an old commanding officer's, one who'd given his life to save Red's. He grabbed her waist and pulled her close, reaching his hand around to—

"Yuck," came Penny's rough whisper. "You guys are gross."

Must've woken up.

Lori withdrew, brushing at his shoulders as if dusting off a jacket. "You do see now? I've got no fix for this. It may be my fault. I don't know for sure. But there's nothing to be done."

He turned and eyed the cluster of flashing red lights atop Cheyenne Mountain, like hemorrhaging stars. "Carter's been investigating this for a while. His angle may pan out. He told me he was getting close." He pointed to the red dots. "In the meantime, we keep moving."

She grasped his arm. "Thanks for not being angry." She leaned in again and pecked his cheek.

He jerked away. "Oh, I'm mad as hell. But choosing to trust you...for her." He pointed to Penny. "Surprised you even wanted to get near me. I smell like cat piss."

"Cat?" She leaned her nose to his neck and sniffed. "No. Just sweat and BO."

Nose to shoulder, he inhaled deeply as he could where the feline's mark had misted against him. Nothing. Had he only dreamed it? No, he'd been awake for certain. He shook his head. Maybe a hallucination. He'd sensed this threat to his family for months, stalking his trail. Now, it was gradually taking form.

Reaching around to the small of his back, he felt for the grip of the .357 Magnum wedged beneath his belt. He held it out to Lori. "You may need this. Got it off the dead Jamaican operative, after he nearly crushed my skull."

She popped out the cylinder and held it close to her face in a faint beam of starlight.

"It hasn't been fired," he added. "They should all be full rounds."

She snapped it shut and wedged it into the front pocket of her jeans, where it bulged like an eighties cell phone. "Tell me about the Jamaican."

He shot Penny a glance, and she lifted both palms, shaking her head. He smiled, turned, and pressed through the branches, out into a growing dawn.

Lori's urgent whisper followed behind him. "What Jamaican?"

He pressed forward, his wounded leg's step always crunching a little louder than the other. Two hundred meters ahead, a crouched shadow slipped beneath the tall, dark cone of a Douglas fir. The wildcat again? Another sniff at his sweater's shoulder, but he smelled only the faint remnant of winter's mothballs. The shape could've been anything.

He tightened his grip on his own pistol and limped toward bleeding stars.

Chapter 21

Pebble Plug

Ripples from the silver lake lapped against the toe of Lam's boot. A low fog only a few inches thick rose from the cold water, early morning rays peeking between trees setting it aglow in two fiery circles, the face of a leviathan rising from the depth. A bass leaped from the water between the glowing blazes, visible only as a metallic flash before it sunk back into the blanketed mist. A splash sounded, but no spray rose through the hazy covering.

He winced at the throbbing burn of the fresh .45 caliber hole in his shoulder. But he couldn't head to the hospital yet. Red and his little girl even now could be being stalked by the same predators who'd killed Andi and put the slug through his flesh. Even in his agony, the crisp, moist air enlivened his hunter instincts.

"You OK?" Elway asked. The tall, slender park ranger had pulled into Dark Canyon just as the first light of morning had struck the generator house's keyhole. He wore crisp green uniform pants, gray poly shirt, and a wide, flat-brimmed straw-colored cap, the illegitimate spawn of a cowboy hat and a sombrero. Unrelated to the fabled Super Bowl champion quarterback named Elway, the man's personality was weak in comparison as well. The ranger had busted Lam two years earlier for poaching elk in Rocky Mountain National Park, but had let him off with a warning. Everyone knew the place was overrun with herds. Sure, not as bad as Estes Park, but they still needed to be culled, or else disease and starvation would set in. Funny how Lam had beamed this morning at the sight of the man from whom he'd always tried to hide.

Lam bent his knees and scooped up a handful of pebbles. "I'm OK. Mind's wandering. Just short on sleep." He thumbed through the wet rocks, comparing each to a 9mm cartridge Elway had lent him. Lam selected a gray one with black dots, rounded from centuries of water washing across its surface, tapered at one end. He stood and tossed the round back to Elway, pausing for a second as a head rush passed.

Elway pressed it back into a spare seventeen-round magazine, slipping the metal container into a pouch on his belt. He studied the dead Jamaican near his feet. The assassin's huge white eyes stared at the sliver of a moon about to set. "You look like hell. You shouldn't be walkin'," he said, as if to the dead man.

"Shoulder stings, but only if I move it." He lied, the wound a bit worse than when he'd helped a farrier buddy shoe a mule. The long-eared beast was eighteen hands tall and had kicked Lam square in the chest. It'd taken him a week to catch his breath.

Elway turned, pointing a brown boot in his direction. "Listen. I believe your story. 'Specially with what went on yesterday on the Peak. But you've got two bodies here and—"

"Three bodies," Lam corrected. "I told you I killed the Jap sonofabitch that shot at us on the way in. You saw the doughnut in the road?"

Elway pushed his brim up with a finger. "Yeah. Figured some kids were just pretendin' to race the Pikes Peak Hill Climb. Road was tore up most the way here."

"That's where the Jap started shootin'. That guy's dead. Plus Andi." Lam pointed to the body splayed in the middle of the parking lot. "And that bastard makes three."

Elway followed him toward the Jeep pickup. "Like I was sayin', you got two bodies, maybe three if we find this other fella. You can count on a good couple days of questions from the feds." He gazed up beyond the tall, bare tree line. "It's like a volcano erupted up there. News agencies. FBI set up camp at the Glen Cove way station."

Lam winced as he leaned onto his back, sliding on gravel, scooching beneath his truck. Gas fumes lifted as he stirred the dirt. Elway had redressed his wound, wetting the gauze with peroxide that soaked through his T-shirt. As he lifted his good arm to push the pebble into the bullet hole in his fuel tank, the Colt 1911 dug into his back. He reached around and placed it on the gravel next to him.

"What the hell you doin'?" Elway yelled.

"Plugging a hole."

"Not that. You got a license for that gun?"

"Ain't mine. It's the dead guy's. Plus, don't need no license if I open carry."

"Lam, you shouldn't have touched it. We've got to leave the scene as sterile as—"

What a numskull. "I told you, someone else shot him with it. I was too busy talkin' to the angels after a forty-five caliber bullet knocked me on my ass. I sure as hell wasn't going to leave it there." Elway reached for it, but Lam snatched it from the ground. "Trust me! I know it looks bad, me alive and three people dead. I'll tell the FBI the whole crazy-ass story. But I got somethin' to do first. Gimme a rock."

Elway jogged to the edge of the parking lot and grabbed a baseball-sized stone. Probably the only exercise the man got in his life. Lam took it and tapped the gray pebble till it was wedged tightly into the metal. The bullet inside the tank clanked with each strike. "Behind my driver seat there's a red-and-blue toolbox. Inside it on the top tray there's a bar of Ivory soap. Get it."

Elway handed it to him, and Lam rubbed the cube hard against the pebble and surrounding bare metal. The dampness of the remaining gas dissolved it into a soft seal. Lam smiled at his work. Soap, a rock crawler's best friend.

He slid out and untwisted the gas cap. "She's a beast. Fill her with both cans."

Elway scowled, but his expression softened when his eyes fell on Andi's body in the truck bed.

"I ain't leavin' her here," Lam said.

Elway nodded, then hoisted a jerrican from the back of his own pickup. A poor excuse of a vehicle. Tiny Ford Ranger, two-wheel drive, bare stock. Probably got stuck the first puddle it drove through. "Feds are on the way. They said to not move anything, to leave the bodies right where they were." He tipped the bucket, and gas flowed into a metal funnel Lam held, the cold liquid chilling his fingers. "If you move her, it might mess up the evidence, stop them from finding who did it to her."

He hadn't considered that. The Jap was dead, but he was working with this Jamaican. If there were others, they needed to pay, too. "We'll put her on the grass near the lake, but I still got something I've got to do first."

"They ain't gonna let you leave, Lam. They've got checkpoints on this road near Cow Mountain. Hell, you know I can't let you go."

"I told you, I'll tell the FBI everything. You tell 'em we were just trying to get the truck workin' and I took off. You've secured the scene. Sure your cell phone doesn't work here?"

"Hell, no. Not for another five, ten miles maybe. Once we're clear of the valley. CB works OK. You need—"

Red had warned him not to tell anyone where he was headed. "No! Don't need the CB. Just need to talk to my wife, let her know I'm OK. Like you said, once I talk to the FBI, they ain't gonna let me see daylight for a few more days. I need to let her know I'm fine first."

Elway tipped up the second can, draining it. Ten gallons. That'd get him a little over a 120 miles. Or sixty on steeper mountain roads. The driver's door creaked as he yanked it open. *Have to oil the hinges.* Lam grabbed the steering wheel with his good arm, lifted a leg high, stepped on the nerf bar, and hoisted himself onto the seat. A burgundy smear of Andi's dried blood streaked the tan vinyl bench seat. The key turned, and the Jeep growled a low, angry note. The Colt 1911 pressed against his skin as he leaned back. He stretched his arm and patted the dashboard. "That's the spirit, girl," he whispered. "Let's go make that call."

Chapter 22

Mother Nature

Pain jolted Penny awake. Her nose stung like it'd been hit with a dodgeball. Her head had been bobbing in sleep, nose smacking her mother's bony shoulder. She slurped up a line of drool like spaghetti, dangling to Mom's collar. Penny had been riding her back, only being woken to climb the steeper ridges, or ones with loose rocks. She couldn't remember traveling far, yet somehow sensed it had been a long time since she'd last been awake. The air was warmer, thicker, and the sun heated her neck. She stretched her arms and rubbed it. *Ouch!* Her skin hurt. Burned, like being at the beach.

Dad was ahead, rounding a fat green bush, stepping up on a black-spotted rock. Moving faster now, with less of a limp. Maybe because it was easier heading downhill.

"I can walk," Penny said.

Mom snorted like a winded horse. "I'll let you...once we get to the bottom...of the hill."

After another minute or so, her mother let go of her legs, and Penny slid down to the path. Her skin tingled, and her feet were numb as rocks. "My legs feel funny," she said, poking her knee with her finger.

"They'll be OK," Mom panted. "They probably just fell asleep. They'll feel like pins and needles."

She straightened and rubbed her palms on the small of her sweat-soaked back. This incline didn't look too hard, and they seemed to be on a trail, though no tracks were in the dust. Penny stopped and pulled up her pant cuffs, just to make sure the tingles weren't a troop of ants on her skin. Mom gripped Penny's arm and held a finger to her lips. "Shhh." Dad was kneeling on the side of the trail a few paces ahead.

After a couple of minutes, Penny took a step, but Mom held her firm. How long were they going to stand here? She turned to ask but kept quiet when she glimpsed her mother's face. So pale, and the black makeup around her eyes had smeared and run down, like a Halloween zombie mask.

A few more minutes, and they slipped closer to Dad. He leaned against a tree, aiming his pistol down the trail. But his eyes were closed. He must be doing his stop, look, and listen. Penny shut her eyes too.

"What'd you hear?" Mom asked.

For a minute, he didn't say anything. Was he OK? She stole a peek. When he finally opened his lids, the whites looked red. Hard, like he was angry. "Nothing."

"Why'd you stop?"

He spoke through gritted teeth. "We're being watched."

Mom knelt next to him. "Where?"

"Don't know," he snapped.

Mom scowled. "Then why'd you stop?"

Her father cocked his head. "I said, we're being watched. No, I can't see them. Or hear them. Just trust me."

Her mother shrugged. "Maybe the Det's got eyes on us? A drone?" She craned her neck and scanned the sky.

"No." He patted the ground. "It's here. I don't get this feeling when it's cameras. We just stepped across a line, somewhere back near that holly tree. Into unfriendly territory."

Mom huffed and stood. Hauling Penny along by one arm, she started up the trail. "You need sleep. If you can't see it or hear it, it doesn't matter."

Penny's feet raced to keep up, stumbling over loose rocks, sliding like skis on ice. When she glanced back, Dad was grimacing, his limp more like a quick skip. "Wait for Daddy. He knows about the woods."

Mom barreled forward. "All we need to do is get to the far side of that mountain. Only another mile or two before—" She froze.

Now what? Penny peered around her mother's waist. The narrow path was a gentle upward slope. Tan, sandy-colored rocks hung over one section, like a big anvil, striped in brown and gray. *Sedimentary rock*, her bug-eyed science teacher would say. Black insects hummed around a hole in the cliff, some shooting in and out on an aerial highway.

Oh. So Mom didn't want anyone to get stung. Well, they could just keep their distance and go around. Still, her mother stood frozen. Dad finally caught up.

Her mother pulled the Jamaican's pistol from her pocket and pointed it toward the hole, but higher. "That what you saw last night?"

What was she talking about now? You can't see bees at night.

Just then, something flicked atop the sandy rock, the size of a chipmunk. It scurried back behind one of the tan pebbles. She studied the empty space it had left, then... *Oh no!*

Penny couldn't pull in another breath. Her stomach burned. The sandy rock stood upon four furry legs. A huge lion, but skinny, with wide padded paws, and no mane. The tip of its tail flicked back and forth. She'd glimpsed its tail, not a chipmunk. Penny shrieked, but Mom clamped a hand over her mouth.

* * * *

Red stepped in front of his wife and daughter. The mountain lion was small, maybe a hundred pounds; not fully grown. Skin stretched taut as a drumhead across its ribs. A young male, and hungry. Not a good combination. He raised his pistol. *Damn it!* He couldn't use his weapon. He glanced at Lori. "Don't shoot."

She was backing away, eyes stretched wide, Penny in tow. "That thing comes near me, I'm shooting it!"

"You'll give away our position." He jerked his head toward a pine. "Get Penny up that tree."

Lori cocked the revolver. "Cats can climb."

He held up a hand. "I'll draw it away. You're defensible up there. Now, up the tree!"

Penny jerked free and quickly scaled the trunk. Lori climbed after her, though not as nimbly. With a lazy bound, the cat dropped twenty feet to the path and stalked toward Red. It had been waiting in ambush for dinner, apparently. With cats, the trick was to look large. Time to test that theory. He tossed a thick branch the size of a pry bar up to Lori, then grabbed another. He ripped off his sweater and held it over his head, hoping to enlarge his silhouette.

Each paw stepped carefully, deliberately in front of the other, as if it were walking a tightrope. The claws punctured small triangular holes in the trail's dust.

"He's faster than you," Lori called. "Beat the shit out of it if it gets closer."

The beast tucked its legs beneath, tensed to pounce, eyes on Red's chest, not his sweater or the swaying branch. The same heat burned his belly as when the cat neared him last night. But that one had been smaller, and black, right? Or he'd dreamed it. No, this had to be the same one. Darkness is deceptive, covering a thing's true nature.

Red placed the sight a few inches over his target. If the animal leaped, he'd be ready. Why wasn't it moving? "Come on, you cocky little shit," he taunted.

Mountain lions were solitary, pitiful creatures. Leaving their family when still young to spend a life alone, on the hunt, ever in the shadows. Nothing in them honorable or loyal like a wolf pack. Such a team ascribed meaning, challenged individuals to stretch beyond their own limited significance. But mountain cats were ignorant of such nobility.

He swung the stick again, and the creature yielded a retreating step, leaving four neat punctures in the trail. Progress. A cool breeze swelled, carrying the scent of wildcat piss. A few more waves of the branch and hushed shouting, and it lay its ears flat against its skull and slinked away.

"Anytime, you skinny coward!" he called after it.

He dropped the stick, tense shoulders slumped. He inhaled cool air. Half of him disappointed he hadn't shot the thing, the other half relieved he didn't have to.

As Red turned back toward Lori, an enormous black bear, at least four hundred pounds, stood on hind legs and fanned fat paws behind Penny's shoe, as if trying to swat a fly. Long black claws sliced the air.

So that's what scared the mountain lion away.

Lori's eyes widened in confused surprise as Red pointed to it. "Penny!" he called.

His daughter glanced down and lifted her legs with a jerk. Losing her balance, she lunged to grab a branch. Lori clutched her shoulder to steady her.

The bear dropped to all fours. Its fur was thick and long, with a shine that meant it enjoyed oily goodness from a trout stream. It shook like a dog coming out of water, sending waves of sparkly brown down its wide back. A short, tan snout punctuated a fat, wide skull. The beast was so large, if it had been brown, he could've mistaken it for a grizzly. It didn't appear angry. Must've thought his daughter's legs some sort of game. Hard to miss those fuchsia sneakers.

It ambled up the trail toward Red. Shit, black bears were supposed to be timid. No way could he outrun it. Though bears could climb, a tree was his still his best chance. Holstering the pistol, he jumped and grabbed a low pine branch and pulled himself up, swinging his good leg over. He climbed one row higher, then drew the weapon again. Its barrel followed the lumbering animal's progress.

What is this, the Nature Channel? Maybe it'll just pass.

It stopped at the base of his tree, turned, and grunted. A great, earthy rumble. Twenty yards back, two black cubs trotted from behind the holly, eighty pounds each, healthy fat rolls undulating as their short legs pumped. The two caught up, and she ambled, apparently unconcerned, as if the three strange creatures in the trees had always been there.

The bears slipped down the hill between rows of aspen, behind a short drop-off next to a thick mound of dark green shrubs. A gray boulder formed a berm on one side, keeping the earth uphill from eroding onto the bushes below. With delicate precision, the mother lifted to her hind feet again, stretched, and clamped a high cluster of red berries between both paws. The whole bush row shook and rattled as she yanked them down. The bottom four feet of the growth all around had been picked clean. A regular fast-food stop for the family, it seemed.

The mother placed the berries on the grass next to the cubs. The young ones munched till frothy crimson dripped from their jowls like blood. Finally, she served herself. The larger of her offspring nosed in while she enjoyed the first taste. A growl and a snap of teeth sent it scampering behind the other. The whole scene was serene, peaceful. A mother, protecting, caring for, and disciplining her cubs. She stood to reach for another clump.

Isn't such a bad thing for Lori to see.

Red glanced at Penny. Her leg was jiggling nervously, but Lori had wrapped one arm around her waist. He stooped to climb down the tree, but just then a low shadow passed across the holly, as if someone was on the other side, about to turn the corner of the trail. Lori and Penny's eyes were still fixed on the bear family. He waved, trying to catch their attention, but their eyes were on the bear.

He drew his pistol.

Around the corner stalked a short young woman, long black hair pulled back in a ponytail so tightly it stretched the corners of her eyes. *Yoga.* She'd changed clothes since yesterday. Holding a Glock 19 in Weaver style, the sharp cut of her triceps was evident. Black stretch pants accentuated muscular calves. Weapon steady, she shuffled silently down the path, beneath Red, toward the bears.

From her position on the road, he figured she couldn't see the animals past the boulder. Next to her pistol, she held a large phone. Her gaze flicked to it, then to the shaking bush. A yellow blot glowed in the middle of the screen, otherwise filled with an aerial view of the surrounding forest. Looked to be thermal imagery, probably from a drone. But the picture display was grainy, so a low-quality camera. Certainly nothing military grade.

Red slipped around to the far side of the tree trunk, hung from a low branch, and dropped, aiming his feet at a thick patch of grass to muffle his landing. Lori had caught his gaze now. She pointed to herself, then Yoga. She drew the .357 Magnum from her pocket and steadied her aim by leaning on a thick branch. At least ninety feet stretched between Lori's tree and Yoga, so she'd need luck as much as a steady hand to hit her mark. Penny climbed to a higher branch, behind the thick trunk and out of sight.

He gripped a bare gray stick the length of a baseball bat and headed toward the path. Ready to jump behind a tree should he crunch a pinecone or dry twig and alert Yoga. He shoved his pistol under his belt for fast access. If all went well, he wouldn't need it. As a stiff gust rustled aspen leaves, he got in several long, bounding strides during the temporary clamor. Yoga was stalking now, pistol aimed toward the rock berm. Knotted calves winced at every step. She set pink Nike running shoes gingerly, picking her way between strewn cones and twigs too. Red crept to within twenty feet. Her musky perfume, or maybe a scent from the bears, wafted past in the breeze.

The bushes shook again, and she froze. Almost at the boulder, she'd be able to see over it soon and realize her mistake—she was tracking three bears, not Red and his family. He risked a few more long strides, nearing to where he could almost reach her with his club.

She inched forward, knees bent, crouching low. Red set his boot soles on the same crushed stalks of grass where her tiny feet had been. If they hadn't made a sound landing there, his should be silent as well. He recalled how she'd threatened Penny on top of the mountain, had even took shots at them while he sprinted downhill on the bike. Now the bitch was hunting his family again. She had to die. He'd swat her head like a teed-up baseball.

He concentrated on the best spot, just above her ear. Raised his stick. Yoga spun around, but the club was already on the downswing. He shifted its vector and swung past her scalp, crashing it on her wrist, breaking her grip on the weapon. The gun landed in a green patch of dandelions. He cocked his fist to strike and— *What the hell?*

His head was slammed to the side, and his ear rang. She'd landed a punch! He turned back just in time to see the other fist flying from the opposite direction. It crunched into his jaw. The bitch was fast as hell. Her blows were light, but quick as a boxer working a speed bag. He sidestepped a kick to the groin and aimed a punch of his own, landing it on her chest. She stumbled backward, enough time for Red to regain his bearings.

She jerked a black blade from a sheath on her belt and lunged for his belly. Red stepped back and sucked in his gut, barely dodging the attack. Well balanced, she didn't overcommit and drew back for another. He slashed with the stick and managed to land a blow to her cheek. The telltale crack of bone, or maybe the stick, and her eye vibrated in a spasm. He thought about his pistol, but needed to take her alive, to find out who she was working for.

Knife fights were the worst. They never went well. Most often, there was little difference in the amount of blood spilled by victor and vanquished. Why hadn't he taken the Jamaican's blade?

As she lunged again, he stepped toward her, closing the distance, and caught her wrists as she thrust the blade upward. A risky move, but one he'd practiced countless times. Before she could draw back, he raised his knee and connected with her chest. She stumbled toward the berm, flailing for balance, mouth agape, searching to replace the air that had just been forced from her lungs. She tripped over a thick branch and toppled just over the boulder, arms whirling.

He reached for her. *No!*

A squeal echoed. One of the bear cubs shot into view, galloping toward the trail. Yoga must've landed on the other one. A growl and a hollow *thump* were followed by a garbled scream. Red inched toward the edge of the berm and peered down. Eight feet below, the huge black bear stood over Yoga, one meaty paw pinning her bloody neck. Nose low, sniffing her face. The second cub cowered a few feet away beneath the cover of the picked green shrub, panting, crimson berry juice dripping from its teeth.

Don't mess with Mama Bear.

He held his breath and backed away, careful to retrace his same soundless steps. Wouldn't be good to attract the attention of the sorely vexed animal. He braced an arm on the rough trunk beneath Lori and Penny to rest for a second. Amber sap had poured from a jagged gash where a branch had been recently torn away. The sticky gel gathered into a frozen flow like melted candle wax. It stuck between his fingers. Drawing his lips back from his teeth, he tried to catch his breath, then lifted a hand and motioned to Lori. "Let's get you down. Can't get stuck here. Need to keep moving."

She pointed toward the gray boulder and whispered. "What happened to her?"

He snorted and spat white froth swirled with black dust onto the ground. "Dead meat."

Lori glared. "You killed her?"

"No. Bear got her." He waved a hand in dismissal. "And I'm fine. Thanks for asking."

She slipped the revolver back into the stretchy front pocket of her jeans. "She could've told us who sent her."

"I know. I wasn't trying to kill the woman."

"Just comes naturally," Lori mumbled.

It did. No sense in denying that. Killing wasn't enjoyable. But it was nice to be skilled at something. An operator. That's who he was. He'd tried to take Yoga alive, but did what was necessary to accomplish the primary mission. In this case, keeping his wife and daughter safe.

Penny glanced down from the high limb on which she still sat. "Don't be mad, Mom. He didn't mean to."

Red sensed there was more in his daughter's response than she'd expressed. She was scared Lori would be mad at her for killing the Jamaican. He gave her a reassuring smile.

Lori opened her mouth, glanced at Penny, then squatted on a branch and jumped down. Thin flakes of bark twisted in the air as they floated and landed in her hair.

He stepped up the hill, away from the trail. A smooth branch a little longer than his father's cane lay next to a tree trunk. The bark had long dried and fallen off, leaving the wood grain bleached and smooth. A perfect walking stick. He grasped it and pointed up the slope. "We'll want to go around. I'd like to try and scare away the bear, to search the woman for what she was carrying. Maybe some ID. Find out who she was. But we can't risk angering the animal." Maybe it was better this way. Yoga had needed to die, and it wasn't his fault.

But she would've called her command center before engaging her target like that. When she didn't report back, they'd send someone after her. At least this way, when her body was found, she'd just been killed by bears. If the drone's thermal display was poor enough quality, the aggressors might believe she'd accidentally tracked those beasts instead of Red and his family. A long shot, but all he had at the moment. As his dad used to say, *Wish in one hand, spit in the other. See which one fills up first.*

Chapter 23

USCG

Carter's eyelids were already shut, but he squeezed them tighter as an ache in the back of his head grew to a splitting pain. He inhaled salt air. Sun warmed the nub of his cheek. A seagull's laugh blew on a stiff breeze. The gust chilled his body. He lay flat on his back, atop a hard surface. It rose and fell, as if suspended in a hammock. He lifted a hand over his face to shield his eyes from blinding sun.

He started to sit, but hands pressed him back onto the rigid bed. "Stay down, sailor," said a gruff voice. The accent was from…where? He pressed his foggy mind to remember. Where was he? How'd he get here?

Rhode Island. That was the accent. Similar to Boston, but only half the attitude. The guy couldn't be too threatening. Eyes adjusting to the light, he dropped his arm. Peering through slits, he studied full, red cheekbones. Blond hair pulled back in a bun. The gentle curves of a woman's face. Her blue cap read USCG in white lettering. Not quite pudgy, but short legs stretched blue fatigues at the thighs. Must be the auxiliary.

But how…where? Recognition flooded in with the memory of straining to pull the rope aboard Javlek's sailboat, just before he hit the water. Sonofabitch must've coldcocked him with that rod he was carrying.

Carter sat up, this time pushing aside Blondie's hands. He'd been lying upon a thin aluminum stretcher on a stainless steel deck. Drops fell from his nose and upper lip. A clear plastic mask covered mouth and chin. Was this woman gassing him? He snatched it off and gulped salt air. A clear hose ran from the mask to a quart-sized green oxygen bottle. His toes squished inside soggy socks, loafers gone, pants lying beside him, flannel boxers soaked through. Where the hell were his shoes? Those were four-hundred-dollar Ferragamos. Somewhere beneath him, near his feet, emanated the rumble of diesel engines at low speed. The small area was encircled by stainless handrails and bulkhead. The craft appeared to be a fast response unit, at least forty feet long, with an enclosed center cabin.

Blondie's voice was low, the tone calming. "Take it slow. Don't stand up."

Carter swiped his thumbs across his eyelids, squeezing water away, then blinked to clear the remaining haze as he shook his hands dry. The boat plowed into a swell, and the craft shuddered. White spray shot up like a fountain despite their slow speed, floating upon air as they drove through it. "What happened?"

"Let's get you situated," she said.

Gripping under his arms, she pulled him to a storage bin. He eased his back against it. Could've done that himself. *Not like I'm a cripple.* Still, the newness of waking from death cautioned him to not resist a bit of aid.

"You were in the ocean for a spell. You remember knotting your pant legs? Turned your trousers into a life preserver. Not many people know how to do that. You former Coast Guard? Got a nasty gash on the back of your head. Need some stiches once we get shoreside."

Carter reached back to touch it, but she slapped his hand away.

"Don't do that. It's bandaged." She held up fingers. "How many?"

"Three."

She glanced down at her hand, then held up another finger. "How many this time?"

"We gonna do this all day? You got four there." One wriggled and she dropped a digit. "Now three."

Another glance at her hand, as if she had to count them herself to be sure. "Uh-huh. You better stay down till we're docked. Lay back on the stretcher."

He waved her off. "How'd I get here?"

Her cheery smile faded. "You've been in and out of consciousness since we pulled you from the water. You've got a concussion for sure. Why don't you tell me your name? And how you got in the water."

The ache at the back of Carter's skull rose again. He reached around to cradle it, but dropped his hand, remembering her earlier rebuke. "We were getting set to tack. Javlek said—"

"He the only other one on your boat?"

"Yeah. Just him and me." Carter had been clocked on the head. Maybe he wasn't remembering it correctly. Could he be wrong? "Never went below, so I suppose there could've been someone down there who could've whacked me. Even so, the prick must've thrown me overboard. Make it look like a drowning."

A corner of her mouth curled up, but then the smirk vanished quickly, as if she were trying hard to hold back a laugh. "No one else you know of, though? Just trying to make sure no one is missing."

Anger burned his neck. "That sonofabitch clocked me with a flagstaff. He'll have to come ashore soon. He called his boat a Bermuda forty, whatever that is. *Mistress Two.* Blue hull. I'm pressing charges. I'll bet—"

Javlek stepped around the side of the cabin, blue blanket draped over his shoulders. His weathered, tanned skin shone pale and thin now. He smiled and sat on the storage bin next to Carter. "Oof," he wheezed.

Blondie jabbed a finger at him. Command in her voice. "Told you to stay up front!"

Carter struggled to stand, but the boat was rocking and he couldn't keep his balance. Blondie had incredible sea legs to stay upright in these waves. He dropped back down on his butt, jolting the pain in his head back up to a scream.

Javlek rested a hand on Carter's shoulder, grip weak. "Thank God you're OK. You look like I feel."

Carter winced as a new wave of nausea rose and fell. "You clocked me, you sonofabitch!"

Javlek let his hand fall to his lap. His gaze wandered to a spinning radar atop the cabin, as if embarrassed. "We both got cleaned. The boom." The blanket slid from his shoulders. "I'm an idiot. That rope of yours got bound in the winch. Happened to me once before. I slipped over to help, and next thing I see is a bright flash. I woke up almost overboard, leg tangled in the same rope. *Mistress Two* was listing hard to port. The cockpit almost filled with seawater. I dropped sail, looked around, yelled for you. Didn't know how long I was out. The radio wasn't submerged, so I called for help. Bilge pumps were running, at least. I cranked up one of the engines so the batteries didn't wear out." His cheeks creased in a smile. "Fired right up, even with the entire motor compartment underwater. Got them breathers airtight. Yes, sir. At least I did somethin' right."

Too many details. The old man was lying, trying to play dumb. But politicians were so hard to read. "The boom got the both of us?"

"Got the goose egg to prove it." He twisted to face the bow. A swollen purple bruise was clearly visible through close-cropped hair. He could've given it to himself, sure, but it was large enough he would've been knocked unconscious anyhow. Javlek pointed at Blondie. "Chief Petty Officer here tried to put me in a neck brace. Told her I weren't no boat goat."

Her eyes narrowed. She held up a clenched fist. "Listen, you condescending sonofabitch! This *boat goat*'s been a sailor her entire life. She could tack your little ship blindfolded without getting whacked in the head and needing the Coast Guard to haul her soggy ass ashore. Just 'cause you're old as dirt and got nailed on the skull don't mean I gotta take any more of your crap." Her cheeks glowed red as a Christmas ornament. Standing in front of them, she was barely taller than the seated men. She clasped her hands behind her back, as if to stop herself from throwing a punch. The tear of Velcro being separated came from behind her. Quicker than Carter's eyes could follow, she clamped a padded cream-colored collar around Javlek's neck. Before the man could get his hands up, she'd cinched the straps tight. "You didn't even know what year it was when we pulled you off your sinking ragtop." She pulled out a thick roll of white athletic tape and wrapped it around the brace several times, overlapping the Velcro.

"I survived a year as a POW," Javlek protested. "I don't need this sissy thing." He slipped both thumbs beneath the collar.

Blondie put her nose right up to his. "You take that off and I will handcuff your ass to the handrail. Your decision, old man." He must've been stroking her the wrong way earlier. She shoved the tape back into her blue trousers and stepped into the cabin. A tall, skinny man in the same blue uniform stood just inside, one hand on the ship's wheel and another on the throttle. Wouldn't a craft this size take at least a crew of three? Where was the other? Blondie slammed the door shut.

Javlek glanced at Carter, worry in his eyes. "Sorry, but I had to piss her off so she'd leave. Listen. Don't tell my wife about the accident. She'll make me get rid of the boat. I just whacked my head on the underside of a cabinet below deck. That's all that happened, if she asks you."

Maybe this guy wasn't bluffing about the mishap. The explanation—the real one—sounded stupid enough. "What's it worth to you? The wife is the least of your worries."

Javlek scooched forward on the storage bin, tendons of his neck stretching the skin tight like ropes of a sail, fear in his eyes. "What you asking for?"

Mistress Two bobbed behind the vessel in the cut of its wake. Why hadn't Carter noticed the sailboat in tow before? A long white line ran to a cleat on its bow, taut and straight despite the distance. The nose of the vessel pitched up, fighting its capture like a hooked marlin. Listing to port, a stream of water flowed like a garden hose from the starboard, bilge pumps still working to empty their load. Naked masts glinted in sunlight. Beneath the boom, a man in blue fatigues stood at the helm.

Carter lifted his chin. "A story like this could be political suicide. Retired vice chair of the JCS isn't safe on the water? A Navy man who can't sail? You'll look inept, or demented, or both. I'll keep my mouth shut, but only if I'm getting paid in information."

A metallic melody burst from the pocket of his slacks. Carter stretched to gather his dripping pants from the deck, dug around in the wet cloth, and pulled out his phone. He thought he'd lost it in the water. His daughter had given him her upgrade for Christmas, and this model was water resistant. COLORADO on the screen. Maybe it was Red! He pressed it to one ear, plugging the other with a finger so he could hear. "Hello?"

Disappointment crashed as an unfamiliar voice came through the tiny speaker. "Yeah. This…oh, hell. I can't remember who he said I'd be callin'. But Red gave me this number. You know him? Guy with a copper-colored beard. Had his little girl with him."

Carter propped an elbow atop the locker, but couldn't muster the strength to hoist himself up. He flopped back down again. "Yeah. Red. He OK? What's going on? Who are you? How'd you get this number?"

The crackle of an angry engine mangled the man's voice, as if he were driving a hot rod. "Name's Lam. Red gave it to me before he left. Told me to call it first chance I got. And to tell you… Wait. What's your name?"

"Carter."

"Yeah. That's it. Told me to tell you he's alive, but headed to Cheyenne Mountain. Who are you? FBI or something?"

Carter pressed a palm to his forehead. "Yeah… Or something. What happened to Red?" He listened as Lam described the last twenty-four hours, how he'd been attacked on his way to work in Dark Canyon. That a friend named Andi had been shot. Then a run-in with a huge Rastafarian in camo. And how Red had foolishly refused to stay in some sort of electric grid. The man's sentences trailed off at times. The guy had been shot, and up all night. Sounded beat. Or maybe Carter couldn't follow his convoluted descriptions due to his own pounding headache.

"I had the generator building wired so tight it'd fry the balls off anyone thought they could get in."

Carter closed an eye as salt spray from the bow cascaded across his face. "Red tell you anything else, besides where he was headed?"

"No. Said for you not to tell anyone else. That you'd know what to do."

Carter glanced at his watch. It'd be six o'clock in the Rockies. What the hell did Red think he could do…and without telling anyone? Did that mean no one in the Det too? Was he supposed to organize some sort of rescue mission? But how, without resources? "Thanks for the call. Sounds like we owe you one. This phone you're on, can I get back in touch with you if I call it?"

"Unless I'm in a dead spot. And they're plenty out here."

"Thanks again. Get that shoulder looked at." Carter clicked off. He glanced at Javlek. The man was gazing mournfully at his trailing sailboat. Maybe he could use the retired admiral's help. He had good connections, though also to Moses.

No. Break it down. What were the facts? Lam said Red and his family had been attacked atop Pikes Peak. In an organized, well-coordinated effort. Sounded like high-stakes players. So the solution couldn't involve Javlek. That man may have helped create this problem. And Red's warning to not tell anyone else confirmed it. So, no involving the Det. Was he worried about a mole inside the organization? Up to now, Carter hadn't considered that being the source of the list on Moses' computer. But if Jamison was correct and Moses was trying to sell the data, it had to come from somewhere. Could be his source was in the Det. As a fusion cell, they certainly had access to intel from many sources. Depending upon how accurate this list was, it could be devastating. And if CIA operatives were named, fatal.

So, the answer had to be below the radar, a local player, someone or something who up to this point hadn't had a stake in the game. Did he know any cops out west? Any of his old FBI connections stationed there? Anything at all? Grace had provided Red's sister's cell phone number, but that woman had only been able to confirm Red, Lori, and Penny had headed to Pikes Peak the morning of the shooting. She didn't know their current whereabouts and was worried senseless. He squinted as bright sun blasted through another wave of bow mist, filling the deck with a beautiful rainbow. Even Blondie was smiling as she stepped from the cabin. He had only one option.

Carter thumbed CALLBACK.

Chapter 24

Scrugs

The door of the flimsy camouflage-painted trailer shuddered under Lam's knock. The metal tinked like a tin can. Still no answer. Old Scrugs must be out hunting, or maybe had a late night at Jo-Jo's Bar and was passed out hungover on the side of a mountain road. Could be shacked up with his obese girlfriend, but they weren't on speaking terms, last Lam heard.

The mechanic had slipped past the feds' checkpoint at Cow Mountain, easy enough for anyone who knew the trails. Driven all the way back out to Route 67, then to Cripple Creek, and laid down an Andrew Jackson for a made-in-China mobile charger. What a rip-off. He'd powered up his phone there in the parking lot and called Carter, just like Red had asked. That had been a disappointment. Turned out the man wasn't a fed. Just a no-count detective of some sort. Why would Red have wanted Lam to call that guy? Then, after they'd hung up, he'd called right back, asking if Lam knew any park rangers or local law enforcement that could be trusted.

Lam had no connections. "I avoid those guys like the plague," he'd told him. And Elway was back at the generator house covering the scene. Even so, that park ranger wasn't any kind of hunter.

Carter had sounded half-drunk. If Red and his little girl needed help, it surely wasn't coming from that guy, either. Now that Lam had been freed from Dark Canyon, it fell to him to figure out how to find Red and his girl. That meant he'd be covering open valleys with mile-long sight lines, so he needed a weapon with more range than the 1911 pistol under his belt. Which was why he'd come knocking at Scrugs's trailer.

He let the screen door slap shut and stepped down the pile of stacked cinder blocks beneath the front door. Bud's tail wagged eagerly. Scrugs's 150-pound blood hound was named after the beer, not short for buddy. The monster shook his head, ears slapping jowls, spraying streams of slobber and a few black flies. *Poor thing.* Lam had once phoned in an anonymous tip of cruelty to Animal Control because Scrugs left the dog outside year-round. But the pound claimed they couldn't find Scrugs's place, then blamed Lam for a prank call. The mobile home was certainly hard to find, tucked high inside a mountain gully with trees and brush growing up all around. No driveway. You just had to know how to look. Like hunting. How to follow a trail. That wasn't something you could teach a desk ranger over the phone.

Lam reached down, patted the dog's head, and rubbed behind his ears. Bud's hind leg twitched in a dead man's scratch. A hinge creaked behind, and the hound's tail wagged. Lam turned and threw up both arms as if shielding his eyes from the sun. "Holy shit! Get some clothes on." Damn. He'd never be able to unsee that.

Scrugs stood behind the screen door, white beard hanging to his chest, yellowed at the tips and a single brown streak of tobacco stain at one corner of his mouth, pale potbelly protruding over stretched-out tighty-whities. "You come on ta my land and gonna tell me how to dress?" The hermit pushed the door open and, with guttural grunts, stepped down the cinder block stack, barefoot. One big toe had a purple nail, as if stomped by a bull. He patted Bud, then pointed to a wooden crate with a large hole cut in one side. "Now, git!" The dog stood and loped off, shaking its head to clear the flies as it went.

Lam grimaced as he glanced into the recluse's bloodshot eyes, trying to keep a straight face and ignore the half-pregnant man. "I need to borrow your Remington 700. The one-chambered 7mm mag."

Scrugs's nostrils flared. He rested hands upon hips, though Lam couldn't really say the man had any. "And...why you ain't takin' your own rifle?"

Lam glanced back at the trail he'd hiked to the house, so the loner couldn't see him think. Should've come up with a story before now. "Saw a small elk herd on my way in today. Didn't bring mine, and not enough time to fetch it. Thought I'd try and bag one, though." Scrugs would know this wasn't the first time Lam had poached while at work.

The old-timer's gaze was steady. "Then why your eyes all puffy? Hungover? Don't look like you've slept in a week. How'd you hurt the arm?" The man stepped closer, slipping a finger beneath the edge of the sling near Lam's neck. He snorted. "Funny. Your shirt's got a forty-five caliber hole in the front." Pale love handles jiggled as he turned back toward his shack and swung an arm, two fingers pointing at the screen door. "Come inside. I'll get ya doctored up. Slug still in there?"

The man hadn't even asked why he'd been shot. He'd hunted many a time with Scrugs. They'd roasted an elk tenderloin down in the gully on a spit over maple fire, sipping homemade brew, and he'd woken the next morning with a rod through his head. Lam stood on the narrow trail, feet heavy as rocks. No way he'd follow that old bastard into his cabin till he got more clothes on. "Slug's out. Passed clear though."

The man stopped and spoke over one shoulder. "None 'a my business, but who you wantin' to kill?"

Lam shrugged. "Kill? No one. Just trying to bag an elk."

Scrugs eased himself down on the cinder block steps, back straight, fingers knotted across his belly. A wave of nausea rose, but Lam pictured him in a red suit like Santa Claus and it finally passed.

The man's voice deepened; his beard trembled as he growled. "You come ta my house, no sleep, shot through the shoulder, askin' me for a rifle, when you got a beautiful Remington thirty aught six of your own settin' at home. Wife seein' another man?"

"No!"

"Then you got mixed up in that shit on top 'a Pikes Peak, I s'pose."

How'd Scrugs hear about that? Maybe he'd been to town yesterday.

The old-timer scratched his beard. "Scanner's been full 'a traffic last thirty-six hours. Even seen a few of them black helos flappin' around the sky like injured ducks." His eyes narrowed. "I think them feds is coverin' up an abduction. You goin' huntin' for an alien?"

Lam suppressed a grimace. *Here we go with the talk about skinny green men from outer space.* "Nope. Not an abduction."

The geezer's overgrown cottony eyebrows lifted. "How you know? Happens all the time! Air Force told the media they moved the command center out of the mountain. It's a lie! To cover up what they're really doing. They're busier inside there than ever. Think they ever needed all that equipment just to track satellites and space debris?" He pointed a pale arm to the sky. "They's got eyes on them UFOs comin' and goin'. Can't do a thing about it, though, 'cause we're outgunned. Aliens come and take whoever they want and do—"

"*Scrugs!*"

The wildness in the old man's eyes flared out. "You come askin' me 'cause you know none 'a my guns can be traced."

Lam couldn't deny that. Scrugs had dutifully purchased his entire collection from private parties, in cash, then disassembled every part and filed off anything that looked like a number. All his conspiracy theory militia buddies who gathered the second Tuesday night of each month in the VFW parking lot did the same thing.

Lam sighed. "I need yours because we shoot the same X. I'm not looking to kill a man, but I need it just in case." The old-timer was half-cocked, but kept a secret even when drunk. Lam relayed his experience the night before to him, Red and his kid running off toward Cheyenne Mountain, and the callback from Carter asking for any help Lam could provide.

"You trust this fella, this Red?"

Lam grimaced as his shoulder cramped. "He took one hell of a beating for his little girl. Patched me up and made sure I was OK. I don't owe him anything, but the guy needs a friend right about now."

Scrugs slapped hands to knees and, with effort, grunted himself upright. He started to hike up the steps. "Fine. I'm comin' with you."

Like hell. "You don't want to come on this hunt."

"You want my rifle, I'm comin'. Plus, what good's a weapon gonna be if you need it? You've got a busted shoulder. You'd be twitchin' all over. Probably shoot his kid. Big mistake... Maybe you start losin' blood. Someone's gotta look after your ass too."

Lam caught the door before it slammed and followed him in. As lax as the man kept his body and wardrobe, the inside of the trailer was squared away. A short stack of *Field & Stream* stood on an oak coffee table next to another neat pile of *Guns & Ammo*. Planted in the middle of the living room was a suede leather recliner, directly in front of a short black woodstove. On a folding table against the wall lay a gray box, a frequency scanner, that Scrugs had demonstrated to him once before. Several other radios stood behind it, mounted in metal mini racks, wires bundled and tucked in a tidy manner. A black Motorola XPS 5000 two-way radio, the same brick used by the FBI, stood in a charger. Scrugs claimed he could eavesdrop on the feds' encrypted frequencies, but Lam knew that was a joke. Like media reporters, he could only listen to the police channels, and the FBI in the off chance they needed to transmit unsecured. Tiny red and yellow lights flashed like a Christmas tree, reflecting off glossy green metal cabinets hung in the kitchen over a shiny Formica counter. Not a single soldier was missing from a twelve-inch-square knife block. "Clean as ever," Lam said.

Scrugs's skin glowed a deathly lime in the florescent light as he waddled back to his bedroom. "Nothin' wrong with being poor, and soap don't cost much."

Lam chuckled to himself. Scrugs liked to poor-mouth, and did a fair job of looking down and out. But he received a regular disability check from the Army, plus Social Security, plus had other income based on how much money he spent on weapons. More than enough for a single man to eke out an existence inside a paid-for trailer.

A few minutes later Lam was flipping through an article in one of the magazines about bow hunting moose in Alaska when a couple snorts drifted in from the bedroom. "You got your girlfriend back there?"

"Jus'…tyin'…my boot."

Who knew speed laces were such an effort. Another few minutes and the old man stepped into the kitchen with the hems of dark charcoal fatigues tucked into knee-high leather chaps, like a World War I cavalry rider. He laid the Remington 700 on the counter. The twenty-six-inch barrel projected from a dark-grained walnut stock. Scrugs had rubbed the wood with three-hundred-grit sandpaper, leaving behind a matte finish that didn't reflect light, like he did for most his weapons.

"She's got three in the magazine, one in the chamber. Reloads with 160-grain soft points, IMR 4895 powder. Overcharged a little, like I always do. Them slugs'll fly just shy of thirty-three hundred feet per second." He patted the Leupold 3x9 power scope tenderly, as if stroking a kitten. "Zeroed at four hundred yards on flat terrain at nine thousand feet altitude." He rubbed fat fingers across the stock's wood grain. "Go a lot farther too. She'll reach out and touch someone for sure. When the Democrats seize power like they're plannin'—"

"Scrugs. What you got strapped to your back?" Lam needed to rein in the man's attention, so the long barrel topped with a flat muzzle brake rubbing the ceiling was a good opportunity. "I've never seen that one."

The old man turned sideways to allow a clear view. The entire weapon looked almost seven feet long, like a thick barrel with a stock affixed. A compact bipod folded against it about halfway up. Single shot, bolt action, whatever the rifle was. Velcro straps ran across its center, snugging it to a black tactical pack. A scope large enough to see Mars was affixed to the top.

"I just bought her last month at the estate auction of a cardiologist in Montana." He grinned. "Lotta good he was. Man died of a heart attack at fifty-nine. I snatched up this baby right quick. A Soviet anti-tank rifle from early World War II. She's a PTRD-41. Fourteen-and-a-half-millimeter bullet. Not much good against German armor, but'll take down an elk at a thousand yards. Even farther, I suppose. The doc had a smith up there add the scope."

A thousand yards? For real? "You can't take that. It's not even legal."

Scrugs frowned. "Why not?"

"Over fifty caliber. After that, it's classified as…artillery…or something."

"Not like what we're doin' is legal anyway."

Lam picked up the Remington with his good arm. "We're not doing anything illegal. Just going on a ride in my truck with a couple high-powered rifles. If you gotta come, bring a different one. Something smaller. Less obvious. More…legal."

The geezer shrugged the pack higher up his shoulders. "I'm comin', and I'm bringin' my gal. Not like you could hit diddly shit with a busted shoulder anyway. You plannin' on shootin' left handed? Who knows where your X would be." He squinted. "I ain't gonna be alive much longer anyhow."

Lam rubbed his eyes with a clenched fist. The old man was always sure he was dying from one thing or another. And as hardheaded as his hound with the scent of blood in his nose. Lam's arm was starting to ache again, so he reached in his pocket, popped the top of an ibuprofen bottle, and swallowed a few. "Whatever. Let's go."

He pushed open the screen door and stepped down. With two, he had to admit, they could cover more ground. If Red and his kid were still alive, he knew exactly where to wait. But chances were, so would any other good hunter, such as friends of the dead Jap and Rasta. Scrugs was lumbering along behind him with that damn rifle barrel waving over his head tall as a pine sapling. Maybe the old man was right, except both of them would be dying.

The image of Andi's dry, empty eyes staring at a night sky full of white dots pricked his conscience. She was a mother. Maybe even now her young children were getting the news of her death. He kicked a pebble down the trail. *No*, he resolved. These predators were part of the same team. The same ones stalking Red and his kid. Lam was a hunter too. If any of those bastards showed up in his scope, he'd be sure to adjust for windage.

Chapter 25

Towers

Penny crept on hands and knees up behind her dad. Sharp pebbles pressed into her palms and shins. He was on his belly next to a tall tuft of blue-green grass stalks, whose heavy heads were bowing in a breeze. His fist gripped his smooth gray walking stick. He'd been lying down for about a minute, next to a dusty clay road. More than a dozen tall steel towers in red and white stood atop a pine-dotted crest ahead of them, like a section from Jackson's Erector Set.

She gasped with the excitement of the sight. Wasn't this finally where they were supposed to be? But there was no Air Force base here. She glanced around, bewildered. Where were the airplanes supposed to land? Dad was staring down a road.

"You doing your 'stop-look-listen'?" she asked, out of breath. Moving silently was so much harder than normal walking around.

He turned, leaning on one arm. "You're getting quiet, sneaking up like that. Yeah. We need to go through this gully, between those two peaks." His cheeks glowed with fresh sunburn, a deeper red than his beard. She'd always liked those whiskers. He used to joke how she'd pulled out tufts of them as a child. "Got the grip of a gymnast," he'd teased. None of her friends' dads had red hair. Some grew beards, but theirs all looked dorky. Dad's didn't. He trimmed it neatly, but the thick red pelt still reminded her of a wild animal. No one else would've known how to protect her on top of Pikes Peak, or from those men shooting at them while they biked away. None of her friends' dads could've run all day with a bullet in their butt, and then fight a soldier twice their size, then keep moving all night long and still be awake now.

Like a lion's claws, Dad had kept this part of himself sheathed. But instead of scaring her, the thought had allowed her to finally fall asleep last night.

He pointed across the trail. "Roads are always where you have to be most careful. Nothing there to hide you. Once we get through that gully, it's a quick downhill hike to the entrance of Cheyenne Mountain Air Force Station. Where'd you leave your mother?"

Penny glanced behind her. "Behind that rock. She had to pee."

Dad pointed at a blackened boulder across the road. Someone must've put a bonfire next to the rock while camping. "Once Mom gets here, I'm going to cross first, to that spot over there. Then I'll wave you over. Wait for my signal. Watch how I do it. Be fast, but light on your feet, like when you just snuck up on me. When you go across a road keep your steps pointed parallel to it. That way, if someone sees your footprints, they don't know which direction you were headed."

Gravel scuffed behind, and Penny turned her head. Mom crept up with a tall clump of grass clenched in one fist. "The road looks hard packed," she said. "But I'll sweep away any traces just in case."

* * * *

Scrugs gripped the rung of a tall galvanized steel ladder, locking on with both fists. He pulled his body flat against the cold metal and sucked in a deep breath, resting his legs. The wheeze of asthma rattled in his chest, but clinging halfway up a three-legged radio tower on the top of Cheyenne Mountain, he didn't dare let go to grab the inhaler from his pocket.

Lam had said the structure was only three hundred feet tall, but Scrugs's lungs told him different. Like his predawn climbs up tree trunks to hunt deer, he'd tried to ascend in silence. But somewhere around sixty feet his lungs began to sound like a chain smoker sucking wind through a megaphone. Stomach acid crept up and soured his throat.

He didn't mind heights. They'd never given him trouble in his high-rise work before he'd retired. After a few years as a door gunner in the Army's 1st Cavalry Division, he'd floundered between construction jobs all over the country, swinging a twenty-two-ounce framing hammer, moving wherever the economy called. But he'd finally planted himself with Houston Steel Erection after meeting Mary in Dallas. She'd gotten pregnant, he finally gave up weed, and after a decade was a site super for several fifty-story projects. Steady on his feet, he used to scramble across girders three times as high as he was now, before OSHA cluttered everything up with fall arresters and climbing harnesses. Since then, a drunken troll with vertigo could work steel construction.

The radio tower swayed not because he was dizzy with height, but asthma was depriving his lungs of oxygen. A breeze blew, and the tower's taut guy-wires hummed a bass note, almost a G-flat. A turnbuckle clattered overhead, as if threatening to break loose. Scrugs craned his neck backward and gazed up. The tensioned lines above all pointed like an arrow to a small steel platform the size of a deer stand another twelve stories above him. The long barrel of the PTRD-41 strapped to his back reached over his head and seemed to aim at the same target. The rifle's muzzle brake swayed back and forth with each labored breath.

Closing his eyes, he considered his options. Go back down and set up atop one of the low shacks that housed the radio equipment. But trees could block his vantage point. Lam and his friend Red, and his little girl, they needed help.

Scrugs started up again, hand over hand, and finally found himself beneath the steel plate. Damn, it looked bigger from the ground. The perch was triangular, the size of a small coffee table. An antenna was bolted to its middle, shooting up another twenty feet. Scrugs reached over, grasped it, and pulled himself atop the platform into a sitting position. He dropped his legs over the edge and locked his feet into the tower struts.

Lam had tried to ascend a neighboring tower, but Scrugs had insisted he'd be more useful across the gully as a spotter. That would give the two the widest field of view to find this Red fella, if he was still alive, if the government hadn't killed him yet. Aliens usually only gave the feds twenty-four hours to silence anyone who gained knowledge they deemed inappropriate. Some friends said the ETs could read minds, but those guys were crazy. They could only erase memory. Scrugs had survived an abduction and escaped, though he couldn't recall most of it.

In the middle of the stand among a half-inch pile of crusted bird droppings laid two steel nuts, extras left after construction. He pinched them between fingers and dropped one, then the other over the edge of the platform. They fell in the breeze and thumped onto gravel. Three seconds on their downward journey resulted in six feet horizontal movement. That was a lot of windage to adjust for.

Lam had cut off the electricity to the tower at a big green box outside that same hut. He'd said the legs of the structure were part of the antenna, putting out a hundred thousand watts. Not that Scrugs cared about the harm radio waves could do. He was dying, not being paranoid like Lam always suggested. The doc at the Veterans' Hospital had finally figured out the reason for Scrugs's heartburn. Stomach cancer. Inoperable. Four months to live. What a kick in the balls.

Glancing down, he searched the base of the other towers, trees, and buildings that dotted the "antenna garden" as Lam had called it, looking for any signs of movement. Scrugs had no problem shooting someone if it meant protecting Lam or his new friend. But if a technician working on radio equipment spotted him doing it, Scrugs would spend the final few months of his life in jail. But no one was moving this morning.

He reached over his head, gripped the long barrel of the old anti-tank rifle, and pulled it from the straps that secured it to his tactical pack. The weapon was a monster, almost forty pounds, but lighter than one would expect from a tool meant to take out armor. He clipped a strap to the antenna a few feet above and used it as a sling to rest the barrel. Not the most stable support, but it allowed him free motion to cover a wide field of fire. Plus, horizontal bars stuck awkwardly from the antenna above his head, making the extra limb of the weapon look fitting.

His wheezing from the climb subsided, and he pulled the stock tight to his shoulder. The cheek rest was nothing but a flat square of metal whose chill goose-pimpled his face. As he leaned into the scope, the road below shot into clarity. He swung the weapon to both sides, testing where he could aim without repositioning. His field of fire was a full 180 degrees, to the pine-covered ridge a thousand yards north, and the entire gully between. The slope of the small valley was shallow, and natural cover grew unimpeded. A trained soldier might even walk through undetected.

A tower of similar height stood no more than a hundred feet to the side with huge white funnels bolted to it. Scrugs had wanted to climb that one since it had a larger platform, but Lam had said he didn't know how to lock out the power. And Scrugs didn't protest once the mechanic mentioned the possibility of his nuts getting fried. He was dying, but still had plans for Saturday evening.

Where was Lam now? Lifting his head from the scope, Scrugs searched northerly, outside the perimeter road that surrounded the thirty-five acres of mountaintop real estate. He noticed his friend stepping slowly as he descended a narrow rock trail, placing boots on either side of a shallow V-shaped washout, making his way to the opposite ridge.

Spotting was one thing Scrugs was good at. He'd enjoyed better than twenty-twenty vision since he'd been a kid. Maybe turkey hunting in Tennessee as a teenager had trained it into him, or his time in 'Nam as air cavalry. Either way, somewhere he'd developed the ability to notice the slightest motion in the wild. His mind would filter out the swoop of a bird, and the skittering of a squirrel, and the waving of grass in a breeze. But if a single tuft parted unnaturally, indicating an unseen danger lurking near the roots, his eyes would lock onto the spot immediately.

He unbuttoned a shirt pocket and lifted out a heavy brass cartridge the size of a bratwurst. He frowned as he noted the black tip and red band encircling the bullet. In his haste out the door, he'd grabbed the weapon's original armor-piercing incendiary rounds. For hunting elk, he used aftermarket solid brass projectiles, lathe turned to match standards, though he hadn't had a chance yet to take down an animal with one. Instead, these bullets had been manufactured well before Scrugs had even been born, meant to bust through armor and catch fire to fuel tanks or ammunition. Worst part was, they cost fifty dollars a pop.

Oh well. Bullets were useless, except for the split second they were screaming through the air. He slipped it into the rifle and, with the clunky awkwardness inherent to most Russian weapons, locked the bolt forward.

A flash of movement in his periphery. Someone had just run across the access road and was huddled behind a black boulder. He swung his rifle toward it and peered through the scope. His X hovered over copper-colored hair. He snatched a Motorola two-way from his vest. The device had proven most useful, much of the radio chatter since yesterday being unsecured since the feds were communicating with local police. He pressed Transmit. He'd agreed with Lam to pretend to be some sort of tree-hugging nature spotter in case the FBI overhead. At Scrugs's suggestion, they'd even set up code words.

"Elk spotted eight hundred yards west of your position, heading east, crossing the road." Where was the kid? Hidden close? The hair color had to mean this guy was Red. But he seemed to be waiting. If he moved another twenty yards, he'd be into thicker forest and harder to track. "Take your camera and move fast. Looks like your lone bull."

Chapter 26

Stump

Red crouched behind the blackened boulder, which had charred coals piled up around its base. Listening, his movement hadn't seemed to have stirred any unwanted attention. The team pursuing them wouldn't want to venture so close to a military installation. Maybe Yoga was the last challenge he'd have to face. Once through the shallow gully ahead, the journey's end was only a half klick downhill. From Cheyenne Mountain, he'd be able to contact the Det and this hellish vacation would be over. He'd take work over this any day. At least then his team was the aggressor and he could stack every conceivable detail to his advantage. Like Jim, his prior commander, had always liked to say, "If you're ever in a fair fight, your tactics suck."

Directly across the dusty pink gravel road Penny crouched behind a sedan-sized mound of cheatgrass. Its heavy seed heads curled and hung limp; their flowing tan whiskers waved over her head. Honeysuckle scent drifted in the breeze. Her gaze was locked with his, waiting instruction.

She'd been such a trouper. The thought of finally getting her to the air base stirred relief. The blurry shadow of a soaring bird passed between them on the road. These two worlds weren't supposed to intersect. He'd always been able to flip a mental switch as a soldier, enjoying being a dad to the kids in one world, morphing to operator when working for the Det. It was what his own father, Tom, had taught him when he'd tried out for the JV football team as an adolescent. "Once you step over that chalk line onto the field," he'd said, "you leave yourself behind. Become another man.

The meanest sonofabitch on the field." His father's smile had been tight and wicked as he'd rested a hand on Red's shoulder. "That's the one place it's OK to forget that shit about being nice and playing fair. Let out the wild man everyone else wants to bury. I know he's in you. Get to know him. Make friends."

Now he considered the conflict between the outside husband and father, and his own inner wild man. An operator. Though Lori had been dragged into this world before, he'd been able to shelter the kids from it. But now Penny was wandering out in the field, innocent and oblivious.

He stared at her knotted pigtails, hanging like the heads of cheatgrass. Was she going to stay his little girl, or had this stirred a wildness inside her? Would she begin to distance him now, knowing who he really was?

Red had certainly done that with his father. The man had been a FiSTer in Vietnam for two years, a forward artillery observer, but the only evidence of his service was a Purple Heart his mother had placed on the mantel and a twitch in one eyelid from viral nerve damage. His feral temper could flare like the flash of a mortar shell.

Was there a point at which Red would no longer be able to switch back as well?

Lori waved, and he blinked, drawing his thoughts back to the present. Glancing at Penny, he curled fingers in a *come here* gesture. She rose to a crouch and crossed the road in a side step, feet pointing parallel like he'd told her. Her legs crossed each other, weaving the way his old coach used to make them run in football warm-up drills.

She knelt behind the boulder at his feet and sucked in a few deep breaths. "Did I do good?"

A shiver climbed his neck.

Lori followed, brushing away their steps with her grass-clump broom. Still, if anyone was looking they would spot the band of swept road. A gust rustled through branches, or was it the distant rumble of an engine echoing across the gully? A motor. Red searched the sky, but only a few contrails of high airliners were visible. No rotor slap, so it couldn't be a helo, and no prop whine. So probably not a drone. Must be a truck coming up the road.

He turned and limped between white trunks of aspen. "Quick. Follow me." Another twenty meters and he knelt behind a bleached rock. He didn't know what to expect. Even if it was just a utility truck, climbing the mountain to work on the radio towers, he wouldn't flag it down. They'd come so far he wouldn't chance it now. Operatives could be disguised as anything, including electricians.

Lori gazed over the rock next to him. "We should keep moving. Who cares what comes up the trail? Another half hour and we can be inside the base."

Thin slices of the road were still visible between the trees. Trodden grass marked their path from the aspens. The motor echoed louder. Among the peaks and cliffs, sound direction was difficult to determine.

Penny slipped her hand inside his own. Her fingers were crusted in brown dirt, and the purple nail polish was half scraped from her thumbnail.

"Let's take a breather here," he said. "Stay low. Once whatever passes, we'll get moving again."

Tires crunched over gravel just beyond the aspen curtain. Yellow flashed between the tree trunks as a vehicle braked to a halt. Had the driver seen their brushed path across the road?

Red drew his Sig from under his shoulder, and Lori aimed her .357 toward the aspen, crouching and resting a wrist upon the boulder. Hinges growled as doors creaked open. He thought he made out a pickup, but trunks and leaves blocked clear sight.

"Mr. Harmon!" shouted a male voice, intonation young. "Mr. Harmon! I am Special Agent Stump with the FBI, out of the Denver field office. We're here to get you to safety."

Like hell. *Stump?* What self-respecting agent would keep a name like that? He ought to shoot the bastard just for not making up a better alias.

"Mr. Harmon. My instructions are to take you and your family to the Twenty-First Security Forces Squadron at Peterson Air Force Base, where you will be met by members of your unit, reunited with the rest of your family, debriefed, and carried home."

Red glanced at Lori. "This guy's a fake. He's not asking for authentication."

Lori curled her lip in a confused look.

"There's a protocol to this. A rescue team asks for an authentication word, to make sure they're not picking up an enemy."

Lori spoke in a hushed whisper. "These guys are FBI, not pararescue. They don't know your exfil secret handshake."

"Mr. Harmon, I know you can hear me. You were taped on security video at Pikes Peak. The man you shot was a fugitive of the FBI, so we were called in. In an effort to identify you, our agency sent the video to other government offices and your organization contacted us. We've been tracking your movements by thermal imaging drone for the last hour. That's why we're here, and how we know you're just inside these trees. Please, let us help."

Lori shrugged. "The Det probably didn't even think of giving them your code word."

For a split second, he caught the glow of a phone screen between trunks. The man seemed to be walking away from the truck. "If he comes any farther, they might be trying to flank us," he whispered.

Lori's breath was hot on his cheek. "Friend or foe, they know where we're at."

"I can't outrun them, but you and Penny can."

"Mrs. Harmon, I have your supervisor, Stacy Giles, on the phone. She can vouch for us." Dry leaves crunched as Stump walked toward them. "I'm going to leave it just inside the trees here. You can talk with her. Then we can get going."

Stump stepped slowly through the aspens, hands raised. In one palm was a small gold shield, his creds. In the other a phone. He wore tight blue jeans with cowboy boots and a brown T-shirt. Must've been called in on short notice. Even with the two-inch heel, the man barely broke five feet. Red wasn't even as tall as Lori, but Stump would never have made agent if the FBI still enforced a height requirement. A wedding band encircled his ring finger. If he was for real, this guy should've taken his wife's name. Red kept the blade of his front sight in the middle of Stump's chest.

Just inside the line of trees the agent gently placed the phone upon the grass, then turned and stepped back toward the road. Red stared at narrow openings in the trees, ensuring both men were next to the truck. Yoga had been tracking them by thermal image. Commercial drones with the technology were readily available, used for wildlife surveys. If these guys were operatives, they could've dropped off an entire team just up the road. They could be encircling them now. Maybe Stump was stalling while an ambush closed in.

Red glanced about, but couldn't see more than a hundred feet in any direction through the scrub oak and aspens. A flash of black jeans toward the truck and Lori was running to the phone, bent low. She snatched it from the grass and ran back behind the boulder.

"That was stupid!" he snapped.

She put the phone to her ear. "He knew my boss's name. It's worth the risk." Red flashed his gaze around the perimeter. Still nothing.

Lori crouched behind the rock. "Stacy?... Yes, we're OK. Red's OK too.... Listen, this Agent Stump... OK." She gave a thumbs-up, and Penny silently clapped her hands. Lori held up a finger. "One more thing. Last month's surveillance on Abu Sayyaf in Canada. What was the transaction amount we tracked?"

Impressive. Even if she recognized her supervisor's voice, she was validating her identity. If Mossad was behind the operatives chasing them, they could have the intelligence and resources to impersonate her boss. The technology to accurately mimic a voice had been around for a decade. But one couldn't pretend to know a transaction amount that only Lori and her boss would remember.

She pressed END and blew a sigh. "Stump's for real."

"Can I shoot him anyway?"

Lori stood and cupped her hands next to her mouth like a bullhorn. "We're coming out!" She gripped Penny's wrist and started around the rock.

Red hurried to take lead, pistol still in his grasp but hanging beside him. Too much had gone wrong to drop all defenses now. He squinted at the sun, the burned creases in his forehead stiff as cardboard. As he wove through the aspens, a breeze cooled his cheek. Stump was standing in front of a yellow Nissan SUV, a stick-figured family on the side window indicated the driver had four kids, two cats, and a dog. Must be the agent's private vehicle.

Another man, dark black skin, taller and bulkier than Stump, stood in sandals and cargo shorts near the rear of the vehicle. Not the size of the Jamaican, but his eyes were just as bright white. He stepped closer and stretched an arm to the three of them, bottles of water in his grasp. The safety seal cracked when Red twisted off the top.

Sandals shrugged off a gray backpack. "I'm a medic. Anyone injured?" Slight Southern accent. Georgia maybe.

Penny was chugging her bottle. Water spilled from her lips as she pointed to Red. "Dad got shot in the butt."

Red took a swig, keeping an eye on Stump. "I'm OK till we get to Peterson."

"Mind if I take a look?" Sandals stepped closer.

Red raised his pistol to the man's face. "I said we're all OK till we get to Peterson. Where are your creds?"

Sandals' hands went up, but he didn't flinch. This wasn't the first time a man had a weapon trained on him.

"Red!" Lori yelled. "His badge is on his belt. These guys are here to help."

Sandals slowly turned sideways, pointing down with one finger to a shiny eagle atop a shield clipped to his waist. How'd he miss that? It had only been two days since ascending Pikes Peak, but it felt like a week. No sleep. A long hike. He'd been through worse, but fatigue was starting to dull his mind.

Maybe these guys were for real. Maybe they *were* going to take his family to Peterson Air Force Base. And the Det would have them on a plane in hours. Like breaching a locked door, you never knew what to expect on the other side. But to get through, you had to expose yourself. He lowered his pistol.

* * * *

Penny studied the white-lined stick figures of people on the window of the yellow truck. She'd told Mom and Dad they should get some like it for their car. Her family was big enough, and she was the oldest. Jackson and Nick were a lot younger. But Mr. Stump's family was bigger. Four kids, not three. The tiny outline of two cats and dog stood next to the youngest. She'd asked her parents for a cat before, but Dad had just laughed. He hated cats, or pretended to. And Mom had said maybe, now that they'd moved "out into the boonies," as she liked to call it. Penny missed having neighbors close like at their old house, but enjoyed the dream of putting up a fence around their huge backyard and buying a horse. Now would be a good time to ask Mom and Dad for a cat. Or maybe a horse, and they'd settle for a kitten.

The smallest kid's stick figure had a dress. She was the only one. Poor girl, having three older brothers. Penny had it bad enough, with two younger ones. At least she could tell them what to do.

Mr. Stump had his phone to his ear. He opened the driver's door and sat behind the wheel. "Let's get you guys outta here. Sorry for the mess on the floor. They called me down from Denver stat, and I was already in Castle Rock, so I just came in what I was driving. You can throw anything in the way into the back."

The man who'd given the water opened a rear door. A doctor. "After you, ladies," he said with a smile. His teeth were so white they looked like dentures. Mom crawled in with a sigh, tossing a Mimi dolly off the seat.

Penny had accumulated a hoard of Mimis when she was little. Even though she'd outgrown them, she'd never mustered the strength to throw away her collection, and never knew any other five-year-olds who liked them enough to want to adopt them. Maybe Mr. Stump's kid would want them. Should she interrupt him? He didn't look like he was talking on the phone, only listening. "Would your daughter like some Mimi dolls? I've got a bunch that—"

His ears twitched when he smiled. "That's sweet. You don't need to do that. But I'm sure she'd enjoy talking to you about them."

"How old is she?"

His eyes cut back and forth, like he was listening to the phone. "About your age. Ten maybe. She's crazy about those things."

Penny pasted her best smile, trying hard not to laugh. Was he trying to be funny? No one her age would be caught dead with a Mimi. They'd be teased the rest of their life. That was why she was trying to get rid of them in the first place. Mr. Stump put a finger to his ear and bent his neck, now clearly concentrating on listening to the phone.

As she slid across, she noticed a booster seat in the back cargo area. But the stickers on the window showed Mr. Stump's girl was the youngest. No one Penny's age would need a booster seat.

A knot tightened in her stomach. What had Dad said when he was teaching her to stop, look, and listen? He'd shared his story about how he and his team had stumbled through the woods blindfolded. How he'd learned he'd taken sounds for granted. *Listen for anything that doesn't fit*, he'd said. The white cloth face of Anna, a baby Mimi lying on the floor, was stretched wide in her perpetual cry.

Penny cupped her hands around Mom's ear.

* * * *

Scrugs centered the crosshairs of his scope on the short man's center of mass, the one sitting behind the steering wheel. Who the hell were these guys? And why would Red just let his family get in an SUV with them? Were they using some alien mind control trick? They'd take 'em to the underground bunker out west of Woodland Park, and let the ETs erase their memory. Either way, he couldn't shoot now. The 14.5-millimeter bullet would go clear through the short guy, his seat, Red's little girl behind him, and on out the back without even changing its trajectory. If he was going to take a shot, no one could be behind his target.

Another glance to Red. It was him all right. His copper beard shone in the high sun. His limp wasn't as bad Lam said it would be, but still noticeable.

Scrugs whistled a silent catcall when he glimpsed the wife. Tall and thin, though her blond hair frizzed wildly in the dry Colorado air. The knees of her jeans were caked with pinkish dust and an elbow stuck out a tear in her white blouse. She bent her neck and slipped into the backseat of the Nissan.

The little girl held herself tall, shoulders back. A spitfire for sure. Scrugs still couldn't believe Lam's story how she'd saved her dad. Sounded like she had more vigor than a billy goat after a spring thundershower.

What the…? The wife was opening the SUV's door. But slowly. She gripped her daughter by the hand. It was as if she was trying to sneak out. Why? The short guy wasn't making any threatening moves.

Oh-oh. The driver peeked behind, then hopped out himself, hand on the grip of a stainless revolver. He held the pistol to his side, where the wife couldn't see it. But Scrugs had caught its glint as the man stepped from the vehicle. The FBI didn't carry revolvers. Must be a US Marshal, or some local law enforcement helping in the search. Maybe a game warden. Be nice to shoot one of them.

Scrugs reached into his backpack and snatched a palm-sized device that looked like a mini video recorder. He held the laser rangefinder to his eyes and pressed a black button on top. Eight hundred sixty-eight yards. His bullet would be traveling around three thousand feet per second. A little less than one second airtime to reach the short man. The steel nuts he'd dropped a few minutes ago had taken three seconds to hit the ground and had moved six feet perpendicular to his shot. Two feet horizontal for every second in the air. Approximately.

He reached atop his scope and twisted the elevation knob three notches to adjust for distance, then reversed it two of the clicks when he considered he was seated several hundred feet higher than his target. *This is such a guessing game with so many variables.*

The wife shut her door. Shorty slipped his pistol from his belt. A quick glance to Red, and Scrugs saw the other guy had him looking at a piece of paper, maybe a map, distracting him. Shorty cocked the hammer, then motioned with the pistol for the wife to get back in.

Scrugs had no shot. The bullet would have to go through the driver's opened door, then Shorty. But the wife was behind the man. He might even hit her daughter as well.

He waved his hand as if she could see him from this distance. *Move, lady! Get the hell out of the way!* Scrugs aimed at the center of the man's back, then moved the crosshairs two feet to the side. The breeze was steady, so that should be about right. But still no clear shot. The Motorola clipped to his vest squawked, but he ignored its chatter. He gently squeezed the trigger till it rested against the break point. Exhaled most his breath, then held it. The crosshairs rose and fell each second with the beat of his heart, dropping back to level with his target's center of mass. The mother took a step back toward the SUV. Her ankle twisted on a rock, and she fell to the ground. Her daughter dropped beside her. A beat, and the crosshairs leveled. Scrugs pulled the trigger.

Chapter 27

Mimis

The cold water cooled Red's throat as he tipped the clear bottle and took another swig. He sighed in relief now that the family was finally headed out of the forest. His shoulders hung with fatigue. Drowsiness weighed on him, as if he were drugged. He shifted weight from his aching leg and leaned on the walking stick. Then stretched his neck side to side, fighting the exhaustion. Couldn't let himself relax. They needed to get moving. He stuck his head inside the passenger window to see if the keys were in the ignition. He should just drive them out.

Sandals, the medic, pointed a long, bent finger at the center of a folded topography map, calling Red's attention to it. The faint green terrain lines gathered tightly, almost into a single fat mark that defined the steep border of the Front Range of the mountains. Just beyond the gorge toward which the family had been headed.

Sandals moved his finger along a squiggly blue line. "We're right about here. Fastest way out is…" He stooped and spread the paper onto the ground, unfolding it to follow the line further. Another gust shook the trees and blew a puff of dust behind the truck. The wind cooled Red's skin as it whistled through aspen leaves.

Just like the breeze as he'd snuck up behind Yoga.

A door of the SUV clicked open, and in Red's periphery Lori stepped from the far side of the vehicle. With their low water intake, she probably had to stretch out a leg cramp.

"We'll head out to Route 67 here and..." The medic was trying to call his attention back to the map.

They needed to get on the road. Red knew where they were going. They had to travel all the way around the mountain to get to Colorado Springs. Why'd this guy care about explaining it to him? What Red really needed to do was call his sister, to let her know the family was OK. She'd be worried terribly by now, not having heard from them since heading up on the Pikes Peak Cog Railway early yesterday morning. And Jackson and Nick. They'd be inconsolable. He held out a hand to the kneeling man. "Need your phone."

He glanced back to the SUV, and *crack!* The driver's-side door slammed against Stump in the bright flash of a fireball. It knocked him to the ground behind the vehicle. Lori and Penny were nowhere in sight. The breeze carried the scent of burnt metal. The shot had been an armor-piercing, incendiary round. Trajectory from the east, near the gully.

He stepped toward the SUV. Lori sat on the far side of the road, holding her ankle, mouth agape, staring at a writhing Stump in disbelief. The man clutched hands over his sternum, pulling deep breaths. A sucking chest wound gurgled between his fingers. If some sniper had just hit Stump, Lori'd be next. He waved an arm at her. "Get off the road!"

She clutched Penny's wrist and scrambled across the trail, slipping between a short holly and a dead pine trunk. Red glimpsed Sandals, reflection in the rear window of the SUV, raising his pistol to the back of Red's skull. Red ducked, and the shot shattered the pane. Red swung his walking stick and struck the weapon, but Sandals' grasp remained firm. Another rapid strike and the stick smashed into the man's knee. With both hands Red gripped Sandals' wrist and pulled it across his body, straining to keep the weapon pointed away. He swept his leg in a tight circle and managed to trip the man. They both fell to the ground behind trees, Red atop his arm, pinning the weapon, still aimed away. At least they'd be out of the sniper's sight.

Sandals' wide smile now an angry glower. Did he think Red had something to do with the shooter? "I didn't do it!" Red hollered. "We need to get undercover or we'll be next."

Sandals wound up and punched his ribs with his free arm. A powerful blow. But Red didn't dare let go of his hold. The medic cocked his fist and beat him again and again. With each strike, he grunted. "You... just...won't...die!"

This man wasn't confused. He meant to kill him!

Red couldn't reach his own weapon under his sweater without releasing the pinned arm. He smashed his forehead against Sandals' face, but the punches kept coming. One to the kidney sent fire down his legs. He bit Sandals' nose till cartilage snapped and warm blood filled his mouth. The man jerked his face away, and Red spat the severed chunk back at his eye. Sandals screamed and reached above his head, fingers combing the ground. A black hunting knife lay in the dust. Must've dropped from Sandals' belt earlier. The blade glinted as his fingers wrapped around the handle.

Not good.

Red released his grasp, rolled away, and sprung up. Snatching his walking stick, he brought it down hard on the man's forearm as he raised the pistol. The crack of bone, and the weapon fell to the ground. Before Red could kick it away, Sandals lunged with the knife. Red dodged the thrust, but the man's arms were at least six inches longer than his own. His attacks were quick as Yoga's, but with the extra reach, Red barely stayed out of the blade's path. One slashed into his thigh. He spun away and swung the stick across Sandals' back, sending him sprawling onto the SUV's hood. Two rapid blows to the neck and head, and the medic dropped, eyes rolled up, convulsing.

Red dove behind a thick pine trunk and yanked out his own weapon. Why hadn't the sniper tried to shoot him too? Was Stump one of the enemy operatives, or had he just taken a bullet meant for Sandals? Or Red? Or both? Was the sniper an FBI asset, trying to protect Lori? But why would he kill Stump, if Stump was FBI? Maybe the sniper was—

Hell, this wouldn't get him anywhere. Bottom line: there was a marksman with a big-ass rifle and Lori or Red were his next target.

A glance up and, shit. API ammo could pass clear through the pine trunk he lay behind. He rolled toward the woods and crept up behind the same thick, black rock he'd knelt behind earlier. Lori was in clear view now, across the road. No sight of Penny. Must be huddled in the grass clumps behind her. He caught Lori's eye, and they both glanced at Stump. A puddle of crimson grew beneath his shoulders. His eyes lay wide open, staring toward high wisps of cloud. Breath came in shallow gasps.

But Red dared not try and drag him to safety or he'd get shot himself. The haunting, acrid scent of burning flesh. Earth and seared skin. The incendiary round would have partially cauterized the wound channel. The man could live, but not likely.

Sandals lay ten feet away. The medic had stopped convulsing and would wake any minute now. Red cursed as he glimpsed the man's pistol underneath the SUV. He'd have to shoot him if he woke and rolled for it.

Stump's chest fell, but didn't rise again.

Gravel crunched in the distance under heavy steps. "Red!"

A familiar voice, but who? Lori pointed to her own eyes, then down the road in the direction of the sound. She eased her pistol up, over the boulder. Her position was well concealed by the tall stalks of blue-green grass.

The steps came faster now. "Red! You OK? It's Lam." A flash of recognition and Red held up a hand to Lori, shaking his head. He peeked around the edge of the black rock. A man jogged toward them, fifty meters away, dark brown shirt with JEEP in light-colored block letters. One arm was in the same sling Red had hurriedly tied together early the previous night. With his other he gripped a bolt-action rifle slung around his neck, stock wedged so tightly into his armpit the weapon stuck out straight, ready to shoot.

Was Lam an enemy operative? Had he shot Stump? No. Not with that hunting rifle at least. He could've killed Red anytime last night. Red waved a hand in the air, and Lam slid to a halt. He stuck his head out the rest of the way so the mechanic had a clear view, but kept his body behind the cover of the black boulder.

"What's going on, Lam?" He glanced to his rifle. "Mind aiming that thing away? Why you shooting federal agents?"

Lam pointed the weapon at the road. A Remington 700 of some variety. He glanced behind, nodding toward one of the radio towers. "I didn't take the shot. That was Scrugs, a friend of mine. And these aren't federal agents."

"How you know?"

Moving slowly, Lam pulled out a black handheld two-way the size of a brick from his arm sling. "Two FBI agents were killed on Beaver Valley Road earlier. Report came across the radio just a few minutes ago. Report said one victim's personal vehicle was stolen, a yellow Nissan SUV." Lam pointed the antenna of the two-way at Stump. "When that guy started waving a pistol at your daughter and wife, Scrugs took the shot."

"Just like that? Little man pulls a gun and your buddy takes him out?"

Lam nodded. "Just like that. Guy's cracked. Don't need much encouragement to pull a trigger."

Story was too crazy to be made up. Red slipped out and stepped toward him, pistol still in a firm grip.

The receiver in the mechanic's hand crackled with static. "*Everything OK, Lam? This Red fella gonna go apeshit on ya?*"

A corner of Lam's mouth curled as he lifted the device to his mouth. Red's grip on his pistol tightened, knowing the distant sniper's X was on his chest, but he forced a deep breath and slipped his weapon beneath his belt.

"No. We're good. Thanks, buddy. Unless you see any other vehicles from up there, you can stand down. We'll call the feds, so get that cannon of yours hidden in the bed of my truck."

Red trotted over to Stump and put two fingers to his neck. No pulse. The exit wound in his chest was at least a half inch across. The brown T-shirt well stained, though blood no longer welled from the hole.

A groan from Sandals. His foot twitched. Lam knelt on the man's back as Red rooted through the trunk's contents. He grabbed jumper cables from beneath the rear seat and tied the operative's wrists and ankles. Lori stepped onto the road from behind the grassy cover, gripping Penny's hand. She slipped up behind Red and peered down at the tied operative, then drew her husband into a hug.

"You did good," she said. "We got a live one. Maybe we'll figure this thing out yet."

Red smiled and turned toward his friend. "Lori, this is—"

"*Lam!*" Penny hollered. She ran over and wrapped her arms around the mechanic's waist, smiling and gazing at the man's sweaty, unshaven face. "I told Mom that short guy wasn't real. He was lying about the Mimi doll. Ten-year-olds don't do Mimis."

Another groan from Sandals. He lifted his head from the gravel, then dropped it again. His eyes focused in growing awareness.

Lam tousled Penny's hair. "Well, my daughter Jessica, she's a little younger than you, and even she told me a while back she was too old for Mimis anymore."

Red frowned. *What the hell's a Mimi?*

Lam glanced at him, to Penny, then the tied man. He jerked a thumb over his shoulder like a hitchhiker, pointing toward a log lying beside the road. Enough distance to be out of earshot.

Red nodded.

Lam bent and grabbed Sandals' black knife from the gravel, a straight blade with green paracord wrapped around the hilt. Red felt his stomach tense, but Lam only held it out, handle first. "That man put up an awful fight," he said, winking. "Got himself beat to hell. Lost a lot of blood. May not make it. Might need this to cut bandages." The mechanic slipped Penny's hand into his own. "My arm's hurtin' bad. I see a log up there we can sit at. Why don't you come and tell me all about it, what you did since last night. Your dad and mom need to talk to this fella alone for a bit, before we get driving."

Chapter 28

Pink Pantsuit

Red flashed a US Marshals star to a pale kid with slicked hair and a rosy pimpled neck. The guy must've shaved with a rusty blade. The Geeks on Wheels look-alike studied his badge. Red grazed his two-week-old bullet wound returning his wallet to his back pocket. The flesh had knitted and the hole was covered with a mound of new, tender skin. But he could even walk without a limp now when he concentrated. The slash on his leg had not proven to be deep and was almost completely healed.

Carter planted himself in front of the security guard's desk and flipped open his wallet also, holding an ID in front of Rusty Blade's forehead. As he stood in the middle of the glass-walled foyer, his pressed pants hung crisply down to shiny brown shoes. He looked like the suit displayed on the cover of the *Men's Health* magazine beneath Rusty Blade's coffee cup.

Red grabbed a Jolly Rancher from a crystal bowl on the counter, twisted, and popped the candy in his mouth. He shoved the wrapper in his jeans pocket. Sour Granny Smith apple, a favorite.

Neither of their IDs would do any good here at Merkel Research in Fairfax, Virginia. The building warranted enough CCTVs and security guards to shame the Pentagon. Though it operated as a political think tank for select clients, the primary effort that occupied its employees was financial intelligence for the CIA. If you didn't carry a Merkel ID, you didn't get in without an invitation.

Red shoved the candy into a cheek. "Lori Harmon and Stacy Giles. They're expecting us."

Rusty Blade placed a black handset to his ear and punched a button. "Your guests are here.... Right." He hung up and pointed down a hallway to a door with MECHANICAL ROOM stenciled in red. "Remove all metal objects, everything, and place them in the cabinets in there."

Both men stepped inside the closet, a narrow locker room. Damn tight spaces. How could anyone stand working in even smaller offices? Trapped like a fish in a bowl.

He placed his Sig Sauer in the bottom of one cubby next to his five-inch Spyderco folding knife. Both seemed to whimper as he withdrew his hand, like a pair of puppies left at a pound. He glanced down and tugged up on his fly. Felt naked.

Carter unclipped his shoulder holster and placed it in a locker next to his belt on the opposite side of the room, slamming the door. "Still can't believe you beat that operative to an inch of his life."

Red and Lori had interrogated Sandals using limbs, stakes, and clubs. Brutal, but two days of running for their lives through Pikes Peak National Forest trying to keep their family from being shot had numbed any sympathy for the man. It had taken fifteen minutes of torture, but the mercenary didn't know who had placed the contract on Lori. Typical among such teams. You can't leak what you don't know. Then Lori had torn open the man's pants, placed his own blade on his scrotum, and threatened to castrate him if he didn't provide the bank name and account where his advance pay for the hit had been deposited. Wet teams were usually paid half up front, half upon job completion. Though Red hadn't understood at the time, she'd later explained she could follow the money back to its source and maybe figure out who was behind it.

Red closed the cabinet door. That must've been what this meeting was about. Stacy Giles, Lori's supervisor, had called Carter a few hours earlier, requesting a face-to-face.

The walls of the closet leaned in, as if the lockers would crash down upon him. He stepped outside the door and drew a deep breath. Turning back to Carter, still fiddling with something in a locker, he said, "Maybe Stacy and Lori figured out who went after us in Colorado."

Carter had been right about one thing. Detective work was boring. And slow. In the two weeks following the event, the CIA and the FBI had been mute regarding any progress as to who was behind the incident. Red would ask Lori every day, and even she would only reply, "Nothing yet. My boss is still working on it." How long did it take to lookup a few bank transactions in a computer?

Carter stepped out, and a crew-cut blond man in jeans and red T-shirt waved them to follow. He walked with his neck hunched forward, the nape well tanned, rocking with the familiar packhorse swagger that evidenced his back was familiar with a rucksack. Carter stepped into a millimeter wave scanning stall, like the machines at an airport. Holding hands over his head, his pants dropped to his thighs.

Rucksack motioned to Red next. *Here goes. Never get through one of these things without a strip search.*

The scan complete, Rucksack stared at a monitor, scowling. "What the hell? You got more metal in you than a machine shop." The man stepped close and patted Red's elbow and thigh.

He winced when fingers pressed the still-tender slice from Sandals' blade. He'd learned to not offer an explanation for the titanium plates and screws unless asked.

"I'll bet TSA blows an aneurism every time you try to board a plane." Rucksack escorted them to the fifth floor and, with a half smile, left them in a glass-walled conference room overlooking University Drive. Two blocks down, blue lights flashed in the middle of an intersection, blocking traffic. Every few minutes, Carter pulled up on his belt loops.

A minute later, the door opened and a brunette with shoulder-length ebony-black hair, standing no taller than Red, stepped inside. Pink slacks and suit top looked to be designer threads that Carter would appreciate. Like the ones worn by braless models on the glossy magazine covers in the checkout racks at the grocery store. Her eyelids were brushed a cobalt blue and her fingernails matched, the exact same shade as the tips of armor-piercing rounds. Nice touch. Cherry lipstick drew into a creased smile. Her scent was of roses, the same perfume Red's grandmother had worn. Must've come back in style. Overall, a well put together professional. But her expression hardened when she glanced his direction. She studied him with detached coldness. Like Carter every morning when he glanced at Red's jeans and L. L. Bean commando sweater, or whatever other fashion faux pas he'd committed that day.

Carter broke the silence. "Stacy, this is Red Harmon, Lori's other half."

The lines in her face disappeared as she turned to Carter and grinned. How did that man get on every woman's good side? He'd just smile and say something witty and they'd shove their tits into his face. "Thanks for coming, Detective. But I only invited you."

* * * *

Carter caught Stacy's gaze, willing himself to not gawk at the woman's neon pantsuit. *My goodness, have the nineties come back in style, or has she just never left them? And what the hell is up with the bright blue nails?* Like she'd been finger painting and forgotten to wash her hands. She'd clearly expressed animosity for Red while shooting clay pigeons, but never given Carter a reason. Now, she'd not even tried to shade her scorn. "Red's here at my request."

She squinted, but pulled out a chair at a cheap maple veneer conference table. Carter yanked up on his pants and did the same. Red sat across from her and leaned elbows on the table. Was he goading her? Carter had told him to keep his mouth shut. Hopefully he'd listen.

Stacy brushed the table surface with her fingertips as if she were petting a cat, blue dots swirling on a sand-colored sea. It didn't appear to be a nervous tell. She was considering her words. She'd been fair when he'd dropped in with Grind for questions at her home. She deserved the benefit of the doubt.

Carter sat back and unbuttoned his jacket. He glanced at his watch. "You called me. You have information or need my help? Which is it?"

Her fingers froze. She smirked. "I thought we'd be a team on this, Detective. I told you that investigating Senator Moses had been a pet project of mine for years now." She glanced up at Red, as if trying to read his expression. To his credit, he gave nothing.

"That's not the way I remember it. I'm grateful for your advice, but we didn't strike any deal." He and Grind had been rather eager to leave her home that day. Had he missed an unspoken cue?

Flashing blue and red lights reflected off her eyes. An ambulance must have arrived outside. "I thought it was clear enough. I help you. You help me. Who to allow in. Who to leave out." Her gaze lifted to Red again with that last statement.

Why'd this woman have such an ax to grind with his friend? "Red has just as much at stake as Lori. If we've got some sort of deal here, he's a part of it."

Red opened his mouth for the first time. "Where's Lori? Thought she'd be here."

Stacy turned her chair to Carter. "You discovered something about Senator Moses and didn't let me know. Let's hear it."

That answers one question. She wants to be on the receiving end. But how'd she hear he'd made progress in his investigation? Red must've mentioned something to Lori. "First, Red told me you validated the identity of one of the operatives chasing Red and Lori. One Agent Stump, I believe.

As you know, he wasn't with the FBI. Which raises the question of whose side you're on."

Stacy pinched the bridge of her nose. "I never validated his identity. How the hell would I do that in such a short amount of time? The FBI had so many assets on-site, they didn't even know which end was up. I simply told her there were several agencies engaged in search and rescue. She jumped to conclusions."

Plausible. But Lori wasn't there to confirm. Still... "We received authorization to tap the senator's phones and monitor his home network. His computers."

Stacy started to pet the cat again. "A formality. To legitimize your previously illegal eavesdropping."

He'd not even mentioned that to Red. If something had gone wrong with the unlawful taps, he wanted him to have plausible deniability. Where was this woman getting her information? She was taunting him, hanging it over his head, but to what end? "You can appreciate the need to protect an investigation's integrity. We've recently gathered damning evidence."

White lights flashed in her eyes. "You've linked him to what happened on Pikes Peak?"

That came out of nowhere. Was she making fun of him? "No. I've got lesser charges wrapped tight. I've got other evidence we're still wading through of a more significant nature. National security type of accusations. If my hunch proves correct, it could get him a lethal injection, though I doubt he'd ever receive it." He wasn't going to elaborate on the list of operators and CIA assets he suspected Moses was peddling to the highest bidder. Her bottom lip seemed to stick out. Was she trying to pout? "I can give more, but this deal of yours looks one-sided at this point. Why should I share with you?"

She stood and strode to the far end of the room, bell-bottoms brushing her ankles. That suit belonged in a museum. The cheap leather of her shoes creaked. But she didn't rise to her position in the CIA by being a fashion expert. She was sharp as hell. Maybe the clothes were a distraction to cover something else. But what?

Reaching into a mini fridge tucked inside a credenza, she pulled out a bottle of water, offering one to Carter as well. He lifted a hand in a *no thank you*. She twisted the cap. "When I was young, my grandma came to live with us. She set her watch by Lawrence Welk and Paul Harvey." She tipped up the bottle. "Ever heard of him? He had a radio show where he told *The Rest of the Story*. That's what I've got. The rest of your story."

She placed the half-empty bottle on the table. Red lipstick was smudged around the threads. She licked a droplet from the corner of her mouth. "Let's cut the shit. You are now in possession of evidence that implicates Senator Moses with money laundering in support of his political campaigns. If you're good as I think you are, it'll stand up in court. Big deal. This lethal injection stuff?" She tapped her middle finger hard onto the table. "I want in on it. We need to know if it ties in with what I've discovered."

Whatever. Take, take, take. Carter was starting to feel sorry for Skinny, if that was in fact her significant other. He stared at her chin because her eyeshadow was too distracting, but clamped his lips shut. He'd wait her out.

Finally, she said, "The rest of the story is that I've made significant strides into tracking who funded the wet team that came after Lori."

Red, covering his mouth in a yawn, stiffened and dropped his hand. He opened his lips, but Carter cut him off. "Go on."

Another swig. She was really playing this up. Teasing. Had this woman ever even consummated her marriage?

Then: "Lori told me how she disclosed to you our 'back door' with Mossad, an unofficial exchange of financial intelligence, and how it had gone silent a while ago. Tracking that almost-dead operative's bank transfer has proven to be a challenge, but we did it. With seventy-six percent certainty, it originated with an account controlled by Mossad." She waved a hand in a rolling motion. "It's covered by several layers of corporations, bureaucracy, and old-fashioned friendship, but it's controlled by them nonetheless."

Red had done well staying quiet, Carter mused. But now his face was so flushed his beard appeared blond. With a clenched fist, he blurted, "Who? We can take care of him."

Another swig. "That's just it. We don't know. It certainly wasn't an officially sanctioned event. We work too closely with them. We're valuable. It was an individual. Someone working on their own."

"Then tell Mossad about it. They could find out who authorized the payment."

"Yes, but you're assuming they'd take care of it *and* that we've got nothing to lose. By informing them, we'd be broadcasting we've been spying on their financials for decades. Not good form to tell your neighbor you've been gazing through their bedroom window."

Red stood and leaned over the table, as if he were going to crawl across it. "This is my family we're talking about. I don't care if—"

Carter grabbed his arm, and Red froze, then sat back down. Stacy took another swig and said, "To hell with your family. This is bigger than you. Your peep sight view of the world doesn't cut it when it comes to larger issues of national security." She aimed the bottle at Carter. "This is why I don't like operators. They've got one hammer, and everything's a nail."

Carter had never seen Red angry, but now his eyes glowed bloodshot. He wanted to chew this woman's face like Hannibal Lecter. "At least we get things done." he growled.

Stacy stood this time, planting fingers like roots onto the table. She leaned across it. Droplets of spittle sprayed the air as she spat, "Your organization *getting things done* has destroyed years' worth of asset building! Have you ever considered that sometimes it's better to leave your targets intact? That maybe other organizations have plants deep undercover? People we've been working half a decade to turn? Then they get thanked with your bullet through their skull. After that, you know how difficult it is to rebuild? Your op in North Korea accomplished nothing!"

That's what this was all about.

Red gripped the armrests. "It wasn't for nothing. We plugged a hole. One from inside *your* organization."

"My organization? The kind detective hasn't informed you the list is back on the market?" She glanced at Carter.

Red's eyes narrowed. "Huh?"

Stacy leaned back and crossed her arms, as if appraising a piece of art. "Yeah. All that work you went through. The insertion. The op. The exfil. All of it was a temporary fix. Your name and ugly mugshot, along with countless others like you, plus CIA agents, handlers, and informants. Worst intel breach in our history, back on the market. You accomplished *nothing.*"

Red sank into his chair, eyes dashing back and forth, trying to absorb the blow. "Our op plugged the hole. We fixed all that." Both glanced at Carter.

Carter's gut knotted. He stifled a grunt. How the hell did she know this? He'd kept a tight lid on his investigation. Only a few people even knew about it, and only two knew of his suspicions that Moses was about to sell the list. *She's bluffing.* He scratched his nose. "And where are you getting this from?"

Stacy's blue-domed eyelids glittered in a beam of sunlight. "From you! Just now." She stomped to the fridge and grabbed another bottle. "You play the cool detective, all poker faced. But your pupils just dilated like you were high on weed when I mentioned that. An involuntary response. If that hadn't worked, I'm monitoring your heart rate through your seat. I'd only suspected it before, but thanks for the confirmation." She tipped up the bottle. "See how fun interdepartmental sharing can be?" A coy smirk. "I'm getting goose bumps."

This woman was whacked. Either that, or she was one of the best interrogators Carter had ever seen.

Red rubbed the back of his skull, his face curled in doubt. "Carter?"

"We'll talk later, Red." He pointed to Stacy, taking another swig. The woman was going to have to pee soon. He needed to think. To regroup. But first: "So, how does this fit in with your Heavy Paul guy?"

Stacy wagged a finger as she drank. More lights flashed across the back wall. A fire truck's siren screamed. "Paul Harvey. It's the rest of the story. You've got evidence Moses laundered money. I've got evidence someone in Mossad sent a wet team after Lori. The two have to be linked. I'm going to use Lori as bait to draw out who in Mossad is responsible."

Red was already shaking his head. "Over my dead body. Not gonna happen."

Stacy held up her bottle in a cheers. "Too late, little man." She flipped her wrist, checking her watch. "She's on a flight to Jerusalem. A thousand miles over the Atlantic as we speak."

Chapter 29

Ben Gurion Airport

Lori Harmon stepped from the hull of the Boeing 747-400 onto the gray-carpeted jet bridge. She dropped her small black carry-on and extended the handle, pulling the suitcase behind her. Her lower back and neck ached as she made her way into Terminal 3 of Ben Gurion Airport, Tel Aviv, Israel. She'd never mastered the ability to sleep on aircraft, and the eleven-hour flight from JFK had been no exception. Work sprang for a first-class ticket as part of her cover, but her seatmate had been a gregarious young Hasidic Jew who'd gabbed all night long about his thriving fabric trade in Manhattan's garment district. Men in that sect were normally reserved, so at one point she'd suspected him of shaking her down. But his boring, tedious knowledge of fabric dyeing was thorough enough to convince her otherwise—though not quite boring enough to put her to sleep.

The wheels of her carry-on clicked over the tile seams all the way down the terminal, beneath a blue sign in Hebrew and English reading IMMIGRATION with an arrow. Next to it was mounted a black hemisphere, a housing for one of the many CCTVs. The airport was medium sized by modern standards, maybe one-fifth the size of Atlanta's. A stream of passengers spilled from another jet bridge and merged with her own, like salmon joining the stream. Wheels clicked, heels thumped, and chatter rose in Hebrew and English and French and—she cocked her head to listen—a young voice in Arabic with a Syrian accent whined, "Mommy, I'm hungry." The statement was met with a sharp "Hush!"

Spying a green sign of a stick figure wearing a skirt, she veered off from the traffic and slipped into a restroom. At the mirror she flinched when she glimpsed the stranger reflected in it. Her face was cold death. Saddles dark as charcoal beneath her eyes. It was five in the morning East Coast time, twelve noon local. Lori had cut her hair and dyed it black, a nice complement to the sleepy eyes. But the color would stand out much less in this culture. She'd never used much makeup before, but now she unzipped her travel case and pulled out a cosmetics purse. Lifting a brush, she stroked a rosy-beige foundation onto her cheeks, reapplying another layer. It was mixed with microparticles of silver and titanium. The combination played hell with photos and made her cheeks appear inset, almost hollow, tricking facial recognition. With a black kohl pencil, she stenciled dark eyeliner around her lower lid and in an arc near the bridge of her nose. This look was similar to one in a *Jalouse* magazine she'd seen, but the main objective was to make her eyes appear larger and closer together, almost like Japanese manga. Yet another means to throw off facial recognition. She had no way of knowing whether Israel had her image in their database, but with the revelation the wet team had been funded from a bank account controlled by Mossad, she wasn't taking any chances.

Returning her tools to the bag, she studied her work. Black hair, dark makeup, pale skin, tired eyes. A Goth pushing middle age. Maybe she should've opted for a nose ring. Slipping on Prada glasses, she completed the semidisguise. Tony probably wouldn't even recognize her.

She gripped the handle of her case and rejoined the stream, now just a trickle, still swimming toward Customs. He would be fuming, back home. She'd been carrying a draining emotional heaviness all last week, lying to her husband about the office not making any progress determining who was behind the attack at Pikes Peak. But the deceit would be over after this visit. It was for his own good, and for the kids'. She'd told him many times, secrecy was their only ally.

He'd forgive her in the end. It would only be for a few more days, and the kids would barely notice she was gone. She'd left a list taped to the side of the refrigerator with dinner instructions, reminders to get the mail, to complete homework assignments, and to buy a present for a birthday party Nick was invited to. Tony always spoiled the children when she was out. They often appeared vaguely disappointed when she returned. She'd left a separate note for him on his pillow, explaining what little she could: That this trip was the only way to determine what rogue Mossad agent had arranged for her assassination. And that she'd been ordered not to tell anyone about it, or her financial investigation's progress, as a security precaution.

He'd forgive her. He always did. Never angry for long. A few nights of gratuitous sex and it'd all be forgotten. Not that he was as simple as most men, but at his core he trusted her. Knew she was smart as hell and could handle a simple dead drop.

She passed Steimatzky, a bookstore and newsstand with glossy magazine covers in Hebrew and English. She picked one up with a blonde in red heels and orange dress, makeup penciled in a similar manner as her own, though smudged. How'd the editor miss that before sending it to print? Sloppy, like the rogue Mossad agent. Once her mission was complete, someone else would clean up the mess. Kill them. A different department of the CIA would assess the agent's physical health, social habits, and best weaknesses to exploit. Maybe it'd be a heart defect that could plausibly be accelerated. Or a jealous husband. Or one of the most creative she'd known, a Russian oligarch with sleep apnea who, during a business trip to London, had his travel CPAP malfunction. Three men had strapped him down while another agent had held his mouth and nose closed. The best assassination was always an accident. Not the sloppy crap at the top of Pikes Peak.

Lori followed the stream till it jammed into the back of a long line of travelers divided by black-taped barricades. A row of immigration officials sat fifty feet ahead, shaking heads and staring at screens. Her Hasidic garment district friend waved and smiled as he passed, on his way to a much smaller area next to a sign that read CITIZENS OF ISRAEL.

Others filed behind her. She slipped a hand into her pocket and powered up her phone, building her courage against the text she would doubtlessly be receiving from Tony. The device came alive, but no new messages arrived. Strange. As the line shuffled forward, Lori reviewed the plan. The fintel back door with Mossad had suddenly reopened one day last week. Communication came in gushes, but from a different sender. One never knew who was on the other end, but in her opinion the personality was all wrong. Less helpful. Too demanding.

Stacy had told her to drop the blackmail bomb immediately, so Lori had feigned specific knowledge of the rogue Mossad agent behind the failed operation on Pikes Peak. Said she'd tracked the wet team's funding to them. It was a half-truth, much better than an outright lie. A trade would be performed through a dead drop. The old-fashioned kind, nothing electronic. In exchange for ten million dollars and a copy of the written audit trail as proof, she had promised her silence and that any subsequent investigation into the funding source would turn up empty. Her lifeline would be a dead man's switch on the bank transaction audit. That would keep the rogue Mossad agent from trying to kill her in the future. Because if she were to die, after a few weeks a digital repository would notice her absence and it would automatically transmit an encrypted message, one containing the damning evidence, to the director of CIA Financial Intelligence and the FBI Financial Intelligence Center.

The immigration counter was only twenty feet away now. An agent raised a beckoning arm, and the line moved another few steps. She allowed herself a slight smile. The beauty of the plan was that the trumped-up audit report inside a white envelope hidden beneath the lining of her luggage contained falsified account numbers that Stacy monitored constantly. If anyone tried to access them and maintained a connection for more than sixty seconds, the CIA would be able to trace it to the originator's IP address. Sixty seconds was the magic number she'd been told, no matter how many hops the connection contained. If that didn't work, a tiny software tracking bug was a backup, downloaded to the agent's computer when they accessed the account. By the time the agent discovered they'd been duped, it wouldn't matter. The trap would already be sprung.

Each time she thought of it, her eyes burned. This sonofabitch had tried to kill her and Red, and even threatened Penny. Even more, Stacy suspected they were the ones who had been peddling a list of operators and CIA assets. A security breach that would mean lives lost in the field, and would take decades of rebuilding. She fantasized of slipping into the rogue agent's bedroom. A team holding him down while she clamped his mouth and squeezed his nose till his body ceased to struggle, just like how she'd suffocated the Russian oligarch so many years before. But before he'd pass, before slipping into the frantic panic of suffocation and while still cognizant of his impending doom, she'd whisper, "Your mistake was threatening my family." However, she was no longer a field asset. Fintel analysts didn't do things like that. Not most.

* * * *

Someone nudged Red's shoulder. Then again. He opened his eyes, yawned, and found he was staring at the back of a blue airline seat. His cheek rested on one palm, and drool ran down his wrist. He wiped it away, trying to appear casual.

Another nudge.

It was a thin woman in the seat next to him, gray hair pulled up into a twisted bagel atop her head. Her eyebrows were raised expectantly. "We've landed," she said on a faint gust of garlic breath. "You were out almost the entire flight."

Red stood and stretched, nearly whacking a man in madras plaid shorts across the aisle. Commercial coach was definitely the way to go. All his prior overseas flights had been on Det business, so he'd traveled in the back of a C-17 or C-5 or other military cargo aircraft with earplugs wedged tight, sitting in a nylon-webbed jump seat designed to quickly cut off all circulation past a passenger's thighs. He hadn't slept this well in a long time, even at home.

The jet bridge wasn't connected, so the most eager passengers were still cramming the aisle. He opened an overhead compartment door, then remembered he hadn't brought anything except a phone. Nothing. Not even a toothbrush. He'd marched out of the meeting with Stacy in a fury, and driven straight toward Baltimore Washington Airport to catch the next flight to Tel Aviv. But Carter had been riding shotgun and convinced him to stop by the Det first.

"Let Lori do her job," he'd said. "She knows what she's doing. If you follow, you'll just screw it up."

The detective had been right. Red was no spy. However, he knew how to hunt men. Lori's trip amounted to nothing but setting bait on a hook. But her traveling to Israel on a mission like this was akin to fishing for shark by dipping her feet in the ocean and dropping chum. Stacy had said she had no backup. "No need. It's a simple, old-fashioned dead drop," she'd told him.

Bullshit. Even the best plans shatter once the first shot is fired. You always plan backup. And backup to your backup. And exfil for all contingencies. If Stacy refused to provide it, Red had to. But he couldn't use Det assets. Higher would never have approved. Sending a team of military operators into Israel? Total insanity. And what would the mission be? His team was efficient at killing people and breaking things, not trailing a CIA analyst through Jerusalem to ensure her safety. He was on his own to do this. He knew how to track an animal. Following someone around a city couldn't be much different than trailing soldiers through the woods. Just a change in landscape, right? So he'd grabbed his passport and headed to the airport. Carter would get the kids to Red's parents' house for the next few days.

The line spilled out the doorway onto the gangway. Red exited the plane and stepped quickly down the tiled terminal. He pushed his way to the front of the pack, ignoring sharp comments in several foreign languages.

Lori could probably tell him exactly what these people had called him. But if they wanted to be first, they should've walked faster. She'd already been in-country twelve hours. He had to get to her.

He followed signs to Immigration and arrived before it was crowded. A woman in a blue uniform shirt glanced up from her computer screen and waved him forward, then held out a hand for his passport. He'd received a civilian one with a few fake stamps four months ago as a CIA precaution for all Det operators. "Just in case," they'd said. Now he was relieved to have it.

She eyed the papers and then glanced behind him. A loose lock of purple hair fell down her cheek. "Traveling alone?" Surprisingly good English. Better than some of his operators.

Carter had warned him to tell the truth as much as possible. To only answer the question. "Don't volunteer information, and don't look impatient or annoyed."

"Yes, alone," he said.

Her eyes flashed back and forth on the screen. Carter had said lone males would be questioned the most intently. "Business or pleasure?"

"Business."

She glanced behind her, as if waiting for someone—maybe a supervisor. "And what is your business?"

Lie as little as possible. "I'm a consultant."

She stared, eyebrows pricked, asking for more.

Don't volunteer anything.

"What kind of consultant?"

Immigration officials were trained to look for guilty body language. "Stand still," Carter had instructed. "Hands in pockets is safe. Or hold something, but don't fiddle with it."

Easy enough. He slipped both hands into the pockets of his jeans. "Arms. Primarily light infantry. I'm here at the request of IWI."

The agent wrinkled her nose, as if at a bad smell. She leaned back in her seat and began to raise a hand toward a bald man in the same blue uniform shirt who was standing against a wall as if at parade rest, gazing at the counter of agents.

Red broke in to distract her. "Israel Weapon Industries. They hire me to break their weapons." He smiled.

She didn't. Must not have gotten the joke. "I field-test. They want me to work your defense force's X95 assault rifle. It's the bullpup, with one with the mag in the stock. I—"

"I'm familiar with it. My sister has to carry one." She rolled her eyes. "Even to the beach." She curled a finger at the man.

Damn. Had he said too much? He'd told Carter this wasn't a good cover, but he didn't know anything else. And he had, in fact, field-tested the X95. But not at the request of IWI.

The bald supervisor stepped beside the agent at the tan plastic-looking counter.

"IWI said they'd fax over a letter of introduction," Red blurted. He'd spoken too quickly. Did they pick up on it? Maybe this spy crap was harder than it looked.

The supervisor rocked on his heels, then disappeared through a door in the back wall. A minute later he came out, head bent low as fingers flipped through a stack of papers. He yanked out one with the IWI's familiar logo with diamond-shaped arrows.

Red muffled a sigh of relief. Thank goodness for Brooks, the Det's CIA liaison. She'd given him five sheets of summary detail on his cover, which he'd memorized in the hour waiting for the plane. That was one ability he'd always had. Even now he could envision the pages in his mind well enough to read them, as if in a photo. Apparently the CIA had covers prepared for most major countries.

The man pointed to a phone number. The immigration agent lifted a beige handset and punched buttons. The faint buzz of two short rings came from the earpiece. The man in madras plaid shorts from the plane coughed next to Red, standing at the adjacent agent's stall with his wife and two sons, one barely old enough to walk, pungent diaper almost dragging the floor.

The agent spoke into the handset in Hebrew—at least that's what Red assumed. She glanced at the passport, then the screen. A green glow reflected in her glasses. Was she playing solitaire?

More talk, nods. Finally she stamped the passport and held it out to him. "Welcome to Israel, Mr. Vetin. They said they emailed your hotel reservations to your phone." She glanced around him and lifted a hand. "Next!"

Red stepped to the side, then walked down a wide ramp. He pulled his phone from his pocket and held the power button. "That's as much as I can give you," Brooks had said in her raspy smoker's voice. "A simple cover and a phone I can do without getting anyone else involved. Anything more, and unwanted questions will start coming."

Brooks was a doll. She had to know none of this was above board. He was breaking so many rules right now, screwing around in circles he knew nothing about, but she'd never questioned him.

He continued through a covered atrium with tall, golden-tiled mosaic pillars lit from above. They resembled the Olympic torch carried by runners at opening ceremonies. He located an ATM and withdrew two thousand shekels.

It was dark outside. The air smelled of wet leaves, like rain. Almost midnight local time, but there were two lines of white taxis idling, one against the near curb and another across the street. He leaned against a steel pillar supporting a stretched white canopy—the kind that Lori always said looked like upside-down udders. The phone wasn't secure, but had never been used before. No one would have reason to eavesdrop. He dialed a number Brooks had given him. "It's a local one," she'd said. "But we have it forwarded to the command center."

Carter answered, rapid fire. "Get your shit moving! Lori is headed to the drop now. Stacy just called. Something went wrong. Grab a taxi and I'll give you the sitrep."

Chapter 30

Baladi Supermarket

Lori's phone buzzed on the nightstand next to her hotel bed. Groggy with sleep, she snapped when she realized it was still dark. She swung her feet to the floor and glanced at the screen. 11:30 P.M. It displayed JERUSALEM. Who'd be calling so late? Could be Stacy checking in, routing a call through local switchboards.

She pressed a green button. Before she could say anything, "Warbird" came through the speaker. A woman's voice, Hebrew accent. It was the code word established for the fintel back door. Whoever initiated a transmission would start with it and the recipient would reply with another. But that was through a simple text system. Now it was being used by phone?

"Blue line," Lori said, running fingers through bangs. Where'd her hair go? She yanked strands down in front of her eye. Black. She'd forgotten she'd cut it earlier.

"Exchange will occur at Baladi Supermarket, the one on Taha Husein Street, 1:30 A.M. tonight."

She glanced at the screen again. Had whoever was on the other end of the fintel back door with Mossad hacked her phone? They were playing her, trying to throw off her bearings. Some posturing needed to be expected. It was part of the game. Short time frames meant it'd be difficult to mobilize support or surveillance. Not that Lori had any. Still.

She ground her toes into the carpet. "That's in two hours. I don't even know where Baladi is."

"You'll be able to make it in time, if you hurry."

She could play along, to a point. "I'll drop the package and let—"

The voice was monotone, as if reading a script. "No need. I will meet you there."

Not how it works, sister. "This is a supermarket? I'll do your location, but I'll drop my package and give you a call once I'm clear with instructions where I put it."

The woman's tone hardened. She wasn't used to back talk. Must be higher up in the organization than she thought. Not the low-ranking go-between she'd assumed. Mossad was manned by a disproportionately high number of men. Lori might even be able to narrow it down to a short list of suspects.

"You will do exactly—"

"Shut up!" Lori snapped. "My rules. I'll call you on this same number when I'm done." She punched END, closed her eyes, sucked in a deep breath, and held it. Blood throbbed in her ears. A cricket chirped near her window. A police siren wavered a few blocks away. This had to be the same woman from the message blasts through the fintel back door. What a controlling bitch. Who could live with someone like that?

* * * *

Lori pulled back her hair and pressed a flesh-colored bone mic into her ear canal. The device, smaller than a hearing aid, was invisible to casual observation. The Uber driver slowed his Audi at a stoplight and glanced both directions; then the engine raced as they sped through the intersection. It seemed to be a sport model of some variety, seats tighter than airline coach economy class. Why'd someone that owned an Audi need to drive for a ride-sharing service? Probably couldn't afford the payments otherwise. Turns out Baladi Supermarket was in the West Bank. They'd been through two military checkpoints en route. The guards at both seemed to be set at ease upon recognizing her driver. They'd turned off Route 60 a minute ago. Sweat glistened upon his cheek beneath tight black curly locks as headlights flashed through the windshield.

The man glanced into the rearview and turned a palm open. "Why market? And why this one? Too late for woman. Return tomorrow instead?"

The Baladi Supermarket was open twenty-four hours. It was almost 1:30 A.M. now. "I just need to pick up a few items before morning. We're going on a tour." Passing an empty parking garage surrounded by chain-link fence and rusted sheet metal, the driver's concern appeared warranted.

The streets were becoming darker as they drove farther from the main road, and trash filled several corners. But this market was supposed to be a major store and was situated in a section of the city that attracted a younger crowd. It'd still be busy, even at this time of night.

The vehicle smashed through a pothole, and the driver smacked the wheel. In Hebrew he shouted, "Son of a whore! Fix the roads."

Lori had called Stacy after the control-freak lady had woken her. "Don't change the plan!" Stacy had said. "*You* dictate the drop location and time, not the other way around."

Correct…under most circumstances. But Control Freak already knew who Lori was. She'd already tried to kill her. But now Lori had the threat of the dead man's switch on the audit report keeping her pursuers in check. They wouldn't attempt that again.

This exchange was Lori's only option. If unsuccessful, she'd have to drop off the grid completely and subject the kids to another move, this time further away, breaking all ties with family. She couldn't do that to them. They'd just settled into a new home. They'd leased a horse at a nearby stable for Penny. The boys loved their teachers. Other than a rogue Mossad agent trying to kill her, life was good.

She glanced at her phone screen and verified the bone mic had synced. Her thumb hovered over the local number for Stacy. She'd be fuming, and Lori didn't need that this early in the morning. She'd fill her in afterward, blame it on technical difficulties. The car stopped beside a sidewalk half-covered in sand next to an excavation. A tracked yellow backhoe hulked like a tank near the pit. Across the street on a corner lot was a three-story tan cement block building, light spilling from large street-level windows, the rest dimly lit. The top two floors looked to be apartments. At least a dozen shoppers pushed carts and milled about behind the lower panes. Scarves covered the hair and neck of several women, like Muslim hijabs. Black or white kippahs crowned the heads of the men.

"I'll only be a few minutes. Wait here till I come back and you'll receive a return fare as well." She dropped a two-hundred-shekel note onto the front seat, opened the door, and stepped across the road. Her foot splashed water onto the cuff of her slacks. Across the store threshold, warm humidity heavy with cardamom and saffron brushed her cheeks. Black curls stretched below the pink headcloth of a young lady who stood behind a checkout register plastered with multicolored stickers, as if the decals were trying to conceal hidden damage. The attendant's skin glowed, and she smiled at a lanky teenage boy, the young man's eyes fixed on the floor. She sighed as she pounded buttons and stuffed celery into a plastic bag.

A large supermarket, at least thirty aisles. Yet they were narrow, with barely enough room for two carts to pass. This place must've been an anthill during daylight hours. Drums, guitar, and a violin sang in rhythm as a vocalist called out Hebrew pop lyrics—too distorted to understand. Stamped knives with plastic handles hung from the capital of a short Greek column of faux marble, like acanthus leaves. A young man, square jawed with straight blond hair, restocked shelves with yellow-and-red boxes of Telma cornflakes, a photo of a basketball player about to shoot printed across their front. Israel was one of the most culturally diverse nations in the world. The employee was most likely a Russian Jew.

Or a contract assassin.

At the far end of the store, fruit carts lined the wall, an indoor market. Oranges, grapefruit, persimmons, and pomegranates heaped in piles beneath a false ceiling of palm fronds. This side of the building stood silent, no people. Frozen meals and wine were most likely the staples of patrons this time of night. Across from a display of avocados, neat rows of canned soup were stacked three high, flush with the front of the shelves. *Perfect. Already restocked.*

She pulled the white envelope containing the falsified audit report from her purse and slipped it behind a row of Osem canned tomatoes. The package could lie unseen for days back there. She withdrew her hand, turned, and jerked to a halt.

A man stood in the middle of the aisle. Wide shoulders, gray hair neatly trimmed short, tanned skin, thick neck, but with a belly that stretched a green polo shirt over blue Levis. Jackson's and Nick's steel-blue eyes stared back at her. Both her boys had inherited several of their grandfather's features.

"Dad?"

Her father's mouth opened; then he seemed to compose himself. He pointed to her head. "What'd you do to your hair? You've been blond your entire life."

Stacy had been investigating Lori's father for illegal campaign fund-raising as a pet project for years. She'd tried to keep it a secret, but Lori knew everything that went on in that office. Her dad, a Virginia state senator, had taken flak in the press for illegal fund-raising, but it only increased his poll rankings. Lori had ignored Stacy's obsession with him. Several women wanted to see her father in jail. Some days, she was one. She'd diagnosed the man with narcissistic personality disorder two decades ago. He treated her mom like carpet and been caught in two affairs. God bless that woman for sticking with him as long as she had.

"What are you doing here?" She clenched her jaw. It was all she could think to ask.

"You know better. Never let the other side dictate circumstances of an exchange."

Why was her estranged father in a supermarket in Jerusalem? How'd he know she was working a drop? He'd worked for the CIA fifteen years ago before running for office. Was he still in their employ? Lights fluttered above as a bird flew straight down the center of the aisle. Her father wasn't supposed to be here. He wasn't allowed in this part of her life. "But—"

He stepped toward her. "I'll explain later." He grabbed her wrist. "You need to get out of here."

She twisted her arm free. "What the hell are you doing? You have any idea what you're putting at risk?"

Two pops like an air stapler sounded near the end of the aisle. Palm fronds shuddered, and warm blood splashed Lori's neck. Her father tipped toward her like a propped broom ready to fall. She wrapped her arms around his shoulders in a hug and pulled him to the floor between fruit carts, glancing at a brunette behind him at the end of the corridor in knit charcoal newsboy cap and Glock 17 with silencer.

Blood spilled onto the floor from her father's back and biceps. He lifted a hand toward her face.

Heels clicked on the tile floor, marching toward their position. Shit. Where to run? What about her dad? She had no weapon. Gripping a grapefruit, she hurled it toward the woman. Not even close. Two more pops and her earlobe stung as an apple exploded next to it. She ducked.

Her father labored to draw in a breath.

She wasn't going down without a fight. As Lori peered over, an avocado exploded near her cheek. She lifted the edge of the cart to tip it toward her, but it just rolled. The assassin stepped around it and aimed her pistol at her father's chest. The woman who'd called tonight? The one on the other end of the fintel back door? The rogue Mossad agent? Almond eyes suggested Asian descent. Her hair fell straight and raven black against her neck.

"Kill him and I'll leak the audit trail. You'll be hunted by your own people."

The woman glanced in both directions. The aisle was still empty.

Should Lori scream? Not a good tactic when threatened with a pistol.

The woman pursed purple lips, and a pop sounded from the muzzle. A hot puff of air blew past Lori's face, and her father shuddered as the third projectile sank in.

The assassin trained the muzzle at Lori's chest. A short, shiny metal rod flew and cracked off of the assailant's head, clattering to the floor beneath a shelf. The woman winced. She stepped back and aimed her weapon down the aisle. Another flash of metal, but this one stuck into her gut. A brown shank protruded from her stomach. She clenched fingers around it, and three more pops sounded from the Glock. She strode in the direction from which the shiny metal was flying. This was Lori's chance to escape. Maybe slip out a back door. But…her father.

Another flash, but it bounced off the killer's shoulder. The object clattered to the floor. A steak knife with a cheap plastic handle. Two more pops and the woman grunted. A man was hunched behind a wagon of persimmons, tossing knives like a circus act. More pops and her slide locked back. He tucked a shoulder and rolled toward her, springing to his feet and slinging a blade so hard it stuck out of the back of her neck. A severed artery pumped a stream of crimson across cans of stewed tomatoes. Her eyes rolled back, she bent at the waist, then fell straight forward. Smacking the floor, her head rang a hollow note like a ripe melon.

Lori pressed a palm over her father's chest where a minute ago the same lady had punched a bullet hole. *Don't die on me, you sonofabitch.* Subsonic ammo was low velocity, so the projectile might not have penetrated deeply. Who was the knife thrower? "Call an ambulance," she whispered in Hebrew, though she'd tried to shout it.

A second later a short man was on his knees next to her. He spoke in English. "That your dad?"

The voice was familiar, but… "Tony?" His beard was gone. Raspberry abrasions on his cheeks, like he'd done it with one of the steak knives. His hair was black and shiny.

He slipped to the other side of her father. "Hold the pressure. Let's get him on his side. Need to see the wounds in his back."

Moses winced and grabbed Red's neck. His speech was labored. "Kill...that—"

"Stay quiet. Don't move. She's bleeding out now. Don't need you doing the same."

"No!" he screeched. "Paili Baum sent the assassin. *I'm* going to kill her." He turned his gaze to Lori. His voice a whisper. "I'm sorry. I'm a lousy father. But, no matter what your boss says, I never tried to hurt you. Everything I've done was to protect you."

Lori looked down on him, as if from the ceiling, up in the palm fronds. They needed to run, in case others were close. But she couldn't move her father. Blood pulsed beneath her palm. His heart was racing. "Shut up. Tell me later."

Red pressed his shoulder blade. "He's bleeding bad. Punctured a lung. Going to probe it, see if I can stem the flow."

Her father arched his back as Red plunged a finger into it. His chest heaved. "I'll take care of Paili. Get out, before—"

"Shut up, Dad. I'm not leaving you."

"Yes, you are." He glanced past his feet to the body of the assassin on the floor. "She's not Mossad."

Whatever. "I don't care who she is. Tony, you're hurting him."

"She's an Abergil." He coughed, spouting a mist of blood. "She got an artery. I can feel my lungs filling."

Palm frond shadows waved on his cheek. The skin of his neck sank to a pale green.

"Abergil is Jewish mafia," he said, glancing behind her. "They don't perform a hit alone."

Chapter 31

Losing a Tail

Red's finger probed inside Moses' back. The hole went through a rib, and shards of bone cut his skin as he pressed his pinky deeper. He grabbed a steak knife and cut away the senator's polo shirt in a long slice. The squelching music coming through ceiling speakers sounded like deaf cats mating. Or a Russian trying to yodel.

Lori pressed a thumb against the hole in her father's sternum. She spoke in a hush. "What're you doing?"

"Bullet channel is through a rib. I can't get my finger in to pinch off the bleeding." He placed the blade into the hole.

Lori grabbed his wrist. "You can't cut him."

There wasn't much hope of the man living at that point, but Red had to try. "Give him something to bite on. I've got to slice a passage around the bone so I can get my finger inside." Subsonic round, so the bullet might not have gone much deeper. But no way to know. He'd seen silenced 9mm bullets pass clear through a thigh. And who knew what damage the bullet in his chest had done.

Lori grabbed a thin wooden wheel spoke from the cart next to her and yanked it loose with a *crack*. She bent over her father. "Dad, hold...bite down on this...Dad." Her voice shifted to a whimper, like the whine of a puppy. She slapped the man's cheeks. "Tony, he's not responding." Her short black hair parted around the pale skin on her nape as she leaned. Panic swelled in her eyes.

Red pressed fingers into the warm rolls of her father's neck, against his windpipe. Cardiac arrest. He rolled Moses onto his back and began chest compressions. A sadistic pararescue medic had once demonstrated on a mannequin how the seventies tune "Stayin' Alive" set the perfect rhythm for CPR. Now, the Bee Gees sang in his mind as he counted compressions. What an awful song.

If the senator's heart started again, they'd need an ambulance. Amazing no patrons had ventured down this far end of the store, but there weren't many this time of night and it had only been a couple of minutes. Time only *seemed* to stand still when bullets flew. The shots had been silenced, the struggle brief, and the yodel-mating had muted any other escaping noises.

"I'll keep doing CPR. Get someone to call for an ambulance. Keep an eye. If these guys don't work alone, backup won't be far."

Lori stood and lifted her hand from her father's chest. The next compression squirted a jet of blood a few inches into the air. She dropped back down and covered the fountain. She placed fingers against his neck and her ear to his mouth. Her eyes were moist. Her lips quivered, but she was still holding herself together.

A few more compressions and Red slipped a palm beneath Moses' neck, straightening his windpipe.

Lori covered her father's mouth with her palm. "It's no use. He's gone." A single tear streaked her nose.

Red shoved her hand out of the way, pinched the senator's nostrils, and blew into his lungs. The hole in his back gurgled. "Damn it!" He slammed his fist onto the senator's chest. "I'm sorry, dear."

Lori stood. "We need to get out of here."

Red searched the ceiling. No CCTVs. He jumped up, grabbed the senator's hand, stretched his arm, and scraped the fingers across the assassin's cheek, gouging three streaks. Enough to get the dead woman's skin under his fingernails. He wrapped the same hand around the hilt of the knives protruding from her gut and neck. He grabbed a clump of her hair and yanked it out, then shoved it between the dead man's fingers. Lori seemed to catch the idea, and snatched up the knives that had bounced, wiped them across her shirt, and pressed them against her father's finger pads.

Attagirl.

She reached behind canned tomatoes and pulled out an envelope. Must have been the drop. He gazed at the pistol in the woman's hand. The rectangular outline of an extra magazine protruded from her pants pocket. But he couldn't take the weapon without upsetting the stage.

A squeak from a cart's wheel approached from the front. They turned and sprinted the opposite direction, careful to remain silent. Red slipped around the end of the aisle, picked up two rolls of paper towels, and studied them as if comparing prices. Only a hunched man in black pants and white yarmulke shuffled along twenty meters away. Red ripped open a roll and wiped the blood from his hands, stuffing the dirty towels into his pocket and passing clean ones to Lori. "Anyone notices our sleeves are stained, tell them we grabbed a leaky ketchup bottle." He peeked around the corner of the fruit aisle as a young blond man pushed a cart of boxes into the center. He walked faster than an employee would. He stopped when he glimpsed the bodies and pulled something from one of the boxes. The lights were dim, obscured by palm leaves, but the squared silhouette of a Glock 17 was unmistakable. The same weapon as the assassin.

He'd have to kill this guy as well.

Lori grabbed his arm and ran toward the back of the store. "Follow me."

She must have an exfil. A few rows down, she turned and started toward the cashiers. But they should be moving *away* from people. She held up her hands and spouted something in another language. Must have been Hebrew, because a young woman in a pink headscarf reached below a rainbow-colored cash register and lifted out an IMI Galil assault rifle. Looked like a Grateful Dead fan going vigilante. She thumbed the selector switch one click rearward—full auto. Nice. An off-duty soldier.

Two couples ducked and sprinted toward the front door. A few others squatted low behind checkout racks. No screaming. These people knew what it was to live under the constant threat of a terrorist attack. The woman aimed the weapon toward the fruit aisle. If Red snatched it from her, he could take the man out himself.

Before he could, Lori jerked him down the adjacent checkout aisle. He ran after her outside. She leaned into a freezer and lifted out two bags of ice. "Stay here. Then choke out the driver." She turned and walked across the street.

What driver? Red's taxi had dropped him and sped off an hour ago. Why'd she take bags of ice? Lori approached a red Audi A4 parked in front of a white Subaru. A sporty model. The Audi's driver glanced up from a glowing screen, then scrambled out his door. He grabbed the plastic bags from Lori with one hand, holding the rear door open with the other.

That's my girl. The ice must've been meant to set up the driver so Red could put him to sleep.

As the man dropped them into the trunk, Red snuck up behind and locked his neck into a choke hold. The driver couldn't scream. He struggled for a few seconds; then his body collapsed. Red started to push him into the trunk with the ice, then lowered him to the sidewalk instead. He'd be safer there and come to in a few seconds.

Lori slid through the driver's door. Red followed, shoving her across the console to the passenger seat. "I'm driving. You navigate." Manual transmission. Perfect.

Shouts came from inside the store, echoed by three cracks from the Galil, then pops from the pistol. He shifted into second, redlined the tach, popped the clutch, and they shot forward as all four wheels squealed on the damp pavement. Steered like it was on rails. The turbo whined and gulped air as he slapped the shifter through its gate.

Lori buckled her belt and fingered her phone. Straight black hair, pale skin. She looked like the wife from *The Addams Family*. Kind of turned him on. "What's your exfil?"

She lunged at him and shoved his shoulder. "What the hell was that about?"

With his wife, the line between sorrow and anger often blurred. "What was what about? I'm making this up as I go." He yanked the wheel to avoid a pothole. "You OK?"

"Why'd you bring Dad?"

Bring her father? She trying to blame her mess on him? "I didn't! You did."

She clenched her fingers into fists. "Why're you here at all?"

This was going nowhere. "Always wanted to visit Jerusalem and pick up a hooker. You'll have to do."

She aimed a punch at his chin, but the shoulder strap stopped her swing short. She jabbed at his head with her off hand. He tapped the brakes, and the seat belt snatched her neck. "Calm down and get us back to the airport." He paused at a stoplight, downshifted, and accelerated through the intersection into an on-ramp. No idea where they were headed, but it was away from the supermarket.

"We've got a safe house ten kilometers from here. We can hole up, make some calls, and ensure all's clear before we show our faces in public."

"Who's Paili Baum? That name mean anything to you?"

"No."

"Then we've got a name. You can check her out once we're stateside. Finish what your father started."

"Dad knew he was dying when he said that. Whatever he was planning, it's already in motion. We need to get to the safe house."

Red glanced in the rearview. A streetlight glinted off a white Subaru five seconds behind them. "We're not going to your safe house."

Her eyes bulged. She shouted, "You're out of your depth, Tony! Trust me. We can't head to the Tel Aviv airport without making sure no one is going to be looking for us."

Hadn't they worked through the trust issue back in the forest? Dr. Sato wasn't doing their relationship any good. "I'm the one who just killed an assassin with a $1.99 steak knife. You attacked her with a grapefruit. And missed. I'm not the one out of my depth. Did I mention black hair makes you look like a Goth hooker?" Abreast of an exit ramp, he slammed on the brakes and twisted the wheel. The vehicle drifted sideways, tires trailing smoke. He applied power, pulling into a turn, rear bumper slipping past yellow crash barriers, throttling onto the ramp at ninety kilometers per hour. He glanced into the rear. Four doors. Enough room for booster seats. Maybe Lori would let him trade in the Explorer for one of these.

The white Subaru made a sudden lane change and followed. He yelled over the engine and tire noise, "We can't go to your safe house because we've got a tail. Just verified it."

Down a short straightaway the chase vehicle seemed to gain. Red steered between two storefronts, one with a neon shoe in the window, then made another quick turn into an alley. He slammed on the brakes and cut the lights. "You trust me?"

She turned in his direction, but darkness obscured her expression. "Right now I think you're a cocky, chauvinistic, egotistical sonofabitch."

"You knew that when you married me. But do you trust me?"

"Yes! Whatever. Pull off the road if you're trying to hide."

"Good. Then relax. You'll need to be loose for this." Red shifted into reverse, gunned the engine, and released the clutch. He twisted to see through the rear windshield, and the vehicle raced back down the alley, aimed at the road from which they'd just come. The intersection was dim, and a brown cement wall stood on the opposite side. Lori braced against the seat. As they closed in, other headlights sped toward the same intersection. He pressed the pedal all the way down. Needed to time this perfectly. Past the point of no return. With a *crack*, he collided with the chase vehicle. Metal crunched. Glass crashed. A sharp *bang*, an airbag curtain exploded down the rear windshield, and the car was filled with the acrid, phenolic scent of spent gunpowder.

Chapter 32

Gas Station

Red leaped from the car. The Audi's trunk was folded upward. The Subaru had been knocked from the roadway and was straddling a sidewalk, pinned between the Audi and a tall cinder block wall. One of the chase vehicle's tires was canted, and its strut poked through the hood like a compound fracture. A hot mist of sweet-scented antifreeze rose from the wound. Behind a splintered windshield, the driver wrestled with his seat belt.

Red dove through the warm cloud and landed on the hood. He punched through the windshield, reached between the spokes of the steering wheel, and grabbed the driver's collar. It was the same blond man from the supermarket. A brown mole interrupted a crease on his forehead. Young looking, but his blue eyes were wide. Not familiar with the sting of surprise. No wonder Mole-Man was backup. Red jerked him forward and slammed his face into the wheel. Time to school gen X on the pain of failure. He repeated the motion like the cycling of a rifle bolt till Mole-Man's terror was replaced with the numb glaze of unconsciousness. The shattered safety glass fell out of its seal and lay across him like a crystal blanket. Red leaned into the vehicle and probed the floor with his fingers. They landed on the hard outline of a Glock, and he snatched it up. He patted the unconscious driver's pockets and jerked out two spare magazines.

He scrambled away and slid off the hood. Tires chirped, and headlights turned onto the side street, aimed at the accident. An engine roared as a dark blue van raced toward them, moving too fast for neighborhood traffic. Twin orange marker lights glowed from the edge of the vehicle's large side-view mirrors.

Red hopped into the driver's seat, tossed the weapon into Lori's lap, slapped the vehicle in gear, and stomped the gas. Glass and metal tinkled like wind chimes as the vehicles separated. Three bullets cracked through the rear door, coming from the direction of the gaining vehicle. The alley was narrow with cars lining both sides. He plowed through potholes as the Audi accelerated.

Options? No quick response could come from the Det. Keeping a tight lid on the investigation, Red hadn't involved anyone besides Carter. So, no Hellfire missiles from a Reaper drone soaring forty thousand feet in the air. No response team prepositioned on the ground, either, ready to jump in and lend support. And this screwup was his own doing. He was the one who'd wanted to trail Lori like a lone wolf. It was as if they were right back among the trees of Pikes Peak National Forest, severed from support, scrambling for their lives.

He slapped the shifter into third and sped onto a dark straightaway, dimmed streetlights lining the median. "I can lose the van. But now we're driving a car anyone can spot. Police will pull us over just because we don't have taillights. Need to ditch this one and get another. Maybe at a parking lot."

Lori twisted to see out the rear window, reached, and yanked on the deflated airbag. She grunted with the effort, and it tore loose. "Get clear, then find a gas station. That's the best place to make a trade."

But they needed to avoid cameras. "No. Most gas stations have CCTVs."

She shoved the curtain into the floor and stomped it down. She racked the Glock's slide, shoved it and the two mags of ammo into the waist of her jeans, then untucked her blouse as a cover. "We won't be in-country long enough for it to make a difference." She patted his knee. "You did well, Tony. But brute force won't get us out of the country. We've got to blend in. Disappear. We're not at Pikes Peak. This is a landscape I'm familiar with."

* * * *

Lori gripped Tony's hard and calloused hand as they walked along a cracked sidewalk in front of two-story stucco townhomes in muted browns and tans. Each had a Kia or Toyota sedan parked in front, end to end. Impatiens or pansies dotted window boxes. But just across the quiet street sprouted a tangle of derelict apartments with broken balcony rails and shattered windows. The sidewalk was lined with sedans clad with multicolored body panels and wheels resting on cinder blocks. The air was still and cool, though heat radiated from the pavement.

They'd ditched the Audi several blocks away at the end of another row of houses. They'd backed it up against a hedge to conceal the damage. Another few blocks' walk and they'd be at a gas station they'd spied. Passing a deep green bush, she inhaled the honey scent of blooming camellias and gardenias. She took a deep breath, willing her strides to slow. The walk was oddly...pleasant. A chance to think and enjoy her husband's presence. And he was finally here, in the moment, with her. So often he was present in body, but mentally off on training or planning the next op. Ever since ditching the Audi, for five whole city blocks, he'd listened to everything she said. He was depending upon her as an asset. She wasn't just extra baggage.

She squeezed his hand. "Why'd you shave your beard?"

A streetlight glinted from the corner of his eye. "Carter said it'd be a good idea once I got here. In case I got caught on some TV doing something stupid. Like tossing steak knives at women."

A car passed, and the headlights shimmered on his dark mop. "How'd you dye your hair so fast?"

"Black shoe polish. All I could find on short notice."

Impressive. And it explained why his skull shone like plastic spaghetti. "You look like one of Jackson's Lego men. Darth Vader." She pointed to a fanny pack clipped to his waist. "What's in your man bag?"

Red smirked and shook the oversized accessory. "Empty. Got it same place I picked up the razor and shoe polish. Wanted to blend in. Look like a fem tourist." His eyes narrowed. "Don't tell Carter I wore this thing."

They passed beneath a silver maple, and Red's boot slammed into a section of sidewalk raised by one of the tree's roots. He seemed to study the path a few feet ahead. "Sorry about your fa—"

"We'll talk about that later." Couldn't go there right now. Her father's death had actually seemed to lift her spirits, like an asthmatic receiving a hit from an inhaler. Was elation part of the grieving process? Or was she that screwed up?

A raven flew down the middle of the road, beneath the cones of light cast by streetlights, its shadow slicing down the twin yellow lines, bisecting suburbia from ghetto. A lifetime of pent-up frustration at her father yearned to scream, *Good riddance, you womanizing cheat!* At the same instant, an idyllic child just wanted to hurt at the loss of her daddy. She turned her gaze away from the run-down apartments and searched the sidewalk ahead.

They covered the rest of the distance in silence. A clear, cool summer night. They'd have to come back and visit Jerusalem again, during daylight hours, without the Jewish mafia chasing to kill them.

Turning a corner, she spied three rows of gas pumps beneath a green steel canopy. Fuel vapors stung her nose. As they stepped closer, a woman in an orange Hyundai sedan pulled up. She slipped her keys into the front pocket of blue sweatpants.

Red opened the door of the convenience store, and Lori stepped inside. She darted down an aisle of chips and soda. Two CCTVs only, both aimed at the cash register. Red studied bubble gum while she picked up a tube of kosher Pringles and glanced out the window. The woman gassed her car and returned the nozzle to the pump, then headed for the store.

Lori stepped back outside and stopped her near the door. She purposefully stumbled with her Hebrew. "Excuse you. Which road to Route 60? Toward Rock Dome?"

The lady gazed at her blankly with pink, pudgy cheeks dangling with uncertainty and fists resting on full hips. A smile broadened upon her face. "Route 60?" She spoke slowly, as if to a child. "You'll need to drive south."

As she relayed the directions, Red stepped out of the store, head turned away and coughing over his shoulder as if he had a nasty cold. He slammed into Lori, who fell against the woman, jolting her. She slipped one hand into the woman's pocket, the other around her back, as if to keep her from falling.

Once steadied, Lori turned to Red. In German, she shouted, "Watch where you're going, Aldrik! You could've hurt us!" She brushed the woman's shoulders. Switching to Hebrew, "Sorry, you idiot. My instructions thank you. You injure me?"

The pudgy woman's smile returned, though she rubbed her chest where Lori had collided with her. She fumbled through the remaining directions, explaining a few more turns, then continued on her way inside the store.

Once out of her sight, Lori sprinted to the Hyundai, pulled the stolen keys from her pocket, and started the engine. She accelerated out of the lot. "Gas stations are best because you know the car is full. Sometimes people even leave keys in the vehicle."

She probed the side of the seat, pushed a lever, and slid it back. Woman must've been a pygmy. She thumbed her phone and opened the map app. *Should be a fifteen-minute drive to the address of the safe house.* She flipped a toggle and adjusted the side mirrors, then reached to the rearview. A dark van ten seconds behind flashed into the brilliant beam of a streetlight as it drove past the row of dilapidated apartments.

Chapter 33

Extreme Prejudice

Red sank lower in the passenger seat of the Hyundai and glanced into the side-view mirror. "Looks like the same van." He leaned into his seat belt as Lori made a sudden turn down a side street. The chase vehicle followed. He pulled his phone from his jeans pocket and punched REDIAL.

Carter answered on the first ring. "It's about time! What the hell you doing in the West Bank?"

Like a worried wife. "Love you too, dear." Red imagined him in the command center, staring at an oversized monitor to track Lori's tag moving around Jerusalem. The same fate that would have been inflicted upon Red if he hadn't decided to get back on the field of play. Red's tag, removed by Lam as he tried to dig frags out of Red's bullet wound, was taped to the collar of Roadkill, the family's new mutt. To the Det and anyone else watching, Red was relaxing at home.

He was pressed against the door as Lori pulled another turn. The van continued to follow, though at a distance. They could outrun it again, but their pursuers were hanging back. It was as if they were attempting to be discreet. Surely they knew they'd been spotted. Another variable must be in play now. What did the enemy have planned? Other players on the field? But where? "Need help. Call in Captain Richards. Tell him to get Brooks and all the other liaisons in the command center. I want Joint Special Operations Command, CIA, FBI, NSA, and anyone else that might have assets on the ground in the West Bank. We need to lose a tail, with extreme prejudice."

A second passed before Carter's reply. "You certain? Getting those guys involved will cause irreparable harm to our investigation. Not to mention your misappropriation of resources. You could be looking at jail time."

Carter had been slaving for months on the investigation into who was trying to kill Lori, all below the radar. But now even this operation was a bust. The drop never occurred. All they had was a name. Paili Baum. Red had to gain control, some form of certainty around their situation. "Need to get out of the West Bank. We've got a tail that won't go away. And I think there may be others."

"What are they driving?"

"A blue van. Nissan, I think."

"And you?"

What did it matter? "I don't have time for this, Carter."

"Just tell me what you're driving!"

"An orange SUV."

A shuffle of papers sounded through the earpiece. A faint knock, as from tapping on a table. "Get to Hafez Ibrahim Street. Head east on it. It's a ten-minute drive from where you're at. We'll take care of the van."

Who was "we"? "How you gonna—"

"I need to get things in motion. Signing off." The phone went dead.

Red twisted to peer back through the rear windshield. Two headlights glowed ten seconds behind them, flanked by orange dots. He glanced around the interior of the stolen vehicle. Black pants with dirty brown knees lay in a tangle of clothes on the backseat. A yellow hard hat rested next to it. The scent of stale cigarettes rose from the blue cloth interior. He might find a crowbar or hammer he could use as a weapon in the far back, but if they were caught in a firefight only the Glock would prove useful.

Lori shoved his shoulder. "Relax. It's a van. I can lose him. We can't get the Det involved. You're not supposed to be here. Neither am I. My father's dead. This whole thing needs to never have happened. Get out of the country without anyone knowing we were here."

Covering up problems was Lori's standard operating procedure. But that only meant the issue came back later, with more attitude. The defense mechanism was keeping her functional now, but it wouldn't do anything to get rid of hunters on their trail. Only one way to eliminate a direct threat. Low-crawl below grazing fire only long enough to destroy a machine gun nest.

Red pressed the map icon on his phone. "Keep the van behind us. Get back on Route 60 and head south. We didn't get the Det involved. At least, I don't think so."

"We can't go to the safe house with a tail."

The Hyundai's transmission moaned as the vehicle accelerated. "Slow down. We've got to head to a specific road first."

She slapped the blinker and changed lanes. "Why?"

"Carter hung up before I could ask."

Lori glanced nervously into the rearview. She must have been more worried about the van than she was letting on.

He guided them to Hafez Ibrahim Street. It ran only about two hundred meters. Carter had said to travel it eastward, so he navigated to the opposite end.

Lori began to turn onto it, then stopped in the middle of the intersection. "I can't go here. It's one way, the opposite direction."

"It's four in the morning. No one's going to be on the road."

The alley was paved with square blocks, like large stone pavers. Three-story apartments lined one side, a tall beige hotel the other, rusted-iron stains streaking down corners of windowpanes like tear tracks. Cars crowded both sides, facing against them. They were a fish headed upstream.

Red held an open palm next to Lori's hip. She drew the Glock from her jeans. The metal was warm from resting next to her flesh. She passed him the two spare magazines as well. They approached a cross street and paused at a red sign displaying a raised white hand. The headlights behind them bounced and flashed. The chase vehicle was speeding up. Ahead, the road narrowed until the Hyundai had only inches of clearance on either side. Metal canopies extended from two opposing storefronts into their path, creating a gauntlet. As they approached the narrow passage, their headlights illuminated a man stepping into the middle of it. He wore black pants, shirt, and a dark scarf tied around his face. He turned toward them and—

"RPG!" Red shouted.

The seat belt snatched his neck as Lori slammed on the brakes. A speeding motor roared as the van trailing them raced to close in from behind. Trapped. Shit. Red gripped the Glock, released his belt, and opened the door, but it slammed against a parked car. He raised the pistol to the windshield. A blaze of brilliance and the rocket's trail blew the soldier's scarf against his face as the missile sped toward them. Red dove over Lori, folding her in half and shoving her below the wheel. The projectile screamed overhead, missing the roof by inches, slammed into the van, and exploded with a bright yellow flash. The *crack* shattered plate glass windows. A car alarm sounded. The van veered off course and plowed into a VW bug, its cabin filled with licking flame. The black commando's eyes gleamed in the brilliance. His shadow danced and jumped behind him, surrounded by bursts of orange cast by the fire onto a concrete wall like a movie screen. The man lowered the RPG's empty tube, waved them forward with a curl of his arm, and stepped out of the way.

He must be from Carter, why the detective had to get off the phone. Red slid into his seat. He slapped Lori on the back. "Go. Get out of here."

Lori's wide eyes reflected the orange that filled the narrow avenue. Tires squealed, and the Hyundai lurched ahead. As they passed the spot where the RPG had been launched, the commando's shadow loomed beneath the store canopy with a hand raised in salute.

Chapter 34

Shadow of the Cat

Lori lifted her black travel bag and slid it into the 747's overhead compartment, wheels first as the flight attendant had requested. Halfway in, the door latch snagged on a pocket seam. She pressed the luggage down, but it still didn't move. A Chinese man with gray hair and a young lady with the black lamp logo of Tel Aviv University on her sweatshirt stood behind Red, waiting to get to their seats. Lori shoved the bag, then again, harder, but it refused to budge. She balled her fist and tapped it like a hammer.

Red placed his hand on hers. "I got it."

Five more passengers had joined the line, gaping at her. The college student's mouth was open, red chewing gum on her tongue. Lori's face warmed in a flush. A bead of sweat trickled down her cheek. Her pinky was sore, as if it'd been pounded. She slipped into a window seat and leaned against the cold bulkhead, gazing out at luggage handlers tossing bags onto a lazy conveyor. Red slipped his hands down the sides of her carry-on. A *pop!* and it slid in. His mechanical intelligence was infuriating. As if his fingers were switchblades. He sat next to her and clipped his seat belt. She leaned to his ear. "Did I just make a scene?" Why the hell did she care? Must be fatigue.

He closed his eyes and rested his head back. "You always make a scene, beautiful." He squeezed her knee. "A few eyes may have turned your way. No more than usual."

She released a sigh, but a roil of angst filled her stomach. She had to stay sharp. Couldn't let her guard down. Not yet. Outside, a woman with kneepads strapped against ballooning blue pants tossed a dog kennel onto the conveyor as if it were a trash bag.

Another squeeze on her knee. "Doing OK? Want to talk?"

Her stomach ached, as if it was slowly threading itself through a hole. "Not now. Once we're home."

"Wake me if you change your mind." He tucked a mini pillow behind his head and turned toward her, eyes closed, just as he did every night at home. He had to be exhausted. His chest swelled, and he heaved a sigh, like a bird ruffling its feathers as it settled after a fright. Black smudged the pillow cover now, and she caught the oily scent of shoe polish. A few copper-orange strands stood out from the rest, like stripped electric wires.

"Why'd you follow me?"

His eyelids shook, but remained tight. His lips barely moved. "Haven't figured it out yet? Eight years of marriage. Three kids. Figure we're a set." His chest heaved in another deep breath. "Plus, no one gets to kill you except me. That'd be embarrassing."

She whacked his thigh and crossed her legs. He smirked. She leaned in and pressed her lips against his.

What a patient man, putting up with her tantrums. She should've known better than to attempt a drop without some sort of backup. That's how they should occur, but there had been too many variables on this one. He knew that, but she'd been blind. Why'd she been so anxious to push forward with this drop? Didn't make sense.

A raven twisted in a breeze, circling above the baggage handlers, like an eagle scanning a mowed field for mice. It turned gently, soaring upward, never flapping, carried by a rising thermal from the hot tarmac. Never seen a raven glide like that. Tony's grip relaxed, and he grunted, a long exhale signaling he'd fallen asleep.

She glanced at her watch. 7:14 A.M. local. She'd been awake all night, and now would certainly be so for the next thirteen hours of the flight. She turned to the window. The raven was almost as high as the control tower now. It spun and banked, enjoying the strength of its wings, as if it had no needs. No appetite. No yesterday. She closed her eyes and imagined the view from up there, the humid breeze rising past her feathers, soaring without a care of her own. Her mind drifted with the bird, her body shuddering as a stiff airstream lifted her into the sky, higher until the atmosphere cooled, a cloud mist brushed her eyelids, and the plane, airport, and all of Israel disappeared below a footing of white mist....

Her seat shuddered, and a *chirp* of tires sounded outside the window. She bolted upright. The arced aluminum canopies of JFK Airport sped by as the plane's brakes groaned. Manhattan's bold skyline leveled in the distance, the Chrysler Building's speared apex piercing a line of blue-gray clouds. She licked a crust of drool from the corner of her lips. She'd slept the entire trip.

* * * *

Red stood next to Carter in the marble foyer of Markel Research. The entrance was framed by two walls of plate glass in aluminum frames, the other two of shiny walnut paneling. Hard, like the Spartan images of city apartment flats furnished with concrete table and metal chairs in one of Lori's designer magazines. He'd been able to convince her to decorate with a lodge motif instead of something so sterile. Rusty Blade stood behind the high counter again. His rash seemed to have cleared, or maybe the guy had finally switched razors. No more sour Granny Smith apple–flavored candies in the bowl. Red snagged a blue raspberry, a close second to his favorite.

Rusty Blade returned a handset to its cradle. "You know the drill, gentlemen. End of the hall. Remove all metal objects."

The pair stepped inside the same narrow closet and removed wallets, keys, knives, and pistols. After returning from Jerusalem, carrying his own sidearm had proven therapeutic. He'd been off balance without it.

Carter had refused to disclose who had saved their asses with the RPG on that narrow street in the West Bank. He'd only reminded Red that in his short stint at the FBI, he'd worked in the Counterterrorism Division. But the masked shooter's aim with a crude weapon had been quick, instinctive, and accurate. His salute had snapped like an honor guard on parade. A military asset. But the media had spun the attack as organized crime turf warfare.

Carter clicked the locker door shut. "About time Stacy called us back. Lori give you any idea as to the meeting's topic?"

Red hurried through undressing and jumped outside the cramped space before the walls closed in and suffocated him. Air in the hallway was more welcoming. "Think it's obvious. I told you about yesterday's intel brief. Paili Baum was killed. Poisoned by strychnine."

Carter stepped out behind him, rubbing an eyebrow. "That was old school. And vindictive. Why use an alkaloid that causes such a painful death? There's a message in that."

Without a belt, Carter's pants were halfway down his hips again before he stepped inside the millimeter wave stall. Once the scan was complete, a red dot above stainless steel elevator doors flashed on. Lori stepped out wearing black jeans and a tight white blouse. Dress-down Friday. He'd left early that morning, before she was at the breakfast table. He'd have fun snaking her out of them tonight.

She shook Carter's hand, then gave him a hug. "Good to see you again. And thank you."

His wide frame seemed to swallow hers.

She gave Red a hug and peck on the lips. Her lips were slick and tasted like cherry. He reached for her hand as she led them upstairs, but stopped short. He didn't recall seeing any suits on TV holding hands. Probably a faux pas. He didn't want to reflect poorly on her. And Stacy already held a grudge against him.

They passed the conference room where they'd met a week earlier, into a large corner office with white slatted window blinds. Closed. Even so, beams wedged through the gaps and cast parallel rows of light across a side table where an industrial Bunn coffeemaker perched. It hissed as brown liquid poured into a carafe. Steam rose from the brew through the rays like a stepladder.

Stacy sat behind a steel desk. It was clean but dented by hammer blows, like a workbench in an automotive shop. She wore purple slacks and a lime-green blouse in some sort of stiff fabric. An instant headache. Carter had spoken of her poor taste in clothes earlier, but surely this had to be fashionable. He'd seen a commercial on TV with a swanky runway model in the same colors. The detective stutter-stepped when he entered the room. Stacy was picking at a rock in the tread of her white sneakers. It twanged in a trash can, and she stood, beaming. "Morning, Carter. Coffee?"

The detective's gaze moved to the side table, and his shoulders relaxed a mark. "Please."

She snatched the pot and began to pour into a mug sporting the eagle and crossed rifles of the NRA logo. "How would you like it?"

"Just a little sugar."

She glanced at Red, and her smile disappeared, but a corner of her mouth turned back up. Maybe the woman had left her fangs home, stuck in her husband. "And you?"

"Black, thanks. Like my coffee with coffee."

She handed Red a steaming mug with a kitten in a Santa hat. A bubble cloud read HAVE A MEWY CHRISTMAS. This lady was a professional in her passive aggressiveness. Why'd Carter get the one with the guns? But the java was dark, chocolate, with the perfect hint of bitterness. He itched his nose, took another swig, and sank into a leather seat. Lori stood, leaning against the blinds near the steaming pot, then moved to a chair next to him. Stacy settled behind her workbench, and instantly the mood seemed to settle as her purple pants disappeared from view. "I think we make a good team, Detective. I hope we can work together again."

Carter straightened. "Once my investigation is complete, I won't be under the employ of the Det." He lifted his mug in a toast. "If all goes well, you'll never see me again."

Stacy glanced at the ceiling. Red followed her gaze. Butterflies were pinned to it, arranged in a circle. A mosaic of black and yellow and orange, rimmed with iridescent blues and greens, formed into the image of a happy face. A smile arranged from insect carcasses.

She lifted her mug and gulped. "Too bad. You may be closer than you realize." She turned to Red. "Paili Baum. You have a hand in that one?"

Who the hell did she think the Det was? "We're not the SS. Bullets and knives. No poison. The official word is it was an accident," he huffed. "How do you accidentally ingest strychnine?"

Carter eased back in his chair. It was the first time Red had seen him relax in weeks. "Poisoning takes planning. A person on the inside. Whoever did it, it's been in the works for a long time."

Stacy shook her head. "Nah. Mossad took care of their own." She peered over the rim of her mug to Lori. "Sure you're OK with me talking about your dad?"

Lori nodded. The shadow of a cat leaped onto the floor. The animal must've been outside on the window ledge, casting its distorted form upon the carpet between the slats. The angle of the light made it appear larger than life. Its tail trailed behind like that of the large, dark feline from which Red had hidden in the forest when Penny had been asleep.

Stacy glanced at the shadow. "The detective here had all the senator's communications tapped. We got the authorization to listen in as well because he'd proven Moses had been laundering money. The day before he was killed, he came clean to Mossad." She turned to Red. "What he told you and Lori before he died was the truth. He had been trying to protect Lori. He and Paili had worked together for years, laundering, lining their pockets. Paili had risen to a director in Mossad's political action department. As such, she was in constant contact with foreign dignitaries. A perfect opportunity. I suspect Moses was only one of many. Moses had been trying to put a stop to it, but never enlisted the help of any US agency since it would mean admitting he was a crook. He didn't go to Paili's supervisor, either. Instead, he contacted an old crony in Metsada, their special operations division. Paramilitary ops."

Red sat up. "You saying Paili *wasn't* poisoned?"

"I'm saying that once Moses contacted Metsada, it escalated. I passed my intel up our channels and we tried to snag him, but he was already out of the country. Paili discovered Moses was in Israel and paid organized crime to kill him. I've got a buddy in our Office of Space Reconnaissance. I was told, unofficially, we put a satellite on Paili. The same night Moses was shot, my buddy said six men slipped into Paili's house." Stacy took another gulp. "Poison was the cover story, my guess. Either way, she met a violent death. Mossad doesn't screw around."

The shadow pranced across the floor, making its way toward Stacy's desk.

Lori crossed her arms. "My father said Paili was the one after us."

Stacy tapped the desk. "When you provided Mossad that extra fintel nine months ago, Paili must've thought you were onto her. Mossad was already running their own investigation, and she was covering her tracks. You were marked. Paili controlled the account from which the Pikes Peak wet team was paid."

Red stood and walked to the door, swirling coffee in his kitty mug. "So we're done, then. Moses had Paili taken out."

"Good riddance," Lori growled. "No one's after me anymore."

Carter closed an eye and scratched the lid with his thumb. "But the list?"

Stacy rubbed one of the dents with a finger. Her nails this morning were violet. "That was Paili, not Moses. Turns out she had expanded her services from laundering to blackmail. Mossad doesn't know how she got the list, but when she found out Moses had a daughter and son-in-law on it, she used it against him. She wanted not only her cut of the laundered cash, but Moses' as well. That's when things started to unravel, and Moses was trying stop her. Misguided, but he possessed some semblance of nobility after all." She tapped the divot with a knuckle.

Red sipped his kitty. Coffee was lukewarm now. "Just about wraps things up."

Carter leaned back and stared at the smiley face on the ceiling. "Almost. When you went running off to Jerusalem, you told me to get the kids to your parents. On the trip, Penny told me all about how you'd taught her 'stop, look, listen' in the woods. How she'd figured out Agent Stump was a fake. That got me thinking, and I did my own 'stop, look, listen.' I was missing something. A clue was ringing a bell, but I'd been deaf to it. Then it hit me. Other than those in this room, who knew you and Lori were going on vacation to Colorado?"

The muffled crunch of cat food came from outside. Red poured himself another two fingers and sat back down. "Just the shrink. Sato's the one who told us we needed to get some time away."

Stacy clanked the mug on the workbench. "Carter told me four days ago about her. We dug around. She had more security clearances than I could count. Lots of government agencies sent their high-value assets to her. She had three ex-husbands, all on alimony, and she was living way outside her means. Expensive cars. Second home on Martha's Vineyard no one knew about. I did some tracing, found she had an offshore account and, sure enough, had received payments from Paili. Went back years. I passed it up the chain and was immediately given an order to cease and desist."

Lori straightened. "So, Sato's already being investigated by someone higher up.... But you were referring to her in past tense."

Another glance passed between Stacy and Carter. "I believe it's proper to refer to Sato in that manner."

Lori leaned forward, resting elbows on knees. "Shit, Stacy. CIA can't just go killing a contractor without a trial. What if someone made a mistake?" She stared at Red. "You know about this?"

He lifted his hands. "New to me." The crunching from outside ceased. The shadow turned, bounded across two other windows, then dropped away. "But as far as I'm concerned, if she was the leak, you already said it. *Good riddance.* She might as well have been the Jamaican that pointed a pistol at Penny. The bitch needed to die. That's what you guys are talking about without saying it, right? Someone killed this woman?"

Stacy stared at the floor next to her chair where the feline's shadow had rested. She rolled her mug between her palms. "None of us will ever know. Based on the transactions in her account and the way I got shut down, she's already offshore and being interrogated. Possibly disposed of." She tipped her head back, emptying her cup. "One more for the missing persons list."

Chapter 35

A Taste of Blood

Red's eyes snapped open. 0513. He swung his legs over the edge of the warm bed, sat up, and flipped off the alarm so it didn't sound in another two minutes. No need to wake Lori. He pressed palms to his temples and rubbed in a circle, trying to heat the synapses of his mind. He stood in the ebony-dark room and picked up running shoes, shorts, and T-shirt he'd set out the previous night. Then made his way around the end of the mattress, stepping slowly, curling his toes to keep from jamming them into his dresser's stubby feet. The door closed behind him with the softest of clicks.

The dim hallway was paved in wide-plank heart pine reclaimed from a barn loft that had originally stood on a corner of their property back when they'd first purchased it a few months ago. The rest of that structure had been too rotted to warrant anything other than a lit match. He padded in bare feet across the warm boards toward a glowing light from the living room. One of the kids must've gotten up for a drink in the night and left the switch on.

A familiar solvent scent, mild and slightly sweet, floated down the hall. Standing on the threshold, he squinted at a blazing wagon wheel chandelier, bright enough to light a crime scene. He groped for the switch and flipped it off. The pain behind his eyes subsided. A candle glowed in the middle off the table, dancing shadows of a daylily arrangement in orange against one wall, like the fire after the RPG in the West Bank.

"Hey!" Lori's voice.

He glanced in the direction of the sound. She stood at the end of the table, cradling an artist's brush between three fingers like a cigarette holder, gripping a multicolored palette with the other. A white button-up oxford covered arms and chest, pulled on backward so the collar propped below her chin. The back fell open like a medical gown, revealing bare skin and delicate white panties. Red, brown, and green striped the cloth across her abdomen.

"What you—" His voice was rough with sleep. He grunted, clearing his throat. "What you doing up?"

She circled the brush in the air. "Painting." She stood before an easel with a canvas the size of a jerrican resting on it. A dim silhouette of her shapely breasts quivered on the wall, the candle projecting through the thin shirt cloth. "Turn my light back on."

Red closed his eyes and flipped the switch. After a minute he cracked them open and stepped behind her. Kids wouldn't be up now. He wrapped his arms around her belly and pulled her against him, sliding his hands up to cup her breasts.

She pressed her ass into his groin. "Didn't get it all out last night?" She reached behind her neck and stroked his beard.

He huffed. "Hope I never get to that point."

A corner of her mouth opened and she pulled away, fanning the palette before her nose. "Brush your teeth. You could start a fire with that."

Red pinched her nipples softly and stepped back. "What're you painting? Haven't seen you with a brush in a while."

She placed the palette on the table atop sheets of splayed newspaper. "I woke up last night and couldn't get back to sleep. I kept having this image flying through my brain. Even if I dozed off, there it was. I didn't know exactly what it was at first. Just some colors and movement, but I had to work it out." She pointed the handle at the canvas. "This is what I've got so far."

The painting's background was burnt red with a blue-gray wedge across the lower portion. Yellow lines striped across that section, dividing it in two. A paved road. A prairie falcon with ballooned, brown-flecked chest stood in the middle atop a shiny black raven whose head was craned at unnatural angle. The predator's talons spread open the rib cage of its prey. Its beak was tipped in crimson, and its tawny wings were spread, protecting its kill.

"Nice. Graphic. Should I be worried about you sneaking up on me?"

She touched the beak with her brush, leaving a white highlight, sun glinting off the wet blood. "Don't make it something it's not. Just accept what is. I've had the idea ever since we got back from Israel. Needed to get it out, on canvas, or it was going to drive me crazy."

Red snatched his keys off the kitchen counter. "I'm heading to PT this morning. Need to get to the bunker." He wrapped his arms around his chest. "Taking the team on a swim. Hope the stinging nettles have cleared out."

She stuck out her lip in a coy pout. "Don't wear yourself out."

In the blazing overhead light, her smock hung as thin as a sheer curtain. Colors streaked her half-naked body. A lustful ache filled his belly. Would the team care if he was late? He checked the black-faced diver's watch on his wrist. Fifteen minutes to make a twenty-minute drive. Damn.

Penny stepped into the hallway between them, hand over her eyes and peering through a slit in her fingers. She stumbled as if half-drunk and hugged his waist. A yawn. "Time to get up?"

Red stroked her hair. His wedding ring snagged on a knot. "It's Saturday, princess. No school today."

Her arms tightened around him. "Where're you going?"

"Work."

She stared up, confusion knitted into the wrinkled skin of her scowl. "Why today?"

"Need to keep my team fit and focused. We don't have any bad guys to chase right now, but need to be ready when we do." Couldn't shield her from the reality of his job anymore. She'd witnessed more than most green operators. He grabbed her around her waist, lifted her into a hug, then dropped her down. She made her way back to her room, hand still shading her eyes from the brilliant living room light, staggering in a sleepy stupor. What a trouper. He'd finally confided in Lori how Penny had shot the Jamaican and, to Lori's credit, she'd taken it in stride. For a second, pride had even flashed in her eyes. They had promised each other their daughter would be evaluated by a child psychiatrist, but were still screening candidates.

Red glanced at Lori, smacked his lips in a mock kiss, and gazed at the painting once again. The striped road. His two worlds divided. Yet, they'd been forced together at Pikes Peak. And again in Israel. But the melding had brought peace to their home instead of the stress he'd feared. A dead raven. A falcon. The threat against his family had finally been slain, a task he'd been working for months. Its weight had been lifted, but he hadn't recognized it until now.

His body ached to be stretched, his muscles to be tired, and his skin to sense the chill of salt water. To be alive amid pain. To strain to lead the pack. The taste of blood was in his mouth again.

Recall

In case you missed the first Red Ops thriller, *Recall*, here is a sample excerpt showing the introduction of series hero Red Harmon. Just turn the page to enjoy more exciting drama from thriller master David McCaleb . . .

Meet Red Harmon, a special ops veteran who learns he never left the call of duty . . .

To a trio of muggers, Red looks like just another suburban dad. But when they demand his wallet at knifepoint, something snaps. In the blink of an eye, two muggers are dead, the third severely injured, and Red doesn't remember a thing. Once an elite member of the Det, a secret forces outfit whose existence is beyond classified, Red thought his active service was over.

But his memory is coming back—and a lethal killing machine is returning to duty . . .

Facing an unthinkable nuclear threat, a volatile international power play, and a personal attack against his family, Red has no choice. He must rejoin his old team, infiltrate the enemy camp, and complete the biggest mission of his life . . .

Chapter 1

Three Seconds

Tony "Red" Harmon yawned as he rubbed burning, fatigued eyes with a palm. His cuff slipped back from his watch. 9:47 P.M. Too late for the family to be out. Nick dragged his feet on concrete, cheeks puffy, hand gripping Red's index finger. So tired he didn't even ask for a treat as they walked out of Walmart, past the candy machines. He looked up, snot glistening under a pink nose. Red winked at him, surprised yet again how his son looked like he'd cloned his mother's eyes.

The shopping cart was full of things they needed, but didn't want. School supplies and vegetables. A wheel with a flat spot clacked a steady cadence as Red pushed it under a rush of warm air blowing from above, into the January chill outside. How'd he always end up with the broken ones? He pushed with one hand, straining his wrist to keep the thing straight, pulling Nick with the other. He stepped slowly, careful not to slip on the frozen pavement. Just ahead, little Penny held Jackson's hand so tight his fingers were turning blue. Her head was high. She was obviously pleased Dad thought she was mature enough to guide her younger brother through the perils of the parking lot.

Hope his fingers don't go numb, Red thought.

"Look for reverse lights. They're the ones that'll run you over," Lori told them. She reached for Penny, then tucked her hand back into her peacoat, as if trying not to be too controlling. Narrow hips swayed as she kept pace with the kids.

Red looked back down at Nick, who was yawning again. "Tired, buddy?"

"I wanna go bed." He laughed. "Me too. Been looking forward to it all day."

Lori glanced back, smiling, and lifted her chin.

They passed through a fog of exhaust from an old Ford pickup, the decal of a deer and crosshairs on the back window. The smell of gasoline stung his nose. Their SUV was parked far out, under the same pole as always, the lamp casting a cone of brilliance like a stage spotlight. A few snowflakes whisked through its beam like mayflies in summer. They passed a red Nissan Armada, just like the one their petite Filipina neighbor drove, the vehicle's tires tall as her shoulder.

The Armada was running, but without lights. Penny waited, watching the bumper, then scurried behind it with Jackson in tow. No more parked cars, so she skipped the rest of the way to their new Ford Explorer. Somehow it already had a dent in the quarter panel, and enough fruit juice in the carpet to make your soles sticky as a lint roller.

Penny had just pulled Jackson around the far side when Red heard two thumps—doors shutting. He glanced back. It was the Armada. Three people were following them through the dark, hands in pockets, heads down.

Red passed through a warm pocket of air rising from the pavement. He put Nick's hand into Lori's and reached for the keys. The horn beeped, the door locks snapped up, and the interior lights glowed. "Kids, get in."

He pushed the cart to the rear bumper, leaving it sticking into the traffic lane. The kids jumped into the back and slammed the door, smiling, glad their once-a-week shopping torment was over. Red grabbed Lori's shoulder, opened the passenger door, and pushed her in. The three men stepped past the shopping cart. Red locked the doors and tossed the controller into Lori's lap, relieved as the door slammed shut.

All three wore black jeans low on the hips. Two were tall and sported matching red sweatshirts, hoods pulled up. A tight-fitting blue one covered the third, a short, slender man. He came close while the others stood back. When he lifted his head, the pole light illuminated a Roman nose and light brown skin. The hood shadowed the rest. He pulled a long knife with a serrated blade from his pocket. Its sharpened edge glinted in the brightness. His voice was young and scratchy. "Your wallet, bitch!"

Sure. Take the damn thing. Red glanced to the SUV. The kids were bouncing in the backseat, blowing into cupped hands, unaware. Lori had pulled out her phone and was dialing. She could drive them out if she had to. Red reached to his back pocket and pulled out the wallet, staring at the gangbanger's eyes. They were empty, soulless, like his nephew strung out on meth when his sister had called for his help last year.

Red held the wallet next to his hip for a second, then took a step back. He slipped it into his pocket. What the hell was he doing? His life wasn't worth risking over a couple maxed-out credit cards. His vision blurred, then focused on the glinting edge of the blade. It was as if he were watching his own body from above. His arms spread, hands still as steel. Words surged from his chest, from someone caged inside him, forcing their way through his voice box. "Come and get it . . . bitch."

"Tony!" Lori said again. Only now did Red realize she'd been screaming it. Her eyes were wide, pleading. She pointed to the ground. One of the gangbangers lay on his belly, blood running from his legs and a small pool forming under his head. Red was bent over, knuckles clenched in the man's hair, pulling him off the pavement. His forearm was bloody and he pressed a snub-nosed revolver at the mugger's brain stem. Where'd the pistol come from?

The thug's eyes were closed; he wasn't moving. Dead? Resisting the urge to let go, Red laid the guy's head on the asphalt.

"Tony, you don't have to kill that one." Her voice was shrill.

He backed up, pointing the pistol at the still body. Red licked a metallic taste from chapped lips, breathing fast and shallow as a panting dog. What the hell was going on? A tall man an aisle over held up leather-gloved hands, backing away. He ducked into a Dodge Charger, tires squealing as he accelerated out of the parking lot.

Red slowed his breathing, then turned to Lori. "The kids?" Where was the Explorer? He spotted it a few spaces away. The shopping cart lay to one side, three boxes of number two pencils scattered across the pavement like pickup sticks. He jumped over the mess, landing next to two bloody heaps, the bodies of the other muggers. He squinted as the light reflected off one of the scarlet pools and stifled a retch.

The SUV's rear window was broken. High-pitched crying blasted from inside. He ripped open a back door and saw all three kids in the seat, huddled.

"You guys okay?" No answer, just more crying. He grabbed Nick's shoulder. The boy's frail body was quivering. "You hurt, buddy?"

Penny looked up. "Is it over?"

A smear of blood was across his daughter's cheek, tear tracks streaking through it. He cradled her head, trying to wipe her face with his thumbs, only making a bigger mess with the blood from his hands.

"I'm okay," she said, wiping her nose with a knuckle. "The— the blood. It's not ours."

The debrief room was gray, cold, and Spartan. Detective Matt Carter had designed it to look more like a morgue than a police interrogation chamber. "Three seconds!" Carter said. "Hard to believe." He sat in front of the stainless-steel table he'd bought when the seafood plant across the street went out of business. The shiny, sterile slab and knife slots of the tabletop fit the mortuary theme perfectly.

He felt in the pocket of his tan d'Avenza herringbone sport jacket for the pack of Wrigley's gum. "That's all it took . . . three seconds." He unwrapped a stick, then checked the time on his titanium Tag Heuer. No clocks in his debrief room. It hadn't been a long night yet, he thought. Two delinquents dead. One all but. They'd deserved it, murderous punks. Feeding their habit. If all three were gone there'd be less paperwork. The commonwealth attorney perched, buzzardlike, next to him at the table. Pencil-neck politician. Probably resented being woken up this hour.

Wasn't long ago that Carter had left Chicago's mean seventh district to become a detective in the sheriff's department of his sleepy hometown in New Kent County, Virginia. He still did homicide investigation, but at nothing like the one-a-day burn rate his team had done for years. The whole bloody confusion was still too familiar.

The killer sat across the table. His reflection in the stainless steel was distorted, fuzzy from a surface scarred by years of filet knives. Carter threw the green pack of gum on the slab, then stood and paced, neck back, eyes closed. So, what's wrong here? Stupid question. The killer, Mr. Harmon.

Guy has a good job. Nice family. No record. Acted in self-defense. Video from the parking lot cameras proved it. Even pencil-neck said they couldn't charge him. But Harmon's story didn't make sense. Experience told Carter when a piece didn't fit, something was hidden. But he had to be careful not to overstep legal bounds.

"Mr. Harmon?"

"Yes, sir," he said, scratching his neatly trimmed beard. Eyes were bloodshot, starting to sag underneath. He'd been to the bathroom to wash blood from his hands, but still picked at what was dried under his fingernails. That sweater would never come clean.

"Mind answering a few more questions?"

"Sure. Can I talk to Lori first?"

"Absolutely. No problem."

Carter peered through the small bulletproof window in the gray steel door at an empty hallway. "Looks like Sheriff Jenson is still talking with her. Mind if we go through this now? It'll get you out faster. I appreciate your cooperation. You've heard about the gang problem we've had?"

"I can wait. Rather not come back." The killer took a deep breath and pushed his fingers through tight red locks. "But I don't know what else I can add. Been through it twice. Can I see that parking lot video? I don't understand why I can't remember more."

Never answers my damn question. Knows exactly what he's doing. Poker-faced. "Don't see why not. Maybe it'll jog your memory." Carter slipped out and grabbed the DVD off his desk. Walmart's security manager wasn't there tonight, but the store supervisor gave it over when Carter promised he'd bring it back the next day. Yeah, right.

"Your vehicle was parked near a light. Surveillance camera had a perfect view." Carter slipped the disk into a player at the end of the table and fast-forwarded to 9:49, then pressed *Pause*. "If you honestly don't remember this, well—it's graphic. As graphic as a black-and-white security video can be."

Harmon shrugged. "If I did it, I need to see."

Pencil-neck pulled his chair closer to the TV. "Okay by me," in a nasal voice, as if speaking through a pipe.

Carter put it on slow motion. The closest gangbanger lunged at Harmon with the knife. He deflected the attack, grabbed the man's wrist and locked his elbow, then snapped that arm and pushed the guy's head through the rear window of the Explorer. He slammed a fist onto the back of his neck, slicing it open on the sharp edge of the broken window seal. As the body dropped to the pavement, one of the other thugs pulled a pistol from the front pocket of his sweatshirt. Harmon pushed it away, the gun firing three times into the air. He punched the attacker's neck, grabbed the pistol as the body fell limp, and took aim at the last one sprinting away. That one knocked over the shopping cart in his haste. He was at full speed when Harmon shot twice with his left hand. The gangster fell, only his feet remaining inside the view of the security camera. *Pause.*

Harmon stared at the screen.

"Three seconds!" Carter said. "You killed two people, almost three, without a weapon of your own, and don't remember. Sure you're not a black belt or something?"

Harmon rubbed a knuckle. "Building manager. Like I said."

Time to press. Carter sat and pointed at the screen, rewinding a few seconds. "Look at this. The guy who pulled the pistol. You punched him in the neck. Look at your hand just before that. You're not making a fist. It's flat, like a blade. I saw this guy's body. You didn't hit him. You stuck your hand into his neck, grabbed his throat, and yanked it out. That's why you've got all that crud under your nails. That's only second number two. A building manager, buddy, you're not. The last guy, the smartest of the bunch, runs. Just not fast enough. Two shots. You plant one bullet in each thigh of a moving target. Three seconds."

Carter stood, tipping his chair so it crashed to the floor. Harmon was lying. But what could he charge him with?

Pencil-neck shook his head, as if anticipating the question.

Carter had nothing. Hell, he should thank Harmon for cleaning up. "You can't see the rest in the video, but you scrubbed his face on the asphalt. According to our only witness, the guy in the Charger, you were swearing like a sailor. That's saying a lot coming from a house framer. He thought *you* were the assailant. Thank goodness no one else was packing or they'd have shot the wrong guy."

No reply.

Carter picked up the three-page witness statement from the table and pushed it toward Harmon. "I don't get this. He said you kept yelling, 'Who are you? Who hired you?' as you beat the perp's head against the blacktop. Why were you asking him that?"

Red stared at the video screen and blinked. "I still don't remember any of this. I'm sorry. Wish I could be more help."

Yeah, sure he did. He knew Carter had nothing. "That must've been when your wife got your attention. If she hadn't, you would've been guilty of manslaughter. The first two were self-defense, but this guy was running away. Good thing you didn't kill him. . . . For your sake, that is. NHI."

Harmon furrowed his brow.

"NHI. No humans involved," Carter said.

Harmon squinted, and rubbed the bridge of his nose, as if to clear away disturbing thoughts. "Can I see Lori now?" Hell, this wasn't going anywhere. Might as well order cocktails.

"Yeah. That's enough for now. Let's get you home." Carter turned the doorknob. "I'll see if the sheriff's done with her." He shut the door behind him, making sure it didn't slam.

What was missing? Harmon was evasive for certain, but displayed no signs of it. Carter, if anyone, could read signs. He knew people, personalities, and when the two didn't fit. Could tell when he was looking at the wrong pieces, or when some were missing. Oftentimes, like tonight, he couldn't put it together right away. It all had to bounce around in his mind until the parts formed a meaningful whole. The other detectives in Chicago had called it women's intuition. All the time jealous of his clearance rate. He walked down the hall, head down, thoughts bouncing.

Turned the corner and bumped into Sheriff Jenson's belly. "Oof," said the portly man. "What you find out?" Jenson's long, skinny legs led up to an ample middle, capped by skinny arms and neck. If he didn't know where something was on his gun belt, he'd have to feel his way. Country boy, North Carolina type. Once Carter had settled in, this hillbilly first impression faded. The sheriff was slow spoken, but highly intelligent. Nothing got past him without notice.

"You mean other than don't get on his bad side? Nothing. Just like he said on the ride here, he doesn't remember anything after he pulled his wallet, till his wife started yelling. Can't figure out why I don't believe a word of it. You pull his record?"

"Yep. Nothing in it. Didn't 'spect to find nuthin', nohow. Hell, known his father for years. 'Nam vet, his daddy was. Tony played football with my boys. Get one hand on a pass and he'd bring her in. Not a single fumble, no matter how hard he got crunched. Back then he was small, but you had to add thirty pounds for meanness. Nasty as a boar hog on the field. One time some poor linebacker got between him and the end zone. Bastard woke up four minutes later, five yards back, and six points down."

Carter shifted his feet. "Sheriff. Uh, I've got to—"

"Sorry. Other than a speeding ticket, clean. Talked to his wife. *Damn*, she's a hot number, isn't she? Real upset. Still shaky, so I didn't ask too much. Said he works as a building manager at Varneck's."

"What does she do?"

"Some exec at a think tank, whatever that means. 'Process improvement,' she says. Sounds like bullshit to me."

Carter leaned an arm on the gray-painted cement block wall. "No reason to keep him. Mind if I let Red go home?"

"Who's 'Red'?"

"The killer. You know—Mr. Harmon. Said everyone but his wife calls him Red."

"Huh. Wouldn't have thought he went by that. Once got in a fight with my youngest for calling him 'Carrottop.' Get him. I'll let his wife know they can go."

Carter slipped back into the debrief room. Harmon was still sitting, arms on the fillet table, eyes focused nowhere. "Okay, been a long night. Thanks for sticking it out. Stay in town till we contact you. Go home, get some sleep. Try to put it behind you. Remember, we've got counselors on retainer who can help you guys talk through things. Especially the kids."

"Thanks. I'm sad they saw it, but glad no one got hurt—well, you know what I mean. We'll keep an eye on the kids. They're at my parents' now. Always sleep good there. At least tomorrow's Saturday. We can all sleep in."

The chair screeched as pencil-neck stood. "I'll let you know when a suit's been filed."

Harmon stared at him, blank-faced. "We're not charging you," pencil-neck added, scratching a blotchy red cheek. "But this is America, so you'll be sued by someone. Probably the house framer, for emotional distress. I advise getting a lawyer."

Carter rolled his eyes. "Mind signing the incident report?" He pushed the form toward Harmon. The killer signed quick as a doctor, pen clicking over the knife-marks, and pushed the papers back.

"You ambidextrous?" Carter asked.

"Not that I know of. Think I do pretty much everything righthanded."

Reload

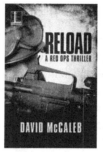

To save his family—and the free world—Red Harmon is back in the line of fire . . .

A sinister enemy is stalking elite military operator Red Harmon and his loved ones. Turning the hunter into his prey, Red uncovers a plot that spans nations and draws him into the remote snow-covered ravines of North Korea. His objective: penetrate the darkest prisons of this mysterious nation to restore national security—and save all he holds dear.
Caught in the danger . . .

Red's not the only one who's been living with secrets. His wife Lori is a lot more than the typical suburban soccer mom she appears to be, and she's stumbled onto something massive. The future of world peace depends on them—and on an enemy soldier with a powerful personal agenda. If Red's mission fails, the balance of superpowers may never recover . . .

Acknowledgments

My debt of thanks in this writing endeavor is enormous. Though my name is on the cover, without the contributions of friends, colleagues, and subject-matter experts, this novel wouldn't be worth reading. Always first, thank you to my wife and family for your continued support for, and tolerance of, my writing. For being the first to ask questions, provide suggestions, and point out error where I had seen none. Thank you for helping me be who I am.

I am always grateful to all the members of my AA group—Authors Anonymous—for my weekly dose of accountability and humility. With a special thanks to Lenore Hart and David Poyer for your patience and sage wisdom in guiding our motley crew.

Thanks to Betsy Glick, FBI Public Affairs, and Agent Cronan, FBI Denver Field Office, for your time and guidance on procedure. Thanks to all the gun nuts, rednecks, and gearheads that I've had the pleasure of knowing through the years. I could never list you all, but you provide more character fodder than an author could possibly ask for. I consider it an honor when I am counted among your number.

Many thanks to my agent, Anne Hawkins. You are an absolute doll. To my editor, Michaela Hamilton, for believing in me, in the series, and your constructive critiques. To Alexandra Nicolajsen, Vida Engstrand, and the entire Marketing team at Kensington for your posts, tweets, interviews, covers, memes, and plethora of other efforts to keep us headed downrange.

Thank you to Google for my last bazillion free searches. I may have spent plenty of time in Rocky Mountain National Park, but never Israel's West Bank. You've provided articles, stories, photos, and videos, and have never complained that I don't click your ads. I cheerfully take you for granted.

Thank you to the entire thriller community of authors. You guys are open, encouraging, and willing to share. An inspiration. Thank you to International Thriller Writers for all the fun and your support. To the superstar authors Marc Cameron, David Poyer, Alan Jacobson, AJ Tata, and so many others, thank you for your willingness to read my manuscripts and provide blurbs.

Lastly, thank you to my readers, for sharing, for enjoying my work, and for letting me know when I run awry. I appreciate each one of you. Please, connect with me on my website (DavidMcCaleb.com), Facebook (McCalebBooks), or Twitter (@McCalebBooks).

I apologize for my thoughtlessness if I have left anyone out. All errors, as always, belong to Trump.

Meet the Author

David McCaleb was raised on a farm on the rural Eastern Shore of Virginia. He attended Valley Forge Military College, graduated from the United States Air Force Academy, and served his country as a finance officer. He also founded a bullet manufacturing operation, patented his own invention, and established several businesses. He returned to the Eastern Shore, where he resides with his wife and two children. Though he enjoys drawing, painting, and any project involving the work of hands, his chosen tool is the pen.

Recon is the third novel in the Red Ops series that began with the acclaimed thriller *Recall*, which was nominated for the International Thriller Writers Best First Novel Award, and continued in *Reload*. Please visit David McCaleb on Facebook or at www.davidmccaleb.com.

Printed in the United States
by Baker & Taylor Publisher Services